SUPERMASSIVE
SUPERSTAR

BY

MARK WARFORD

FIRST CRY DESERT INTERNATIONAL EDITION,
MAY 2020

ISBN-13: 978-0-578-63553-8
Cry Desert Books

www.crydesert.com

Printed in the United States of America

"While we are woven so deeply into each other's memories, time stands still. Only when the intensity fades; when we walk different paths, do we age."

M.W.

SUPERMASSIVE SUPERSTAR

BY
MARK WARFORD

Prologue

Island of Jamaica

There was gunfire on one side of the island, fireworks on the other. A massacre and a party. Protestation and celebration. Blood brothers and soul sisters, united until the break of day.

Sublime and still as eternity, a bush-covered ridgeline carved a crooked path above the tumult of civilization. And the land was colored green as emeralds, and it folded into the blanket of a low and lumbering cloud base that swelled with soft, silent flashes.

The heavenly paparazzi allocated form and function to a diesel 4x4 as it plowed a rutted mountain track, its bulk slewing against mud banks that were axle deep and thick with undergrowth sucked from the sodden earth. The vehicle ran dark except for the faint glow of an instrument panel comprising a sole speedometer, with its needle long deceased, and a radio crackling with the languid, lyrical counterpoint of bass and backbeat. Against muted strobes of lightning, the driver's hands on the steering wheel were smooth and fine-boned and tanned to honey brown, and she commanded the vehicle with deft touches of accelerator and clutch, never straining the engine beyond its capability.

At the crest of the mountain, the lane narrowed, falling away like a silver thread winding to the shoreline two thousand feet below. The 4x4 slowed to a stop and the engine was cut. The driver stepped from the vehicle and lit a cigarette, inhaling deeply. She dug her heel into the soft ground, saw how the descent glistened with the lethargic, syrupy swell of tumbling limestone gravel and chips of razor-sharp shale. Thunderheads, depleted of their payload, now loped northward and the sky broke out into a jeweled canopy and the woman brushed strands of snow-white hair from her face and blew a steady stream of smoke that curled before her crystal blue eyes, dulling the reflection of the glittering sky like a veil had been drawn over a vivid dream. She watched as city lights faltered like snuffed candles. The power wouldn't be back on until morning. And that was a good thing. Rain-soaked blockades would be abandoned in favor of rum-soaked bordellos. Islanders living the island life.

The woman pulled a backpack from the passenger seat and set off walking, skirting the saturated track, choosing to cut a fresh path down through the forested incline. Overhead, the jagged wingspans of swarming bats beat the air like errant drummers accompanying the song of blackbirds perched upon the branches of Soapwood and Juniper Cedar and from within tangled stands of climbing bamboo.

She emerged from a curtain of dense foliage and stepped onto a sheltered beach carpeted with black sand that spread to the ocean's edge, disappearing beneath phosphorous breakers that announced their arrival with cannon-like bombast. In the center of the clearing stood a small stone cottage with a thatched roof prickly with fingers of straw pointing to various points of the cosmos. Against the seaward wall, a waist-high picket fence guarded a manicured rose garden and in the midnight moonlight, rows of multi-colored flowers swayed dutifully in time with the onshore breeze.

The woman entered the property and moved about in the half-light, at ease; at home. She discarded muddy boots into a plastic tub and undressed further as the shower came to temperature. She washed away sweat and grime and boiled water for green tea and came to lay naked on a nest of crumpled silk sheets spread upon a king-size four-poster bed positioned squarely before the open front door. Another squall was marching across the horizon, intermittently blotting out clusters of stars and she sat in silence, watching; transfixed by the movement of the distant boiling sea.

In the dim light, she set her cup on a bedside table and her hand brushed against an envelope. Her heart skipped a beat. She froze, as if the very act of moving, breathing even, might break a carefully woven spell. She read the note by the light of a single candle:

> *My dear,*
> *Time is all we have. I'll be waiting.*
> *H.T.*

The first words she had spoken aloud in many weeks crossed her lips buried in a deep, soul-emptying sigh,
"One more, and then it is done."

Chapter One

The Railway Tavern, White City, London
June 1978

"Listen, ...right, Jimmy Page is an artist. Bob Marley and David Bowie and Pete Townshend are artists. The Commodores? Lionel Richie? *Easy like Sunday morning?* Fuck off."

And so, it begins.

Fez Bramble spits a shedload of expletives into a chipped beer mug and the words are immediately drowned by swirling dregs of tepid, brown liquid. He drains the brew and bangs the heavy glass onto a faded bar towel, blowing a soft, wet belch through pursed lips, bringing the chewed aroma of a cheese and onion sandwich up for another go-round. His eyes water like twisted taps and he drags a crumpled shirt sleeve across his mouth.

"And what's all this, *Everybody wants me to be what they want me to be,* nonsense. Who the fuck is he, if he's not him?"

"You're too literal," Harry chucks out. "You gotta feel it; you gotta relate."

Fez rolled his eyes. With head shaking, said,

"I can relate to the fact that it's a load of bollocks... a truckload of bollocks... a truckload of safe..., sweaty..., bollocks."

"How can it be safe if it's bollocks? If it's safe, that means everyone likes it, and they probably paid money for it, so it can't be bollocks."

"Exactly, it's bollocks because it's safe. It's safe for grannies and smoothies and..."

Fez stalled. The pints were kicking in.

"...wankers that..., well, you know, just wankers."

And then with a finger jackhammering Harry's chest,

"Listen to me, you simply can't be that popular and be respected."

Fez rocked back on his heels, flashing a big, toothy grin, pleased with himself for the rare show of profundity.

"I know 'bout this stuff," he said.

Harry frowned and dug deep.

"The Stones are respected."

"Yeah..?" Fez said.

"And they have hits..."

Fez shrugged.

"...the Beatles and Bob Dylan and ELO and Queen, they're all respected."

Fez chewed his lip, his expression settling like a bag of frozen peas. "So?"

Harry said, "Even Rod-fuckin'-Stewart is respected, and he doesn't even write songs."

"I dunno," Fez said. "He's knocked out a couple. But, c'mon, he's Rod-fuckin'-Stewart, no one expects him to do anything except croon and shag birds."

Silence.

"True."

More silence.

Harold Floom had stepped wide awake into dreamland. He lounged there, happy as can be, eyes glazed, mind-a-wandering. Fez called it a *"rude, fuckin' habit."* Harry said he couldn't help it, said that it was an affliction, and a pretty cool one, *"...a self-afflicted superpower. I can switch off the chatter anytime I want to."*

Fez ribbed him, said he was a freak, but deep down he knew that Harry was a prodigy. *"The boy doesn't say much, but he can play anything."*

Perfect pitch was the one and only hand-me-down from Floom Sr. worth acknowledging. Big bands had been his Dad's thing – the wailing brass, the shiny suits. In their house, Glenn Miller was God. Trouble is, along with an appreciation of silky, saxophone harmonies came an appreciation of fine liquor and subsequently, a tendency to knock seven shades of shit out of whoever stood closest by. Add to that, two failed marriages and a bevy of debt collectors drumming on the front door day and night, and life at 37 Bloemfontein Road was the perfect breeding ground for such an affliction.

The mindless barstool banter that drove Fez to distraction on this particular summer's eve regarded Harry's worship of anyone that played the keys. 'Cause Harry played the keys. And Lionel Richie played the keys. And in some distant corner of Harry's mind, he undoubtedly toyed with the idea that, given the right circumstances, they could be friends. There they'd be, seated side-by-side, taking turns banging out delicious, soulful melodies, both decked out in one-piece pantsuits that glittered like disco balls, with flares so wide they'd snap like firecrackers at every stride. This wasn't a new phenomenon. Recent ivory strokers that'd been floated as potential chums included Stevie Wonder, Steve Winwood, Keith Jarrett, and Ray Charles - didn't matter if it was rock, soul, jazz, blues, or the perpetual cat-squeal of his granny on her accordion, keys were keys.

Fez waited, mouth agape, but Harry dreamed on, staring into the middle distance as if he was choosing a paint color. He blinked eventually, issuing a soft and uneventful riposte, "It's romance, mate, you just don't get it."

"You don't have an ounce of romance in your bones," Fez said. "You shook like a fuckin' wet dog when Pauline Fisk asked you to dance last Friday night."

"That's different."

"How?"

"She was eating a pickled egg."

"So?"

"And then she sneezed."

The lads laughed the way real mates do - hearty and breathless and long.

A sudden and distorted fracas interrupted their tear-inducing repartee. It was blowing from an overhead speaker and in unison they turned toward the barman.

Pengo Crane.

He was caught mid-gyration to a screaming guitar workout. Shirtless under a thin paisley waistcoat; sporting a ponytail of such astonishing fineness that it hung limp and virtually invisible against the ivory paleness of his neck. The waistcoat had its failings, too. When not tugged to the beltline, it fell just shy of an abnormally large belly button that Fez swore, *"Follows you every time he moves. It peeks out like a fucking cosmic, third eye."* It was quite the legend.

The music waned and Pengo fed another 50p coin into the jukebox. Twenty plays-worth of Sly and the Family Stone, Marvin Gaye, The Stranglers; Graham Parker, Roxy Music, and Jimmy Cliff.

"Vital music," Pengo shouted out. "Ignore it at your peril."

Suitably re-energized, he slouched back over a crossword puzzle. It was a big book. Like you get at roadside service stations and airports. He'd had it for two years and every checkerboard page had at least one clue answered. He was a man of discipline, was our Pengo. The answers to each puzzle were printed in the back, but he'd never looked. Not once.

He tapped a fat ballpoint pen against his lips and the naked form of a voluptuous hula dancer was slowly milked into view.

The lads mulled the idea of soliciting his views on the subject du jour. This was dangerous territory. Overheard out of context, the topic could be grounds for trouble. Bar talk wasn't street talk. The waist-high span of mahogany was most definitely a confessional; a safe zone for conjecture and assumption in equal measures – but only as long as you faced the soft yellow lights illuminating hanging bottles of the working man's holy water. Spin 180 degrees and spout an unchecked disregard for man or beast into the ether of the great unwashed, or, in this case, glorify a celebrated balladeer and funk-master who was entirely comfortable wearing a bedazzled jumpsuit, and you were likely to invite a swipe of retribution via a balled fist or the stomp of an ox-blood Doc Martin. With the baton-waving, riotous chants of miner's strikes echoing across hill and dale, and the weekly parades of car-toppling, high street-smashing football hooligans nurturing the prejudice of England's youth, taking personal offense to a stranger's bout of verbal gob-shite was commonplace, regardless of its intent. A spilled pint would get you a smack in the mouth. A lingering ogle at some tasty crumpet, likewise, with an added kicking from a mate or two for good measure. Show up dressed in some provocative garb: ripped T-shirt, ripped jeans, leather jacket, etc., or deride a rival soccer team's meager achievement, or stiff-arm some tipsy chick's not-so-surreptitious advances, and the entire pub clientele would swarm to the decade's most thriving of gladiatorial arenas - the nearest car park. Life was never so difficult as being out for a quiet drink.

Heads made a slow revolution of the bar. It was empty. Thankfully.

Fez threw out the challenge.

"Two pints if you please, Pengo. And 'ere, what do you say to Harry's obsession with Lionel Richie?"

"The Commodores," Harry corrected. "And it's not an obsession; it's an appreciation."

"Bollocks! You fuckin' love him."

Pengo set the crossword book aside and reached for two fresh pint glasses from an overhead rack and both lads issued short, involuntary gasps as the waistcoat ascended.

"Look away," Fez whispered. *"Save yourself. Look away."*

Pengo dropped his arms and pulled on a bright, blue ornate handle painted with a turn-of-the-century horse and carriage that was the trademark logo of *Old Nag Bitter*. He was greeted by the splutter and rush of gas and bubbles and froth.

"You wanna wait while I change the barrel?"

"No," Fez said, "Whatever's on'll do."

Pengo surveyed the selection of beers as if he was unsure what was running and what was empty. He pulled on an unlabeled white handle and was pleasantly surprised to see cool, brown ale gurgle into the soap-spotted mug.

"I think Mr. Richie's vastly underrated," Pengo said.

"YES!" Harry flung both arms skyward in victory and he drilled a bony finger into Fez's sternum. *"Under-fucking-rated!"*

"Underrated? How?" Fez pushed back.

"He's given us - we the people, that is - ballads about the self; aspirational ballads. Not just syrupy, stars-a-twinklin' bullshit. He's written some glorious melodies replete with silken love arrows aimed and loosed straight at the heart…"

Pengo paused mid-pour. His brow furrowed.

"…relatable, that's what his songs are, yeah, relatable, to anyone and everyone. Defy demographics, that's what they do."

"Demo-what?" Fez said.

"Demographics - class, culture, race, whatever. They're the songs you pine for as you summon up the courage to ask some tart to dance and, I'd wager, it's what you'll let her play in her bedroom while you're trying to get your greasy mitts up her skirt. Without Lionel, you'd still be standing against the wall like packs of clowns, wrapped up in your finest polyester, shitting bricks, worried the lights'll soon be up and you'll be trudging home alone, stinking of Shawarma and fags, rounding out the night kneading that inchworm between your legs."

Pengo enjoyed the sound of his own voice and was dismayed to find his pearls of wisdom completely lost on the two bundles of chin fuzz propped against the other side of the bar.

"Yeah, but what about the music; the arrangements?" Harry said.

"Oh, I don't know about that stuff," Pengo said.

He set the beers down. "You'd best ask Beecher 'bout that. I don't concern myself with the notes. I just groove on the psychology, man. That's £0.76p, gents. Who's paying?"

Fez dug deep and dropped a crumpled pound note on the bar. "That's gonna be hard 'cause we're supposed to audition for him, and he might think we're twats."

"You two, and Beecher Stowe? In a band?" Pengo scoffed. "Leave it out."

"It's for the telly. Some kid's show. He's miming to one of his tunes. Well, we'd be miming, he's singing live."

Fez screwed up his face, turned to Harry, said, "Whatchya think, shall we ask him?"

"Go on," Pengo said. "He doesn't bite. He's in the back lounge."

Pengo watched their bravado turn to jelly and then returned to his crossword.

Oh, shit, they were nervous now. Neither had expected this. Beecher Stowe was the real deal. He'd been on *Top of the Pops*. In a backing band, mind, but, still, on TV is on TV. You can't fuck with that. And he was older. Only four years. But, still.

"What if he thinks you're a tosser just for asking?" Fez said.

"What, like he's a fan *now*? We'll just be having a conversation. Muso to muso; something he might respond to; something that might actually be a little deeper than, *Whatchya, mate!* You know, like maybe he hadn't considered that point of view."

"What, that Lionel Richie's a twat?"

"No, that Lionel Richie is responsible for the whole ballad thing."

"That's Pengo's idea. You were on about some arrangement or something or other."

"Yeah, but maybe Pengo's thing is better. We should open with that. And then we can ease into the arrangement stuff."

"Maybe. I dunno. He's a frosty fucker. What if he asks you to name some songs?"

"I know a couple."

"You can't go in there with just a couple. You gotta know album tracks and bootlegs. Beecher doesn't fuck around. It's like going into a brothel holding a flaccid cock. You've got to be able to stand your ground - you gotta be erect."

Harry winced, and a little warm beer dribbled from his left nostril.

"I only know what's on the jukebox."

"What? You mean you don't have any records?"

"No.., not as such. Maxine works in Mickey's Records. I can't be buying Lionel-fucking-Richie, can I? She'll think I'm a..."

"Twat?"

"A pop boy."

"Is that why you keep carrying all that jazz shite around - that Felonius bloke?"

"Thelonius Monk. Yeah.., well.., she said it was popular."

"Does she like it?"

"Dunno."

"Jesus. How'd that ever come up?"

"I saw a picture of Keith Richards holding one of his albums and I looked for it and she saw me in the jazz section and from then on it all got a little weird."

"Whatchya mean weird?"

Harry's crooked mouth turned up at the corners, said,

"Let's just say my jazz collection is fuckin' stellar, mate."

"Holy fucking and shitting Jesus."

Pints were lifted. This was big. A walk-up. Unannounced. They moved awkwardly into the lounge, across an expanse of crimson and yellow carpet dotted with stains of puke and spots of blood and black-rimmed craters of cigarette burns. The smell of wood fires and fried food was heady, and the lights were dimmed like kerosene lamps and the half-moon booths wore patches of tatty green velour that were smooth and waxy. The sounds spilling out of the jukebox were low, but unmistakably Van Morrison: *"We were born before the wind; Also younger than the sun..."*

A lone figure was stretched out in the middle of a booth, feet up, boots scuffed and veined with scratches. A half-empty mug of Guinness and a pack of Marlboro cigarettes sat on respective beer mats. His head was down and his hands were painted by strands of wavy, black hair falling thick and long across the pages of a notebook that rocked with the press of his writing.

Harry whispered, *"Oh, fuck, he's working."*

"Don't worry 'bout that," Fez said. "Go on, ask him. He'll tell ya straight. He knows fuckin' everything about music."

"Nah.., let's forget it."

"Coward."

"Fuckin' not."

"You're such a knob." And then. "Beecher.., Beecher Stowe!"

What now?

"Whatchya, mate!" Fez shouted a little too loud. And they were in.

"Oh, shit," Harry muttered.

The pair moved like conjoined twins, inching across the swath of frayed rayon that lay before them like they were navigating a bed of hot coals. On the jukebox, Van the Man gave way to the gated backbeat of Elvis Costello's *Pump It Up*. Without raising his head, Beecher returned the greeting.

"Alright, fellas?"

"Whatchya doing?" Fez said.

Harry groaned.

Beecher said, "A little writing."

He looked up, studied the pair – an early embrace of White City's black-suited punk attire and a gallon of peroxide bleach painted the boys with the patina of a film negative. Beecher supped his ale and smiled approvingly, "Looking good, chaps."

Fez pushed the comradery a little too far. His eyes dropped to a battered case leaning against the wall.

"Is that a guitar?"

Harry coughed.

Beecher pulled a cigarette from the pack and dragged a Swan Vesta alight. He sucked in through one side of his mouth and blew out the match from the other. As far as the lads were concerned, they'd just witnessed a miracle.

"Yeah, just got it. '58 Sunburst Strat. Swapped the Cortina for it. Needs a little work." And then with a wink, "I think this one might be a hit-maker."

"So, how you gonna get to gigs then?"

"I'll be on two wheels. Snooze said he'd lend me his Triumph when I need it. It's no use to him since he lost his license."

"I heard he was chasing someone 'round the North Circular an' he wasn't wearing a helmet," Fez said.

"You heard right. He was chasing the bloke that stole his helmet."

"Brutal."

The group offered up a moment of silence, each visualizing their own version of Snooze Silver, with trumpet case looped over his shoulder, laid flat on the tank of a 1968 Bonneville, dodging lorries and buses and capital day-trippers, trailing a three-foot-long, carefully coiffured mane of platinum hair like it was Isadora Duncan's scarf.

Fez regained his focus and blurted, "What do you think 'bout Lionel Richie?"

Harry choked. His knees buckled, and he sat down on the edge of the booth and then immediately stood.

Beecher was amused. "You aw'right, Harry?"

Fez pushed Harry aside, "Yeah, he's fine. You see we was talking about ballads and stuff and democratics and arrows and we was wonderin' what you thought 'bout all that?"

Beecher said, "I know there's a question in there somewhere."

"The quality of his arrangements," Harry chirped in, "...we were discussing the quality of some of Lionel Richie's arrangements."

Beecher nodded. "Well, have you heard him on the radio?"

"Yup."

"...and have you seen him on the telly?"

"Last night, actually," Harry said.

"Well, then, nuff said. You see, music isn't about technicalities, it's about how it makes you feel. And he makes a lotta people *feel*..."

Harry landed a fist squarely into Fez's back with a resounding, "Eh, what about that then?"

"... and that's what sells. And so, 'round and 'round it goes."

"But you didn't say if you liked him."

Beecher leaned forward on both elbows, turned to a clean page in his notebook and began to write.

"No, I didn't."

Harry squinted, but the scrawl was upside down and illegible, nonetheless.

"Ya doing a book?" he ventured.

"Playlists," Beecher said. "I'm spinning tonight at the *Cube*. You should come down. It's free until ten."

Heartfelt or not, the invite was received as such. Chests swelled, and pulses raced as the wallet-stripping, ripped jeans-reality of expensive drinks and dress codes was gently set aside. Bob Marley was up on the sound system, *"I wanna love ya, and treat you right..."* Beecher flicked back a page, scribbled through a title and made a note of the song. He leaned back in the seat and closed his eyes, drumming the pen in time to the beat. Fez and Harry supped and nodded and smiled. They scanned the room. *Fuck.* No one here to see this.

"...Ja provide the bread, we'll share the shelter." Beecher let out a deep sigh as he opened his eyes.

"Music is love," he said. "...and you should never have to ask if someone is in love."

The crash of a tin tray and pint glasses smashing in the outer bar intruded. Beecher gathered up his belongings, scooted out of the booth and hefted the guitar case onto his shoulder. Fez and Harry followed like dutiful puppies. The trio found Pengo crouching, cloth in hand, a soggy cigarette butt hanging from the corner of his mouth and a good six-inches of ass crack spilling from too-tight *Brutus* denim.

"Rough day, Pengo?"

"It will be for the little bollocks that left a bag shoved under that stool."

Harry's eyes widened; he said nothing.

"I wanna use the cellar for some auditions," Beecher said. "You cool with Sunday afternoon?"

"No worries, man. I'm closing at two 'cause Mum's not well. Gotta do the dinner. I'll leave the key."

Beecher nodded his thanks.

Harry prodded Fez in the middle of his back.

Fez shook him off and stuttered, "B.., Beecher, you.., uh.., still okay with us trying out?" Fez said.

"Of course, lads. No promises, though. We'll start as soon as the pub's emptied."

Fez and Harry struck the poses of hardened professionals. Beecher lit another smoke. Pengo wiped at the floor. On the jukebox, the delicious, opening piano progression of *Easy* by the Commodores kicked off. The trio drank it in.

After a spell, Beecher said, "Killer solo."

And for a moment, time stood still.

Chapter Two

Beecher lied.

Sort of. He *had* been writing out lists, just not the 45's he would spin that night. The treatise he thumbed through now on the top deck of the number 57 bus to Hammersmith was his life story. Or as it would be, one day. Everyday events, carefully annotated; diary entries, suitably polished; observations, noteworthy encounters, song lyrics, and his wardrobe, all stroked down into a six by nine journal with a silver *Mont Blanc* pen. An accidental gift from a nameless lady.

He opened to page one and read aloud, softly,

"Beecher Stowe, that is my name, and this is my band..."

Chills. Every time. The future foretold. Writing it down made it real. And he needed it to be real. 'Cause everything else wasn't.

The bus hit a pothole deep enough to swallow a Ford Anglia and rocked to a halt. Beecher lifted his eyes and watched the traffic in the opposite lane come to a standstill at a red light. He looked down through the smeared window dirt and made out the shapes of the tops of heads bobbing into the saloon below. Voices grew louder as the younger folk ascended to the upper deck.

He silently willed, *"...that's it, lads, stay at the back,"* and as if by magic, the gaggle of mouthy brats flopped onto separate bench seats with feet immediately muddying the scarlet tuck and roll upholstery. *"...good lads."*

Beecher flipped through the pages and read on,

"...she said that if my flaws are visible, I must be doing something right. And if I lost my money and then I lost my spirit and then I lost my will, she'd always be with me. But not until I'd learned the true meaning of rock 'n roll. 'Cause she cares so deeply about this crazy way of life."

He closed the journal and then he closed his eyes. And there she was. Blonde, beautiful. But she was a blur, her face obscured by clouds and dreams and desire. She moved like melting butter and she spoke in accents. He rolled the pen in his fingers and the engraved letters pressed into his flesh. The word *ROAM* outlined the span of his thumbprint. He replayed their one and only encounter, now a year past, for the thousandth time: a gang of Teddy Boys; a single organism of velvet drapes and brothel creepers had spilled from a rusty Ford transit, fueled by lager and arrogance, bellowing in unison the lyrics to *'Be-Bop-a-Lula'*. Beecher was up at the front, top deck as per usual. Winding his way down Baker Street. Literally. Half asleep, head nodding against the glass. A woman stepped from a doorway adjacent to Portman Square. She came to the curb, parting the boisterous crowd. The louts scoffed at her finery. Crotches were grabbed in mock salute. They encircled her, braying like mules. Beecher came fully awake. The bus wasn't stopping. The woman stood her ground, unfazed by the spitting, *Brylcreem'd* vipers. She opened her purse and withdrew a pearl-handled Baby Browning. To a man, the Teds buckled at the sight of the pistol, stricken by immediate sobriety, spilling over parked cars in retreat, blurting fractured obscenities: *"Fuck.., get out of it..."* *"She's mental..."* *"Get outta the fuckin' way..."*

The scene cleared; the handgun was replaced. Beecher was mesmerized. The woman shielded her eyes from the glare of the sun and glanced at the upper deck and smiled. Her teeth were white and perfect; her eyeliner heavy with drama. But it was her mouth and her lips. They were Bardot's lips, sculpted and painted fire-red by masters. She drew them into a pout and raised the palm of her hand, sending an imaginary kiss directly at Beecher. He leaned forward, unconsciously, too suddenly, whacking his forehead on the glass. A midnight-black Rolls Royce Silver Shadow glided to the curb and the woman issued a conciliatory frown. She sealed the purse's clasp, wrapped the shoulder strap around its bulk and dropped the bundle into a nearby wastebasket. A few silent words were exchanged with the driver of the vehicle and then she stepped gingerly into the opened rear door. The car nosed into traffic and slipped from view.

Beecher raced to the rear of the bus, sprinted down the spiral steps and bolted off the platform. Traffic was jammed solid at all corners of the intersection, but there was no sign of the car anywhere. It had simply vanished. The bus revved and spewed a thick, black cloud of diesel exhaust and clattered off, leaving Beecher to weather the bleating of car horns and the inevitable abuse of impatient drivers. He walked to the wastebasket and peered inside. The purse sat among soiled newspapers and flattened soda cans, stained now by the dribbles of tar-colored liquid and greasy smears from wadded chip papers. Beecher weighed his actions for a moment and then retrieved the bag, walking quickly across the street and through the open gates of the park. He found an empty bench and sat, a little nervous; a little excited. He probed and explored the exterior of the bag and squeezed the supple white leather and it collapsed easily under his grasp. He popped the clasp and spread the mouth and his mind raced: *"Guns were rare amongst fellas, let alone women. What if she'd killed someone? What about fingerprints?"* He pulled a handkerchief from his pocket and covered his hand. *'Cause that's what detectives do.* He reached in and with a rush of dismay, found the interior empty but for a solitary, silver pen. He upended the bag and shook it and then sat, feeling foolish. His mind had played tricks. *The distance? The light? But why did the Teddy Boys scarper?* No, she had a gun, for sure. He rolled the pen in his fingers, felt the inscription, read the word, *ROAM*. The breeze picked up. The warmth of summer washed over him with the scent of cut grass and Beecher closed his eyes. He felt the woman's lips brush his cheek. He was startled and suddenly embarrassed. But he was no longer alone. He was a witness; an outsider, and she spoke to him and she laughed with him and when he reached for her, she vanished. *Fuck!*

The No. 57 rattled as it slipped into gear and yanked Beecher back into focus. He stowed the journal inside the guitar case. Music was drifting up the stairs from a market stall - the Bee Gees were in full flight, *"Listen to the ground; There is movement all around; There is something goin' down; And I can feel it…"*

Outside, a commotion. A woman, weighed down with a trio of kids and a trio of shopping bags, running and yelling. She scythed through onlookers as if she was fleeing a burning building. The conductor spied the wayward troupe through dirty windows. He sneered, *"Not today, missus."* All morning he'd been brusque and officious, rattling the leather change purse and ratcheting off lines of perforated tickets, riding the ruts of the route like a longboard surfer. Now, he raced to the open platform at the rear of the bus, dinging the bell with such voracity he might as well have been signaling the driver with Morse code. He was the master of his domain, and here, *"…rules is rules, darlin'!"* Hopping on the back of a moving double-decker might be every UK citizen's right, but so is suffering the wrath of every shitty conductor.

The bus proceeded to lurch away from the curb and the woman slowed and dropped her bags, spitting in disgust. Her kids toed the cement as if this was always the way. The conductor issued a satisfied smirk and ran a flat, pink palm across his thinning locks, pasting a few errant, greasy strands back into place. And then it started to rain. Heavy. Third time today. Summer showers on a summer evening. Sheer joy in a Cornish garden. On the Goldhawk Road in Shepherd's Bush, misery came to play, dreary and gray and the city groaned under the oppressive weight. Three stops later, Beecher cradled the guitar case and stumbled down the circular stairs. He stood alone on the open platform inhaling exhaust fumes, turning up his collar against the slanting rain. As the bus slowed, he timed his exit perfectly, hitting the ground at a full run, jogging the last few steps, avoiding the inevitable push of soggy passengers anxious for a seat in the dry. Beecher bounded through the door of the *Giggling Sausage* without breaking his stride.

Snooze Silver was behind the till, counting the day's takings. The sharp clatter of forks and knives on cheap china and the rustle of tabloids underscored a disc jockey bleating out the day's news from a scratchy medium-wave radio.

"Whatchya, Beech! Nuffin' like a little rain to shift a few fry-ups."

He zipped a wad of fivers like playing cards.

"Gis egg and chips, will ya, Snooze."

"On the way."

Snooze lifted a wooden serving hatch, bent double and shouted, "...one egg and chips, Maureen."

In response, two deep hacking coughs, and then a woman's voice, "With sausage?"

"With sausage, Beech?"

"Go on then."

Back through the hatch, "With sausage."

Again, the woman, "Mushrooms?"

Snooze relayed, "With mushrooms?"

"Might as well."

"With mushrooms."

Snooze remained stooped. Silence. A fridge door handle pulled. A rattle of plates. Here it comes...

"We're out of sausages. How 'bout a bit a' bacon?"

Snooze found Beecher nodding before he opened his mouth.

"Perfect," he shouted back.

Beecher scanned a crumpled *Daily Mirror*. The bold headlines screamed - *Hostage of Hate is Freed: Kidnap gang dumps priest on roadside.*

"Nasty business that," Snooze offered. "What's the world coming to?"

"One might say the same about this 'ere named establishment never having any sausages."

"They go, mate. Early. Since the Odeon is being refurb'd, a full English is impossible after six a.m. Never had it so good."

"They're doing it up just for me. New seats, new stage, new bogs. You'll see. Across the marquee it'll say, BEECHER STOWE * TONIGHT * SOLD OUT."

"It opens in two weeks."

"Best get the grub out then. We've got work to do."

"We still on for Sunday?"

"Absolutely. Should be good."

"Any movement with the single?"

"Haven't heard anything. Arch is still doing the rounds."

"You trust that bloke more than I would."

"No choice, I'm just not a salesman. Don't have it in the blood."

"Yeah, but has he got it in his? He talks a good game…"

A swing door to the kitchen pushed open. Maureen. Late fifties. A looker in her day. Wears a ring, but never hitched. *"Chased after too many married ones,"* she was fond of saying, *"…guess I should've let a few single ones chase me."* She carries a knife and fork in one hand, a steaming plate in the other. An unlit No.6 hangs from her top lip, glued by a cocktail of saliva and crimson lipstick.

"'Ere ya are, pet."

She slid the plate in front of Beecher, gave him the silverware after a quick wipe, and reached into her apron for a Bic lighter which was duly wheeled at the tip of the cigarette. She pulled out a chair and sat down with a loud, satisfied sigh.

"What're my two favorite rock stars up to today then?"

"Still on the prowl," Beecher said.

Maureen chuckled and the collar of her blouse fell open, revealing a cleavage that was smooth and dark and weirdly irresistible. Beecher always stared. Maureen knew everyone stared. By now, it was all part of the greeting. That, and the oxygen-depleting fog of her perfume. She settled in for a chat.

"Snooze says you're both gonna be on the telly. That's exciting."

"Yeah, some contact of Arch's. He's set us up as one of the 'Sounds of Tomorrow' on that kid's show, *Razzy Pop*. We have to mime to the music and sing live. Everyone does it."

"Is that the one with the games and that bloke that plays the teakettle?"

Snooze says, "No, that's on the Beeb. We're gonna be selling our soul on the one with the adverts. Goes out Thursday at half-past five."

"What song ya doing?"

"A new one. It's called, *Supermassive*," Beecher said. "It's the one they thought worked best, so we're touting it as the new single."

"Ooh, I say, where can I buy it?"

"Nowhere yet. We've only got one copy."

"Never mind."

The words were exhaled in a cloud of thick smoke.

"I'll be watching, though," she said. "It's so exciting. I'll get Freddie to bring the telly down from upstairs. We'll have it on in the café."

"How's he doin'?" Beecher said.

"Good days and bad. There's just no work, and he can't labor anymore 'cause of his back. If we didn't have this place, we'd be out on the street."

Maureen's eyes welled with melancholy.

"I think of my poor ol' Mum in the war and I'm just thankful we have a roof over our heads."

"You deserve more than that," Snooze said.

"Bless you, Snoozey."

Maureen stood and dropped an inch of smoldering cigarette butt into a half-empty teacup where it landed with a faint fizz. She gathered a few dirty mugs and plates from the adjoining tables.

"All will be well in the end, you'll see," she said, backing through the kitchen door.

"He's not right, you know," Snooze said. "Freddie's been talking 'bout doing himself in."

"Not in front of her, I hope."

"I dunno. Found him in the back alley, wanderin' and mutterin' like a vagrant, and he had the dogs out, tryin' to get 'em to sound off at the neighbors as revenge for the racket they make of an evening. He's also threatened to get the debt collectors out, 'cause he knows her at number 47 gave a false address on the hire purchase forms when she bought that new fridge. I was out there for two fuckin' hours. The only way to coax him in was with a bunch of grapes. Mate, it's desperate."

"Have you had the Doc out?"

"He won't come anymore. Says we keep wasting his time. Reckons Freddie is faking it."

"Faking what?"

"Everything. All of his ailments. Says he's doing it so's he can stay on the dole."

"It's no life for Maureen."

"I know, she reckons if the council gets wind of it, they might shut down the café. Says they're looking for any excuse to knock the building down and put up some posh flats."

"Who'd wanna live here?"

"Exactly."

Beecher pushed the last, slimy mushroom into a soup of egg yolk and with a wedge of burnt toast, scooped it onto his fork. With lips smacking, he pushed the empty platter away.

"Do us a tea, Snooze."

He opened the tattered notebook and jotted a note:

Freddie and Maureen. Lost in the system. Who are we if we don't look after each other?

"Still at it, eh?" Snooze stared at Beecher through a cloud of steam rising from an electric kettle. "How's it coming?"

"It's getting a little heavy in places, you know, like a proper book."

"You sound disappointed."

"I've gotta join the ideas together at some point. Didn't think it was gonna be this much of a heavy lift."

A pulsing synth and a monotonous bass line rattled the little transistor radio's speaker and Snooze reached up and twisted the volume higher.

He sang along, "*Who are you.., who, who; who, who...*"

Beecher slotted in with perfect harmony as an errant ray of sunshine speared the Venetian blinds and lined the café with strips of soft, yellow light. And for a moment, handclaps and backbeats and distorted guitars brought time to a standstill.

Chapter Three

Six miles away, three black cabs wound their way along Belgrave Place. The first two were empty of passengers. The third carried a woman. She was blonde and elegant, a snow queen transported through temperate canyons of opulence. At number 25, they stopped.

The single passenger alighted. Standing; waiting. She pushed black Ray-Bans into place and smoothed the wrinkles from a royal-yellow wrap dress. Black stockings and white stovepipe boots rounded out the attire. The hubbub of West End traffic and construction workers and frantic shoppers had been replaced by the chirping of songbirds and the inevitable sense of calm propagated by old money and proud buildings and manicured garden squares. A brace of uniformed doormen greeted her, eyes trained to the deck, ushered into action by a third suited gentleman. The cargo of the cabs was unloaded. Four elegant trunks with matching cases. The woman stood aside, wordless until a clumsy mistake sent one of the cases spinning into a murky puddle. A weary glare penetrated the green lenses. She advanced and inspected for damage.

"I'm sorry, ma'am," the porter said. "I'll make sure to polish out any scratches."

"I'm sure everything's fine," she said.

The suited overseer approached.

"Good morning, ma'am, I do apologize for the mishap."

"It wasn't your fault, and all seems to be well."

"Will you be taking afternoon tea?"

"Not today. I'm going to take a walk. But I should like to have supper early." She checked her watch. "Say, around 6:30?"

"Very well."

"And ask Chef to prepare salmon for two. I am expecting a guest."

"Of course."

The last of the bags were carted inside and seeing all was clear, she dispatched the cabs with a wave, turned on her heel and set off toward Belgrave Square Garden.

Hans Tomek leafed roughly through a copy of the Financial Times, yawning and crossing and uncrossing his legs. In the mottled shade of a Great Oak, the warmth of the day was passing and he appreciated the creep of cooler air gathering at the base of his neck. He scanned the articles, mouthing dreary comments as the mood took him.

"Tedious; fabricated; most definitely not a murder; faulty technology; a pointless merger, it'll fail miserably, all responsible parties should hoist themselves over the railings of their penthouse terraces; tedious, tedious, ah, that's better..."

The dog-eared pink pages showed *Aeon Records* riding high in the market on the back of multiple successful albums and a handful of top twenty singles. His decision to float the company on the exchange two years ago was finally paying off, which meant his stable of Ferraris was about to gain a prancing horse or two. In black, of course. He folded the broadsheet and set it aside and his eyes darted impatiently around the square. An elderly woman tore chunks of bread from a loaf and scattered them on a patch of grass, all the while uttering random chirps and clicks, but no birds flocked. She clocked him sitting alone and shuffled toward the bench, hoping no doubt, for a little tolerant exchange. Tomek let out a sigh, accompanied by a deep, guttural rumble from his throat. He leveled his gaze at the woman and with the mildest contraction to his facial muscles, brought a furrow to his brow that could have hosted a parked bicycle wheel. By chance, the carpet of fallen leaves at the woman's feet fluttered awake and began to whirl and dance about her legs. She paused mid-stride as the improbable vortex gained speed, encircling her now static form. She batted at thin, dry stalks nipping at patches of exposed flesh that raised thin, ripe tracks on her pale, blotchy skin and quickly backed off, issuing delicate squeals of frustration and soft pleas for help. Retreating to the gates, she was rewarded as the commotion fell silent and the ground underfoot was again appropriately inanimate. She glanced back at the man on the bench. He doffed a black Homburg in her direction, his expression now light and amused. The woman was unnerved, and she shuffled cautiously toward the path through another pile of leaves, and with her footfall finding no obstruction or contest, made directly for the street.

Tomek stretched and yawned again. A hearty, satisfying yawn. He reached into his jacket and retrieved a pocket watch and flipped the cover open. A black and gold face with raised Roman numerals. The time read one-minute past six. He snapped the cover closed, looked up and the snow queen stood before him.

"You're late," he said.

"Not at all, I was watching that little display."

"Nature intervened. I think she was looking for a friend."

"And that's certainly not you."

"She'd do well to thank me for sparing her the embarrassment of having to justify why I'd be interested in the price of a pint of milk, or how the No.52 from St. John's Wood never seems to keep a proper schedule, or how her varicose veins are worse this time of year because of the heat or the humidity, or any number of inconveniences."

Tomek narrowed his eyes and said,

"Anyway, there's too much chatter in this world. A London square should be a place of sanctuary and solitude – a place to exhale; a private place."

"How thoughtful."

"It's been precisely one year. How've you been?"

The woman acknowledged the newspaper at his side with a slight nod. He moved it and she smoothed the back of her dress and sat down.

She said, "I was sad to leave the tropics."

"You like playing castaway?"

"I like being me."

"Who are you, if you're hidden from view?"

"It's not a deserted island, people come and go."

"Much like the British weather."

Both heads cocked skyward in appreciation of the impossibly blue sky. And then she said, "I hope you're hungry, we're having salmon. I know you like it."

"Indeed, I am famished. Shall we walk?"

"Can we just sit a while? These warm evenings are so rare."

Around the square, streetlights preempted the rising dusk, flickering to life with a distinct raspy hum. The woman was holding a small, black envelope. She tapped her leg with its spine, her eyes trained on the swaying branches overhead.

Tomek propped an elbow on the seat back and stroked her hair. His fingers brushed her neck and they were hot as naked flames.

"Have you found someone else?" Tomek said.

"No," her voice almost a whisper. "But I will."

He reached back for the newspaper.

"Have you seen how well *Aeon* is doing? We'll close the second quarter of 1978 beating out every other record company. So much is owed to you. Without your eye for talent, we'd have closed up shop months ago.

Instead, millions of satisfied customers get to listen to some inarticulate, unimaginably obtuse, angry voices, spouting their utter dissatisfaction with the very society that is paying hard-earned money to keep them in hookers and heroin. Quite extraordinary work, my dear."

"If merit was all that counted to be successful, the charts would be full of pompous soloists," she said. "Everybody needs somebody to speak on their behalf. Don't you think it's an artist's prerogative to have an inflated opinion of himself?"

"Or herself?"

"Or herself."

Tomek lifted the Homburg and pushed his hand through wavy black hair that was as thick as sheared wool. A bead of sweat had sealed the leather brim to his flesh and he wiped away its residue.

"The question is, can we be both advocate and spectator?" he said.

The woman stroked her own mane, brushing silky, white strands from her fingers and following their languid, coiling fall onto the grass.

"I can."

"You *are* special, aren't you?"

"Well, I'm alive."

"And you count your blessings?"

"Of course, I don't need reminding."

"Excellent. That means I can expect another bout of good fortune and the echoes of rousing applause in the near future?"

The woman tapped the envelope.

"One more, that was our agreement."

Tomek took the envelope and opened it. He withdrew a folded rectangle of thick card that was brittle and creased with age. A photograph. Black and white, yellowing at the edges. The picture was of a gathering: two men with arms draped over each other's shoulders in mutual admiration as two women looked on.

"After all this time," he said.

A moment of silence passed between them.

He said, "Take off your sunglasses."

She did.

"There, that's better. Such incredible, deep wells of honey and caramel. I miss their suspicious gaze. You are bound to me in so many ways, but your eyes are what I will remember. Do not hide them from the world."

She blushed and reflexively raised a hand to her cheek.

"It just takes one voice, Eeva, …and it's got to come through you."

"So you say."

Tomek stood and extended his hand.

"Now, let us dine on that fine salmon and prepare ourselves for the days to come."

Eeva rose, hooking her arm through his elbow. As they walked, clusters of leaves shimmered in puddles of summer rain and a solitary wood pigeon swooped clumsily down onto the grass and gorged itself on the drying bread. From a basement window across the square, *'It's Now or Never'* by Elvis Presley called through the wrought iron railings.

Tomek said, "One of those will do nicely."

Chapter Four

"Check, one, two!"

A universal proclamation as predictable as the ensuing squeal of feedback from a rented P.A. system that wasn't so much on its last legs, as it was in need of its last rights.

Beecher and Snooze huffed and puffed, lugging gear into the gloom, bemoaning the Railway Tavern's dwarfish cellar and its hive of silver beer barrels sprouting arteries of plastic pipes. Thrown in for good measure was the inexplicable pervading odor of stale cabbage that raised the eyebrows and watered the eyes of all that entered. Once the set-up was complete, Beecher remained at the door and guided fresh sets of nervous hopefuls, lackluster wannabees and absolutely never-wills down the comically narrow corridor christened for the day as, *Audition Alley.*

The musician's stations were set against the metallic backdrop – a bass player's rig was first up, followed by a Rhodes electric piano resting on piled crates and finally a kick drum, snare, one floor tom, one cymbal and a hi-hat glinting in the shadows at the far end. Snooze had snagged himself a bar stool underneath the only window, albeit one that was sealed shut by twenty years-worth of toxic paint on the innards and a similar pasting of street grime on the outer pane.

Fez and Harry sat like stone-faced gargoyles atop a nest of empty barrels, covering their faces every few minutes as they took a few sneaky swallows from a crate of *Bell's* whisky Pengo had stashed in the cellar as a back-up for New Year's Eve festivities. The lads had donned matching leather jackets and tartan strides for the occasion and from their perch, they studied the cavalcade of prospective sidemen with utter disdain. Word had spread like a dose of the clap. A professional paying gig and a shot at being on the telly drew every semi-pro and rank amateur out of dank bedsits from Brighton in the south and Bristol out west to Manchester and Liverpool up north. They came with their arrogance intact and their girlfriends by their sides and their hair products freshly applied. Some brought dogs, others brought Mums and Dads. The best of the crop arrived on time; the worst rolled up late and stoned. And like jilted lovers, Fez and Harry hissed an endless stream of whispered criticisms: *"perv;" "cock;" "wanker."* Not a single prospective bandmate escaped their scathing, scotch-soaked rebukes: *"dope-head;" "he's just here for the dosh;" "fuckin' hell, he's a she!" "what a cunt."*

Beecher had worked up a routine that consisted of five minutes of group jamming whereby he would call on the respective musicians to take a brief solo. Rarely did the proceedings amount to more than a mild cacophony. The auditions started precisely at 3:00 p.m. and by 5:30 p.m., eight drummers, four keyboard players, and six bassists had been dispatched with forced optimism, *"Great guys, I'll let ya know."*

"Snooze, these blokes are fuckin' charlatans," Fez said. "Beecher should let us have a bash and be done with it."

"Steady on you two, let him do his thing. You'll get your shot, just be patient."

Another hour passed, and another set of musos were paraded in and duly tolerated until the last of the scheduled misfits packed up his borrowed guitar and shuffled away up the cellar stairs. With the clatter of boots on stacked barrels of bitter and lager, Fez and Harry presented themselves for duty.

"I dunno if I'm up for any more nonsense today," Beecher said. "You've seen and heard the best and brightest from every county. Not much to look at, eh?"

Fez was emboldened by the scotch.

"Coulda saved you a lot of time and trouble," he said.

He snatched a pair of drumsticks from his back pocket and brandished them like a chef about to sharpen a knife. Snooze nodded at Beecher, gave his trumpet a quick polish with the tail of his shirt.

"I'm up for it," he said. "Can't hurt."

"Right, then." Beecher slung his guitar over his neck and clicked the standby switch on his amp. "Assume the position, gents, you know the drill by now."

Fez scooted along the makeshift corridor and sat at the drum kit. His heart was racing, and he belched a lungful of whisky breath and felt a little sick. The scent of moldy vegetables blended with the alcohol and he brought up a tablespoon of bile that scorched his throat and once there, he coughed reflexively, and it shot up the back of his nose. He almost cried forcing it back down.

Beecher said, "A little 12-bar in 'E'. One, two..."

Harry didn't wait for the full count in. The alcohol had had the opposite effect on him. He was relaxed and impulsive. He smashed a two-handed chord down on the Rhodes and caught Beecher unawares. Then he toyed with some scales. Up and down the keys, soft and bluesy, teasing faint melodies from the overdriven piano. Fez picked up on the noodling and set the hi-hat alight. Beecher was motionless. Snooze's jaw dropped. They were off. Sure, it was 12-bar, but it had... *feel*. The explosive energy was immediate, with melodies built and layered like cheeky young rock 'n rollers tiptoeing right up to jazz's door, ringing the bell, and then sprinting away with an anarchy-laden, *"fuck you, live for today,"* slap across the face.

With his left hand, Harry hammered out a bass line that would have made a metronome weep, and with eyes closed and head gently nodding, wandered the upper reaches of the ebony and ivory with his right hand searching for that elusive pot of gold. He was utterly and completely lost in the music. Snooze blasted a few brassy stabs here and there, finding his way into the groove, but mostly he watched. And then came Fez's first resounding snare crack. He had been dancing lightly across the diminutive kit, but now his hands were like electric paddles bringing a dying heart to life. *"CLEAR!"*

Beecher's smile said it all. He waded into the deep end, his guitar lines coaxing and cajoling; willing every new round of notes to explore hidden territories of sweet anxiety. Twenty minutes later, they eased off the gas and Harry tinkled out the intro to The Rolling Stones', *Fool to Cry.* Snooze picked up the melody and soared. And they climbed the mountain together. Like a band.

On the path outside, a crowd of pub regulars mingled at the locked doors, smoking roll-ups and trading mindless banter, counting the minutes until opening time like inmates awaiting parole. As every new chord progression took flight and escaped the confines of the cellar, Beecher's crew whooped and hollered with excitement, and the patrons gathered closer around the pallid bloom of light pushing through streaks of dried urine and oily mud coating the half-moon window. And one by one, they tuned out the rumble and crash of city traffic at their backs. And they listened.

Chapter Five

Eeva was exhausted. Shallow breaths were all she could muster. Sweat glistened all over her naked body and she writhed and moaned, awake yet seemingly drowning in mid-air. She tilted her head backward and saw beneath her that the bedroom whirled like a lighted carousel. She gasped and grabbed at her belly. She probed her sex, sinking her fingers deep and she called out, but the words were smothered by his mouth. She bit down on his lip and longed for his flesh to fuse with her own. It was him. Again. From beyond the void. Faceless, but not voiceless. A man of his time. Immediately, she came with a release that emptied her lungs and left her skin electric to the touch. And then she fell into the darkness of sleep, so exhausted and so complete.

The alarm clock on the bedside table was set for 3:00 a.m. It displayed gaudy, ivory hands spread wide, promising the time of 2:50 a.m., ticking loudly in anticipation of its release. But it was denied prematurely by the smack of Eeva's palm. She stretched and curled into a ball and felt the damp patches of her tears as they were absorbed by the fabric of the pillow. She reached out in the muted light and explored the empty side of the bed and wondered if it would always be this way. She knew he could only come to her in her sleep and a singular weight of emptiness filled her gut and she shut her eyes tight and willed the sadness away and soon the ache subsided.

Eeva reached for a glass of water and found it empty. She crawled from the bed and made her way to the bathroom. The moon-glow spilling through parted curtains painted her reflection in the full-length mirror with hues of purple and blue and she regarded her body, and it was toned, and her limbs were long and lithe, and her hair tumbled about her shoulders like tropical clouds. She gulped three glasses of water in quick succession and wiped her mouth, drawing parallel winding trails of lipstick on the back of her hand. The waxy, crimson stain showed jet-black in the half-light and she read aloud the shapes of letters, "S, S".

A bead of sweat trickled down her spine and she shivered. Eeva traced the lines with two fingers and then she scrubbed at the markings with a wet towel until only a patch of ripe, bruised skin remained.

Chapter Six

The guard at the gate was Sidney Butcher. His name tag said so. He was a towering stalk of wheat with a nose that clung to rosy cheeks like it had been glued on. In harsh, direct light, the span of his nostrils cast no shadow. Take a half step sideways, however, and Sid's character was defined. As both a child and a teenager, he'd have fought and cried and hidden and triumphed, all because of that breathtakingly-barbed slab of flesh. He greeted Beecher with neither smile nor frown.

"Name?"

Sid's voice was a broken baritone, cultivated by single-malt scotch, brown ale, and pipe tobacco. He leaned out of the guardhouse window and was suddenly alarmingly close and a pungent, mothball musk arose from his cheap suit and the stiff green visor of his peaked cap grazed Beecher's forehead.

Again, he asked, "C'mon, young fella, what's the name?"

Beecher took an instinctive step back and the drops of rain clattering on the tin shed's roof found their way along corrugated grooves and dribbled down his neck. He lifted his collar, said,

"Beecher Stowe."

"What kind of band is that?"

"No, that's my name."

"*Struth.*" Sid's eyebrows arched. "What's the ban...?"

On a walkie-talkie, a wavering voice cracked small and metallic through a distorted speaker. The voice was agitated to the point of tears.

"*Sid, they're all over the place. What am I supposed to do? They're climbing over the back wall!*"

A frustrated shake of Sid's head set the nose into motion and Beecher was sure he felt a draft.

"Deal with it, Barry. They're teenage girls, not terrorists."

"*But one of them kicked me.*"

"If they get onto the soundstage, I'll see you get more than a kicking..."

Back to Beecher.

"C'mon, mate, I haven't got all bloody day. What's the name?"

"I don't know what you mean. We're here to do a song on *Razzy Pop.*"

"No kidding. See that line of vans?"

Sid's finger rose from his clipboard and without looking up he gestured at an airport-sized, grass field crammed full, nose to tail, with nondescript Transits and Combis and cattle trucks.

"They're all here for the pop show. Well, not the cows, they're here for *Farming Today* which shoots on the adjoining… anyway, that don't matter."

Beecher threw him a shrug and a blank look.

"I don't want *your* name," Sid said. "I log the talent by song title or band name."

"Oh, right you are." And then, with a broad self-conscious smile, as it would be the first time he'd said it out loud with any sense of purpose, "Supermassive."

"Two, S's?"

The walkie-talkie again.

"Sid, they've broken through. It's a fuckin' stampede. And they're stabbing at us with their pens. And they're all squealing and shouting…"

"Fuck me!" Sid blurted into the radio, "Bring the car 'round."

"I believe it's three," Beecher said.

"Three what?"

"S's."

"Oh, yeah, right. How many in your party?"

"Four. Do you need their names?"

"Nope. All done."

Sid pushed the heavy cap to the back of his head and smoothed strands of hair that showed as one grease-laden, dark line. He scribbled some notes on the clipboard and began to scrawl on four plastic badges, pausing to issue a thumbs-up to a forlorn young chap standing alone in the drizzle, wrapped from neck to shin in a neon-yellow rain cape. In due course, the single-bar security gate rattled skyward.

"Wear these at all times, otherwise you'll get thrown out. Make your way around the back and look for a parking space at building six. You'll need to get your gear over to building eight, 'cause that's where they shoot the show, but DO NOT park at building eight, you'll get towed, and then thrown out."

Beecher accepted the credentials one-by-one as they were inscribed and he sauntered back to the van, oblivious of the concrete skies and the persistent rain and the rainbow-swirled puddles. Today he was a rock star, doing rock star work, at a rock star venue.

Behind the steamed windscreen, he saw three faces peering out. He saw their lips moving with questions, comments, and concerns and he felt inexplicably taller. The nerves, he expected, would come later. For now, there was calm and order. It seemed only natural that the rusty Ford Transit shrouded in a fog of its own exhaust fumes represented his entire future.

The door squeaked open and he hopped into the driver's seat.

"All right, lads. We're in."

They milked the ride onto the lot. Eyes peeled, looking for celebrities in every darkened doorway. Harry thought he saw Joanna Lumley, but it turned out to be a leggy cleaning woman carrying a mop. Snooze bemoaned the bygone days of classic British entertainment as they passed a billboard promoting yet another American cop series. Fez was uncharacteristically quiet.

Beecher noticed first.

"Not feelin' it, Fez?"

"Yeah," and then with a pang of profound and sublime sadness, "...I just want it to last."

Harry rested his hand on Fez's shoulder. One day of employment had been promised to the lads. Theirs wasn't the luxury of being a permanent band member. Beecher had been clear 'bout that, *"No guarantees, lads. Too many unknowns."* It was a father talking to his kids: *"Yes, we're going on holiday; no, we're not staying for ice cream."* Fez and Harry shrugged off the brevity of the gig. What else were they gonna do? Sit in the pub? Go 'round Harry's house and knock out some of the day's hits on piano and drums, just the two of them, prancin' around like gits and then pack up, get some chips and watch telly until it closed down at midnight? Maybe they'd go to the movies if they could scrape up the cash. But it was all shit, anyway. That left going back to the *Railway* and supping a few pints and arguing about Lionel-fuckin'-Richie. No, this was staggeringly awesome. Even it was for just one day.

At building three, a chipped and fading plaque spanned two, towering stone columns:

Crown Television Studios: where the dreams of tomorrow are made in color for today.

"Probably used those in *Cleopatra* or *Ben Hur*," Harry mused. "They re-use everything at these places."

"This isn't Hollywood," Fez said. "...it's Brentford."

"Behind these walls, we could be in Oz," Snooze chimed in.

Harry was laid flat on piled amps and drum cases, "Can we get a tour of the studio, Beecher? You know, after the gig?"

"I don't know how long they'll let us hang around."

"But we can ask, right?" Harry persisted.

"Sure thing, we can ask."

The wipers aquaplaned over cascading water, but through the murk, Beecher saw a pink dress dart between the cabs of two parked lorries. He stomped on the brakes and everyone shot forward, sounding off with the appropriate biblical rebukes, *"Jesus..," "God's sake..." "Mother Mary.."* A blue anorak and denim skirt hanging over black Wellington boots was braver. She came up to the passenger window, cupped her hands and peered inside. Snooze looked back, a little horrified. The girl saw his trumpet case and squealed, "Over here!"

In two's and three's, they came, surrounding the van, tiny hands drumming on the body panels, rocking the Transit to the limit of its already compromised springs. The girl in the pink dress appeared out front, hands planted firmly on her hips. She studied Beecher through the insignificant slash of the wipers, saw no panic, only confusion.

"Back off, girls!" The shout was lathered with authority and purpose. "It's not them."

The statement echoed around the van and the banging and rocking ceased as if the feed of electricity had been cut off.

"Trudy says it's not them."

"Well, who is it?"

"Who gives a fuck?"

"Back undercover girls!"

Beecher wound the window down.

"Who you after?"

The girl raised an umbrella and came to the driver's side. She was barely a teen. A duffel bag was slung across her budding bosom like a bandolier.

"Not you," she said. "Someone famous."

"How d'ya know we're not famous?"

"You didn't hide your face."

"Simple as that, is it?"

"Yeah, and you're not wearing sunglasses."

"But it's raining," Beecher's naïve expression triggered an exasperated reaction that said, *"lost cause, this one."*

Time was marching on. She checked her watch and signaled to her mates. They moved off in a cluster, tight as a pack of wolves, the scent of celebrity still fresh in their snotty noses.

"There ya go, lads," Beecher said. "First taste of stardom. How'd ya like it?"

Fez was brutally honest, "I dunno 'bout you, but I nearly pissed myself."

"I wonder who they're after?" Harry said.

The Transit's wing mirrors suddenly glowed brightly with the reflection of headlights. A motorhome was bouncing along the driveway. Its powerful diesel engine hummed like a ship's turbine as it drew alongside, sloshing regally through standing water, painting the Transit with a wash of oily slime.

"Hold tight, Harry," Beecher said, crunching the van into gear and following along in the muddy wake. "I think we're about to find out."

The motorhome lumbered confidently past building six, but Beecher obeyed Sid's instructions. He swung the van into an empty parking spot and shut off the engine. This is as far as we go, lads."

"We're gonna get soaked," Fez said, feeling it was his duty to state the bleedin' obvious.

"We need a trolley," Harry said.

"We'll wait 'ere while you go 'ave a look 'round," Fez said, eyes a' rolling.

"No need," Harry said, quick as a flash. He was pointing at a golf cart tucked under the overhang of a loading bay.

"I bet they use that for movie stars," Snooze said. "…for getting them around the place, so's they don't have to muddy up their finery."

"Well, it's ours now," Fez said. "I'm sure they won't miss it."

The lads scurried out through the rear doors of the van like hungry rats. They probed for a bit, flicked a few switches.

"No key," Fez said.

"Just press the accelerator and go," Harry said. "It's electric."

Fez clambered behind the wheel and set his foot on the pedal. Nothing happened. He stepped on it a few more times. Still nothing.

"Fuckin' hell, maybe the battery's dead," Harry said.

Fez made a sour face and gave the cart a final petulant stomp and all hell broke loose. The cart came instantly awake and shot from the loading bay like a spanked mule. Harry's toes received a double smash. Fez panicked and locked the steering, completing a chaotic circle on two wheels, bringing it up just short of the Transit's grill. He took a breath, peeked out from beneath the flapping, canvas canopy, saw Beecher and Snooze howling with laughter.

"Beats walking," he said.

Building eight was as cold as a wartime hangar in the depths of winter. Built atop a 30,000 square foot slab of concrete, the structure seemed to suck the damp from the surrounding soil and corral it in the massive shed for all to bear. The stage crew milled about, all clutching mugs of steaming tea with hands wrapped in fingerless gloves. Some wore wool jackets, others opted for heavy sweaters and knit caps. Outside, the temperature nudged nicely into the 60's; within the corrugated cavern, it was twenty degrees cooler and would remain so until the studio lights came fully on.

Beecher's band was wide-eyed and shivering with anticipation as Fez steered the overloaded cart through a set of double doors and parked next to a flatbed lorry loaded down with cables and rigging. The smells and sounds of the television studio were electric. Power tools raged and sheets of plywood crashed and splintered as they were fitted onto drum risers. Coils of lighting cable were hoisted aloft on squeaky pulleys and colored lights began to pulse like distant stars. The lads absorbed everything in mind-numbing detail, not caring in the slightest at being shunted to-and-fro at the insistence of a floor manager's abusive shouts:

"For the tenth fuckin' time, you can't just fuckin' hang around! Find somewhere else to bleedin' stand."

"He's just busy," Harry said. "We should move."

Meanwhile, Beecher was on the hunt. He had a name, and he had a description: Colin Cox, assistant director. A wiry skinhead; *Billy Whizz*, if he were a real person and not a character in a comic book. Everyone Beecher asked had seen him; no one knew where he was.

"He's like the wind, that one."

"I find it works if you just stand still and wait for him to do the rounds. You won't wait long."

"In the café, or in the control room, or somewhere in between."

And finally, "He's in the bog."

An electrician wearing a hangover like a horror mask, said, "We had a little, pre-show curry last night. Cox'y didn't fare so well if you know what I mean."

Beecher loitered outside the gents for a few minutes. A few stagehands came up to the portable toilet and knocked and received a muted, *"fuck off"*, for their trouble. The band had a call time of eleven o'clock, and it was now pushing midday. Beecher's concern must have been obvious. A tap on his shoulder and a comforting, *"don't worry, mate, it's always like this,"* spun him around where he was greeted by Smiler Davy, currently sitting at number two on the British charts with his catchy, thrashing ode to British society's inevitable downfall, *'Bermondsey On My Mind.'*

"Oh, shit.., wow, cool!" Beecher felt like a slobbering schoolgirl as soon as the words left his mouth. "Sorry, it's our first time on this show; or any show."

"They'll soon have you losing your mind with boredom and frustration," Smiler said. "By the time they get these lights up, it'll be lunch, and the union mandates an hour and a half, minimum. So that takes us up to two, or two-thirty before any of the gear gets set up, and then they let the audience in around five or six. If you're lucky, you'll get time to do one run-through, block out a few camera-moves, and soundcheck all at the same time."

"They said I was supposed to report to the assistant director no later than eleven a.m."

"They do that to keep everything on schedule. Mind you, some bands are total cunts, showing up late, completely pissed. You'll know them by the fact that they never get invited back, and without the telly on your side, the song disappears, and then so does the band. There are more musicians that've royally fucked it up now working in *Sainsbury's* than you'd ever fathom."

The sound of a toilet flushing and a door latch sliding introduced Colin Cox to the daylight. Squinting; shuffling from the gloom, white as a sheet. At the sight of Smiler, he was soon skidding across the floor, clipboard clutched to his chest, hand outstretched in anticipation of welcoming the star of the show. Smiler backed off, issuing a brief wave and a, *"…we'll be in my trailer when you need us."*

Beecher felt a tug on his jacket. He shouted his name at the crestfallen director, along with a hasty apology, and hurried after Smiler.

"That's not gonna go bad for me, is it?" Beecher said.

"Nah, mate, he was only gonna lord it over you; tell you how important he is, and how he runs the show. He's a bit of a weasel that one, zipping around with his hair on fire about one bullshit thing or another. But you're in luck, for today only, I'm having a sale on advice for up and coming artists – real inside stuff; stuff that will make your hair curl."

Colin watched his lead talent melt into a forest of parked vehicles, then heeled and headed in the direction of the control room. He stopped short twenty paces from the soundproof door. His stomach growled like a drain emptying and a whistle of gas crept out of his ass. You could have heard it from twenty feet away. He checked around, thankfully no one was near. He regained his composure and moved on, slower now. He spat a few directives at a grip and a boom operator lost in casual banter, but that too was cut short by another disturbance in the gut - this time, like steam escaping a radiator. His next stride was cautious, but it still proved too ambitious. The ensuing evacuation would be heralded at Crown Television Studios forevermore. Unfortunately, Colin's uniform of corduroy flares and platform soles expedited seepage, so every involuntary shiver and shake distributed a coffee-colored puddle of reconstituted Biryani over the concrete floor. There was no point in denying it; no walking this back. Might as well let it go. It would've taken the actual *Billy Whizz* to outrun it. A full minute passed, immutable and seemingly eternal. Colin just folded his arms, bowed his head, and shat.

From the gantry above, Fez and Harry and Snooze might as well have been at Disneyland. They leaned on the railing, swapping countless, *"did you fuckin' ever see something like that?"* looks.

"We've been professional musicians for exactly six hours and forty-seven minutes," Fez said. "I'm gonna be writing a fuckin' book before the day's out."

Smiler's motorhome was everything Beecher had read about in magazines and seen in the movies. Yes, it had two televisions. Yes, it had a bathroom and a shower. Yes, it had a refrigerator and a stove and a separate bedroom and a lounge and fluffy beige carpeting, everywhere - even on the walls.

"That's so no one can hear the shagging."

"No, way..." Beecher was mid-sentence when Smiler cracked up.

"We're not all animals."

Smiler pulled a tea kettle from a cupboard, filled it with water from a plastic jug and set a tiny gas flame alight.

"Cup 'a tea?"

"Yeah, lovely. No sugar."

"So, what're ya doin' on the show?"

"I have a song that we've been touting around, seems to have got the attention of someone here. Good enough, they said, for the *Sounds of Tomorrow* slot."

"Excellent. We did that spot with our first single when I was in the *Royals*."

Smiler tapped a picture frame screwed to the wall. A sequence of Polaroids showed five pseudo-punks lounging up to their armpits in a bathtub filled with pseudo-puke, each holding a gold record. The scrawl read: *The Royal Bastards, in honor of selling out, completely.*

"Wankers," Smiler said. "Everything was bollocks. We couldn't play a note, the piercings are fake, and there we all are, raving it up, sitting in a tub of rice pudding."

"Song was good though," Beecher said.

"You liked that?"

"Yeah, killer solo."

"Played by a bloke in his fifties. Great player, mind."

"You didn't want to play on it?"

"Contractually, we weren't allowed to play on the A-side. Flip it over and you'll hear us in all our pathetic glory."

"Don't think I heard that."

"You and everyone else."

"What about live?"

"When we did gigs, we'd sing live, mime to the track. Everyone does it."

"Sounds like cheating."

"That's why I left."

"Worked out alright, though, …for you, I mean."

The kettle whistled, and Smiler poured boiling water over a couple of teabags. He pulled a milk bottle from the fridge, gold-top, the good stuff. He scooped out the thick band of cream from the neck and dropped it into the cups.

"Well, yes and no. If you treat this rollercoaster ride as a business and not a passion, you'll be fine. Just don't wear your heart on your sleeve until you get a few hits under your belt."

Beecher felt a shiver of doubt creep up his spine.

"Whatchya mean?"

"Study the charts. See what's selling, and then see who's listening," Smiler said. "Give 'em what they want for a while and see how it goes."

The on-sale advice was coming across a little hardboiled. Not so much a route map to success as it was a precursor to fucking things up. Beecher took stock of the dirt under Smiler's fingernails and his heavy, bloodshot eyes. What passed for the unshaven, renegade-with-a-grenade look on camera, was, up close, patchy stubble carpeting acne scars.

Smiler changed tack.

"Put it this way, if your song takes off, you're gonna think it was all you. Trust me, it is everything *but* you."

"But it's my song, and the public would've bought it."

"The public will buy the sound of a bagpipe being shagged by a rabid dog."

Beecher grinned.

"Art is not commerce," Smiler said. "But commerce is art. Your job is to feed the machine. And it's insatiable, mate. If it ain't you, it'll be someone else; some other fashionable git, swooning and crooning."

"So, the business is just pretty maids and slaves, all in a row."

"Ha, that's good, I like that, make a great album title. No, you see, the business, when it works, is a finely tuned machine, but no one knows enough to be able to predict what's next. It's not like tea bags, where you expect every bag to taste the same. You can't do that with music. The public are a fickle bunch of twats. All it takes is some asshole with a new haircut to change the direction of popular music – with no warning. Your best stuff might be coming on the next album, and it might be the natural evolution of what you've been playing. But if you're playing rock or reggae and the teenagers want disco, you better have something in the pipeline that fits, otherwise, news of your latest release will only be useful for wrapping tomorrow's fish n' chips."

"What about Dylan and The Who and Stevie Wonder and Jagger and Richards? They do alright."

Smiler topped off his teacup with water from the kettle, lit a smoke. Beecher pulled out his own pack and shared the light.

"They wouldn't make it today; the business is bigger than the act. Never used to be that way. Those fellas only survive today 'cause they've got an audience built-in from a decade ago. This is 1978, man! See how easily punk is killing rock? Now imagine what it's like in the boardroom of these fuckin' record companies – the same old, white dudes that signed Olivia Newton-John and The Osmonds are having to get to grips with the likes of The Clash and The Buzzcocks. Give me a fuckin' break."

"How do you keep doing it?"

"I keep one foot in each camp - a little rock 'n roll; a little anarchy - and never release a single that's over two and a half minutes."

"That's it?"

"Oh yeah, and never smile."

"Smiler don't smile?"

"The boy's gettin' it."

Beecher slurped the tea. He suddenly craved sugar. He'd never met a rock star and didn't know what to expect. Maybe they were all like this? Smiler was a million-seller, probably jaded. He seemed straight, maybe too honest; a little too giving. He'd had a friend like that at school. Ronnie Carp. They'd shop-lifted their way across Hammersmith. Doing every newsagents in the borough was their goal. Almost made it, too, until Ronnie got pinched for dropping a glass jar of Sherbet Lemons from under his jumper. Fuckin' thing smashed into a million pieces and the owner's dogs scoffed the lot and one of them died as a result. Tragic. What was worse, Beecher wasn't in the shop at the time, he was watching the bikes in the alley. But Ronnie talked himself into a right ol' stew; gave too much away and the shop-keep had rung the police pretty sharpish.

Fast forward fourteen years to the snug confines of a shag-carpet wonderland, and Smiler was giving off the same vibe – too many details, and the cops were coming to take Beecher's carefully, cultivated dream away.

Smiler was on a role.

"As long as you understand that there is popular music on one side, and great music on the other, and that those two monsters rarely get the same billing, you'll be alright."

"Who gets to choose?"

"If you ever find out, let me know."

Smiler tapped his ash and studied Beecher for a long moment.

"You're not like the rest; you're a bit of a grifter, aren't ya?"

Beecher shrugged a, *"Dunno, am I?"* and said, "Which side are you on?"

"The side that pays the most."

"You're known for your albums, now."

"Ah, that's just marketing. People still only come to the gigs to hear the old stuff."

"Does that bug you?"

"Not in the slightest. Once the clapping starts, all is well."

Smiler didn't smile. He fiddled with the handle of the teacup, lit a fresh butt and coughed.

"Listen, mate, resist what you can, and embrace what you can't. Each of us is perfectly imperfect. I thought making music was what this shit was all about. What did I know? I was eighteen. I stumbled on a decent song; a tune that brought little girls to their knees. I wasn't the first, and won't be the last."

Smiler held the cigarette between uneven teeth, smacked the table in a mock drum roll.

"Build for the future," he said. "And don't forget, there's always *Sainsbury's.*"

A rap on the door; a stagehand with an update.

"Ten minutes, Mr. Davy."

Smiler summoned his best Captain Bligh, shouted back, "Very well, make ready on the foredeck!"

The levity waned, and Smiler brought out a bottle of brandy from a cupboard under the seat. He swigged from the bottle and offered it to Beecher.

"A little Dutch courage," Smiler said. "Makes the waiting bearable."

"No thanks, I don't want to miss anything," Beecher said.

"Know what I'm gonna miss? I'm gonna miss this..." Smiler tapped the label. "...the free booze. How much is a pint these days?"

"Depends. About forty pence for a pint of Guinness at the Railway in White City."

"Jesus, I used to pay that for scotch."

Beecher said, "You sound as if you're about to give it all up."

"Writing's not on the wall, mate. Literally. When you don't see your name graffitied anywhere, time's up."

"Time to retire?"

"Time to grab the silverware and scarper."

"You must have made a mint these past years."

"I've done alright. Easy come, easy go."

"Houses, cars, guitars?"

"House and car? You're in it. I buried a guitar, though. In Epping Forest. The tax man can go fuck himself. He's not getting that. It's a beauty. '58 Les Paul. Not a scratch. Played it once on..."

"Sunset Ghetto?"

"Yeah, how'd you know?"

"Guessed. Biggest hit 'an all. That solo was fat. Like Peter Green. His playing, that is."

"I like you, Beecher Stowe. Make sure you look me up when you've finished with all of this. We'll go for that forty-pence pint."

"Might be fifty-pence by then."

Smiler scooted off the edge of the couch and hitched up his trousers. The knees stood proud like dessert bowls. What had once been smooth, black velvet was now flat and patchy with all the chic of a worn sofa.

"Let's go make good for the boys and girls, shall we?"

Chapter Seven

"We'll bring you on stage about one minute before we roll tape. Be ready with your instruments and be looking out for the count. Just do your song and don't worry about the cameras, they'll be moving all over the place, and try your best not to look into the lens. The director used to work on films and he loses his mind when bands play to the camera. When the song ends, the audience will clap regardless, so just have fun. If you need me, ask for Fergus."

Mary Fergus was a stunning, mousy Dubliner with a boyish figure and crayon-red hair. Officially, she was the second assistant director, but in Colin's absence she'd been bumped up and as such would be shepherding Beecher and the lads through their one and only rehearsal and the live performance.

"I'll not earn any more money for being nice, so mind you do as I say, when I say it," she instructed. "If I point to you, that means I need your immediate attention."

Snooze was smitten. Harry and Fez were intimidated. Beecher was thankful she wasn't Colin.

"You been doing this long?" Snooze struggled for a good one-liner.

"Oh, fuck, you're not thinking of asking me out, are ya?"

Straight to the point, like a kick in the bollocks.

Snooze played dumb.

"I'm, uh, new to this," he said. "…just looking for some professional guidance."

"Well, alright then," Fergus said, with suspicion scrawled all over her face. "Seeing's you ask, about eight years, straight outta school…" And then with eyes peeled, said, "…but I had a year off when I had my daughter."

Wait for it. Here's where they always caved. You'd see it in a sudden shuffle of their feet, or a quick fiddle with their outfit, or a cough, or a stutter, or an uncomfortable silence. Or all of it at once. Best of it was, she didn't have a kid. A few scares, all with the same bloke, but he was long gone. She was twenty-six and ambitious as fuck.

"You okay there, trumpet man? Any more questions."

Snooze took it all in his stride. "No, ma'am, thank you, I remain at your service."

He was a charming bastard; she'd give him that. He had a sweet nature. But they all did in the lead up to, and sometimes during, the first shag.

A photographer weighed down with entirely too many cameras hovered at Fergus' shoulder. If a case of herpes had legs, this would be it. His shabby, denim-on-denim garb was as wrinkled as he was miserable.

"Am I shootin' these blokes?"

The band looked around expecting to see another group standing nearby.

"Shoot everyone that performs on the show, Ronnie. How many fuckin' times do I have to tell you?"

The photographer took another jab,

"Colin says the photos are useless if they're not of the headliner. He says no one cares; he says no one remembers, and no one gives a shit."

Snooze raised his trumpet three inches from the photographer's ear and blasted two bars of the galloping solo from *Penny Lane*. The photographer folded like a dirty blanket and shot a line of piss down his leg.

"Pretty memorable now, eh?" Snooze was more interested in Fergus' reaction than he was with the whiny little shit's.

Beecher spread his arms in admiration, couldn't have been prouder. Fez and Harry wore ear-to-ear grins. Ronnie skulked off, cameras bouncing on his belly, left index finger plugging his inner ear.

Fergus nodded in approval.

"Nice breath," she said.

Chapter Eight

Traffic moved slow enough through the curtain of slanting rain for Eeva to window shop. Music was a religion in this part of Chelsea. So was bondage. Every sensitive runaway with Mum and Dad's caustic threats still ringing in their ears made a beeline for the King's Road. The uniform was as vital as the war paint. And this is where you got it all - ripped, faded, painted, glued, stapled and chained. What you could do with a bolt of tartan was limited only by your imagination, rather than your bank account. Eeva balked at the DIY fashion, but this was prime hunting grounds for disgruntled, malleable youths. They moved in herds from bedsit to café to pub to café to bedsit like anarchistic peacocks - shagged stiff, stuffed to the gills with beans on toast, stoned on Moroccan weed and pissed on *Carlsberg Special Brew* – all courtesy of the mind-bogglingly extorted, taxpaying British public. The more assertive members of the tribe had their dripping noses shoved into a Melody Maker or NME, looking for instruments they couldn't play, so they could join a band that couldn't play, from which they would forecast a loud and distorted end to a shitty and unforgiving world. For this, they would be adored by their peers, loathed by the public, pandered to by nervous record companies, and vilified by the nation's media. A zero-sum game and an insidious recipe for the evolution of a globe-shattering industrial complex.

"Pull over here, please."

Eeva was vigilant. She spied a ripped denim jacket and an abused guitar case and a close crop of orange hair. The girl was stumbling about in a daze, drenched to the bone, thick tracks of mascara bleeding down her cheeks, pleading in vain to every unwitting soul that crossed her path.

The cabbie obliged, pumped at squealing brakes and bumped the curb with a curt, *"Oops, sorry."*

Eeva passed a few pound notes through the glass and stepped out, gliding gracefully under a silver umbrella. She was dressed as though she belonged – black suede heels, black PVC trousers, black satin blouse, black lace gloves, studded leather bracelets on both wrists, black lipstick and eyeliner, and a back-combed wig of such volume as to make a gin-soaked Elizabeth Taylor recoil. The hair was black, of course.

The girl saw Eeva and made straight for her.

"I'm gonna 'ave a fuckin' baby," she yelled at the top of her lungs. "...a fuckin' baby!"

"Okay," Eeva said.

"Can you help me?"

The girl's eyes were perfectly dilated, and she babbled a stream of nonsense for half a minute, said,

"I only let him do it without a bag once and he goes and gives me a fuckin' dose and the Doc says I gotta take some medicine, and then when I go back for more, he tells me he's looked at my piss and I'm gonna have a baby. I can't have a fuckin' baby!"

With these last words, the girl dropped the guitar case and collapsed. She sat with both feet damming the gutter and rafts of trash and King's Road runoff spilled over her already sodden *Chuck Taylors*. She shoved a bottle of antibiotics into Eeva's hand.

"And now, I've gotta take these every-fuckin'-day."

Eeva shrouded them both from the elements, said, "Why don't we get a cup of tea? Maybe I can help out."

They were crouched on the pavement outside the *Bow Tie* cafe and the smell of frying bacon and poached eggs and pans of grease churned Eeva's stomach. The girl made as if to faint and then just as suddenly, recovered. She stood, said,

"I'd prefer a pint."

Of course, you would.

The Trafalgar pub was a short and shaky amble down the street and the girl hugged the guitar case like a newborn for the entire way. From twenty paces, the stench of stale beer and stale bodies clung to the façade of the building like aluminum foil encasing rancid meat. Once inside, the girl was greeted by a mountain of pasty, pink flesh with bulging eyes, three chins, and sporting a pair of pierced nipples joined by a chain-link of safety pins. The woman would come to be known as, Pedo File.

"You strippin' tonight, Fiona?"

"Not for you, you dirty ol' slag."

Hacking laughter followed as the girl pointed to a pack of Silk Cut on the bar.

"Come on, flash the ash."

"You still owe me from last night," Pedo said.

Fiona sucked the cigarette alight and answered through a cloud of smoke, "I'm signing on tomorrow, I'll get ya back."

A television over Pedo's shoulder broadcast a man being suspended from a helicopter, held, apparently, by nothing more than wallpaper paste. It was enough to captivate the women for the duration of the commercial.

Eeva took a seat. She laid a crisp, five-pound note on the table.

Fiona snapped her fingers.

"Landlord, a pint of bitter, if you please, she's paying."

The girl danced over with the guitar case and set it on the floor. She grabbed the fiver, fetched her beer, came back and took a chair.

Eeva said, "So, Fiona is it? How are you feeling?"

"Miserable. Well, better, s'pose."

Fiona supped the beer. She was wrapped tightly in the self-righteous malaise of the self-contained, expressing not an ounce of concern or interest for another's well-being.

"So, who is the lucky father-to-be?"

Eeva would soon tire of listening to Fiona's luckless wanderings. The mock tragedies would be duplicated in every borough across London – an altercation or a bout of abuse or a pending conviction would drive strays to the big city where they would hide in plain sight. For the truly broken, the reformation would be swift – survive or die. For the casual and the petulant, episodes of fertile discovery were only an ounce of hash or a groping, scabies-ridden shag away. Eventually, anger and resentment would build, and the winds of remorse would unfurl a city-sized, canvas sail, and the tempest would howl and blow the lucky ones back into the arms of their loved ones. For others, like Fiona, the tunnel was never-ending and extremely dark.

"I thought he was a good bloke, you know, the type that has a laugh but knows when to be tender and caring."

"A rare breed," Eeva said.

"He was gonna make it big, and we was gonna buy a house in Deptford where he's from. I called him, Big D, 'cause of his wotsit, *and* his name's Derek. And he called me his little fucky-pot. I fink it's cute, isn't it?"

"Sounds idyllic."

"He didn't want me to take my clothes off no more, said it makes him look desperate. Well, if I don't strip, I don't have any fuckin' money, and he sure as fuck don't have any, and he was always happy to take mine. He's a racist fucker an' all, givin' my hard-earned dosh to those National Front skinhead pricks. He shaved his head last week, thinkin' he's so hard."

The willingness for a stranger to exhibit such indiscretions left Eeva cold. She didn't see a young, intelligent woman in her sexual prime navigating the floodwaters of love and companionship, she saw flesh turned blood-side out; she saw insatiable arrogance and dumbness.

"Did you tell him you were pregnant?"

"Yeah, …an' he fuckin' slapped me, didn't he?"

Not hard enough.

The rhetorical nature aside, Eeva was tiring of this girl's ranting.

Fiona's voice cracked exasperated, "Who'd do that? Anyway, so, I waited until he was asleep and took his fuckin' guitar. That'll teach the bastard. I'll sell it and go to fuckin' Paris and have the kid and he won't fuckin' ever know."

She took a long drink, with hands shaking. Her fingernails were bitten to the quick and flaked mustard-yellow polish. Fiona scanned the room, caught Pedo eyeing her up. She smiled back, wished she wasn't skint, knew that at some point of the evening she'd have to finger the ol' tart to get a couple of quid. She looked at Eeva as if for the first time and said,

"I'm not a whore."

"I didn't say you were."

"Just sayin'. I'm gonna be a singer. Well, I was gonna be a singer. Derek says I was good."

"And now you have his guitar."

"Too fuckin' right."

As if to validate her new possession, Fiona flipped the silver catches and spun the case for Eeva to see. She lifted the lid ceremoniously to her chin and smirked,

"Whaddya think of that?"

"It's empty," Eeva said.

Fiona's outrage was climactic. She beat on the case with fist and boots, yelling and crying. She tore the lid from its hinges and ripped out the lining, tearing every last fiber into ragged fingers of crushed blue velvet. In the pandemonium, a theme tune began to belt out from the T.V.

"Hush your nonsense," Pedo said. "I love this show."

She sang along with the syrupy, hook-laden melody.

"RazzyPop on a summer's day;"

"RazzyPop will chase the blues away;"

Pedo's rattling bulk sent the chrome struts of the barstool into whines of squealing protest.

"City lights and electric skies;"

"Get on board, let's go for a ride;"

51

She was on her feet now, dancing, with breasts colliding like two airships in distress.

"RazzyPop, live your dreams today;"

"RazzyPop, now it's time to play."

The cymbal-crashing finale was accompanied by Pedo inflating and popping a *Salt 'n Vinegar* crisp bag against her head. She returned to her perch, breathless and sweating, and from the looks of her reddened areolae, clearly excited. Eeva noticed Pedo's eyes were tearing up. There was a sad dream afloat in there, somewhere. Half a bottle of vodka would set things right. Seal up the tomb, nicely.

Eeva surrendered Fiona to her elemental misery. She stood and caressed the spiky orange hair and a wash of food coloring stained her fingertips, and a glimpse of the future pulsed through her pores. Paris, indeed, loomed on the horizon. A baby would flourish in the womb, but it would never see the light of day. Fiona would avenge its hidden life long before a name could be etched into a stone marker. The pub was deserted but for the three women and a sole barman, swabbing beer mugs with a ratty towel, eyes fixated on the television.

An airy jingle played, *"Sounds of Tomorrow, coming atchya today, hey!"* Eeva moved to the door.

"...and now viewers, meet some homegrown lads, all the way from White City, with their brand-new single..."

She set her hand upon the brass pull...

"...Su-per-mass-ive Su-per-star!"

...and froze.

Chapter Nine

"What does it matter if the piano's not in tune," Fez was incredulous. "You're fuckin' miming."

"I can't mime," Harry said. "I don't know how to. I have to hear something or else it feels wrong. And if it feels wrong, it'll look wrong."

"The playback volume is rubbish, too." Snooze was up for a groan. "That Smiler bloke was way off the beat."

The group was huddled in a darkened cove strewn with lighting stands. Harry sat mournfully staring at an upright piano painted with rainbows, and dogs and cats leaping, and kids frolicking across electric-green meadows clutching colored balloons. *Razzy Pop's* ghastly hand-drawn logo was smack in the middle of the confusion.

"I can't let Maxine see me playing this fuckin' toy on national television."

"So, you're pissed off 'cause of the way it looks?"

"Would you wanna be seen plonking away on this piece of shit?"

"No, that's why I brought my own kit."

"How was I gonna drag a fuckin' piano down 'ere?"

"What about your electric, you coulda shoved that in the van?"

"Again, national television; debuting a *ROCK* song; playing a toy."

The stage curtain drew back, and Fergus's silhouetted figure brought Snooze to stand at attention.

She said, "Where's your fearless leader?"

"Gone for a slash, can I be of any help?"

"Are you the lead singer?"

"Nope."

"Then, unfortunately not."

Fergus shot a glance at Harry.

"What's your misery, and why have you got the *Play Day* piano out here?"

"The stagehands brought it out, said we were to use it for the show."

Fergus burst out laughing and Snooze's heart skipped a beat. It was a beautiful, lilting, and incredibly sexy laugh, not like the screeching, teeth-scratching cackles he was used to.

"It's your first time; they're fucking with you."

She unclipped a walkie talkie from her belt.

"Nice one, Eric. Now bring the Yamaha to stage eight. You have nine minutes to air."

On the main stage, the audience roared with laughter as a sketch featuring several clowns culminated in a custard pie fight.

"That's seen the back of that, thank God," Fergus said. "I'll be adding clowns to the list of creatures never to work with. You can't tell if they're serious or taking the piss."

She scanned the group, noticing their stage clothes.

"I'm liking the outfits lads, very classy. Whose idea was the all-black?"

Her answer came soon enough as Beecher squeezed by a stack of amplifiers and presented himself, front and center. The hair was pushed back, and he was clean-shaven. He wore a buttonless, thigh-length jacket with silk lapels over a high-collared shirt, both midnight-black to match his hair, and form-fitting black trousers brandishing six metal studs along each outer seam. Under the glare of the stage lights, flecks of gold in the jacket cut the air like a thousand suns. The ensemble was completed by the drop of a white silk scarf, bound high and tight at the neck.

"Not late, am I? Just warming up the pipes."

"No, right on time," Fergus said. Her mouth went dry as she was caught off guard. With little more than a few yards of velvet and a shiny belt buckle, the unassuming civilian had transformed into a head-turning presence. She stuttered a little, but finally got out a, "Nervous?"

"A little, in a good way," Beecher said. "How long we got?"

She checked a stopwatch affixed to the clipboard. "Exactly eight minutes and ten seconds. We're on a commercial break now, and when they come back, they'll do some pop news while they set the stage, and then it's *Sounds of Tomorrow*. Do just like we rehearsed, the playback will begin before the curtains part, start playing as soon as you hear the music and keep going until the end of the fade, even if the cameras swing away."

Fergus felt odd; a little school-girlish. She'd sorted through truckloads of pretty boys in her time on the show, but Beecher Stowe evoked something unique. Not charisma, although he had that aplenty. It was something else. She busied herself with papers on the clipboard. *What was it?* The word she kept settling on was, *purpose*.

In the damp air, the show's theme tune spread throughout the sound stage like a ghostly vapor, chased by the cheers and yelps of an audience made up entirely of that particular mutant that is part attack dog, part hissing viper, and part lascivious bat - the teenage girl. Three chuckling hosts were soon off and running with vapid gossip and lackluster news and views from the entertainment world. Each presented an often erroneous, *"did you know?"* or an edifying, *"on this day,"* segment that elicited a positively sanctimonious level of applause due to the over-active thumb depressions of the halfwit whose sole responsibility it was to illuminate, on cue, four 'CHEER NOW' signs that were suspended around the complex like public-relations guillotines.

The final dressing of the stage was executed with surprising precision. Formerly ambivalent stagehands now descended from the rafters like a horde of denim-clad Ninjas. They sprouted from trapdoors and rushed from the wings wearing fixed stares and moved silent as clouds. The drum riser was wheeled into place; speaker cabinets were stacked two high and four abreast, with four amplifiers gracing their summit. Two microphones were planted on previously-taped X's, and a gleaming Baby Grand and Hammond organ were slotted into the frame. Beecher shouldered his guitar and wound a lead from the backline to his mark, and then he checked that everyone had assumed their positions. Over his right shoulder, Harry brushed his fingers lightly across the highly polished ebony and ivory; behind and slightly to his left, Fez stretched his wrists and whirled his arms and cracked his neck. He'd have to reproduce every groove, tom-tom roll, and cymbal crash perfectly, and his sticks would most likely never strike the kit. Lastly, Snooze twirled his trumpet and licked his lips, claiming his patch with a sauntering, sneering menace.

Fergus looked on, proud as punch, and as the lads settled in, it suddenly made sense - the piano; the drums; the clothes, all black and white. She made her way across the studio floor and stared up at Beecher as he adjusted the angle and height of the microphone.

"You planned this," she said, acknowledging the visual effect with a wave of her hand.

Beecher winked, strummed a few silent chords, said, "Not everyone has a color telly."

Fergus retreated to a podium behind the line of cameras.

"Clay figurines one and all," she said, "awaiting the breath of life."

With the stage set, heavy curtains were mechanically drawn with a monotonous whir and for a moment, the cacophony of young voices raised in celebration was muffled. Beecher clocked his mates, wordless; nodding. Spotlights at his feet awoke and the heat was immediate and welcome. He hummed a few notes and a surge of panic swept over him like a rogue wave.

"Fuck, that's the wrong key."

He stepped back from the microphone, cleared his throat.

"Try again."

A demonic call and response had begun.

"No, no, you stupid fuck, wait for the track. Don't piss around, now."

He gripped the neck of the guitar tight, too tight, and the blood drained from his knuckles. The instrument was mute, stripped of its voice. He silently picked out the song's melody and muscle and brain connected. He closed his eyes and she came to him, summoned from the abyss, with smoky-blonde hair framing ruby lips.

On the other side of the curtain, an airy jingle played: *"Sounds of Tomorrow, coming atchya today, hey!"* Beecher filled his lungs and came fully awake.

"…and now viewers, meet some homegrown lads, all the way from White City, with their brand-new single, Su-per-mass-ive Su-per-star!"

The backing track spun up and the opening melody shimmered like a fairground after dark, underpinning haunting vocals built from stacked harmonies sung in a dusty cellar:

You said I'd never be anybody,
You said I'd never be anyone…

The first beat dropped, and the overhead studio lights blasted Beecher's face like an industrial furnace. The playback was loud and driving and as clear as a *Sky-Blue-Sky*. Through a haze of manufactured smoke, Snooze saw Fergus throw him a thumbs-up. She danced along, and his heart soared. He twirled the golden trumpet like a gunfighter, passing it between outstretched hands, pausing only to stab at running melody lines with syncopated blows. The studio floor began to shake; there would be no miming today. Fez slammed the skins like he was putting out a fire and Harry was finding soul and passion and joy in every unused corner of the backing track. Beecher raised his game. The guitar in his hands came alive and sang sweet and distorted, and his words flowed like warm honey poured into a vat of molten steel.

Come on and play;
Come on and play me for another fool;

The groove was relentless, driving the audience to its feet in one convulsive, unified swell.

Carry a weight you cannot bear;
And witness mercy fail;

Building to the chorus, the band held back the heads of stallions.

If you fear your tomorrow;
Then come and sail away;

A neutron bomb was ignited; an anthem of empowerment was born.

Supermassive Superstar your life;
Let me see your super magic eyes;

The reins were cast off; the starting gate lifted.

Hey! Hey! You don't save my soul;
You don't get to follow me or follow through;
We're caught up in a super storm.

Sweaty hands clapped in time, and tiny, liberated fists pumped the air - this was no longer a teenage wasteland. The droning tedium of the show was being eradicated by rhythm and by heart. In the control room, the director was shaken from his stupor, roaring at cameramen to keep pace and cover the band and the audience and the individual players, all to no avail. The ferocity of the performance was drowning the feeble headphone signals leaving the technicians to ad-lib all of their moves - which they did to comical effect, careening and colliding in a wheeled dance of confusion.

In a slobbering, clamorous rage, the director burst out of the soundproof shack as one indignant mass of flailing arms and flapping gums, *"move, damn you, move!"* The bleachers spilled their contents to the floor, flattening guard rails, and tangling cables, plunging the studio into a frenzied scrum of panicked stagehands and adolescent jubilation.

Beecher saw out the song with what Snooze would later describe as, *"frenetic grace and rapturous poise,"* and the band brought the final bars of the tune to a close with all eyes locked on their leader. They'd done it; they'd torn the fucking roof off. Smiler Davy had been the same age when the hurdy-gurdy strains of his innermost conductor converted foe to follower, laying glory and riches at his feet for a decade to come. Beecher Stowe wondered if this was how it happened? It seemed so easy; so fantastically uncomplicated - once you were in the door.

As the curtains closed, the resulting cheers sent audio meters to their stops and most all of the technicians flung their headphones to the ground as if they'd received an electric shock. Amid waning whoops and hollers, the director signaled wildly for the three unhinged hosts to cut to a commercial before sinking quickly to his knees, bracing his fall with an expanded palm laid flat in the smeared residue of freshly dispensed, teen urine.

Snooze was off the stage and into the wings as soon as the floor manager gave the nod. He sauntered up to Fergus, deep in her work, logging timesheets and staffing requirements for the next show. He leaned on her podium, said,

"So, maybe worthy of one drink?"

She toyed with him.

"I heard the crack about the playback, thought you might enjoy a little boost in the proceedings."

"Did ya like that? Beecher's alright, isn't he?"

"Based on that song alone, I'd say some changes are afoot."

"I'll take that for a, *yes.*"

She swept a curtain of red curls from her face and continued writing.

"I didn't say it was gonna change for the better."

Snooze feigned disappointment.

She relented.

"One drink," she said. "We wrap at eight, I'll meet you upstairs in the bar."

"Are we allowed in?"

"As performers, yes."

"Performers? Cool."

He backed away with a dramatic bow. As he walked, he lifted his trumpet and played the romantic motif from, *'Love Story.'*

Snooze found Fez and Harry lounging on flight cases and managing the attention of roadies and stagehands and a few bewildered young strays from the audience as they lined up for hugs and handshakes.

Fez obliged; Harry shyly resisted. Snooze inserted himself with great confidence. Beecher held back, half-hiding, spectating from a storage cupboard, shirtless; toweling off.

"Not yet, lads; not for me," he said. "…don't want to tempt fate."

From the battered guitar case, he retrieved the T-shirt and jeans he'd worn earlier and laid the Fender in its molded embrace. He folded his stage shirt, jacket and pants and laid them carefully across the strings of the guitar. All dressed and packed-up, he faced his band with a beaming smile that said, *"What about that, then?"*

Harry was up first, "Sorry, Beecher. It came out of nowhere; I got carried away by the moment."

"We all did," Fez said. "…and it was fuckin' magic, eh?"

Snooze reported, with a satisfied grin, "Fergus saw us right on the sound."

"I only wish Arch had been here," Beecher said.

"He's bound to have watched it somewhere," Snooze said. "If he didn't, there's even more reason to sack him."

"He got us the gig, though. You've got to give him that."

"Your attachment to that wanker is beyond me."

Snooze tread carefully, but of all the times to make a point, this was a cracker.

"He says it takes time," Beecher said. "I've got to take him at his word."

"The only thing I'd take him for is proof that a scrawny, bald bloke, with no talent, no obvious form of income, no ethics, morals, personality, or manners, and a complete disregard for personal hygiene, makes for a first-class con-man. He'd have you believe the music business is built upon trust and respect."

Fez and Harry picked up on the rising tension and moved off to continue reliving their moment in the spotlight. Snooze draped an arm over Beecher's shoulder.

"Look, mate, every record company in London is gagging for something new; something to get the kids looking their way. Did you see the response you just got? Arch Pudding has had an album's worth of that class of material in his bag for months. Song after song, all groundbreaking stuff. You shoulda been on that stage years ago. I'm telling ya, he ain't been playing your music to anyone unless there's something in it for him."

Beecher listened, but he'd heard it all before. He felt his mind beginning to wander.

Snooze backed up, the air was getting a little heavy; he realized he was killing the good vibes, but he was high from the gig and he needed to vent.

"You only keep him on 'cause all those years ago he said that you'd make it; that you'd be a success."

"But it counts. When you're in the dark and someone shines a light, even for a second, it counts; it's like you'd just been given wings."

"Except he didn't say it to you, did he? He said it to your Mum as he was fleecing her for that nasty wallpaper he'd hung in her bedroom - opportunistic little cunt, that he is. And what are the odds he made it all up just to score a few extra quid?"

Beecher scoffed, "Nah, he wouldn't do that..." and then, "...would he?"

"The point is, Beech, he ain't your good luck charm, and he's no knight in shining armor. You're gonna need some proper management if today's response was anything to go by. Anyway, fuck all that," he said, "Let's go celebrate. Fergus said we're allowed in the staff bar and, wait for it, our drinks are *gratis*! How fuckin' cool is that?"

Chapter Ten

Arch Pudding loathed Albert Bridge. Because that was his real name. Well, to be exact, it was Alberto Francisco Bridger. Born in 1952 to a wealthy English landowner and a Spanish actress, the spectacularly-overweight bambino was christened in the Church of the Immaculate Heart of Mary, moreover known as the Brompton Oratory in Kensington.

As a nipper, he was the epitome of, 'a little shit.' Stunted by nature physically and mentally, he was enrolled and subsequently expelled by virtually every upper-class institution in the Greater London area, and later on, disowned, excommunicated, cut-off and ultimately tossed into the streets by said parents on the eve of his eighteenth birthday after narrowly avoiding a lengthy prison sentence for possession of cannabis. Appealing with a fervor one might reserve for cheering on F.A. Cup Finalists and Grand National winners and offering evidence that Mick Jagger had been found guilty of the selfsame crime and subjected to a mere two-hundred pounds fine, Alberto found his lackluster defense falling on decidedly stony ground.

So, the street life it would be.

Broke, but with attitude to spare, he camped out that first night on the Chelsea embankment, clinging to a bottle of *Strongbow* and munching on bags of cheese and onion crisps, staring up at the underemployed toll houses, wondering if he broke into one and flagged down a few cars, how much he could make before the law got wind of the impromptu enterprise. He imagined the headline in the Daily Mirror, 'A Bridger Too Far.' He shrugged it off and decided if he was to ever prosper in this city, he should cast off the moniker of his birth. With nary a thought, a bridge became an arch, which in his spottily-educated mind was a stronger, more powerful structure, and the following day, napping upon the sticky velour upholstery of a SoHo movie theater, he misread the credits of a foreign film and granted himself the smugly-pretentious surname of, Pudín. It was a good year and a half before an exchange student from

Madrid drunkenly informed the patrons of the *Rose and Crown* that his chosen handle was, literally, pudding. Arch embraced the epithet with the gusto of a market trader shifting a lorry-load of fresh strawberries, considering it to be a useful ice-breaker during some of his more nefarious business dealings.

As the years progressed, Arch honed his wit and his charm, and spread cons and scams across the western boroughs like a venereal disease, nicking cars and selling them off piecemeal, stashing the excess cash under the floorboards of a squat in a Shepherd's Bush listed building that had zero chance of ever being torn down. The purchase of three, four-door Cortina's in 1975 established Arch in his first legitimate self-owned business venture: Pudding Cabs. Belaboring the dessert metaphor, Arch had each car painted a garish shade of lime or raspberry or lemon and across the doors, a thoroughly consumer-tested slogan informed the public:

"Pudding Cabs makes everyone else, Jelly-ous!"

Trouble was, as a taxi service, you'd have been better off unicycling to your chosen destination, as the company's *'on-time'* rate paled embarrassingly against its *'never showed up'* ranking. Not once, in the service's brief history, was the diminutive fleet ever roadworthy at the same time. Electrical problems and brake failures and bald tires were considered no-sweat issues, but the obstacle that would invite the eventual demise of the business was that of engine overheating. During the summer heatwave of 1976, reluctant passengers could be seen sharing the back seat with a fifty-gallon drum of drinking water and such an array of coolant hoses and clips that, connected end-to-end, might have spanned the English Channel.

Like a cockroach during a nuclear test, Arch always rebounded. Running the cabs had put him front and center with certain ladies of the evening looking for more profitable representation and Arch saw this as fate conspiring in his favor. He traded in the fleet for scrap and with the paltry profit burning a hole in his scrotum-chafing tennis shorts, splurged on a 1965 Ford Transit, in barely running condition. A single mattress, some bench seats, a few old cushions, some blacked-out windows and a handful of pine air fresheners transformed the old builder's van into a limousine, of sorts. Not only was Arch able to provide suitable, if not always reliable, transportation, but he allowed the ladies to conduct their business on the move if it didn't inhibit the ebb and flow of his trade.

"No kissing and cuddlin,' girls. Milk 'em, fleece 'em, and dump 'em."

And apparently, working in everyone's favor, a couple of weak springs and a wallowing suspension expedited certain physical endeavors to the point that the van soon attracted a cult-like following - a radical evolution for this time-honored profession, he thought.

For the most part, the bookings were a chance for Arch to have a cup of tea and a slash at any number of cafes en route, or, if it was a discrete, suburban affair, a tilt of the mirror, a crank of the radio, and a scan of the racing forms would suffice until the deed was done. For the use of these amenities, he suggested a contribution of thirty percent of the takings. If a little added security was on the cards, or multiple customers had been engaged for a single 'show', the contribution to Arch Pudding Enterprises rose to fifty percent, with the option to reduce percentage points in lieu of a blow job or a tank of petrol. Either way, fluids would be dispensed as part payment.

Plans for expansion were ultimately scuppered when the Transit was stolen and used in an armed robbery and crime-scene fingerprint experts turned up the identifying digits of several high-ranking police brass from all over the home counties - along with a few lesser-known members of Parliament. Arch was subsequently placed on a national watch list even though he hadn't ventured north of Hemel Hempstead in his life.

Nevertheless, you guessed it, he rebounded. Straight into the arms of Lola. Wrapped in her loving embrace, Arch was invisible. From the crown of her bleached barnet to the chalky residue powdering her cracked heels, she extended a mighty, six feet six inches. Were it ever necessary, Lola could cradle Arch like a newborn and consume a Doner Kebab ladled with all the trimmings and spill not so much as a drop of garlic mayo onto his balding pate.

"Shame 'bout the van, Arch," Lola said, layering mascara onto eyelids that drooped like friar's hoods. "I 'fink we was onto a good 'fing there."

She paused with the make-up brush poised in midair like a conductor's baton, as if something obvious had crossed her mind.

"It's not often a girl can earn a few bob *and* get the shopping in at the same time," she said.

As was her way, Lola howled at her own joke, peeling back her lips to reveal two prominent incisors pasted with globs of mauve lipstick.

Arch was still a little morose over the whole episode.

"I'll get it back at some point," he said. "...then I might sell it ...or rent it out as, well, just a van."

Lola threw him another, *"shame,"* and then returned to meticulously painting and decorating a face that had seen, up close and personal, every penny-pinching grifter, every bent copper, and every sleazy magistrate from Tower Bridge to Heathrow across two decades. To her, criminal activities were nothing more than alternative employment. She honestly knew of no one that worked a straight nine-to-five.

"Don't worry, love," she said. "A little pilfering on the side will keep the wolf from the door. Dutch Terry calls it *'sharing'*. He says thievin' is just a redistribution of wealth."

"Well, he should know," Arch said, "…'cause he did twelve years in the Scrubs for doing a fuck of a lot of *'sharing'*."

Lola let out a belt of raucous laughter, "Don't worry 'bout it, my love, gawd knows the blokes that I see, the ones that have all those posh cars and big houses, didn't get 'em through hard work. They're all on the bloody take."

Lola dipped the spiky brush into a tube of black goo and her tongue inadvertently flicked in and out and Arch shivered in anticipation each time the thick pink dart made an appearance. It was during the ensuing fumbling and slobbering that the epiphany struck:

"I'll keep going," he said.

"Yes, yes, keep going," Lola huffed impatiently.

"No, I'll keep going with the management, like I was doing with you and the girls."

"Whatever …just keep …going. I haven't been this close in ages. Must be all this talk of money."

Arch slid from Lola, not so's she'd notice, and zipped up, recoiling at the scent on his fingers as he stroked the few tufts of straw that passed as his hair back into place.

"Except I'll go legit," he said. "I'll find a band or a singer and take 'em to the top. I can do that Lola, I can."

" 'Course you can, darlin'. My little Arch can do any 'fing he sets his mind on."

"I'm done with all the shenanigans; all the knocked off motors and the weekend markets. I'm gettin' rid of it all."

"Don't forget 'bout Lola, will you?"

Arch glanced up, oblivious to the peeling wallpaper and the thin cloud of cigarette smoke hanging at eye level and the sight of Lola reclining on a bed of off-white linen, surrounded by stuffed animals, fishing crumbs of skin from between her toes with freshly varnished nails.

"Of course not," he said, "I'm gonna do it right this time."

With that decided, he unbuckled his trousers and shuffled back under the duvet to finish what he'd started.

Enter Beecher Stowe. Or rather a handwritten advert hanging in the off-license on the corner of Godolphin Road:

Up and coming songwriter and
multi-instrumentalist seeks
professional management.
Tel: 01 899 4367
Ask for Beecher.

"Oi, Manoj, what's all this?"

Arch had only stopped in for a pack of cigs, a bottle of Bell's and a couple of veggie samosas when kismet landed a right hook in the form of Manoj's new notice board. The proprietor was elated. It had hung for over a month without a single comment and truth be told, out of the three notices on display, only one was genuine. Manoj emerged from a narrow aisle topped with party-size cans of Watney's Red Barrel, said,

"I am providing a service to the community. If you have a washing machine or a bicycle or a dining table to sell, then this will be cheaper than paying for a one-time insertion in the local paper."

"Except only people buying fags and beer will see it."

"This is true, but it is still cheaper than the paper."

"So, you're gonna make a profit from punters that have less chance of selling their gear than they would if they dropped it on the curb and shouted like a bleedin' Town Crier?"

"Well, if you must look on the dark side, then I suppose that is true," and then he repeated, "...but it is still cheaper."

Arch paid up and packed the whiskey and the snacks in a duffel and slung it over his shoulder. He unwrapped the cigarettes and handed the discarded cellophane wrapper to Manoj for disposal. He flipped the box lid open, pulled out a butt and sparked it to life.

"Let's see what's for sale then."

The board was not such a grand affair – an upended pallet faced with quarter-inch plywood nailed at each corner and painted a queasy unmellow-yellow. Hoping to add to its appeal as the budding cornerstone of neighborhood information and commerce, Manoj had cleared a space next to a spinning rack of newspapers, comics and nudie mags.

Beecher Stowe's note was pride of place. Smack bang in the middle. Eye-level, if you were Arch Pudding. Ads to the left and right advertised a push lawnmower with missing blades and three Goodyear remolds, respectively. Arch pulled Beecher's request off the board and heard a loud gasp from behind the counter.

"No!" Manoj said sharply. "The gentleman has paid for an entire week. The ad must stay on the board. You have to bring your own pen, or I can sell you one."

Manoj retrieved a tub of Bic biros from under the glass counter and waved a small notepad.

"No need," Arch said with a wink, tapping the side of his head with the card. "It's the phone number for the Railway."

Manoj looked confused.

"The pub. Pengo Crane's pub."

Manoj came to the board and reattached the card, straightening and fussing. Arch drew back the sleeve of his jacket, saw that eleven a.m. was approaching.

"Opening time," Arch said. "All of a sudden I fancy a pint. Good effort, Manoj. Have a lovely day."

Chirping birds and the clattering of diesel buses and taxis, and barking dogs and kids yelling at the tops of their lungs, and the discordant sirens and chimes of ambulances and ice cream vans were all part of London's rich, sonic tapestry - the clip-clop of shod hooves across buttery-smooth cobblestones as a line of mounted police sought to block the entrance to Loftus Road on a Tuesday afternoon, not so much.

Arch turned onto the Uxbridge Road with a spring in his step and crude nuggets of plans and schemes rolling around his head like so many loosed dice. He was brought to a standstill by the swish and stomp of twenty beasts with riders shrouded in protective helmets and vests. Adding to the unrest, a nonsensical noise swirled in the air like a sour odor from the neighborhood beyond - hate had pitched up on his home turf for a spot of lunch and it had brought intolerance and racism as its special guests. The National Front was on the move, and Arch Pudding's precious England was buckling before his eyes as a generation of skinheads swept into view screeching ideologies that had been crudely scratched into the bloodied flesh of their foreheads, and would soon be spray-painted across buildings and shopfronts and onto the bonnets of cars.

Arch was rooted to the spot, listening to the abusive, mob-driven chants and the crash and smash of bricks and stones hurled and rejoiced by men and boys alike.

"Best get out of here, mate," a fresh-faced copper said, from up on high. "This is gonna get ugly, sharpish."

A half-empty bottle of cider, or piss, shattered inches from Arch's foot. The copper threw him a, *"told ya"* smirk and then took a direct hit on the side of his head. Fragments of yellow glass dotted his cheek and he immediately put his heels to the horse's flank and rounded in the direction of the attack. Arch wiped splatter from his jacket and backed away. He'd go the long way 'round, by the launderette, and so set off at a pace. He didn't want these fuckin' yobs to completely ruin his day.

"They wouldn't stone or bottle or brick the pub, would they?"

After all, where else could you swap stories over pints of cool lager after an exhausting day of storm-trooping and Nazi-saluting and fist-fucking a capital city's pride? The football wasn't on, and it was too early for the clubs. Yeah, the pub was hallowed ground.

Arch raced along, with head swiveling, panting like a whipped dog, cursing the diversion. Overhead, he noticed curtains twitching – the semaphore flags of suburbia – and down below, front doors slammed, and bolts slid and mother's in frilly, flour-dusted aprons shouted for unseen children, scolding loudly in the way frightened parents do.

"Fuck," Arch half-spoke, half-thought. *"Lola. She'd be out on the game, strolling her regular patch opposite the park. If they march up toward Notting Hill, she'd get a taste of it, full-on. Ah, she'd be alright; she's a big girl. Like to see one of 'em tangle with her. She could be mouthy, though, especially if it was gonna cost her a date."*

The Railway Tavern regulars had spilled onto the street, most still clutching their pints. In the middle of the crowd, Pengo Crane held court, assigning duties to bouncer-looking types, promises of free beer for a week seemed payment enough.

"Whatchya, Arch," Pengo said. "You heard about all this rubbish? Some coppers were just in 'ere sayin' I should close up 'cause a mob was making its way up the West End."

"National Front wankers," Arch said. "Makin' a hell of a racket, smashing shit up as they go."

Arch Pudding's labored breathing provoked a, "You alright, mate?"

"Whaddya mean?"

"You don't look well."

"That's 'cause I been fucking running," Arch coughed and slapped his belly, "…and I haven't run since I left school."

"Do you think they'll come down this far?"

"Who'd ya think I was runnin' from? You should get these blokes inside and lock the doors. Anyone left out here is gonna get mixed up in it whether they want to or not. It's fuckin' madness."

Pengo jumped up on a stack of beer crates.

"Look lads, me Mum's not well, and I can't have these yobs creating a fuss indoors, so I'm closing up 'til they've moved on."

A cascade of groans signaled a sluggish acceptance that this particular Tuesday's regimen was being royally fucked with, and for the Railway regulars, that was akin to overthrowing a government, or at the very least running out of beer. Where others saw a file of mindless, unemployed factory workers supping pints courtesy of Her Majesty's handouts, Pengo knew that these were men with shattered dreams leaning on each other in a time of need. As he'd seen the brewery's profits rise, so he'd seen the aspirations and dignity of good, honest men plummet like falling autumn leaves. This year alone, three familiar faces had disappeared from the line-up. Normal, chatty blokes, always quick with a laugh, loving the soccer and the horses and the telly, each taking their own lives, leaving young families to bear the cost of their inescapable redundancies.

"I'm nothing, Pengo." Albie Dove had said the night before he hurled himself off the Westway overpass. *"My ol' fella was right, I've actually amounted to nothing. I get up every day and I don't know where to look for a job. I just wander around and then come here, 'cause I can't face the wife; can't face going home in the middle of the day. It's the same routine: café, pub, park, café, pub, home."*

Albie was always the last to leave. Pengo had locked up, bidding him a good night, half-coaxing, half-pushing his sloppy form out of the door, watching him stagger along an empty road under the glare of an irritable streetlight that had suffered too much abuse at the hands of bored teenagers and their homemade catapults. For a moment, Pengo had been captivated by Albie's elongated silhouette as it sparkled intermittently through the wrinkled stained glass and he heard clearly the warbling of, *'Mull of Kintyre'*, sung completely out of tune. Albie was thirty-six years old and had worked as a bricklayer since he left school at age sixteen. His family had always lived in and around the 'Bush, and he had a lovely wife, Theresa. They'd met on New Year's Eve at a fancy-dress party, right there in the Railway. He'd been dressed as Virgil, pilot of Thunderbird 2, and she'd come as Lady Penelope. A simple coincidence or a good omen? They didn't care, they were shagging in the cellar by the time *Auld Lang Syne* had hit its second verse. Fast forward, with two kids and another on the way, and he's out of work going on eighteen months. Why that particular night would be different from any other, Pengo would never know. Every man has a breaking point, and when it comes, he thought, he bet it was as much of a surprise to the afflicted as it was to his family and friends. Albie Dove was never what he'd call a close friend, but he *was* a mate, and you can never have enough mates.

The sounds of the city were muffled and distant, suppressed by an approaching carnival. But instead of music and laughter, there came taunts and jeers, and the enraged braying and caustic songs of anarchy in full voice.

Arch had ducked inside the pub and was helping Pengo move tables and chairs and drape cloth tarps over three horseshoe-shaped booths that sat beneath the twelve-foot stained glass window - the pride of the Railway Tavern. The artwork depicted a train platform with gentlemen in top hats and ladies with full skirts engrossed in greetings or bidding teary farewells, and hawkers pushed carts of apples and sacks of flour, and a newsboy waved newspapers like signal flags and eclipsing it all, a great, black engine rose from the siding like a mountain of fractured iron, billowing steam in dense silver clouds.

"I need two more sheets, they're down in the cellar," Pengo said. "Get 'em for us will ya, Arch?"

The stairs to the cellar were a narrow winding affair and Arch was halfway down when a head turned the corner, looked up with a, "Sorry, I'll go back down."

All that Arch saw ascending from the gloom was a set of piercing blue eyes staring through a curtain of midnight-black hair. The voice was measured, with no discernible accent, and even standing three steps below, still towered over Arch as if he had been sitting down.

"Beecher," Arch said, a statement more than a question.

"Correct."

Arch proceeded with a quick explanation of just exactly who he was and why he was there, all the while still standing in the cramped passageway.

"Trouble's a brewin," Beecher said. "Best get Pengo squared away and then we can chat."

"Nice one," Arch said, "…nice one, indeed."

With every treasured and breakable object packed out of sight, the trio stood like soldiers peering over battlements, eyes peeled up the street and down. The marchers could come from either way. As the sweep of the minute hand hit the top of the hour, they came from both. Flags and banners held high with atavistic pride. They appeared first as reflections in the launderette's darkened windows. Vile slogans were broadcast in myriad colors and raised voices issued abrasive and unified directives, shouted directly at the line of policemen keeping pace with shields raised and truncheons wavering in white knuckle grips. A solitary car's windscreen was speared by a banner pole in a provocative, infantile challenge to authority, but there would be no retribution or arrest.

"Fuck me," Pengo said. "That's Ivy's car; her from the Post Office, she uses that to ferry her old man around since his hip's been on the blink. Why don't they get the bloke that threw that pole?"

"'Cause the rest of 'em are waiting just for that," Arch said. "Take one out, and you gotta take 'em all out."

A heavy thunk on the roof of the pub drew stares at the ceiling.

"Bottle," said Beecher. "Full, by the sounds of it."

Another thunk, this time followed quickly by two more. A couple of skinheads decided now was a good time for refreshments. Excited voices broke away from the pack and prowled outside. Pengo pulled Beecher and Arch to the floor. A face pressed against the window; nostrils flared against the stained glass. From below, the skinhead's pale, emaciated dome looked like someone's blind grandad had been a bit plucky with a straight razor.

"Oi, landlord, you open?" the voice bellowed, and then a palm slapped the glass. "Are you fucking open?"

The howl of the crowd advanced with a sickening rush. Random smashes of glass punctuated every hysterical chant. Another thunk on the roof and an orange fireball swallowed the light, and then an almighty cheer.

"They're gonna burn the pub down," Pengo shouted.

"Nah, they wouldn't, not in front of the police," Arch said.

"Yes, in front of the fuckin police!"

The hiss and crackle of shortwave radios and the clatter of hooves on concrete broke through the celebration and more faces pressed against the glass and the dark cones of coppers helmets danced like puppets atop the railway platform artwork.

"In 'ere," Pengo shouted. "Three of us."

"Stay in there," a mounted policeman leaned down from his saddle, "you'll be alright, the fire blew itself out."

Pengo eased his head up and met the copper eye to eye.

"What about the march?"

"The tail end is winding through now. Should be clear in…"

His measured assurance was interrupted by a couple of angry shouts that preceded a half-brick being hurled through the pub door's crown glass window with an almighty crash. Both horse and rider were immediately off to run down a pair of brazen, soon to be bruised, skinheads. Arch brushed shards of colored crystals from his jacket and stood up for a look.

"That's twice today. Who dishes out agro on a Tuesday bleedin' afternoon?"

"Why not on a Tuesday?" Beecher said.

"Well, it's not even the middle of the week, is it? There's been no time to settle in."

Pengo and Beecher frowned, utterly confused.

"Tuesday's are all about acceptance. It's when we let go of the past."

Shakes of heads.

"Look, Monday's are, oh fuck, another week; Tuesdays are, might as well get on with it, stay up and watch, *The Old Grey Whistle Test,* take the pulse of the nation's youth; Wednesday's are, 'right, we're amongst it, we're in the groove, might grab a pint at lunchtime, or have a stroll down the market – fruit and veg are always the best midweek; Thursday's are, through the worst, might wander up the bookies, have a look at the racing forms, and then stop by the butcher's and order a nice joint for the weekend, perhaps pick up some sausages for a fry up; Friday's are, out with the lads, ten pints of lager, forty fags, and a chicken vindaloo; Saturday's are, down the West End for some shopping with the missus, along to the QPR if they're not playing away, catch up again with her indoors for Scampi and chips in a basket, back home in time for *The Professionals, Match of The Day and Parkinson;* Sunday's frankly are just dinner - roast beef, a big slab of Yorkshire, slice of gooseberry pie and lashings of custard, see what Melvyn Bragg's got going on the *South Bank Show* - usually a load of bollocks unless Pete Townshend's in the studio or some black fella's dancin' or singin' - and then an early night and get ready for Monday."

"Not one for structure, then?" Pengo said.

"The point is," Arch said, in his most professorial tone, "…dishing out agro is for a Saturday. This is Britain, we've grown accustomed to a little bottle smash-and-dash on a Saturday. On a Tuesday? Fuck off. These cunts need a slap."

Pengo, Arch and Beecher paced about the empty lounge bar, meeting often at the expansive window, gazing stupefied at the parading racists like tourists at the zoo, each puffing a chimney stack's worth of No.6, and Benson and Hedges, and Embassy Regal. About their heads, the smoke mingled with the sweet aroma of hops and stale perfume. Outside, other than a few screaming police cars, all was becoming quiet on the White City front.

A thumbs-up signaling, *"all clear"*, from the last mounted copper, and Pengo slid the heavy bolt and opened the doors to an empty yard. So quiet was the car park that the tinkling and whistling of the fruit machine Arch had on the boil could be heard clear across to the adjacent row of shops. Beecher wandered over to grab a few newspapers and bottles of vinegar to try and lift some of the more explicit comments that had been spray-painted onto the pub's windows by one of the National Front's lesser intellects. The slogans scrawled read:

'KOONS GO HOMO' - presumably meaning, 'home,' but perhaps not, and; 'PAKE BASTUDS' - clearly, 'Pakistani bastards,' which wasn't so much an affront to the current immigration policy as an endorsement, or even criticism, of Asian contraception, or lack thereof.

"Good lad," Pengo said. "Should come off with a bit of scrubbing. I'll send Arch out to give you a hand."

Beecher scrubbed; Arch talked. Endlessly. Nothing appeared off-limits. From the sordid details of his nighttime activities with various ladies of ill repute to the dodgy dealings with scrap yards around the home counties. Beecher learned that Arch hated drugs, abhorred toffs, was fanatical about Queens Park Rangers, despised Chelsea – the team, the borough, and, for some unknown reason, the bridge. The pint-sized orator craved kebabs for breakfast, thought tea was best MIF (milk-in-first), drank coffee black with no sugar, kept no pets (although he'd like a dog because *"dogs are loyal and loyalty was the cornerstone of cornerstones,"*), would like to be rich but would settle for being well-off, and hadn't missed an episode of *Coronation Street* in four years.

With a bottle of Sarson's emptied and two copies of the Daily Mail wadded into a soggy mess, the windows gleamed once more, perfectly cleaned of racist vitriol. Arch sensed his one-on-one time with the lad was drawing to a close. Time for one last question:

"So, just how serious are you about this music lark?"

Arch posed the question with an unlit cigarette hanging from his bottom lip, hands at the ready to strike a match.

"It's all that I am," Beecher said, still down on his knees surveying his work. "…and not because I can't do anything else. I could have gone to university…"

"…but you had a dream and you saw your name in lights?"

"…no, I was gonna say…"

"…you had a visit from a dead blues singer, and he told you to follow your heart?"

"…no, my Mum plays…"

"…some of your songs to a Hollywood agent and he said you were a shoo-in for superstardom?"

"…no, she plays bingo down at the Roxy every Friday afternoon and the manager needed someone to call the numbers and when I held the microphone…"

"…you saw yourself on stage with a backing band made up of the greatest artists of all time?"

"…no, I got a nasty shock from the metal and when the electrician came to fix it, he said I looked like a rock star."

"That's it? An electrician said you reminded him of someone?"

"Not just someone, a fucking rock star."

"Did he say which one?"

"No, but it doesn't matter. It set me off and I bought a guitar with my earnings and I never felt more at home."

Arch drew deep on the cigarette. He laughed in that, "*you don't know shit, kid,*" kinda way. He sauntered up to Beecher and went to drape his arm over his shoulder but then Beecher stood up and Arch made to straighten his own collar.

"The entertainment world is like a pit full of crocodiles and man-eating tigers," Arch said, suddenly earnest and educated.

"Lots of bared teeth on show, but they ain't smiling. They'll take you for all your worth and throw the rest to the dogs. But it just so happens that I'm looking for some talent to manage; someone to shelter and nurture, and keep 'em from potential harm. It's fate that brought me into Manoj's gaff this morning, and then meeting you here during all this nonsense. It's the universe conspiring in our favor. Whaddya say we have a listen to your tape and see if there's anything there?"

"It sounds killer on the pub speakers," Beecher said. "I reckon Pengo won't mind me spinning it up, seeing as he has no customers."

"Nice one," Arch said. "Nice one, indeed."

They walked back into the pub like two excited schoolboys. A lopsided alliance had been forged. Beecher pulled the cassette from its case, pressed play, and time stood still.

Chapter Eleven

Eeva sheltered under the spreading, summer canopy of a solitary ancient Oak. A steady deluge of tepid rain rapped hard all around and raised a curtain of mist to her waist. It came from the waxy skin of decaying leaves, and clumps of saturated soil and dead insects - a billion soft tears ascending into the atmosphere where winds from all points of the compass would push and pull and swipe at its mass. She felt the damp air lay heavy on her skin and rubbed her palms together and they were cold, and she slid them into silk-lined pockets, and she waited for the stranger to come.

A whistle announced his presence.
Not for her.
For a dog. A border collie named, Jackson Browne. The dog spun on a sixpence and raced across the meadow, mouth agape, running low, a sleek, sodden missile of white and black. A gnarly, splintered branch clamped between his teeth was dropped at Beecher's feet with a flash of eager eyes and an impatient shuffle of muddied paws.

Beecher lobbed the stick and sent the dog headlong into marshland that swallowed the animal entirely. He set off along the trail, twirling a leash and whipping blades of soggy grass into the air, rejoicing silently as the wind picked up and took the rain in its embrace and whisked it off to the east; to the dirty smudge on the horizon; to London town where it would fall on shoppers and footballers and traffic jams and council houses and castles.

The amplifying light separated the Oak from the dismal, threatening sky, building form and wealth into the mighty limbs and painting highlights of green and gold where dark shadows had ruled only moments before. And the light fought through the heavy canopy and Eeva was immediately irradiated. Her hair, already blindingly-white, glowed brighter and she pushed it from her face, and her ruby lips parted, and she spoke.

And Beecher froze.

"I've been watching you and the dog for some time," Eeva said. "You must enjoy the rain."

"Hate it," Beecher said, and then caught the negativity. "I mean, I prefer it when it's sunny." *Fuck.*

He stepped closer. She wore dark glasses. A little bit Bardot; a little bit Marilyn - if they were hotter than the sun. He saw himself in the reflection, moving awkward and slow. He stood taller and shoved the bunched leash into his pocket.

Eeva said, "I wasn't sure which hill you might climb but your friend assured me you'd be along at some point; said you walked every trail in the park. Such a beautiful place."

Eeva turned her face and scanned the lush, rolling downs and Beecher's gaze followed.

"My friend?"

"The landlord of the Railway Tavern said I might find you out here, with the dog."

"Jackson Browne."

"Nice guy."

"No, Pengo is the landlord. The dog is Jackson Browne."

He saw her cheeks crinkle under the glasses.

"He won't answer to anything else. Go ahead, try it," Beecher said.

Eeva stooped down, "Here, boy!"

Her voice was tinged with an accent that Beecher couldn't place. Sounded exotic. The dog had its nose buried deep in a pile of leaves. At her command, Jackson Browne looked up as if he'd pushed his snout into a live electrical outlet. He spun in a complete circle, raced to her side, came to heel and laid in the dirt with paws crossed. Eeva and the dog both looked at Beecher as if he was an alien.

"He doesn't seem to mind," she said. "Perhaps he's just messing with you."

"That's a first," Beecher said, snapping his fingers and repeating the call, "Here, boy!"

Nothing.

Again, "Here, boy!"

This time with a couple slaps of his thigh.

Zero interest.

"Well, would you look at that. Eight years I've known that dog. It's Pengo's Mum's, she's not been well, and he doesn't get out much."

Eeva stroked Jackson Browne's neck and fluffed his ears and received a grateful whimper in return. She stood up and introduced herself.

"My name is Eeva. I've been looking for you. I saw you on television last week and was very impressed."

As she spoke, a warm breeze drew up the valley and ruffled the edges of her skirt and her skin was bare and her thighs were tanned dark as chocolate. She caught the skirt self-consciously and smoothed it. Beecher was shaking now. He dared not offer his hand, she'd think he was possessed, or tripping.

It's not her, can't be. Coincidence is a motherfucker. Get it together.

He said, "So, what brings you out here?"

Oh, yeah, that's getting it together, nice one..., nice one, indeed.

"I wanted to meet you."

"How come?"

"It touched me, you know, the song and the performance; how you looked."

"You must've liked Smiler, then. He's something special."

What the hell are ya doing? She paid you a fucking compliment.

"Nah, seen him before, same old songs; same old act. You were fresh. It felt like you were going somewhere."

"It was our first show."

If she takes off the glasses, I'll know.

"I was taken by your name."

Beecher squinted a confused, *"Oh, yeah?"*

"Family connections?"

The penny drops.

"Oh, oh, yeah… no. I don't think any of my ancestors ever amounted to much."

"Well, that appearance should put that right, now that people have heard the song."

"Yeah, the kids seemed okay with it. Got 'em up and movin'. Hopefully, it'll be on the radio soon, my manager is still sorting out the details."

And then she mouthed, softly:

Supermassive Superstar your life;
Let me see your super magic eyes;

Jackson Browne sprang to his feet and barked and panted and wheeled about her legs. She continued:

Hey! Hey! You don't save my soul.

Beecher wanted to scream that they'd met before, in some other dimension; at some other time – the skinheads, the purse, his journal, the pen for fuck's sake; the pen!

Go off on that tangent and she'll think you're fucking deranged.

He watched her lips part; he could sense how soft they would be. Another breeze whipped up and brushed the canopy and a thousand lighted crystals rained down from wet leaves, encircling their bodies, filling the void. Beecher's hands flew to cover his head, while Eeva's hands remained in her pockets. She remained perfectly dry. Beecher shook out his hair and Jackson Browne followed suit.

"Guess I'm standing in the wrong place," Beecher muttered.

"But at the right time," Eeva said. "I want to introduce you to someone. He owns a record company, well, he owns many things, but his record company is a particular source of pride. It's how he speaks to the world. He commits his time to very few artists, but when he does, great things happen."

"Do you work for him?"

"Sort of, I just know you and he will get on like a house on fire."

"Who is it? Which label?"

"Aeon Records."

"Haven't heard of them."

"They do a lot of international work."

"I haven't even been to France."

"Would you like to go?"

"To France? Yeah, I wanna go everywhere; I want to see the world."

"How about touring the U.S.A.?"

"That's a pretty awesome dream."

"Doesn't have to be. Come and meet him, let's see what we can work out."

"Just me? Or the band?"

"Just you, for now. It's more intimate."

At this suggestion, Beecher felt a little dizzy. He shuffled over to the trunk of the Oak and leaned against the damp bark. Looking past thick branches and through the netting of emerald-green foliage, he saw that dual rainbows tapered outward from the hillock, extending like translucent bridges, arcing high to the horizon, being gently cleansed of their multi-colored radiance. It was like the end of a fairytale.

"So, shall I set it up?" Eeva's voice had an excited, playful edge.

"Yes, absolutely," Beecher said. "I'm just not used to anyone wanting to receive me or the music. I won't know what to say."

"You don't have to say anything, just listen. This could be the ticket to your dream."

"When do we do this?"

"Soon. I'll call you."

"I don't have a phone."

"At the pub, then. Is that okay?"

"Yes, the pub is good, yeah, call me there."

"When's best for you," Eeva said. "Morning or afternoon?"

"Anytime. I can come anytime."

"Good," Eeva said. "I think the rain has had its say. Shall we walk?"

"Which way'd you come in?"

"Let's just follow the rainbow, see where it leads."

Chapter Twelve

"You should've warned me you were gonna keep Jackson Browne out all day," Pengo said. "Mum's been going berserk which means her blood pressure's up, and I've had to have the Doc 'round. He says she could take a turn for the worse if she gets out of her routine. She's not well…"

"Didn't plan it, Pengo. Time just got away from me. As you can see, the mutt is tip-top. The evening was so warm, and the downs were so, so fucking beautiful and the trees…"

"Warm evening? Trees? What're you on about, mate. It's been raining all day, that's why Mum has been losing her mind. Last time Jackson Browne was out in the wet he had to be taken down the vet 'cause we couldn't stop him from shivering."

"He's fine, look at him, Happy as a lark. He'll be hungry though, neither of us has had so much as a dry crust since this morning. You know, Pengo, I've given you some shit over the years about your dreadful taste in clothes and women, and that disgusting, inedible, macrobiotic hippie-dippie shit you choke down for dinner, not too mention the fact you haven't bought a drink in your entire life, but sending that woman my way was a stroke of genius. Thank you, brother, …and you *are* my brother, you know that, don't ya? I'm tellin' ya, we will walk tall as multi-millionaires, you and me. And we'll have matching yachts, whatchya say to that?"

Pengo shuddered at the thought of spending even one night on the ocean and twirled his little finger inside his bellybutton, a sure sign he was confused.

"Mate, you're delirious, I haven't the foggiest fucking idea what you're on about but keep it coming, it's good to see you smile."

Chapter Thirteen

Beecher swam from the abyss, clawing and kicking and coughing. He surfaced on a sea of ruddy-blue velvet pillows and course army blankets and paper-thin cotton sheets that reeked of mildew and cat piss, only to find Harry and Fez, bent double, tenderly whispering.

"Telephone, Beecher. You awake? Some bird's going on about a meeting, said she'd hold on."

The bedclothes were knotted about Beecher's naked body like the peaks and valleys of a mountain range, and he came upright wind-milling all four limbs, catching Fez on the chin and Harry square in the bollocks, and they both went down, hard.

"Fuck, guys," Beecher shouted, "...what the fuck?"

The lads cowered and massaged and whimpered. Three weeks ago, they were nervous about uttering so much as a passing, *"Hello,"* to the anointed local hero, and yet here they were today, on bended knees, set aglow by the life-affirming rays of a vibrant summer sun as it pierced the Railway Tavern's attic window like a bundle of golden spears, facing his improbably-stiff, morning cock.

"Phone call," Fez eked out. "Downstairs. In the bar."

Beecher gathered the sheet into a hastily-tied robe, rolled off the mattress and stumbled down the winding stairs, two at a time.

The lads upheld a respective moment of silence.

"You could run a flag up that thing," Harry said, with an equal mixture of shock and appreciation.

True to the morning routine, Pengo was in the lounge and Bob Marley was on the jukebox. Opening time was a half-hour away. A time of peace - the subtle clink of glasses, the squeak of the taps, the gentle gurgle of water - this was his thinking time. The telephone handset was cradled in the cash register's open drawer. Beecher came through the doors wearing a sheen of sweat.

"Take it easy there, champ, she's still on," Pengo said quietly. "I just had a word with her. Nice lady; likes a bit of reggae, so you're all good."

Beecher gulped some water from the tap and wiped dribbles from his chin with the back of his hand. He picked up the handset and immediately coughed.

"Sorry, hello, sorry, I just had a drink, sorry."

"How are you?"

"Yeah, good."

"You were sleeping."

"Yeah, can't get off and then can't wake up."

Beecher clocked Pengo's head shake, met his eyes and saw the grin and the pity.

Fuck, what am I sayin'?

Eeva's voice was distant and distorted across the phone line, *"I'm going to send a car for you. It should be there around three p.m. Bring any tapes you want him to hear. You'll be staying overnight, is that okay?"*

"Yeah, I guess so. Will you be there?"

"Of course."

"Yeah, just checking. It's just, you know…"

"Don't be nervous, it's just a meeting."

"Yeah, yeah, 'course, just a meeting."

"See you later."

"Yeah, bye."

Beecher hung up and sidled over to the bar, adjusting the sheet as he climbed onto a stool.

"Today," he said. "At three o'clock. She's sending a car."

Pengo wiped dried lipstick from a beer mug, gave it a once 'round with a damp towel and put it back on the shelf.

"What about Arch?"

"Haven't told him."

"Good, the little shite doesn't need to know 'bout any of this. He'll only fuck it up, take my word."

Beecher fiddled with the frayed corners of the sheet, then picked up a beer mat, peeled off its outer skin and then stared at the shredded cardboard unknowingly.

"I feel bad, though, a bit of a prick."

Pengo found another mug stained with dregs of ale or backwash or.., it didn't matter. Under the tap it went, a quick rinse, a quick wipe, and back on the rack.

"Go ahead and feel that way, right up to the point you're signing a recording contract and then maybe you'll realize what a wanker he's been for not gettin' it done sooner. Fancy a pint?"

Beecher sighed and nodded a polite, *"No, thanks."*

Chapter Fourteen

"Fuuu," Snooze started it;

"...kin," Harry continued;

"... 'ell," Fez rounded it out.

Theirs was a joint exasperation as a Rolls Royce Silver Cloud glided into the Railway Tavern's car park. The car was silent as fog and dressed out in coal-black trim with tinted windows all around.

Beecher fussed with his hair. He was geared up – black coat with satin lapels, leather trousers, a little tasteful jewelry, the works.

"How's it look, lads?"

Snooze ran his eyes over Beecher and then stared out the window, said, "the motor looks the business and so do you, mate." And then with a wink, "Just you remember who makes those songs sound as good as they do."

Beecher looked small and lost and pale.

"I'd never forget that, Snooze," he said. "You and the lads have done me proud and I'm looking to repay you as soon as I can."

"Go on with ya, I'm just fuckin' with your head."

"You know, if this works out, I want to put a real brass section together, with you as the leader. And maybe we'll get a proper bass player, free up Harry's left hand a bit."

"I wouldn't have it any other way," Snooze said.

"Only if it goes well," Beecher said.

"*When* it goes well," Snooze countered. "Now, be gone. Go get us some cash."

"Wanna take some snacks, Beech?" Pengo shouted. "I can bag up some leftovers from lunch."

Fez jumped in, "Yeah, just what he needs when he's trying to snag a record deal, one of your fuckin' cheese and onion rolls. The inside of that Roller will smell like Harry's scrotum after he's rubbed out one of his dailies."

The levity was badly needed, and it broke the tension beautifully.

"Better get out there sharpish, Beecher," Harry said. "The locals are gathering. It'll be on blocks and they'll have the wheels off before you know it."

"Right, here goes nothing," Beecher said. "Wish us luck."

Beecher left the pub with a nervous nod and a wave to the lads as they goofed at the window. He wasn't halfway to the Rolls when the back door of the car opened of its own accord. Not a squeak, not a stutter. The interior was as dark as a cave, and the smell of fine leather and cigar smoke beat off the toxic bouquet of bleach and cheap soap powder spilling out of next door's launderette. Beecher scooted inside, and the door shut just as soundless as it had opened. The band members were solemn now; sudden orphans, peering longingly through the leaded squares of the pub's bay window as the car pulled slowly away.

"You know," Harry said, "We may never see him again. Like in that movie when that bloke goes into that spaceship."

"*Close Encounters,*" Snooze said.

"No, the one where the guy goes a little mental and pisses off his family and makes models of some vision he's got in his head."

"Yeah, *Close Encounters of the Third Kind,*" Pengo said. "It was on TV at Christmas."

"I didn't see it on the telly."

"I don't care where you saw it, you just described the same fucking film that was on the TV last Christmas."

Fez sparked up a joint and caught the remainder of Pengo's obvious frustration.

"And you can put that out, right now. I'm not having any nonsense that'll bring the fucking coppers in here. Where'd you get that, anyway?"

Fez looked a little meek, "From Nana, she's got a drawer full, ready-rolled."

"Jesus-fucking-Christ. Don't go through her things."

Pengo was dialed up now. The strain of taking care of his ailing mother was bearing down like a battleship.

"You asked me to dole out her pills," Fez said, "...and she pointed me to the drawer and there they were, like little, white soldiers on parade. She said you wouldn't mind, seeing as you got it from me in the first place."

"Well, she was wrong. I do mind, 'cause it's the only thing that keeps her quiet through the night, and money's tight right now, so there won't be any more buys for a while."

Fez snuffed out the joint and handed it to Pengo. He reached into his jacket pocket and pulled out a clear plastic bag of the finest, Grade-A smoke money could buy.

"All the way from Morocco, fresh as spring flowers and sledgehammer-strong. This stuff'll wipe out your fuckin' memory, and it's on the house. Nana's been like a Mum to me and Harry over the years."

Pengo was taken aback. Words of compassion coming from the face of this annoying little shit was a rarity. But Nana was a soft spot and he'd hit on it. She was a tower of strength for many a punter. Didn't matter what their station in life was, she'd dish out advice or a hot meal or float them some cash, no questions asked. When Harry's Dad had done his usual number and gone ape-shit and wrecked the house, it was her that put the lad up, and it was her that held him tight when the racking sobs finally came.

"Come on," Harry said. "Beecher's out doing the business, we need to send him some good vibes."

Nods of agreement domino around the bar and Pengo punched *B45* on the jukebox. He reached behind the unit and turned the volume all the way up. Robert Palmer sings,

> *"Said the fight to make ends meet keeps a man upon his feet;*
> *Holding down his job, trying to show he can't be bought…"*

The nods of agreement turned into nods of approval.
And they listened.
Each of them lost to their own place in time.
"What a band," Snooze said. "What a fucking band."

The Silver Cloud floated through the terraced canyons of White City and Shepherd's Bush, picked up the Great West Road at Hammersmith, crossed the Thames at Chiswick, and descended into the leafy sprawl of true suburbia. Greater London, it was called, but south of the river was another world; a self-contained universe of affordable housing and serene parks and bloated supermarkets and gaggles of raincoats squeezing into smoke-filled train carriages with packed lunches squirreled away in faux-leather briefcases. Within the span of a single bridge, the vibrancy and vitality of the metropolis was discarded. This was the land of the wide-boy and the myopic accountant, co-existing like tiger and snake. Accents were buttered and refined in some boroughs and clung to like sodden, cockney lifebelts in others. And here, the weather was observed with the zeal and enterprise of WWII air-raid wardens curtailing a Luftwaffe airstrike.

"*Brolly or no brolly?*"

"*If you miss the 8:15, you might get caught out. Go on, take it. Better to be safe than sorry, eh?*"

"*Supposed to be nice tomorrow.*"

"*They said that last week and look what happened.*"

'*I know, I nipped into Marks and Spencer's and I hadn't been inside but ten minutes and came out and it was teamin' down.*"

"*They never get it right.*"

"*There's money down here,*" Beecher mused.

This was album territory. Where an artist could stretch out, try new stuff, and the kids would buy it because the parents had spare cash. He observed a couple of suburban punks - hair spiked with beef dripping and leather jackets strategically paint-splattered and decorated with a few of Mum's safety pins - nothing donned or applied that couldn't be removed before Dad got home. The two were just young girls, minding their own business, walking amongst shuffling grannies and street sweepers and postmen and paperboys. Tradition, be damned, there was comfort on the fringe. To offend is to belong. They were valkyries and the *Marquee* was Valhalla, home to a three-chord band fronted by a spitting and vomiting, howling banshee deriding every aspect of the British society their grandparents had most likely died for.

More casualties floated beyond the smoke-tinted barrier, seemingly small and utterly content.

"*It's no life,*" Beecher thought. "*Or is it? Maybe they have it down; maybe reaching for the stars is for chumps? Whoever gets what they really want, anyway? Get a job, get a wife, get a house, get a kid, get a...*"

The Rolls came to a stop and a cheerless adolescent, still of school age, pushed a pram across the street.

"*Children pushing children. Yeah, it's no life.*"

The partition window whirred down.

"We should clear this traffic soon, sir," the driver said. "I'll have you there in time for tea."

"But it's only two o'clock," Beecher said. "Where are we headed?"

"Down south. On the coast, near Portsmouth. Just another hour or so once we get moving. Would you like the radio on, sir?"

"Yeah, that'd be great."

He felt awkward and alone.

"I'm Beecher," he said.

The driver locked on Beecher's face in the rearview mirror.

"William. Billy, if you like. Been that way since I was in short trousers."

"The south coast it is then, Billy."

Beecher rested his head on the window. His mind was racing; thoughts folding in on one another - half-baked lyrics, incomplete stories, and fantastic dreams. The tools of writers. And with the words came pictures. Or maybe it was the other way around. Without images, there can be no words.

"Don't pull at the threads," his mother would scold every winter when the Aran sweater was retrieved from a ratty cardboard box and admired for its longevity. Greeting the daylight next would be a pair of purple fingerless gloves knitted two sizes too small, causing his strangled fingers to wriggle out like bent bicycle spokes.

"I promise, I'll do you a new set next year," she'd say. But she never did.

Beecher closed his eyes and journeyed back in time. Sights and smells; the texture of woolen hats and socks and scarves, all the colors of the rainbow. A concession of unconditional love.

"See me then; see me now. Riding in a car. Not just any car, a fucking Rolls Royce. On my own, all on my own."

The words tumbled. He pulled at the thread.

"On my own. Out in front, singing on the telly." And then… *"Who the fuck do I think I am?"*

The car ground to a halt next to a double-decker bus. Inside, there was standing room only. Lower-deck passengers scanned the car from the Spirit of Ecstasy's wings extended in perpetual flight to the soft glow of crimson taillights, settling their curiosity on the blacked-out windows, seeking the mystery within. And the Rolls' dark, opulent eyes stared back. And Beecher stared back, swaddled and safe in a womb of leather and suede. He surveyed the crowd - mostly women, chatting happily all at once, pressed into their seats clutching shopping bags stuffed with freshly-baked loaves, and gaudy cereal boxes, and sprigs of leaks and broccoli spilling from brown paper bags and finding purchase under fleshy chins and resting against pale necks.

"They have each other," he thought. *"And I am alone. I guess money doesn't really matter. Until it does."*

Beecher wanted them to see his face. He tried to lower the window. No joy.

"Can I have the window down, Billy?"

"Back ones are disabled," he said, "...something about dust and dirt mucking up the interior. I'll put on the air conditioning."

A cool breeze immediately whipped about Beecher's legs.

Too cool.

"It's alright, mate," he said. "I'll do without."

The traffic cleared, and the pace picked up. They were motoring now, smooth as silk.

"How'd you like it?" Billy was fishing.

"Another world," Beecher said. "How fast are we going?"

"Ninety-five. She'll do the ton, easy."

"Feels like what being rich should feel like."

Outside, row houses and narrow streets gave way to wide, tree-lined carriageways which in turn gave way to open fields as green as new money. The whisper of rushing air was disturbed. Beecher looked to the sky, colored teal blue through the tempered glass, but it was cloudless and empty. An industrial roar arose, abrasive and insistent. On the road, white lines blurred as one; a single stroke of the artist's brush, broken only by shadows from above. Riding the divide, a motorcycle blew by, the rider tucked tightly, almost fetal.

Beecher blinked and the machine vanished.

Another disturbance, this time two percussive barks invaded the cabin. Dual silhouettes whipped past the car, joining the lead bike by heeling sharply into the Rolls' lane, setting up a tight arrow formation.

Billy was unfazed. Beecher twisted in his seat, saw three more black devils bringing up the rear.

"What's going on with these bikers?"

"Nothing to worry about," the driver said. "These are the Outriders, they'll be accompanying you to the lodge."

"What lodge? Why do we need an escort?"

"I assume because you are a V.I.P."

"And the lodge?"

"A residence on the cliffs. I call it the lodge, but I guess it's more of a villa with forest on three sides. The patio has the prettiest view of the channel."

"I'm sure I don't warrant any kind of escort."

"Are you carrying any valuables, like jewels or anything like that?"

"Nope."

"What about money, or..," Billy spun his head and with a whisper and a wink, said, "...druuugs."

"Nope."

"It's you then."

Beecher checked out the curious entourage, leading and trailing like dutiful railcars. The cadre moved through traffic as one fluid organism and Beecher's excitement turned to anxiety. His palms were suddenly smooth with sweat and he rubbed them on his thighs and shiny smears painted the black leather. This wasn't how he dreamed of being signed. Where's the West End meet-and-greet, and the one-on-one's with journos from the major music mags?

Dearly beloved, Beecher Stowe could've been a major celebrity had he not fallen for the first blonde that suggested he might have a certain 'star quality.'

"We begged him to be patient," said his manager, "...but he just wouldn't listen. He never listened."

The leader of the Outriders raised a gloved hand and the procession slowed, departing the main highway in favor of a succession of narrow lanes, eventually turning onto an unsigned, tree-lined gravel drive that wound through stands of Yew, Holly, Oak and Redwood, with a canopy so dense all sunlight was eclipsed to the point of total darkness. Beecher pushed his face through the partition like an anxious child, throwing Billy a nervous smile and focusing intently on the sulfurous beam of the Rolls' headlights.

The caravan slowed to a crawl. And the minutes ticked by. And the car ambled along in the blackness in pursuit of three red stars. And then the canopy relented, and the stands of trees were broached like the walls of a medieval city, and soon the car was rolling through an expanse of terraced gardens bathed in golden sunlight. And Billy hummed a nondescript tune, tapping his fingers in time on the polished-walnut steering wheel.

Without prompting, he said, "Be yourself in there. Whatever it is you're selling, just be honest."

"Do you know this guy?"

"I've delivered a few people down here. All like you. Young, nervous."

"Musicians?"

"Don't know. It's been made clear that it's not my place to ask," he said, "...got a family to feed, if ya know wha' I mean."

Billy ceased his tapping and gripped the wheel tighter with both hands.

"Remember where you come from. Try not to be seduced by words, they count for only so much."

Beecher nodded, and Billy nodded, and for a brief moment their faces were mirrored in doubt. And with the final bend rounded, a French chateau manifested from thin air.

The Rolls crunched over a gravel drive, coming to rest before a cavernous stone vestibule. If intimidation was the order of the day, it worked. Beecher stared at a palace. Round-turreted towers pointed at clouds, and lead-paned windows were as tall as doors, and lanterns burned in more openings than could be counted. Ivy spread like green arteries across every surface, winding over stone-carved faces that issued equal measures of appeal and disdain. Beecher alighted and brushed creases from his clothes. A few birds chirped, otherwise, silence. From the shadows, a man approached. Black coat and tails, pallid skin, hair pushed back, silver or gray Beecher couldn't tell. He carried a silver tray which he extended a few inches and Beecher saw what looked like three sugar cubes of varying sizes aligned on a white towel.

"For your refreshment."

The voice was soft but guttural, accented strongly of German.

Beecher was about to respond when a heavy oak door opened, and a voice rang out."

"Emil, nicht für diesen gast, er ist nicht der eine."

The man immediately lowered the tray and stepped back. He adopted a smug expression as if to say, *"Your loss."*

A woman, mid-sixties, maybe older, beckoned Beecher to enter. The man with the tray received a second volley of her invective.

This chick is pissed.

"I have an appointment," Beecher said.

"The woman softened into perfect English, "We've been expecting you. Do you have any luggage?"

Beecher shook his head and checked out the entrance hall. From the checkerboard floor to the tin-clad ceiling thirty feet above, walls of Mahogany paneling displayed gilt-framed paintings declaring a blood-and-guts theme of war with cavalries charging on battlefields, infantries engaged in hand-to-hand combat, squadrons of biplanes tangled in chaotic flight, and ironclads under sail in rough seas. Suits of armor, shields, spears, animal skins and the requisite stag's head - a monarch, sixteen pointer – provided only slight relief from the artistic theatre of destruction. The woman stood patiently at his side as he completed a full turn.

"Follow me, sir."

From the entrance hall, four narrow corridors extended into blackness. Muted footsteps and the ticking of clocks, all set to different time zones, accompanied the short stroll. They came to a double door, brass knobs and latches, more carved faces, eschewing stone for wood. These were kinder, less threatening, somehow. Once opened, streaks of sunlight speared another hallway and the sweet smell of jasmine and lemon trees subverted the odor of age and decay. Twenty yards more and Beecher entered a magnificent, glass-walled conservatory open at its widest point to the splendor of the gardens. Rising from a table on the patio beyond, Eeva stood attentive, catching immediately the sinking rays of summer in her platinum hair and shadows were drawn crisp and black across her ivory skin. She moved to greet him with arms outstretched.

"Beecher Stowe. The immensely talented, Beecher Stowe. Come and meet my friend, I've told him all about you."

"I didn't know you knew that much about me," Beecher said, fumbling. "H..h...how are you?"

"I'm excited you've come down."

The scent of her perfume floated on the changing breeze and it was light and flowery, and Beecher's pulse quickened.

Christ, I'm gonna fuck this up.

As if reading his mind, she whispered, "Don't be nervous, just be yourself."

Billy's words, exactly.

Eeva took his hand and her grip was firm and she led him to the table.

Hans Tomek did not rise. He looked through umbrella shade with obsidian eyes that showed no point of light.

"So," he said dully, "...why you?"

Beecher saw a man in black – silk shirt, waistcoat, trousers, socks, shoes; a man befitting the signing of a death warrant.

"Why me, what?"

Tomek shifted in his chair, crossed and uncrossed his legs.

"Why should I invest in you? We have artists that are doing very well and I'm not one to follow fashion, so I'm not given to knee-jerk signings. So, why you?"

Beecher felt Eeva's hand slide from his grip as if he were a yacht that had loosed its moorings and been left to drift without an anchor. And the sea was boiling, and the sails were luffing. She had moved from his side, but the faint aroma of her perfume lingered, and he willed his nerves to calm, and his skin cooled, and he brushed stray locks from his forehead, and said,

"Because I am not any other artist, and because I am clearly not fashionable, and because I wouldn't be here if you thought I was."

"Perhaps."

Beecher's stomach churned. Tomek's stare was cold and intense and unblinking. The man offered no warmth and no courtesy. An opening salvo had been dispatched and now there was silence except for the distant whine of a gardener's power tool creeping and swirling around the patio. Beecher shifted from one foot to the other. He looked around for Eeva.

Gone.

"Heart, by default, sells records," Tomek said, turning his head away, eyes roving the finely-manicured grounds, "...it's an annoyingly necessary ingredient in this business. It's the only body part that can turn sound into money. Try creating an empire without it," he scoffed.

Tomek poured coffee from an engraved silver pot, then hovered the spout over an empty china cup. Beecher declined the offer, thought the pot looked like Aladdin's lamp and wondered if he gave it a good rubbing whether he might be granted a chance to sit. He stood in direct sunlight, overheating, regretting the leathers. He wavered on his feet and grabbed a chairback for support.

Tomek continued, "Having an abundance of heart means little ditties can be relatable to every person, forevermore – housewives, farmers, cab drivers and market traders alike. All it takes is a distinctive voice and a sweet melody and, voilà! Cash flows like a river of snowmelt."

He looked up at Beecher, measured and challenging.

"Now, why do you suppose with all the talent, in all of the world, is that so fucking difficult to produce or predict?"

Beecher made to answer, or rather his lips parted in the hope that something resembling an intelligent response would emerge.

There was no need, Tomek wasn't giving up the floor.

"A hit on the radio can mirror your deepest fears or your burning desires or your soul-emptying aches, and irregardless of the sentiment, I am of the opinion that it remains the only way to speak to the world as a whole. Creating and selling music is at once the most insidious, immoral and life-affirming undertaking in all of the arts - and it is what I do best."

He stood and presented his hand with a transformative smile, showing perfect white teeth and laughter lines etched deep at the corners of his mouth.

"I am Hans Tomek, President of Aeon Records, and you are Beecher Stowe, artist extraordinaire."

"I'm lucky Eeva caught the show," Beecher said. "It was our first time appearing on the television, or anywhere, for that matter."

Tomek motioned for Beecher to sit and a second wave toward the house prompted the delivery of a pitcher of lemonade and a solitary glass.

"Maybe something cool to drink?"

The man with the tray approached uttering the same phrase, "For your refreshment, sir."

"Take some," Tomek encouraged, "...have a drink. We grow the lemons right here on the estate. Something about this location, I think this is the only place in England that gets enough sun."

Beecher poured and sipped and then upended the glass. The liquid was sweet and syrupy.

"Good?" Tomek inquired. "We make it special for our guests. A little recipe I picked up in South America."

Beecher refilled and drained the second serving.

"I don't run my artists in the traditional sense," Tomek said. "No radio plugging and no autograph signing. The deep end is where you learn the trade. Out on the road. We do not promote upfront. Once an artist has turned the heads of a local crowd, that's when we swoop in and inundate the market. There are too many genres converging onto one minuscule radio dial to hope for that elusive hit. This means that only the true believers are gonna get a shot. The other companies, for all their marketing promises and big-dollar advertising and fake talent, will have to be content cultivating a litany of one-hit wonders. You'll find those poor bastards years later, pushing junk to hookers and bags of weed to high-schoolers, or eking out a living as an insurance broker or car park attendant, and they'll lament the days gone by as if they were cheated out of fame and fortune. That's what you get if you have nothing to say."

He took a beat, watching his new recruit process the information.

"So, what say you, Beecher Stowe? And if you think your ass isn't on the line right now, then you and I have no future."

The gardeners were coming closer; the buzz of their tools was invading his space.

Stall, drink more.

He finished and poured another.

It's not supposed to be this way.

"I'd like to think my work is more conscious than heartfelt," Beecher said. "I'm in this to say something, not be something."

"So, you're a radical?"

"Hardly. I believe in me, that's enough."

"So, you're a loner?"

"Saves on petrol."

"That's funny."

"I don't think I'm meant to do anything else."

"How do you know? You're twenty-three."

"Twenty-four. By now, I think it would've occurred to me that I was wasting my time."

"You can sell yourself any number of lies and believe them all."

"This isn't a lie."

"How do you know?"

"The kids like it," he said. "They'll hear what I'm saying."

"A bunch of soppy teens?"

"They'll listen when they're on their own, that's when it'll sink in. That's why you have to write what matters."

"Bold words for a young musician."

"I don't feel so young."

"Hard life?"

"No more than anyone else."

"I once met a young woman whose family had been killed by drunken soldiers. Shot to death, right before her eyes."

"Okay, not such a hard life."

Tomek pulled a thin cigar from a black case and with gloved hands, lit it and blew a ruler-straight line of black smoke that was lost amongst lengthening shadows. Beecher reached into his jacket, felt the outline of the pack. Force of habit, he decided, and chose against it.

"I've always worked on the assumption that it's how you process what you see that shows wisdom beyond your years," Tomek said. "Where do you think that comes from? Instinct? The cartoons you watched as a child? The broken home or the fistfights in the schoolyard or listening to the endless shilly-shally of two-faced politicians?"

"I guess it comes from your upbringing, and your mates. And from the street."

"And there's no lonelier place than the streets."

"Well, it's not exactly New York or Paris. It's White City and Hammersmith and Shepherd's Bush."

"It's all relative. Your struggle to understand the ways of the world is no different than a swindling Wall Street banker, or a mother of twelve in a New Delhi slum, or some beret-clad charlatan that swans up and down the Champs-Élysées. We're all at the mercy of our surroundings. Everybody starts local and aims for the stars - Elvis, The Beatles, The

Rolling Stones, Bowie – they all made a name close to home. If it's honest and true, it can't work any other way. You'll connect with these people first because you speak their language."

"What about Dylan? He had to leave his home to be heard."

"Some might say he found his natural home. Anyway, the world would've found him, sooner or later."

"You sound so …sure."

Tomek flashed a, "Yes, I am."

"The music business is like a game show," he said, "…there are three doors of opportunity. You get to choose only one: you can play what the *people* want to hear, in which case you'll last as long as a pint of milk in the midday sun; you can play what *you* want to hear, in which case you might as well buy a dog and settle for that particular brand of unconditional loyalty…"

Beecher shifted forward in his seat. The mysteries of modern times paled by comparison.

Who was Jack the Ripper? Who killed JFK? Who gives a fuck?

"That's two," Beecher said. "What about door number three?"

"Door number three? Nobody knows. Whomever walks through that door never returns."

Beecher's expression gave everything away. Hurling the pitcher of lemonade against a wall would feel pretty good right now.

Tomek smirked.

"The point is, young fella, are you willing to walk through that door?"

Beecher sighed, part disappointment; part relief. His head was swimming like he'd had one too many tokes of Fez's weed. But it felt good, made him want to dive deeper.

Tomek switched gears.

"If you see hate in the streets, what do you do?"

"I don't understand."

"Let's say someone you care for is being beaten up. What do you do?"

"Did he deserve it?"

"Does it matter?"

"Of course. I know a lot of trouble makers; guys that want to burn shit down just to feel the heat."

"Would you write about it?"

"It's all I write about; it's all there is to write about. With every other bloke out on strike, or out of work altogether, there isn't a great deal of joy being spread in our manor."

"It sounds uniquely depressing."

"All I know is that here and now you can be hated for –

Your money;
Your religion;
Your beauty;
Your ability;
Your opinion;
Your weight;
Your success;
Your failure;
Your accent;
Your race;
Your color;
Your possessions;
Your illness;
Your compassion;
Who you love;
Who you don't love;
Your age;
Your friends;
And your dreams.

Beecher rounded out the oration with, "You can be hated for all that you are."

"Hate is a necessary evil," Tomek said, with that mixture of smile and sneer. "It's all part of a balanced diet, and it's ugly, and it always will be."

Beecher finally pulled out his smokes, sparked up and dragged hard. He felt the smoke burn his lungs and he refused to exhale. This guy was getting to him, making him say stuff; making him confess golden thoughts; thoughts reserved for writing and emoting and conjuring melodies from thin-fucking-air.

It's not supposed to be this way.

"Of course, the flip side of that list," Beecher said, "…is that you can be loved for exactly the same."

"Ah, the romantic appears, wearing his cloak of, "One love, everything is gonna be alright."

"If hate were a rabid animal, we'd shoot it," Beecher said. "If it were a virus, we'd invent a drug to wipe it out."

"Here, honey, don't forget to take your anti-hate pill."

"I took one yesterday!"

"I know, but you're going over to Tommy's house after school and they have that dreadful mauve carpet that always upsets you. And they'll probably pray or sing or who knows what."

Beecher spat a surly, "Evolution has stalled."

"Interesting," Tomek said. "You're angry and conflicted. I like that."

"Enough to give us a record deal?"

"Perhaps. There are conditions, though."

"Of course, you'd like us to tour first, build up a following."

"Oh, no, those are just the details, and given the response from your first outing on the television, we might do well to cut out the middleman and send you straight across the pond."

"I don't know anything about America. How are they gonna understand what I'm saying?"

"Once you create a buzz; once you get the troops onside, the kids will start talking, and then the press will start writing, and sure as everyone wants a taste of what they don't have, the records will start selling. That's when they start to learn your language. You don't have to speak theirs, you just keep on doing whatever it is you do."

Tomek flicked the cigar over his shoulder and Beecher followed the embers' fall, noticing a mound of ash on the patio with blackened stubs protruding like grave markers.

Tomek continued, "I'm talking about committing body and soul to a lifelong dream. If you can't imagine yourself doing anything else, it shouldn't be a problem. Consider it a contractual pound of flesh."

"Then it's about money?"

"Eeva will explain."

"Will that be today?"

Tomek shrugged.

"She keeps a unique schedule; I just pay the bills."

Beecher nodded, not even knowing what he was agreeing to.

The sun was playing hide and seek with soft clouds and the diffused light painted shades of purple across a lawn of yellow and pink blossoms and the sea breeze had found strength enough to penetrate the forest canopy with a cool, salty bite. Tomek suggested they took a break and reconvened in an hour or so. He pointed at the luxurious grounds.

"Take a stroll," he said. "Imagine all of this to be yours. Who knows, maybe one day, it will be."

With that said, he stood. Hans Tomek was taller than Beecher by a few inches but rangy and angular, and the flesh of his face was smooth and hued as bronze as a sculpture. He set a black hat on his head and a coat around his shoulders and took his leave along a cobbled path that cut the garden in two. Beecher waited five minutes, smoked another cigarette, wished he had a joint, and then wandered out into the grounds as instructed. He was unhurried, pausing every few steps to brush the petals of a flower or wipe water drops from waxy leaves. He sat on a weathered bench, feeling the press of his imposed isolation. A disturbance drew his attention to a line of tall hedges. A shower of stale bread was ejected from an opening and ten quacking Mallards raced from the undergrowth to peck and squabble over the morsels. Beecher wandered over and found an entrance to a maze. He met the old woman, backpedalling, scooping crumbs from a bucket and dropping them in her wake.

"I've never been in one of these," Beecher said.

The woman said, "You'll not want to wander too far inside."

She pointed to a patch of bare earth not twenty feet along the path.

"That's as far in as I go to chase these blasted ducks back into the pond."

Beecher peered inside. Dirt gave way to gravel and it was raked smooth and the hedges squared, and even in the failing light, seemed perfectly navigable.

"Overgrown in there, is it?"

The woman curled her mouth, turning snippy and impatient, lobbing handfuls of bread, peppering the ducks on their heads and backs, seeming not to care.

"I wouldn't know, I told you, that's as far in as I go."

Beecher's curiosity was ignited. He sidestepped the waddling frenzy at her feet and wandered inside. The trail was windless and silent as church, and he strolled with arms outstretched, the tips of his fingers brushing leaves of Hawthorn and Purple Beech on each side. His fingers snagged the sharp teeth of Blackthorn and Blue Pine and he copped a couple of bloody scratches. He was becoming lost in thought, turning over the conversation with Tomek, wondering what his place was, and where was his power. Beecher pulled up abruptly as if suddenly awakened. He turned around to face the old woman at the entrance.

She had vanished.

So had the entrance.

He spun in a confused, *"what the fuck"* circle, first one way, then the other. Walls of green topped out at fifteen feet and seemed to converge to a point equidistant, fore and aft. Beecher tried to retrace his steps in the loose gravel, but the ambient light provided no shadow or relief.

Stupid fuck, shoulda grabbed a handful of breadcrumbs.

He brought out his Bic lighter and held it to the ground and the flame danced erratically, casting nothing more than a pathetic glow. Beecher stood and pushed his hand into the foliage, parting leaves and branches, finding only blackness. A dog barked nearby, and he trained his ear on the sound.

Good boy; keep it up.

He followed the direction of its impatient wail, treading lightly, careful to mask the cereal-bowl crunch of loose stones underfoot, but the animal's protest grew weaker and soon faded. No bend or corner showed ahead; it was just an endless, screened enclosure. He thought to count his steps and he spoke aloud to no one.

"Alright, couldn't have taken more than fifty steps on the way in, whichever way that was. So, I'll carry on, do fifty more, turn around, and take one-hundred back."

Beecher reeled off each step, "One, two, three... forty-eight, forty-nine, fifty..."

He stopped. Same story, flanked by nothing but wall, and further ahead, more gravel path. He turned and was beginning to count off the extended paces for his return when mischievous sounds of scuttling beneath the hedges gave him pause. He stooped down and again withdrew the lighter. This time the flame spit like a welder's torch and he adjusted the fuel to a lower setting. At ground level, he heard breathing, deep and rasping. The orange cast given off by the lighter couldn't penetrate the undergrowth, but it was more than enough to highlight a pair of eyes set too wide for a small animal.

Pinpoint reflections. Gone, then back.

Blinking.

Beecher jolted backward and let out a quick shout.

"Jesus!"

The hedge erupted, shaking and convulsing, spitting dead leaves and dry sticks from its core as though a storm had broken out in its midst. Beecher pressed against the opposite hedge and felt the sting and scrape of thorns invade the lining of his jacket. He rebounded and started running, legs pumping like steam pistons, the smack of his boots resounded like struck cymbals as his feet plunged into the loosely-packed gravel. He began counting. Fast.

"*One, two, three, four, five... sixty-two, sixty-three, sixty-four, sixty-five...*"

He felt a disturbance in the air. It pushed from the earth, reverberating, like drumming.

Thud, thud, thud, thud... thud, thud, thud, thud...

Gaining in volume, coming up behind, at speed. Beecher shot a glance over his shoulder, his eyes straining into a curtain of gloom. Coastal fog boiled up between the hedgerows, sucking all remaining light from the sky. He slowed, losing count, thought of abandoning the exercise all together when a blood-curdling growl scythed its way through the air.

Fuck this.

He ran again, this time with his heart slamming against his rib cage.

The rhythmic pounding closed in.

His mind raced as fast as his legs.

No weapons, only stones.

Beecher stumbled as he scooped up handfuls of ammunition and filled his pockets.

Thud, thud, thud, thud...

The beast was almost upon him.

It's now or never.

He pulled up quick and lost his balance, somersaulting into the arms of bare branches and the claws of thorn bush. He came to his knees, shouting and hurling a granite hailstorm into a translucent wall.

"Go on with you! Fuck off!"

More stones took flight; more hysterical yelling resounded throughout the maze. He emptied his pockets and dug in vain at the path all around, finding only clumps of dirt and webs of exposed roots. His breathing was labored now, coming in short, snatched spasms. The beast came out of the night with laser-red eyes and a torso of disease and corruption and bleached claws dripping with the purulence of a shredded gut. Beecher screamed, shuttling in retreat on grazed knees, with arms raised and hands shielding his face. The beast leaped, and Beecher charged backward through the hedgerow, shredding his jacket, gouging flesh from his palms, rolling to a halt on the freshly manicured lawn. And here the light was blazing, and the grass emanated warm and damp from the day's heat.

Beecher curled into a ball, shivering uncontrollably and waited to be taken. Through the evaporating mist of settling terror, he opened his eyes and stared at the green wall, stately and still, and the resonant croak of common toads and the petulant chirp of wood crickets filled his ears and his breathing eased, becoming shallow and steady. He became aware of a presence nearby. It was the old woman, deftly scattering breadcrumbs from her bucket, shooing greedy ducks from under her skirt.

"C'mon, my little duckies," she said, with a voice that was rife with scorn, "...or I'll have you in my pot."

Beecher tried to speak but his voice was cracked and dry and no sound was declared. He watched the gathering move off beyond the tree line, making no further effort to appeal for help. He fingered the grass and felt a ridge protruding from the earth and pulled his body closer. It was a ledge, with fresh, Alpine air pushing upwards to the heavens with the force of a winter's gale. He tilted his head into the blast and looked down and through streaming eyes saw a small settlement and a parade of lights, all colors of the rainbow, and he saw his band in full flight and exquisite melodies filled the air, and Tomek's voice was invasive and shrill, *"There are conditions; there are conditions..."* The carnival passed, and the gale abated, and Beecher rolled onto his back. He drifted on clouds of mindless thought for a few moments, and then pulled his torn jacket tighter around his middle and rested his head in the crook of his arm. And then, he slept.

Chapter Fifteen

"For fuck's sake, Pengo."

Arch Pudding was beside himself with rage.

"I've been nothing but good to you, and now you've gone an' pointed the kid right smack into the mouth of the lion."

Pengo was cool and still, perched on a barstool.

"It was his choice."

Opening time was a half-hour away. Time enough to grapple with his crossword puzzle. He was stewing over eleven down.

"Hillbilly frying pans, six letters. Anyone?"

"Wankers," Arch shouted.

"Nah, too many letters. It does end with an 'S', though."

Arch paced.

"You might as well have told him to go strum his guitar on the bleedin' motorway, he's less likely to get fuckin' run over."

"Banjos," Snooze mouthed through a yawn. His head appeared from the confines of a booth. He slapped shut a dogeared anthology of American jazz and pulled himself upright.

"The clue, try banjos."

"Nice one, Snoozy, there's a pint of special in the taps for you when you're ready."

Arch continued with his puffy-chested outrage.

"Why didn't someone call me and tell me he was talking to a record company?"

"They came to him, Arch, and you weren't around," Snooze said. "Like you weren't around when he was supposed to meet with those blokes that were coughing up some free studio time; like you weren't around when he came off his bike and smashed his wrist; like you weren't around when he had all of his gear nicked by the same idiots you said would sort him out with a new fuckin' amp. In fact, I can't remember a single bleedin' time you've been around when you're actually needed."

Snooze was up and twirling his trumpet, coming closer and closer, and Arch wasn't seeing the menace and the disgust and the desire to shove the instrument up his ass, sideways.

Pengo jumped in between them.

"It's not a conspiracy, Arch," he said. "He's as loyal to you as the day is long. But you need to find an exit, sharpish."

"I've put a lot of money into that lad, what about that?"

"Bollocks," Snooze said. "That was money he earned for *you,* driving your harem of ladies all over the city at all hours of the night. You've used him as an excuse to get a foot in so many doors you've lost count."

"Nurturing talent is a slow process," Arch said, lifting a tonic water to his lips, "...you wouldn't want him to be taken advantage of. And 'ere, Pengo, slip us a squirt of gin, will ya? I'm feelin' a bit anxious with all this news."

"You know the rules, no alcohol out of hours."

The drink never made it back onto the bar. Snooze set the trumpet aside, picked up a heavy ashtray and winged it at Arch's head, scraping the bridge of his nose, taking the glass from his hand like he was on the wrong end of a clay pigeon shoot. The resulting smash brought Harry and Fez from the lounge for a look-see.

"He's gonna get a good hiding," Fez said. "About time."

"Can he take him?"

"Snooze is a wiry fuck, and he's got skills. I saw him lose it with some guys in the café once. They wouldn't pay their bill, said the food was rubbish. He fuckin' did all of 'em, *then* took their money, *then* called the ol' bill. Yeah, he's pretty special."

Pengo put his back to Arch who by this time was cowering against the fruit machine, whining something about attempted murder.

"Ease up Snooze," Pengo said. "You know Mum's not well."

Pengo turned and stared Arch in the face.

"You need to wake up. You treat people like they owe you a fucking living. Beecher Stowe is the only loyal mate you've got around 'ere and it wouldn't surprise me if you'd blown that completely. Now, pay up for the damage."

"I didn't throw it," Arch bleated.

"Well, I say you did, and I've got witnesses on my side, and seeing's as this is my pub, pay up."

Snooze was strutting in the background.

"Yeah, fucking right," he said.

"That's enough Snooze," Pengo warned, "...don't make it any worse than it is."

"Just sayin'," Snooze grabbed his trumpet and slinked off blowing a few lines of, *We are the Champions.*

Pengo sat Arch down. It had been a while since he'd looked at him this closely. His hair seemed to have been cut by a lawnmower, his skin was blotchy and wore the pallor of sour milk; his clothing was frayed and dirty, and he was giving off an odor that was a cross between week-old cabbage water and, well... piss.

"Have you been home lately?"

"Not since last Wednesday."

"Where've you been sleeping for over a week?"

"On a bench, behind the bakery."

Pengo shook his head.

"Go on then, what have you fucked up now?"

"I can't go home," Arch said. "They know where I live."

"Who knows where you live?"

"I laid a bet. It was a good bet, a sure thing."

"Horses?"

"Nah, I'd be smilin' if that were the case. Old Les down the bookies takes the money upfront so there's no worries. But, see, I chanced on some bare-knuckle fights down in Streatham."

"You went south of the river and laid a bet? Are you fucking mental?"

"I met the fighter and his manager, and they seemed straight. I watched him train. You shoulda seen him, he's a fucking monster."

Even in the face of defeat and impending bodily harm, Arch mustered enthusiasm for his motives.

"What was your stake?"

Arch hung his head and Pengo swore that a solitary, glistening tear dribbled down his pudgy cheek. It was so unlike Arch to show any kind of emotion. He was as empathetic as a locked china cabinet filled with dusty hand-me-downs from generations past; pointless shit kept behind murky glass that elicit waves of guilt as you imagine Granny spinning in her grave like a barrel of weekly lotto balls for not upholding some ridiculous family tradition. Nevertheless, there they remain.

For Señor Pudding to display such obvious remorse the stake must have been big. Pengo dove straight into the deep end.

"Like maybe he'd emptied Beecher's account of all of his savings."

"You, cunt," Pengo said, straightening in his chair, "...you fuckin', selfish, sleazy, two-faced, moronic, cock-sucking, shit-eating, cunt."

Arch doubled over as if someone had just kicked him in the balls.

"I was gonna put it back. Honest, I was. With interest," he whined.

"That's all the lad has in the entire world," Pengo said. "He's worked for years to get that money together. He's played at every shambolic wedding and Bar Mitzvah this side of Reading, all for a pittance. And topping that off, he's done stints behind the bar here every weekday since... well, I can't even remember..."

Pengo glanced at the large rectangular ashtray in the center of the table. Maybe Snooze had the right idea - three pounds of green, brewery-branded glass that would penetrate Arch Pudding's skull with hardly any effort at all. He could mash his brains to the consistency of a rustic soup, then get Fez and Harry to bag him up and stuff his tubby, malodorous frame into some dark corner of the cellar where the rats could nibble on his rotund little butt cheeks for eternity.

"...and you took every penny he'd earned to fuel your fucking gamblin' obsession? I don't fuckin' get you, the lad's on the verge of making it big in an industry that pays huge and you go and rip him off for a few hundred quid. You're a laughingstock around 'ere, Arch, and the sad thing is that you never used to be..."

Pengo's voice trailed off. He reflected in silence as a few of the more notorious episodes of Arch Pudding's activities returned to haunt him. Such as the time Benny the scrap dealer wanted to rip Arch limb from limb for stitching him up on some supposed insurance write-offs.

"*They were just cars,*" Arch had pleaded.

"*Yes, but they weren't your cars, and they weren't write-offs. You sold him paperwork on thirty perfectly good motors you didn't own.*"

"*No, see, that's where you've got it wrong. I sold him the idea of thirty motors. He wasn't supposed to come and get them, he was supposed to get the payout from the insurance company proving that he'd scrapped them.*"

"The point is, Arch, despite your failings, you didn't fuck over your mates. Until now."

Pengo was spitting-mad and drops of saliva were raining into Arch's left ear.

"Benny was a mate. And Beecher is a mate, *and* he's supposed to be your fuckin' client. It's a wonder you still have any kneecaps."

Arch started to sob. His heft bounced gently on the tattered upholstery much like his namesake, a soft, pink blancmange.

"I don't know anything about the music business," Arch said.

This confession, coming at any other time, might have been deemed admirable. As of now, it just felt like another play for sympathy.

"I never did," he said. "I just wanted to be close to something real. And Beecher's so real. He creates something out of nothing. Do you know how rare that is?"

"I do," Pengo said. "All of these lads are real, and everyone's got a story just as brutal as yours. It might not be exactly the same but it's brutal nonetheless."

"Why does everyone hate me?"

"As my ol' Mum says, "What's not to hate?""

Arch wiped at his eyes with a bar towel. He fingered a pack of No.6 for a cigarette, found only fibers of dry tobacco and crumpled tin foil.

"You show the world what you want them to see," Pengo said. "...and I reckon you're so busy having all the answers, you can't see you're behaving like a prize twat."

"Snooze has got it in for me 'cause he wants to manage Beecher."

"Fuck off. Snooze Silver has been watching out for that lad for years, way before you came along. He just wants what's best for his mate. If he had his way, he'd be smoking a joint the length of a baby's arm while knee-deep in a recording session at Muscle Shoals."

"What's it all got to do with fish?"

"You demented fuck. Muscle Shoals is a recording studio in Alabama." Pengo clocked the ashtray again.

"Aretha Franklin? Otis Redding? The fuckin' Allman Brothers?"

Not a crease or a curl of recognition. Arch Pudding's expression would have made a blank sheet of paper look like a relief map of the Andes.

"Fuck, mate, do you even like music?"

"I wasn't allowed it when I was a kid. My Dad said it was corrupting and I wouldn't grow tall if I listened to it. Fat lot of good that did."

"When Beecher gets back, you tell him everything that's happened, and how you're gonna pay him back, and that you wish him well, but you can't be his manager. You free him up from all the guilt and bullshit and bow out with a little dignity."

Arch sighed, lost in brooding thoughts.

"If these South-siders get a hold of me, there's no telling what they'll do."

He hadn't heard a word.

Chapter Sixteen

"And she's hooked to the silver screen; But the film is a saddening bore;
For she's lived it ten times or more..."
Beecher awoke to the sound of Eeva's lilting voice. He surfaced from
the blackness of sleep, numb and cold, and she moved from a writing
desk and added a heavy, wool blanket to the sheet covering his body and
he shivered a meek, "Thank you."

"You've been out for a few hours. The gardeners found you on the lawn;
nearly ran you over. I'm worried you might have a fever."

The shakes subsided, and Beecher made a move to sit up, thought
better of it and shifted to rest on one elbow.

"I honestly don't know what happened. I was talking to the old woman
and then checked out the maze and, ...I don't know, here I am."

"Maze?" Eeva sat on the bedside, she hesitated, then asked, "Old
woman?"

"Yeah, the lady that showed me in, she was in the grounds rounding up
the ducks."

"Oh, yes, ...Greta. I never know where she hides out."

Eeva reached across and placed the back of her hand against his
forehead.

Man, she smells so good, like summer.

"You do have a slight fever. I think it's worrying you. I'm going to run
you back up to London before it gets much later. It'll give us a chance to
talk about a few things."

Beecher shifted under the bedclothes and realized not all was present
down below. Bare ass and ball sack were being caressed by some swanky
silk sheets. He spied his T-shirt, leathers, and boots on the opposite side
of the room, folded; arranged like they were for sale.

"I think I was supposed to have dinner with Mr. Tomek," Beecher said,
a little embarrassed. "I don't want to disappoint him, 'cause, you know, he
gave me the time and everything, and I think we had a good chat."

"Hans had to leave a few hours ago on some urgent business. But don't worry, I assure you he was impressed..."

Eeva covered Beecher's hand with both of hers and locked her sea-blue eyes into his gaze.

"...more than I've seen in a very long time."

Beecher would cherish that intimacy forever - the tone of her voice, the gentle squeeze of her hand, the line of her jaw, the ruby lips. Baker Street flashed before his eyes. Looking down from the top deck, all over again. He would finally get to ask her. But not now.

"I should get dressed," he said.

Eeva smiled.

Her look said she knew he was naked. She pottered about the room for a full minute, opening and closing dresser drawers. Beecher rustled the covers, made to get up, sneaked a quick peek at his pale flesh but couldn't quite summon the courage.

Not exactly beach-ready.

Eeva took to grooming her hair with a silver hairbrush the size of a small spade. Long, slow, purposeful strokes. Beecher settled back and watched. She sat before a simple mirror and closed her eyes and hummed, familiar, soft and delicate.

"Bowie," Beecher said. "A genius."

Rays of setting sun spilled through French doors and wrapped her in an amber cloak that shimmered like a desert heat haze. The wall before her was dotted with black frames containing photographs that were sun-bleached and curled with age. They captured a gentle time, open fields and streams, a farm perhaps. Beecher's eyes were drawn to a picture taken from the banks of a small lake. Two children, both girls, ankle-deep in the water, fishing rods in hand, grubby faces beaming with delight. Ivory curls dropped to the shoulder on the smaller of the two, while ebony locks cascaded to the waist on the other. The dark-haired girl was taller by the span of a single hand and rail-thin. The long shadow of the photographer intruded across rippling water and the moment was serene and longed for. Beecher scanned the room further. Wardrobes, with doors gaping, revealed racks of clothes embracing the appeal of different generations – contemporary outfits of denim and leather were sectioned from colorful skirts and blouses sewn from nylon and polyester and acrylic, which in turn stood apart from ensembles of earth tones in wool and chambray and tweed and linen. There were other items, too, formal gowns of velvet and taffeta and silk, but it was within another closet that Beecher paused his survey. Simple garments; outfits of purpose that were not in keeping with the collection, such as overcoats and dresses that were weathered and frayed and stained. Beecher's thoughts flitted again to his first sighting of this platinum angel – her sadness and her poise - and somehow these articles seemed not entirely out of place. The survey continued.

Trinkets of all shapes and sizes adorned the tops of dressers and were of polished silver, and glass vases sprouted fresh flowers, and against the walls, mahogany racks supported countless pairs of shoes and boots. He turned his gaze to the shuttered windows and felt warm air bathe his face and the smell of cut grass was invigorating. He came on to his knees with the blanket wrapped at his waist and found that Eeva's bedroom commanded a stunning view of the estate. In the courtyard below, the old woman and the man with the tray sat together on a bench, sharing a cigarette, and from the copse at their backs, birdsong filled the coming night, and it was from this vantage point that Beecher noticed the gentle slope of the lawn and how it was bisected by a gravel road. But he saw no maze. He observed tool sheds and scattered lily ponds, and he saw rope swings swaying gently from the arms of the stately-old Oak, but no maze was revealed beyond.

"*Drugged, mate.*"

Snooze's forthcoming opinion would not be short on drama.

"*They fuckin' drugged your ass. And they probably raped you. Have you checked your sphincter for misuse? All of those posh fuckers have sexual hang-ups. Like politicians and public schoolboys, they love a bit of working-class cock. Dirty rich bastards.*"

Eeva opened her eyes as if awakening from a dream. She dabbed at her make-up and then moved to the sofa where Beecher's clothes lay, throwing him a sly look, said,

"Still not dressed? Bathroom's next door. I'll be downstairs when you're ready."

Eeva was on the phone when Beecher appeared on the landing. He felt like an eavesdropping intruder. He tried to creep down the wide, creaking staircase unnoticed but worn treads protested with an obstinate wail.

She was seated in a dark alcove, mouthing words softly; nodding mostly. The whining steps caught her attention and she turned and smiled. It was brief and barely notched the edges of her mouth, but it was a smile, and Beecher saw it as a sign to continue on down. If he could've jumped, he would have. Finally, throwing caution to the wind, he galloped the last few stairs, landing with a muted thump on a Persian carpet so large that it consumed the entire width of the entrance hall. Eeva waved him to the front door and there he stood, more nervous, he thought, than when he had arrived. He was startled from his thoughts by the sound of the latch being rattled as if struggling to be drawn. Beecher stepped forward to assist in sliding the slab of wrought iron when the heavy door began to push inward, slowly, as if a reluctant wind was acting upon its bulk. Beecher was about to lay hands on the edge of the door when a beaky nose and hooded eyes shot into view. The man with the tray was breathless, and his brow sweated bullets of exhaustion and a sliver of his tongue poked into view and snaked across dry lips.

"I'd say it wouldn't take much to wear this fucker out," Beecher thought. *"A rise of steps or a stubborn jar of pickled onions or a hastily unfurled centerfold."*

The man's bony fingers toyed with the door latch for a moment, accompanied by a little wheezing and a little profanity. Beecher left him to it and sought the comfort of a chair in an adjoining alcove. The booth was lined with crushed velvet on the walls and ceiling, blood-red in color, and smelled strongly of damp and mold. The air in the confined space was dead, absorbing all ambient sound. A telephone sat center stage. Regional phone books were neatly stacked, and a notepad and pen rested alongside the handset: pushbuttons, no less, cutting edge stuff. Beecher read from doodles and scribbles on the pad. The only legible words: *USA tour dates?*

The man ceased his fiddling with the latch and flicked his head from side-to-side, found Beecher, and with a tut-tut of disapproval, shuffled towards him, tray extended.

"Fuck, not again."

This time, no refreshments. Instead, he offered a key attached to a leather fob. Beecher looked at the object and then at the man.

"What?"

The man spoke with a cracked voice straight from a Hammer horror movie.

"For the car, sir. It is ready when you are."

Beecher took the key. A pendant in the shape of a leaping cat dangled, glinting silver and blue.

Cleared of his duty, the man heeled around and set off, the empty tray still raised in service.

Eeva led Beecher into the courtyard. She seemed renewed, with a spring in her step.

"Have you ever driven a Jaguar?"

"I've never even ridden in one," he said.

"Well, let's do something about that."

Beecher noticed her accent had softened since their first meeting. There was a lightness to her tone, and she was quick to laugh, almost giddy with enthusiasm. She wore very little make-up, enough only to frame her piercing blue eyes, and under a new summer moon that shone bright as a searchlight, her skin was smooth as cream.

The walk to the garage was by way of a winding lane that descended sharply into a narrow, tree-lined ravine. The road was brightly lit in places with incandescent bulbs that were strung like Christmas lights within the canopy, promising the effect of distant stars pulsing in outer space. From the crest of the hill, Beecher saw a grouping of what looked like horse stables facing open pasture.

"The garage?" he asked.

"Yes, I had all of the barns converted. I don't work the land and keep no animals, other than dogs. I keep cars and some motorcycles down there away from the main house. I have mechanics working at all hours and the noise can grate on the nerves if you're trying to sleep."

"What are they working on?"

"All sorts. I used to race rally cars, and this was a great space to test any improvements we made. The land is too hilly for farming, but it makes for an excellent circuit. You should try it."

"I meant to ask you where you're from," he said.

"I've spent a lot of time in Switzerland, but my family is from Austria."

"And now England?"

"I come here in the summer, can't stand the rest of the year, too wet…"

Beecher acknowledged the paleness of his skin.

"Yeah, I guess I'm used to it."

"…and people can be quite miserable."

"It's an English birthright," he said. "A good ol' moan and groan. I'm sure we've been to war for less."

"But then I see them at the seaside," she said. "…with ice creams and sunbathing in deck chairs, fully clothed, and it's all sweetness and light. I don't understand, if there's such an improvement to how they feel when the sun shines, why don't they move to a warmer climate?"

"Roots, history, jobs, family. Wanderlust is for the privileged and the eccentric. Someone's got to keep the home fires burning. Folks have grown accustomed to yearning for their two weeks by the coast. It's like craving a favorite meal. Cornwall was our venue. Rockpools, sandcastles and grassy hills and cream teas. The air was sweeter and the sun somehow brighter. A bat and a ball were all that I needed. And no matter where we went, I always made a new friend. Never saw them again, of course, but that didn't matter. Oh, except for once. My mate, Snooze. The trumpet player in my band. Met him in the shop at a caravan park in Newquay. He was crying 'cause he didn't have enough pennies for ice cream. I made up the difference and for eight blisteringly hot days, we were inseparable. We made all kinds of pacts to keep in touch, no matter what. Turns out, back home he lived two streets away. Saw him the first day of school and it was like greeting a long lost brother."

Beecher was falling back through time, seeing his skinny frame chasing about bare-chested, with matchstick legs sprouting from bright yellow shorts decorated with ship's anchors and compass wheels, making his grandmother rock with laughter as he shooed seagulls from the quayside.

"Maybe it's an island thing, not wanting to give up on ol' Blighty after defending her honor for a thousand years. We had a lot of West Indians moving into our manor and the first thing we'd ask them is, *Why here? Jamaica is sunny all year 'round.*"

"And what did they say?"

"In the first year, the answer was *"jobs,"* and, *"we get a better, safer life."* The government dangled cash and over they came. These days, I'm sure most of them would happily go back but by now, the whole family's come over and settled into new lives."

"Seems to lack permanence. A proud nation reduced to little more than a work farm."

"I think we've exported a fair share of irrational behavior over time," he said.

"How do you feel about money?"

"What do you mean?"

"Is it a driving force or a means to an end?"

"I've earned exactly two thousand and forty pounds as a professional musician, and that took just over three years. So, I'd say it hasn't been an issue, 'cause it hasn't been an issue."

Again with the smile; again with the giggle.

"My father was a concert pianist," she said. "One of the best of his time. He loved performing but had to run a music store to support the family."

"In Austria?"

"Vienna. It was a beautiful place behind an old theater. We sold all of the instruments of the orchestra, especially grand pianos. When the Nazis demanded he complied with reporting all Jewish-owned property, he refused because we had no family money; we were only brokers for instrument manufacturers, but they chose not to see it that way."

Eeva took his hand for support as they navigated the steep drive. With fingers intertwined, it was a lover's grip, warm and safe against the cool sea air. Her leopard-skin boots sported stiletto heels - better suited to the ensemble of a leather biker jacket and skin-tight trousers than stepping out on gravel and hard-packed dirt and skipping over the occasional murky puddle.

She gazed up at Beecher and he felt excited with his world becoming so unpredictable. For him, this was a courtship.

"I'm not so young anymore," Eeva said.

The words fell from her mouth in a sudden and desperate confession; a burden released, like doves taking flight in a clatter of wings beating against stagnant air, taking their bodies higher and higher. For Eeva, the confessional was the smallest and darkest of rooms and its walls pressed tight against her breast.

Beecher saw the veil had slipped and chose to ignore it, said nothing. He realized that he held both of her hands and their bodies were aglow in silver light and the forest all around slept with a profound stillness. In this moment, only the air moved, lifting strands of their hair and sending leaves skipping along the winding path.

Eeva pulled a small wallet from her jacket pocket. It held a single photograph, a family posing before a storefront – at far left, a woman of middle age; in the center of the frame, a second woman was seated, most likely in her late twenties to early thirties. Standing slightly apart were two men, with hands clasped and shoulders embraced. The elder of the two wore clothes that were unremarkable in every sense, while the other was resplendent in high collar and tails. Even with the ravages of time stripping away the image's contrast and marking the emulsion with subtle creases and tears, Beecher recognized the well-dressed man immediately as Hans Tomek. He felt a chill run down his spine and a stir in his gut. The canopy of darkness and the failing light only added to the feeling of dread. He took the picture from her hand, turned it over and read,

Hugo Keller und familie, Vienna, 1938.

He flipped it back and did his best to divert his eyes from the likeness of the younger woman. He uttered the first words that came to mind.

"These are your grandparents?"

"No," Eeva said. "They are my parents..."

She stated the fact with pride.

"…the picture was taken in front of our store."

Beecher let his eyes drift to the center of the photo. The woman's hair was as white as Pacific clouds and his head started to spin as if he'd been drugged, and acid boiled to the edge of his stomach.

Similar or the same?

Her poise, the crossed arms, the chin held high, her expression set in an unforgettable smile. He cleared his throat, stalling, thoughts racing. He knew that smile; he'd yearned for that smile, and now he felt like a voyeur. He shuffled his feet and bought time by feigning interest in the surrounding world, wiping the hair from his forehead, opening and closing his jacket. He finally tapped the photo with his index finger.

"And this?"

"…is me," she said. "The day before my twenty-fifth birthday. I worked in the store every day and helped my father with instrument repairs in the evenings. On Saturdays, I traveled with him to concerts. I took care of his clothes and booked the hotels, and when he performed, I was his page-turner."

Here comes the smile.

"Before the war, I saw all the cities of Europe from the best seat in the house."

Beecher handed back the photo and they continued walking, slower, saying nothing for a few steps, and then Beecher sighed, said,

"It's incredible, isn't it? You wait for what seems like forever for a taste of…I don't know…satisfaction; just a glimpse of what living your dream might feel like. And then you sail right up next to it and it's just like every other day."

"What do you mean," Eeva said.

"Tricks, cons, let-downs. Humans working humans, getting what they can. We're not a very complicated species, are we?"

"But *we* are all we have," Eeva said, "…unless you have some gift for talking to the animals."

"Two hours ago, I was asleep on your lawn, dreaming all kinds of weird shit. For all I know, I'm still in it."

"I'm sure you're not."

"Yeah, maybe."

Beecher gestured to the photograph in her hand, now hanging by her side. With a quickening pulse and smoldering anger, he said, "Why did you show me that?"

"Because sooner or later you would have asked, and I cannot lie."

"Asked about what?"

"That depends," she said. "The conditions. You would've asked about the conditions of your contract."

"Beyond making records and getting paid?"

"Yes."

Beecher was at a crossroads: straight ahead there was complete ignorance; go right and seek the treasure; go left and search for her soul. Going back, he submitted, was not an option. He tilted his head to the night sky.

There's always up.

So up he went.

"Eeva, please tell me what the fuck is going on."

"Do you have a cigarette?"

Beecher pulled the pack from his jacket and took out two, lit them both, handed her one.

"Not a habit, you understand," Eeva said. "I haven't smoked in quite a while."

With that, she inhaled deeply, and the smoke was ejected in a long lazy river. Beecher watched; waited for the inevitable cough. But it never came.

She began.

THE NIGHT OF BROKEN GLASS.

"Before there was sentiment and pity; before brother was pitted against brother, we lived a quiet life. Not prosperous. We housed and fed and clothed ourselves, and we were protected by laws, and we worked and traveled freely. Nine months before the photo was taken, Hans Tomek came into our store with an order for many instruments – oboes, flutes, clarinets, brass and two grand pianos, one for his home in Salzburg, and the other for a house he kept on the banks of Lake Neusiedl. He said he was a collector and from the look of his clothes - finely-tailored suit and polished brogues – he was undoubtedly wealthy. He carried a walking cane that he used as a pointer and a prop. He visited many times and would sit with us for the evening meal and often stay in our guest room, saying he preferred it to the hotel. On occasion, he would take my mother and father aside and speak to them of the changing times; he even warned them of the impending union with Germany to which my father scoffed at the very thought. Tomek was not drawn to argue, he accepted my father's views as fear and concern for family and business alike, but his foresight was confirmed less than three weeks later. In Vienna, it started with isolated beatings in back alleys, bodies being discovered that were bruised and battered beyond recognition.

Then came the night of broken glass. Mobs filled the streets like floodwaters from the Danube. We saw the sharp points of orange flames topping out above the synagogue and we saw the firemen standing by, idly, laughing as it burned. Hordes of men prowled the streets, brandishing lumps of broken concrete and wooden clubs, shattering store windows and driving Jews into the street. These barbarians had been our neighbors only days before, now they screamed for our blood, saying we were a plague.

Tomek returned the following morning, this time with an entourage riding motorcycles. Six in all, evenly split, men and women. They looked to be my age, dressed in black as he was, but not threatening; not a uniform. I guessed that they were some kind of security. Tomek said that he could save my family; give us safe passage across the mountains, but we would need to leave immediately and abandon everything. My mother and father were adamant - they would stay put. Somehow, I think the immediate threats weren't as daunting as setting off into the unknown and losing everything they had worked so hard for. But they asked Tomek to take me as far from the troubles as possible. I was not a child and I refused to hear such nonsense, but they pleaded with me to go. Tomek continued trying to persuade them to come with us but his voice fell on deaf ears. So instead, he made assurances, to them, and me, even as the mobs approached our store. He said for as long as I stayed close to him, he could guarantee an elegant life for me; a long life."

Eeva hesitated as if she was struggling to relive the moment.

"So, I agreed; to what…I didn't know."

She took a final drag of the cigarette, crushed the butt into pulp under her stiletto heel and moved from the path and sat on the branch of a downed tree.

"The last time I was in Vienna, we stood as a family at our window. We watched and waited, silent and still as mannequins, and there were all of these instruments lining the walls, and it was as though they had no place in this world, not with this vile hatred filling the streets. It felt like they had been stripped of the ability to make the music of romance and love."

Eeva asked for another cigarette and then changed her mind, waved it off.

"In the street, a woman was being held aloft, her back was arced unnaturally. She screamed and wind-milled her arms, striking out at bobbing heads. Her clothes were shredded and ripped, and she was naked below the waist and her skin was milky-white and lined with scarlet tracks like she'd been dragged over rough ground. The crowd bayed like feral animals and set upon her with fists and boots each time she was lowered. They came closer to the storefront and my mother recognized the woman as the wife of the baker. She slammed her hands on the glass and made a move to the door. Tomek blocked her way and my father wrapped his arms around her waist, and held her so tightly and she was beside herself, sobbing uncontrollably at the sight of her young friend being repeatedly clawed and stomped.

The people in the crowd were not only thugs and thieves, they were merchants wearing expensive suits, and lowly-paid factory workers, and university students, and rich women wearing diamonds and pearls. And they all clapped and shouted, holding children high on their shoulders for a better look. I couldn't understand the depth of their disgust for us. For all my life we had tolerated mistrust, and there was always a feeling that no matter how hard we worked, we would never belong."

The questions that had formed in Eeva's mind all those years ago, were now cemented within her heart. For her, it was the ultimate penance, one she would never understand.

"Tomek seemed to rise above this as if he could foresee the magnitude of what was to come. He said vulnerable humans fear isolation more than they do hunger. They will go as far to deprive themselves of independent thought to remain vital, like dogs in a pack, and they will hunt and kill at the will of the mob. He said he would never allow that sense of frailty to be present in my life, and I believed him."

Eeva wrung her hands so tightly that Beecher could see dark patches of blood pooling under the ivory sheen of her skin.

"The crowd eventually parted, and two men held the woman's arms outstretched while others beat and kicked her in the stomach. They left her on her knees crouching in a pool of blood and the crowd let out a barbaric cheer. And then came a sound that I will carry to my grave. My mother's cries were of absolute despair, getting louder and louder. She screamed, over and over, *Sie ist schwanger, Sie ist schwanger.*"

Eeva's blank stare misted over and she turned her face to the ground.

"What is it?" Beecher said.

"The woman was pregnant."

The air was stifling in the shelter of the trees and Beecher extended his hand and brought Eeva to her feet. They walked on until the soft glow of the garage porch lights broke through unobstructed. The road would be flat now as the next two hundred meters dissected a pasture, smooth as a billiard table, abutting the tree line like a great, green sea. They stepped from the forest and the air moved once more and the night sky teased the sparkle of its jewels through towering columns of cumulus clouds.

"My parents knew they had to leave," she said. "They had no choice."

Beecher's head was swimming with confusion, kept rubbing his eyes in the hope he'd wake up.

C'mon, Dorothy, click your heels.

He was unnerved by Eeva's story. To embrace it fully he'd have to ignore the bleedin' obvious, or as Snooze preferred, *"You know that itch beneath your bollocks? Scratch at your peril."*

"Are they... here? Your mother and father."

"After Vienna, they never recovered. They clung to each other, but it was impossible for them, being in hiding and crossing borders like common criminals. The years in Tomek's care have been kind to me. Perhaps it was my age. Not so for them. They died a little over a year later, within weeks of each other. They're buried together on a hillside in the Jura Mountains. It's a beautiful place, brushed by the sun for nearly the whole day."

"I'm sorry," Beecher said.

"At least they didn't suffer like so many others," she said. "That's all that matters."

The path forked and Eeva did not hesitate in choosing her way. She lightened the conversation, sharing anecdotes of land clearing and numerous off-road driving mishaps and out of nowhere Beecher realized he was hungry... no, *fuckin' starving*. He conjured up the image of a cheeseburger the size of a dinner plate. Mustard only, no ketchup. Lettuce and tomato and three rashers of bacon. Toasted bun and a shovel's worth of chips. He pictured the café, and Maureen chattering on about her lumbago, and Snooze leafing through the Exchange and Mart trying to find a new exhaust for the Triumph.

"If that fuckin' lorry had signaled when he should've..."

Eeva's voice seeped into his daydream the way rain finds its way under a closed door. Beecher snapped back as she began talking about Tomek again and her empathy was honest and utterly believable.

"Hans Tomek is of our world; he is just not of our time."

She spoke soft and clear, observing Beecher carefully, spoon-feeding him the fantastic tale, waiting expectantly for the rapid blinks, and the deepening furrows, and the heavy sighs that would be wordless with disbelief.

"He fell between two worlds," she said. "He says it's like two lights blinking at different rates. One light represents your present and the other, your past. Extraordinary events bring them together to shine as one. And for that split second, it is possible to pass physically between the two states of being."

She wrinkled her nose and her eyes grew wide as if she was reading a fairytale to a child.

"He says if you were able to live long enough, you'd see it in the twinkling of the stars."

"And how long would that be?" Beecher was curious.

"Oh, I don't know, a few billion years, maybe longer."

"Well, as long as it's within reason."

She became serious again, "He said it was like falling into a void or settling into the deepest, dreamless sleep, except you're conscious the entire time. Sometimes he sees himself in both worlds, but he's certain it's just memories fighting each other for significance."

"How does that explain the..." Beecher struggled with the phrase, although given what he was being told he wasn't sure why. "...aging business?"

Eeva continued, not missing a beat.

"Because Tomek is not of our time, for some reason those he touches most deeply eventually become embraced by his aura, and the passage of time..." she searched for an appropriate word, "...slows. I cannot explain it more than that because I am living it."

"Try," Beecher said, "...please."

A long silence passed between them and Eeva stood with her head bowed as if in silent prayer. She lifted her head to face the cooling breeze and fine strands of silver-white hair were pushed from her face and the picture was complete.

She said, "While we are woven so deeply into each other's memories, time stands still. It's only when we drift apart; when the intensity fades, do we age. Does that make sense? I don't know how else to put it."

"But aging is life, and life is aging."

"...and time is unstoppable," she said.

"Yes, exactly."

"And yet, here we are, bearing witness to a miracle."

"I don't believe in miracles."

"What do you believe in?"

"What I see."

"Utilizing only one sense out of five. That's not very adventurous."

"You know what I mean."

Beecher ran his fingers through his hair and shook his head in frustration.

"Clearly, this shit's too weird for me," he said, and then as an afterthought, "So, how does he get back? Can he go back?"

"And the circle is complete," Eeva said, with a wry nod of her head. "Do I see a hint of faith creeping out from behind those suspicious eyes?"

"I've dropped this far down the rabbit hole..."

Her sudden laughter caught him off guard and he recoiled.

"Oh, we've only just begun," she said.

"No, seriously, if you expect me to buy into this... whatever *this* is, how does he go home?"

"Tomek has spoken often of the need for a grand event. I didn't understand back then because there was no context. But he tells me it's coming soon, a time when the world will share in the birth of a solitary memory; a recollection of such vivid and extraordinary clarity, that it will once again connect him with his own world. And then he can go back."

Beecher wanted so much to contribute; to be witty and profound. Instead, he fell mute.

"Tomek is on a quest," Eeva said. "He is out to create that event. I can't think of how to say it any other way. There is a darkness to him, and I sometimes feel paralyzed in his presence, but he has made good on his word, time and time again. When it came time for the train cars to be filled with frightened faces, stripped of all their worldly possessions, Tomek kept us hidden and safe, far away from the madness."

"That's a long time ago," Beecher said, the nagging doubt now circling his head like an impatient vulture.

"I know," Eeva measured her response. "I know it sounds absurd. I don't expect you to lose your reason, but as sure as we've just stepped from a forest into an open field, there's an explanation that won't embarrass you. We just have to settle on it."

Beecher paused, affronted by the remark.

"Why would I be embarrassed?"

She smiled, said, "A lack of knowledge can be just as frightening as facing a snarling tiger. Are you above pride?"

"I dunno, what do you think?"

"I think we are a lot alike."

Beecher looked her up and down - the leather outfit hugged every square inch of her body; blonde hair tumbled like a waterfall, streaked violet by the light of a silvery moon; her eyes were wells of infinity and her lips, rose-red, glistened like morning dew under the summer sun. This was not the woman she had described as working for her father in a music store in Vienna.

But it could be.

This also was not the naïve victim that had born witness to man's inhumanity and survived only through the intervention of a stranger; a stranger that floated on the back of time as if it were an endless wave bound for a distant shore.

But it could be.

Beecher found the meandering path of his life reflected strongly in her voice. What he'd considered as a secret stash of hopes and dreams, now seemed manufactured. He imagined a train station and a ticket seller's window. He pictured lines of people waiting patiently for their turn at the window, hands upturned and expectant, hungry for the gift of knowing where the fuck they should go next. He'd stood at that window his entire life.

We are the same.

All he could say was, "Maybe."

"I'm just messing with you," Eeva said. "You'd have to have a pretty thick skin not to feel a little overwhelmed."

Beecher let out a deep, satisfying, lung-clearing sigh.

"I saw Jimi Hendrix when I was seventeen," he said. "Packed into this tiny jazz club in Brentford - sweaty walls, black and tans in pint mugs, lots of posing and politics, chicks my age digging blokes ten years older. At four minutes past nine, I had the world bang to rights - a week's wages stuffed in the front pocket of a new pair of Levi's and a sweet '62 Norton Dominator parked outside that looked the part even though you'd be lucky to go fifty miles without the electrics sizzling into molten strings of plastic and copper spaghetti. Didn't matter a jot; everything made sense. At five minutes past nine, a black guy with a paisley shirt open to the waist and a terrifyingly impressive afro that probably had its own moon, slung a battered white Stratocaster around his neck, climbed on stage, plugged in and life was literally never the same. *That's* overwhelming. Everything else is part and parcel of life's jelly trifle - sometimes you get a big scoop of cream, mostly all's you get is a spoonful of soggy sponge and a few tinned tangerines."

"You just went there."

"What do you mean?"

"You just went back in time. You were there, I saw it in your eyes."

"And yet I'm still here."

"Because you live here, this is your time."

"It's a memory, not a vacation. You know, I'm cool with your story, even though part of me thinks you might be bat-shit crazy; probably had a few too many acid trips."

"Wouldn't know, I've never touched the stuff."

"Then maybe I've been smoking a little too much of what my drummer sells."

"Does it make you sleepy?"

"Your story, or the weed?"

On cue, a flash of the brightest smile.

"No, I don't get tired," Beecher said. "I do like to disappear into music, though. It's like food. I go through different tracks, listening to intros and solos; you know, get a little paranoid that I might never be able to create something as unique."

"And when you're not high?"

"Then I don't give a shit. I like what I write."

"Tomek says that's what distinguishes a true artist from a charlatan."

"Except charlatans seem to make a better living."

"My mother used to say you can't hurry a good stew, and every time my father would reply, …but I'm hungry, *now*."

"He's got a point."

The garages were larger than Beecher expected. Twenty-foot ceilings, windowless on the sides, sporting skylights that spanned two-thirds of the roofline.

"How many cars?"

"It's not nice to ask a lady her age, or how many cars she has."

"Ah, that must have escaped my peasant upbringing."

"It's a new rule, it starts now. All I will say is that every one of them was purchased brand new, and all are roadworthy. Just grab any key and go."

The lock to the first unit opened at the touch of a switch that was neatly obscured by a vintage motor oil sign. A heavy clunk announced a shining steel bolt lurching free of its clasp and an airtight seal between the barn doors relaxed with a faint hiss. Eeva instructed Beecher to grab a wrought iron handle and walk one of the doors outward while she did the same with the other, sending a resounding squeal reminiscent of a medieval drawbridge crying out into the still of the night. The doors were lined with Oak planks cut thick as a fist and bolted to heavy-gauge steel supports and the leading edges rolled on industrial casters. To Beecher's dismay, only one lumpy shape was revealed in the otherwise empty cavern. Eeva set the overhead lights ablaze from a master breaker and the spotless confines were revealed. It was clear this structure wasn't for storage - polished tile lay underfoot, pristine workbenches were arranged like surgical workstations, immaculate toolsets decorated two walls, with shelves of glinting spare parts covering the third. In the center of the room, a silk-cover draped a cylindrical object. Eeva entered.

"My second home," she said.

"Perhaps a tidy up is in order," Beecher said, sarcastically.

Eeva threw him a self-satisfied smile. She lifted the corner of the silk and pulled, hand over hand, wadding the cloth against her chest, her eyes never leaving his. She watched the line of Beecher's smirking mouth settle and his eyes widen to the point of watering profusely. The slow tease of a bulging wheel well gave way to the iconic headrest fairing and open cockpit of a 1956 Jaguar D-type XKD-606 wearing flag-blue metallic paint. Beecher was sure he had never stood in the presence of anything as beautiful, present company excepted.

"It's a D-type," Eeva said with such obvious romance that Beecher felt a stir in his loins.

"Of course," he said, "We use them to haul around the band's gear."

He was silent for a moment and then inched closer, wordless with awe, finally issuing a whispered, *"Fuuuucck."*

Beecher felt like a kid again, staring into Pop McCallister's sweet shop on the Fulham Road, reliving vivid and indelible memories of painted-wood shelves stretching from floor to ceiling lined with glass jars sporting silver screw lids, each brimming with candies all colors of the rainbow. He was calling up the past; calling up a schooldays-morning ritual: stopping off for a quarter-pound of mouth-puckering acid drops. The challenge was to make one wee ball of hard-boiled bliss last for the entire laborious cycle up to the hallowed halls and perpetually muddied fields of *Sir John Medgrove Comprehensive*, an institution of secondary learning that engorged the malleable brains and the insatiable bellies and the blossoming bosoms and biceps of girls and boys from ages eleven through sixteen. Within this Victorian edifice of dark hallways and damp walls, the constituents of England's future would consume facts and figures, and soggy steak and kidney pudding, and boiled cabbage and watery mash potatoes and, once-a-week, a gastronomic diversion - treacle sponge and custard - a dessert that assured open season on the weak and the timorous as trades and threats went hand-in-hand with surrendered dollops of the sweet, syrupy bounty.

Here too, physical exertion was specifically and abusively dispatched into the student body with cross-country runs undertaken only, it seemed, when the skies were heavy as dirty laundry and spilled freezing rain like it had been summoned from a celestial hose, and co-ed swimming lessons that drove ebullient hormone levels to their polyester-blended apex as virgin reeds of thrashing humanity made the migration of herds of gazelle crossing the crocodile-infested Limpopo River look like a lazy, summer paddle.

The school was a drafty chamber of horrors, populated by teachers with sour faces and equally miserable lives. It subscribed to the typically-British, mid-60's dichotomy – one foot striding toward the promise of post-war, modern academics, while the other was cemented in the obsessively time-honored conventions of daily assemblies, replete with hymns and notices and contagious yawns and coughs and muffled laughter, and the inevitable scoldings and detention slips. Bike-shed smokes of shop-lifted fags and slobbering and fumbling knickers-down feel-ups were commonplace. Lunchtime scraps were always a crowd-pleaser, especially if they were broken up with a vengeful and snarling, "*I'll fuckin' get you later,*" ringing out across the soccer pitch.

Back to Pop McCallister's.

Beecher had come close in his quest for confectionary tantra. It happened one fine spring morning, May 3rd, 1965. Young Master Stowe had popped a marble-sized nugget into his gob, set it into his cheek and kicked off from the curb with a bloody-minded intent to succeed. Precious little traffic clogged the West London arteries, so several flower-strewn verges were deftly wheeled over, two hilly roundabouts successfully summited and descended at full tilt, and a bollock-smashing crash narrowly avoided as errant tree roots and rising paving slabs sent bared shins sliding across jagged pedals, gouging chalky-white ravines into tender flesh. Victory had been within his grasp until a troupe of Morris dancers, striking up their seasonal prancing and jingling and clacking of sticks, barred direct access to the school's gates, making any detour, in salivary terms, completely impractical. Those eight dickheads, strutting and whooping like demented fairies, cemented a granite-like touchstone into the delicate fabric of his youth that, for a good many years following, would submit Beecher to becoming a literal *Pavolv's Dog* as the sound of tiny bells stimulated the flow of saliva in his mouth, drawing his immediate and irrational ire. And may God help you if you happened to be skipping.

With the Maypole being dutifully wrapped, Beecher admitted defeat. He sat atop his trusty steed, wiped at the bloodied tracks lining his legs, tongued the last of the sugary orb into juice and emptied the balance of his stash into the lining of his blazer. He chucked the paper bag away before entering the school grounds as any sign - let alone being caught in the act - of eating, sucking, or chewing during lessons guaranteed a trip to the Headmaster's office. Here, a set of sadistic swipes courtesy of a gnarled willow cane would be dispensed. Choose palms-up, and you could expect four to six of the best. But you'd have to have nerves of steel. The tendency to flinch was pure survival instinct and served only to piss off the executioner. Choose the backside, and you'd be bent over for a minimum of ten whacks. The dilemma was thus: see it coming or hear it coming. Beecher's advice to any first-timers was to preach the science of the act.

"All I'm gonna say is, bend over. You see, the speed of sound is slower than the speed of light, and believe me, you're gonna see it comin', and you're gonna fuckin' flinch, you're just gonna."

Most opted for the latter as by the third whip, so much blood had rushed to your head from grabbing your ankles, you were more or less deaf anyway.

Of course, the sticky sweets would've been completely lint covered by 10:00 a.m., but they would be sucked clean, nonetheless. Two hours of European History with the stiflingly-dull Mr. Fleedon Squires, a human rake with coke-bottle glasses, a complexion like a battered prune, and breath of such rancid toxicity that it was known to singe nose hair at ten paces, fell either side of the mandatory milk break. And with the crotch-sweat aftertaste of tepid moo-juice plaguing the entire classroom, a little confectionary respite was deemed worth the risk.

Young Beecher's daily ritual would inevitably include a homeward-bound visit to McCallister's emporium, inviting an unhurried stroll amongst the magnificently oversized jars where the selection was studiously considered once more. Maybe it would be the indulgence of a *Sherbet Fountain,* or perhaps a handful of *Black Jacks* and *Fruit Salads* – it depended on the day, mood was everything.

Beecher settled into the Jaguar's driver's seat and the intense aromas of oiled leather and burnished wood and burned gasoline teased his senses to the point of being hypnotic.

"I'll definitely have one of these," he said, squeezing the steering wheel until his knuckles turned white. "One day."

"Why wait?" Eeva said. "You drive."

The bark of the straight-six power plant echoed around the forest like the rebirth of an ancient legend. Waves of smooth, saturated air rushed across the diminutive windscreen drowning every uttered syllable and precipitated streams of salty tears from unprotected eyes. Eeva was ecstatic. With her blonde locks encased in a vibrant yellow scarf, she shouted with joy, encouraging him with a stern, *"put your foot down,"* and a mocking, *"it's not a limousine; it's a race car. Show it who's boss."*

And he did.

What self-respecting, 24-year-old budding rock star, with a beautiful and complicated woman by his side, belting through the languid English countryside at midnight in the summer of 1978, could resist such an invitation? Up and down the gears, pushing into blind corners, Beecher tested his own confidence. He spun up the revs, felt the press of the bucket seat in the small of his back and rejoiced as the chassis flexed under his feet with nervous bites and tentative shudders.

"You're the driver," Eeva said, with her mouth only inches from Beecher's ear. "The car is waiting for you."

He downshifted coming into a bend.

"Now," she said, "...trust me, hit the gas, now!"

He pressed the accelerator hard and the car dug in like a leopard clawing at the stomach of its fallen prey. Overhead, ice-white streaks shot from the midnight moon spearing a thousand arthritic tree limbs as the Jaguar exploded from the last of the forest thickets onto an abandoned dual carriageway. A road sign indicated the turning to Brighton, eight miles ahead, and Eeva pointed and Beecher nodded. She raised out of her seat and brushed her lips against his face and said,

"Breakfast on the pier, we can watch the sun come up."

London was less than an hour's drive north but might as well have been a million miles away. Beecher was sinking deeper and deeper into Eeva's world. She made him want to write and perform; to be more than he'd ever wished for and it was intoxicating. His breath came in short snatches and the Jaguar drifted across the seam of white lines splitting the ribbon of black tar and Beecher felt the warmth of Eeva's hand rest upon his own, guiding the speeding bullet gently back over the divide. She tapped the bezel of the dashboard clock, reached down and turned the dial of the radio and a soft, yellow glow highlighted the AM band just as an after-hours disc jockey was whispering a few final thoughts. The disembodied voice was belaboring the first listen of a new song and he spoke of being moved and empowered, and he shared a personal story of neglect and mistrust, and he lamented the love he once held for another, and how he wanted to make amends and how the song had given him the space to think and to act.

"I think we're missing out," Beecher said wryly.

"Oh, I don't know about that." Eeva threw out her widest smile yet. "I'd wager the forces of good are conspiring in our favor tonight."

Beecher was poised to respond, unsure if he'd misheard when the night became graveyard still and the disc jockey dropped the needle on the song in question; *his song.* A shiver raced the length of his spine as the first few bars emerged like a bejeweled carousel whirling to speed, and in an instant, speakers that were concealed in the footwell and mounted discretely behind the walnut dash, pounded in their housings loud as jackhammers, pushing waves of sound from the racing car that were suddenly visible. And they were painted fire-engine red and electric blue and sunset orange, and they pulsed with sparks and flashes, and they spiraled into the shape of an infant tornado, building higher and higher, swallowing sheets of clouds and clusters of stars.

"I know you wanna kiss me," Eeva sang along, riding both hands in the warm night air rushing over her head.

Beecher felt the mechanical chorus of the classic engine mimic the beating heart of the music, and he pressed his foot to the floor and the bones of the car stiffened, and the open fields and the clusters of trees fell away to blackness as the Jaguar released its bond with the earthbound carriageway and motored atop a rolling luminous path that swerved and swooped with hilly delight. And it was carried ever higher, surfing the backs of turbulent winds that had pirouetted north across the upper latitudes from the muggy tropics to the chilling Arctic gyre. And the eye-watering streams spilling down his cheeks now channeled emotions from the farthest edge of his soul, becoming thick, salty tears.

Beecher rested his head on folded arms and marveled at the lights of twinkling cities and abandoned motorways and rivers and lakes as black as tomorrow dotting the landscape below. The vehicle steered through banks of thick clouds, and showers of balmy rain brushed their faces like the bristles of a painter's brush. And Eeva began to speak and her voice was as clear as spring water.

"If you are humble, your instinct will always see you right. Remember, your gut is your mind's worst enemy. Never ignore it. Only when you are left alone with your thoughts will you tumble into the abyss of self-doubt and self-hate. Your mind will kill you if you let it. It will embarrass you and it will intimidate you. And when all is said and done, the last sound you hear will be that petulant child in your head; the one for whom you allotted all the power, cackling like a deranged demon, cheering on your demise. It's a fight, so don't think it's easy, but you've broken free, Beecher Stowe. Now ride this wave, all the way to the shore."

Sunrise, 4:47 a.m., Brighton Pier.

They sipped strong black coffee and munched on cold Cornish pasties with legs dangling over a lumpy, green sea. A fisherman sat nearby on a wooden stool. He mumbled quietly, indifferent to their presence. He baited three rods and set their respective hooks adrift on the outgoing tide. A flask of tea and yesterday's Daily Express crossword poked from a ragged leather satchel and Beecher was reminded of Pengo's pre-opening ritual.

"You need to get back," Eeva said. "They'll be waiting."

"Who?"

"Your band. They'll want the low down; the nitty-gritty; the salacious details."

"I wouldn't know where to begin."

"Start with the song, everything else is gravy."

"Do you think they know it was on the radio?"

"I do."

"It was past midnight. They'd all have been asleep."

"You're in Hans Tomek's world now. His reach is infinite."

The fisherman roused from his newspaper and checked the lines. More satisfied mumbles. Beecher watched as the man resumed his pose on the stool, hunched and cross-legged and seemingly content, and was a little envious. He'd craved success for so long that the prospect of having it felt intrusive. Beecher Stowe, a man in search of a dream, he knew that guy; he liked that guy. Beecher Stowe, professional and successful, was a stranger, not to be trusted.

"It's not what it seems," Pengo had warned one night when they were lost in their philosophical meanderings over pints of Guinness. *"You get used to your lot in life; you get used to wanting and never having, and you get used to going without."*

"Without what?" Beecher asked.

"The stuff you dream about; all that nonsense you tell yourself you need - the big house, the adoration, the money. People are creatures of habit, they can't just change horses midstream without consequences."

"That doesn't apply to me. I want a career that doesn't rely on working for someone else."

"Well, that's where you're gonna come up short, 'cause we all work for someone else."

"No, in a factory, or a warehouse, you know what I mean."

"Beech, you're not listening. When dreams become a job, most folks let them go. When everything you stand for; everything you've sweated for, is at the mercy of some corporate wanker looking to make a few quid, or at the whim of a bunch of teenagers snacking on the latest groove, you gotta admit that you're working for someone else."

"I'm not looking to be a one-hit-wonder."

"Trouble is, you don't get to choose."

Those words haunted Beecher. He tipped out the dregs of his coffee and watched the black liquid spill and snake seaward where it was quickly consumed by the boiling froth of a breaker rebounding from the legs of the pier. He stared at the beach, thick with pebbles and crushed shells. Shops and hotels along the front were blinking to life as curtains were pulled apart, exposing pinpricks of soft, incandescent lamplight glow.

"Pete Townshend slept under this pier when he was a lad," Beecher said. "The memory of it inspired him to write an album ten years later."

Eeva was silent and studying. The arrival of the morning sun had brought along with it a brisk onshore breeze that whipped golden tangles of hair over her nose and mouth, leaving her eyes alone to betray her thoughts.

Beecher said, "I'm afraid that I might not be cut out for a business that can dispose of me so easily."

"Oh, hush!" There was scorn in her voice. "You're ten minutes into this; you have no idea what the new day holds, let alone what's down the road. You just said Pete Townshend was inspired by a ten-year-old memory. Do you like his work?"

"I do, very much."

"Would you say it was a seminal work?"

"Absolutely. Probably the best he's done."

"Do you think he wrote it from a place of fear?"

"No," he checked his answer, "...I'm not sure I know what you mean."

"Everything starts with fear - first steps, first bike ride, first kiss, first school, first job..."

Eeva stood and held out her hand and Beecher followed. They strolled in silence until a door banging off its latch drew them into the dilapidated Palace theatre. Once the toast of music hall tradition, its innards now suffered from misuse and neglect. Where once, bright lights illuminated grease paint on the faces of entertainers, now greasy stains carpeted the damp floor and broken boxes and rolled linoleum and seats wearing tattered upholstery absorbed shafts of sunlight that intruded through windows caked with grime and mold. Eeva led the way out.

"Fear drives the car," she said, pointedly. "...until you take control. You are a bandleader - where you go, others will follow. I'm not talking about your mates, that's a given. I'm talking about people that look to others for answers. They're not like you, so don't try and relate to them. If you do your mind will seize upon it and tie you up in knots and ensure you are never fulfilled. You have to step out into the light as if it's your birthright."

Eeva spun around and thrust her arms overhead and on cue, a squadron of Starlings shot from beneath the pier and executed a fantastic display of coordinated flight. It was as though a vast, velvet cloak was being draped about invisible objects and then immediately retracted. The birds fell at the mercy of the wind and then shot to the heavens, gyrating and folding upon each other from within, stretching and soaring and spinning.

"Do the work that lays before you," Eeva said, "...and trust in the timing of your life."

Beecher was mesmerized. He looked first at the cavorting flock and then at Eeva and then back to the sky.

"You make it all sound so..., fucking..., simple."

Eeva's expression changed. She was no longer elated, she was pleading. Her eyes were wide and moist with welling tears, and her mouth tightened into a thin, determined line.

"Trust me," she said, "I know a lot about wasting time."

Chapter Seventeen

10:59 a.m.

Beecher made three attempts to push his way through a crowd of regulars that were waiting like anxious puppies for the sign of a swishing curtain and the resounding, metallic clunk of a heavy bolt being drawn. Attempt number four found him squeezed and hunched beneath one of the many chins of a transvestite known to the neighborhood as, Herbie because of, well…, *"Her-Be,"* a bloke.

"Give us a little breathing room, will ya Herbie?"

"Beecher, you ol' horse thief, thought you'd be living in a mansion by now. I heard the song, mate. Top form. One of the greats."

Herbie was having a day off from the heels and the tights, *"too bloody hot for that lark,"* but for some reason, a generous helping of peach-colored spackle remained glazed across his thick, black stubble in defiance of the rising thermometer.

"Glad you like it," Beecher said. "It's been a long time coming."

Pengo's cheesy grin appeared behind the curtain. 11:00 a.m., on the dot - opening time to the citadel; to Aladdin's cave; to four hours of uninterrupted, alcohol-induced idleness. This day, however, would be different. There was business at hand. Floor and ceiling catches were released, but doors were not swung wide.

"Hang on, lads," Pengo said. "I need ten minutes to sort a few things out."

He may as well have delivered a batch of cheese rolls smothered in dog shit, such was the outcry. The odor of stale beer was heavy on the breaths of the huddled bodies as a chorus of *'fucks'* rang out, despondent and disgruntled. Pengo reached out his hand and beckoned Beecher through the final inches and closed the door. The slam of the bolt triggered another round of insults.

"Tough crowd," Beecher said.

"Not bad for a weekday. If it was a Saturday, they'd have skinned me alive."

The lads were gathered, all supping orange juice per the pub's strictest rule, *"no alcohol before opening time."*

Beecher stood before the band, said nothing, reached into his jacket and dealt the airline tickets onto the bar, painfully slow. He tapped each ticket in turn and read aloud the name printed in bold type.

"Finnius Alouicious Bramble; Harold Mabel Floom…"

Fez lost it. Snooze resisted for about three seconds, and then collapsed, gasping for breath.

"Mabel?" Fez asked, with tears streaming down his face. "Who the fuck is Mabel?"

"Leave it out, Fez," Beecher said, noticing Harry's growing blush. "This is serious stuff."

He continued, "Sidney Peter Silver; Pengorick Crane."

"No middle name, Pengo?" Fez's mouth quivered like an electrocuted snake.

"Nah," Pengo said dryly. "Mum thought about naming me after my ol' granny, then thought better of it. She said it might've proved troublesome; said it might've got me a kickin' or two in school; said it might've caused me to take up knitting."

"Well, come on then, what was it?" Harry said, praying for a little redemption, the wheels of his imagination working overtime. Until…

"Oh, fuck off, all of ya!"

Harry's cheeks burned scarlet as he submitted to the contagious laughter, and when all had died down, Fez reached out and ran his fingers across the rectangles of thin card like they were shiny bars of gold.

"We're going. We're really going."

"We certainly are," Beecher said. "London Heathrow to New York's John F. Kennedy airport. First class."

"I've never been on a plane," Harry said.

"You haven't even been on a bleedin' ferry," Fez said.

"I've never had the need."

"You don't need a need. You just fuckin' go."

"Why? Where?"

"France. For a laugh; get pissed; chat up some French birds."

"When did you ever do that?"

"I didn't say I'd done it. It's just what you *can* do."

Snooze shook his head at the mindless banter.

"See what I've had to put up with?"

"I was gone for one day," Beecher said.

Snooze grunted his response.

"One day is an eternity with these morons."

"Okay, lads, listen up," Beecher said. "We'll meet here for a briefing and to check passports. A van will pick us up at 9:00 a.m. sharp and the plane takes off at midday. Other than my guitar and Snooze's trumpet, all of the instruments are being supplied at the other end."

"Can I bring my sticks?" Fez said.

Pengo stepped up, "I'm sure they have drum sticks in America, Fez, but go ahead and bring your own if you must. One pair, mind, not a fuckin' suitcase full."

Beecher had retained Pengo in the role of caretaker and road manager as he was the only member of the party that had visited the U.S.A. It'd been a brief visit; one day. The result of winning a national Sunday newspaper competition for sending in the best drawing of London Bridge on the occasion of it being dismantled, shipped across the Atlantic, shuttled through the Panama Canal, steamed up the Pacific coast, and rebuilt in the Arizona desert. The picture was drawn with pen and ink, bold and incredibly detailed, which was truly a shame as it was printed the size of a postage stamp between the daily horoscope and an Ad for women's crotch-less knickers.

"Awesome," Fez said. "Tell us again where we're going, Beecher. Will we see the Statue of Liberty?"

Snooze's turn, "It's a fuckin' concert tour, you dip-shit, not a family holiday."

"Day one, arrive, 4:00 pm," Beecher read from his notebook. "Transfer to the Plaza Hotel in Manhattan – you'll be sharing rooms, so pick your partner. At eight-thirty that night, we'll do interviews at KBIG and KCOK, New York's leading rock n' roll radio stations; dinner at nine-thirty with record company folks for me and Pengo to sort out some logistics; free time for the rest of you."

Harry shifted on his stool, began to speak, stuttered and stopped.

"Out with it," Fez said, with a hearty slap on his back.

"What do we do for money?"

Expressions of, *"oh, yeah,"* wiped across the faces of the band.

"You'll be given twenty dollars every day that will go against your salaries. That'll cover all of your meals, with plenty left over for a beer. Also, at the tour's end, you will each get a bonus that will be a percentage of the profits."

Fez was quick with, "What's the percent?"

Pengo was even quicker, "If the tour is a wash then it doesn't matter. Ten percent of nothing is nothing. You worry about playing your heart out and making Beecher sound good and keep the punters happy."

Beecher dialed down the tension of the group. Mind and body were fraying at the edges, and he was barely holding his own shit together. The papers in his hand were creased like cheap bed sheets; standing still was impossible; even breathing seemed a chore at this point. For long moments, the sheer volume of this turn of events drove him into a walking coma. The pretense of being busy and vital helped soothe the crying baby in his gut. Thankfully, Tomek's operation was unflappable. His flunkeys had prepped the entire tour in less than a day - flights; hotels; cars; catering; interviews; receptions; wardrobe; instruments; passports; and if so desired, the obligatory rock 'n roll companions. Ladies. Escorts. Groupies. Snooze called them, *"Females of the opposite sex."* Beecher imagined that a single, nubile courtesan from Tomek's world could de-stress the entire band while sipping a cup of Earl Grey and not spill a drop. The thought of it sent another rush of confusion pin-balling around his head and he reached for the nearest empty stool.

"Alright, lads, I've made copies of the itinerary for everyone. We have ten cities on the books; that's ten opportunities to leave 'em wanting more. Let's do this as if it's the only chance we're ever gonna get."

Beecher acknowledged each elated grin and nodding head in turn. He breathed deeply; sighed deeper. Spirits were high and the banter was jovial. A light breeze filtered through a louvered window and lifted a pair of lacy, net curtains like a twirling dancer's skirt. It carried with it the scent of cooked jasmine rice and ripe bananas from Dalal's market, sweetly masking the odor of damp beer cloths.

"Sheila's cooking," Pengo said. "We'll be alright for some grub, lads. I'm betting..."

He didn't finish.

Hellfire slammed the pub doors and the deadbolt was sheared from its clasp and the two slabs of heavy oak buckled and hinge screws were ripped from the door jamb as easy as pulling birthday candles from a cake. The shock waves arrived first, driving the air from the room, compressing and suffocating. Next came the blast wind. Hurricane-force. A scattershot of stones and debris, eviscerating bodies and amputating limbs. Shattered glass from the stained bay window showered the bar, sparkling like cut diamonds. The regulars that had been bunched into the doorway were piled like a basket of dolls, with hair and clothing scorched from their bodies. Blood spatter painted whitewashed brick like poppies under autumn rain. Beyond, in the car park, the blackened, contorted shell of a Ford Cortina spat ragged flames beneath a cloud of tumbling black smoke.

And the cries arose.

At first, feeble and nondescript.

And then, louder and panicked. A female voice from outside lamented, *"my baby, my baby."*

Silhouettes bolted before the raging fire.

In the foyer, limbs were mangled and separated, and the once impatient voices were silenced. Except one. Herbie was on his back, smothered. Blinking and confused. He tilted his head, found Beecher.

"I saw it, Beech," he said. "I didn't hear it, I just saw it go up; like a fucking volcano, mate."

Beecher crawled over to Herbie. The big man was buried beneath bodies that flinched and jerked in the throes of dying.

"Help us out, Beech," Herbie said, "I can't fuckin' breathe."

Beecher grabbed at a beckoning hand and pulled, and another body moved. He screamed through strings of saliva, "Where's your fucking hand? I can't help you if I can't find your fucking hand."

Pengo and Snooze came to his side. Head wounds were bright scarlet against pale skin.

Beecher raged, "Help us out, Herbie, help us the fuck out."

Snooze spit up in his mouth and acid raked his throat.

Herbie stared back. At nothing. He blinked red mist from his eyes and his voice was soft and unhurried. He heard, but he did not see.

"Where are you, Beech?"

"I'm here, mate. I'm right fucking here."

So, by the collar, they pulled.

And the mound of bodies contorted as one entity.

Herbie's shoulders came free and his arms found purchase and he flipped onto his belly and he pushed himself upright.

And when he stood, he smiled, wide and thankful.

And the stubble was gone.

And the pink flesh was gone.

And no tears fell.

Beecher supported Herbie across the rubble and walked him clear.

He settled the big man and made to return but the darkness beckoned and he obeyed.

Beecher felt the first slap and denied it. Until it came again.

"Wakey, wakey, time to go."

The voice was drawing him from the abyss. A deserved place. He had failed his friends and he was cold, and it was dark, and he hung by one hand over a pit of infinite blackness.

Another slap.

He shouted to his assailant, "I'll let go. I mean it, I'll let go."

A needle pierced his arm, sharp and invasive, and the drugs flowed warm as tropical rivers. And there was harmony once more and it was divine. He sought the light but a curtain was drawn and flashes of blue and red whirled against a waterfall and there were screams in the darkness. Beecher retreated.

He ran from the confusion.

He ran to exhaustion.

And then he slept.

THE DAILY RECORD (evening edition) reports:

Coded warning came from man with Irish accent, say police.

Fifteen people were killed, and 12 others injured, many of them seriously, after a car bomb devastated the forecourt of the Railway Tavern in White City, London today.

The injured were taken to intensive care at Hammersmith Hospital. The victims are aged between 18 and 65.

The chief constable for West London, Mr. Clarence Wood, told a press conference that it was the most horrific and cowardly attack he had ever witnessed.

The bomb exploded at precisely, 11:10 a.m., a time believed when the forecourt area would be populated with shoppers at Dalal's convenience market, and patrons arriving to the Railway Tavern. An eye-witness recalled the Ford Cortina as having been parked overnight.

Following the incident, heavy traffic throughout the boroughs of White City, Shepherd's Bush and Hammersmith prevented the ambulances reaching the scene in a timely fashion and many of the injured were taken to hospital in personal cars and taxis.

Target not specified

Mr. Clarence Wood told reporters that a coded warning was phoned by a man with an Irish accent to regional newspaper offices at 10:45 a.m.

The caller said that a bomb had been placed in a car at a White City pub but did not specify which. The caller went on to read from a prepared statement denouncing the British parliament and their policy on immigration.

When asked if recent threats by the Provisional IRA to escalate bombing campaigns in the UK were related, Mr. Wood declined to comment.

Chapter Eighteen

The Outriders carved along the Westway through lanes of sluggish traffic with the gleaming black Rolls in their midst. Roaring exhausts announced the motorcade well before the ominous dark shapes bulldozed their way through bleary-eyed commuters who were startled to attention as three pace setters struck a trail upfront, zipping between chrome bumpers, aggressively blocking and shadowing, opening a clear path for the Rolls to purr by unimpeded. Three more riders pursued in tight formation, acting as a rearguard to dissuade any protesting drivers from acts of retribution.

They exited the motorway without slowing. The riders were at a full peg-scraping, knee-dragging lean as they turned onto Wood Lane and headed into the enclave of White City. The procession soon encountered roadblocks of police cars and foot patrols, waving and slowing and redirecting. Tomek's entourage peeled off into the side streets; the heart of city-planning decay, where scruffy kids kicked through the collateral damage of riotous football-hooligans, hurling slabs of broken concrete at already smashed windows, catching the ire of shopkeepers intent on refurbishing vandalized storefronts and shattered market stalls. The Rolls glided silently through solemn, deserted avenues like a feather brushing silk, coming to a halt an alley's width away from the scene of the explosion.

The front half of the Railway Tavern was gutted from sodden floor to craggy roofline. The blast had exposed the entire frontage of the Victorian structure leaving fingers of shredded timber and rows of chipped, blood-red bricks gaping in the mouth of a monster.

Hans Tomek found Eeva in quiet conversation with an officer standing guard at the perimeter. They were observing uniformed forensics units kicking through mounds of saturated rubble, gathering evidence in meticulous detail. Tomek laid his hands on her shoulders, and noticed at her feet lay a scarred section of Mahogany that was once the bar top. Splinters of oak stood proud like calcified stalagmites for its entire length. In the depths of the cavernous facade, a suited detective wandered the room and was seen to brush against a panel of peeling plaster. His black sleeve was instantly alive with pinpoints of light and he brushed at the tiny reflections and watched with dark amusement as fragments of colored glass took flight like grains of sand shaken from a beach towel.

Tomek's voice was mellow and precise, "He'll recover?"

"Yes," Eeva said. "The boys were sheltered from the initial blast. Mostly cuts and bruises. They will all be released later tonight or tomorrow morning, along with the landlord's mother. She was in bed upstairs."

"A late sleeper," Tomek noticed.

"I understand she hasn't been well."

Tomek walked the perimeter, his disgust compounding at every step. Eeva hung back. Death had its own peculiar scent. As did alcohol when spilled. The combination was putrid.

Tomek returned, said, "Do we know who's responsible?"

"The police aren't giving anything away, but word on the street is that some splintered faction of the IRA has joined up with the National Front. They're making a little cash on the side; marketing their bomb-making skills."

"A crash course in how-to-end-the-world, eh?"

"I guess so. I can ask around some more. The men are tight-lipped, but the women have had enough. Two kids under the age of three were killed outright, and one is in intensive care - a boy, age six; the shop owner's son."

Tomek said, "Why does mankind persist in getting it so wrong?"

He lit a thin cigar and pondered the scene, imagining and absorbing. The premises spoke to him, told him tales of jaunty times, and barroom scuffles, and secret, flirty kisses, and drunks with obscenity-ridden mouths.

And it told him of the life of Beecher Stowe.

"Let's learn what we can about the heathens that did this," Tomek said. "Pay any price."

Chapter Nineteen

"I guess the tour's off," Beecher said.

Eeva adjusted the dressing on his neck.

"On the contrary..."

Her touch was delicate; her bedside manner was tender and compassionate.

"...yesterday, you were a rising star; today you're a hero."

"That's ridiculous. I did nothing heroic."

On the other side of the curtain, a nurse dropped a bedpan and it slammed to the floor and its contents dribbled out frothy and shiny on squares of polished tile.

Eeva shrugged, "How many times do I have to tell you, it doesn't matter what *you* think? People will perceive what they want to. About you, they choose, *hero*."

"What about the lads? They suffered just as much. Harry's coping with nasty gashes on his arms and legs and Fez hasn't said a word. That's not like him at all. That top's gonna blow at some point. And Pengo and Snooze? They were there helping me get Herbie from under that..."

"One at a time," Eeva said. "A face is a face. You have it; they don't. It's not personal, it's your wheelhouse, so own it."

The smile that painted her face was empty. It showed in her eyes and the set of her shoulders. She was distant and she was burdened.

"The press is going crazy for the story, all over the world," Eeva said. "Strangers are grateful because your involvement gives them something in return: a lifeboat when the ship is sinking. Sometimes, all we need is a single image to keep the ghosts away."

Eeva picked up the previous day's edition of the *Daily Record*. On the front cover, photographed against a backdrop of the smoldering wreckage, Beecher Stowe guided Herbie's hulk from the pub into a waiting car. The picture was captioned:

> *Rock musician, Beecher Stowe, survivor of the Railway Tavern bombing.*

An editorial began:

> *The young star's debut single, Supermassive Superstar, is an allegory for a better life. We must consign this horrific event to the dungeons of cowardice and pessimism. I implore you to listen to the words of this brave young Briton. Heed his message, and then rise up and make this world fit for all regardless of race or creed or color or religious ideology.*

Beecher stared at the wrinkled page. Not at himself, at Herbie. The big man was destroyed, physically and emotionally. His bulk was now pathetic and small, and the rags of his clothing fluttered at his legs and his hair was blackened and torn as if plucked by ravenous birds. Beecher's left arm was clasped about Herbie's waist, his right cradled a bloody elbow. The sadness that leaped from the page was palpable and Beecher shook with anger, and with fear. One minute, his pulse raced with the heat of revenge; the next, he was calm and controlled. He thrust the paper aside.

"I just wanted to do this..., thing..., these songs."

"You didn't want to change the world?"

"Into what?"

Eeva gathered her coat and bag.

"I'm sorry," Beecher said.

"For what?"

"I don't know. I just feel like apologizing."

"I have some work to do for Hans. I'll call in later. You should get some rest. You might have delayed shock; it can be serious."

"I'm fully embracing anger, pain, misery, fear, confusion, panic and anxiety. Shock can wait its fucking turn."

A hint of her smile showed like clouds retreating from the sun but like the English weather, it was soon gone.

"What about Pengo's mum?"

"She's okay. Well, I'm not sure exactly what ails her, but the doctor cleared her for any wounds from the explosion. Pengo said he'd be along to see you once he'd taken her to stay with someone called Moochie."

"Moonie," Beecher said. "Auntie Moon. Lives in Cricklewood. Not family, just calls her that. She went to school with his Mum."

He scooted up in the bed.

"So, you met Pengo. He's something else, isn't he?"

"I'm not sure I'd use that word, but, yeah... there's some depth there."

"He scares most people first time out. I've seen him lean into a group of girls and smell their perfume. Chin to eyebrow. Complete strangers. Not one of them said a thing. He's got some sort of calming influence around women."

"And you want him as your road manager?"

"Bloody right. I'd trust him with my life."

"You generally do if they're the ones booking your travel."

"He's like a brother. Closer, maybe. I dunno, never had one, but I expect the feeling's mutual."

A ward sister swung by pushing a stainless-steel cart piled high with covered platters. She was an older woman with kind eyes and a strong regional accent.

"Salad alright for you, Mr. Stowe?"

When she spoke, Beecher couldn't help but imagine the blustery, wind blasted moors of Devon and Cornwall.

"At 8:30 in the morning?"

"I'm afraid it's that or jelly and ice cream. Kitchen's overwhelmed. It's been bedlam. Never known a night like it. Such a shame. Those wretched people; they need stringing up."

"Salad is fine, Sister."

She lifted the lids on all but the last platter and satisfied with her choice, delivered the tray on a rolling table along with a plastic beaker of cloudy tap water.

Beecher made eye contact with Eeva as he slowly and dramatically revealed the contents of the plate. Three leaves of limp lettuce; a whole tomato; two hard-boiled eggs, still in their shells; a sliver of orange cheese, and a solitary pickled onion that left a vinegary slug-trail as it rolled freely around the plate.

Beecher winked at Eeva, said, *"Hero?"*

She slipped on her leather jacket, nodded and took her leave.

The morning was bright and warm and Eeva flagged down a black cab with instructions to take her to Chelsea. The ride would be just long enough for her to change her look, donning the black wig, smearing on purple lipstick and eyeliner, and with a heavy sigh, ladder a perfectly good pair of silk tights. The cab pulled up in front of the deserted Trafalgar pub and Eeva asked the driver to wait. She went across to the side entrance and rang the buzzer. After a fashion, the human blancmange that was Pedo File, popped the latch and stuck her head into bright sunlight.

"Wha'choo want?"

"I'm looking for Fiona, I was here with her a couple of weeks ago."

"She don't live here. Try the flats above the Keyhole or the Seventh Veil up in Soho. She strips there in the week."

"Actually, I'm really looking for her boyfriend, or ex-boyfriend, Derek. I don't know his last name."

Pedo reached into the pocket of her drab, terrycloth robe and pulled out a pack of smokes. She lit one and sucked on it until her eyes bulged. The belt was loosely tied, and it found no purchase around her expansive waist. The robe parted fully. She was naked underneath but didn't flinch. Two fat breasts with areolae the size of painted saucers rested on a stomach that hung to her midriff like a collection of Egyptian scrolls. A thin, black line of wispy pubic hair sprang from in between thighs that showed no daylight. Eeva noticed her feet were bare, showing tiny scabs at the indents of her toes.

Pedo's eyes crinkled and day-old mascara flaked onto her pudgy cheeks.

"Has that wanker got you up the duff as well?"

"Yeah," Eeva said with a dirty grin, "...and I've got something for him, too."

"His name's, Derek Brinks, and you didn't hear that from me. He hangs out with a bunch of mental fucks and I don't need their grief around 'ere. Last I heard, he lives in some squat on Beaufort Street, down near the Embankment."

Her interest was piqued.

"So, wha'choo gonna do then?"

Eeva turned away. Over her shoulder, said,

"Read about it in the papers."

"If you get into trouble, you come back here to me. Pedo will keep you warm, darlin'."

The cab door slammed. Visions of Pedo's heft squatting and sweating and writhing persisted and Eeva shuddered at the thought. She shared the destination with the driver and asked if he might make a quick stop at a bank on the way. He stepped on the brakes sharpish and turned in his seat.

"You thinking of doing a runner? 'Cause let me tell you what happened to the last creep that tried..."

"No," Eeva waved a twenty-pound note at the divider and he snatched it. "I just need to do a little business. I won't be too long."

"Alright, sorry love, I get all sorts 'round 'ere. There's a Barclays across the way. Will that do?"

"Yes."

Derek Brinks was a complete unknown but odds are he was skint - and by now in possession of a severely bruised guitar. A wad of bank notes from a pretty girl might grease the wheels of his ideological loyalty. She replayed another conversation with Beecher as though rehearsing lines for a play. The drive back to London had been at an easier pace. Eeva was at the wheel and she talked and the Jaguar had hummed along dutifully.

"Women especially are sold a flawed story - that chasing immortality, with lotions and operations and therapists, is a reflection of our worth, but none of us can contend with its reality. Without aging, the stages of our lives are no longer precious. To outlive others is to assume life is a race. Being near Hans Tomek has taught me that we are born with this wonderful stress; to make the most of our allotted time."

"Why didn't your parents survive?"

"Tomek said it wasn't part of the bargain."

"But they could have?"

"I don't know, maybe. Tomek saw in me a way to help make others' lives better."

"But not your life?"

"It hasn't been written fully yet. Everyone has their own struggle. Mine is no different."

"Because it's relative to you?"

"Yes."

"And now, to me?"

"I hope so."

Beecher's eyes were set on her profile.

"So, where did he come from?"

"You must ask him yourself. You must bring your own prejudices and decide if you wish to embrace them or let them rest. If you believe it, you'll feel it. In here."

She touched her left breast and Beecher's gaze lingered.

"Tomek says each of us exist at many different moments in time; that we can be transported to these points if our will is strong enough. Well, he's looking for a way back."

The car slowed further as traffic bunched up crossing Kew Bridge. A line of pasty-legged tourists crossed before them. Heads were on a swivel and fingers pointed as they sought directions to the Gardens.

Eeva's voice became somber, "The darkness rises within him every so often. I've learned to accept it. He has no tolerance for failure."

"So, what's the price of failure?"

Beecher asked this question as if he were stepping out onto a frozen lake.

"He can take things from you," she said. "Important things; treasures you hold dear. I saw him empty a man's soul and it was the saddest most destructive act I've ever witnessed. It was soon after the war. There was a sense of opulence growing in society that he detested. People were getting rich from the suffering of others. He had encouraged an artist to express this sentiment, hoping that he might connect with the mistakes of his own time; trigger something deep inside. The artist painted the most glorious and disturbing portrait of the atrocities. It was intended for Tomek's eyes only, but the man was greedy and sold it and then mocked Tomek for his enduring naïveté.

The prospect of notoriety and wealth corrupts all who revere it. On the surface, Hans Tomek appeared quietly disappointed though a river of ice moved in his veins. He left that man withered and dying, empty as a shell."

Beecher pictured the artist, paintbrush in hand, abandoned to a life of artistic dementia and the strength of his own passion rose like acidic bile in his throat. To no longer comprehend the invisible art; to be stripped of melody and harmony; to wander aimlessly through life exorcised of the healing power of sound churned his gut sour. He balled his fist at his side and tried to stem the jolts of adrenaline from coursing uncontrolled in his blood. Robert Johnson had stood at the crossroads and made an historic deal, a journey both celebrated and lamented in the annals of contemporary music. Beecher Stowe had played those exact notes and sang those exact words with childlike ambivalence, lost in the repetition of rhythm and cadence. It was only now he understood.

"You can't just remove music from people's lives," Beecher's voice cracked, and his breathing slowed.

"Time is memory," Eeva said. "Hans Tomek has chosen to speak to the world on terms that humanity cannot comprehend. There simply is no precedent."

"Are you his only link?"

"To what?"

"To, …*us*, I guess."

"Good gracious, no. There are hundreds; probably thousands. You see… how do I put this? I'm the only one that has ever delivered."

Beecher was on edge; his mind racing, trying to fill in the blanks. It was like waiting at the cinema for the show to start. The curtains part; the lights go down, and... nothing.

"At some point we're gonna have to devise a code for when I don't know what the fuck you're talking about," he said. "Maybe I'll slap my cheeks, or burst into song, or simply stare into space."

"Temper, temper."

He realized she mocked and flirted with the same set of her eyes, *slightly narrowed,* and lips, *tight.* He wondered what they looked like during love-making.

"So, who is he? Really?"

She slipped the Jaguar down a gear, revved the engine to its symphonic apex and shot between a line of stationary and stupefied drivers on her left and the petrified and hurriedly braking oncoming traffic on her right.

"He is our father," she shouted.

Eeva waited patiently for an elderly pensioner to gather her income for the week. With arthritic fingers, she counted the coppers and the silver and three single notes into a purse embroidered with the face of Queen Elizabeth II as she would have appeared upon her coronation.

The teller looked on from behind a sheet of Perspex that looked as though it served double duty as an ice rink. It was a new edition to the bank, futile as it may be, following a recent spate of armed robberies in the western boroughs. Ranks of nervous employees had refused to come to work unless proper security measures were introduced. So, with the project assigned to the lowest bidder, a suite of security upgrades was purchased. Unfortunately, the installer had misrepresented his product and the effective proximity of its ballistic integrity, stating that it would hold up against multiple rounds of buckshot sprayed from a sawn-off shotgun. He was true to his word only if the blast was initiated from fifty feet away. In the confines of the tiny building, the safeguards were nothing less than visual deterrents. A stiff sneeze courtesy of a summer allergy would have it vibrating like a loose guitar string.

"You'll be alright now, Mary," the teller said. "Keep that money out of sight until you get down the post office and let them sort it out for you. Alright, m'love?"

The elderly woman hissed and scuttled away.

"To hell with the post office," she said under her breath.

The café, the bookies and the bingo hall beckoned, in that order, and she smacked her lips in anticipation of tea and biscuits and a good natter.

"Next!"

The teller was a dour, chubby man with sausage fingers and chewed nails. He punched and stabbed at a miniature Casio as if he was balancing the national debt. Eeva noticed his neck was dotted with sprigs of wiry beard spurned by the repeated use of a cheap electric razor. They stood proud against a stained and fraying shirt collar that was fastened with a perpetually-knotted tie. His window was a self-ordained pulpit; a place where no customer was spared some sort of financial indignation, albeit from a mid-level manager whose primary responsibility was cashing weekly pension and dole cheques. He reacted to Eeva's request to withdraw five hundred pounds with a suspicious sneer, asking her to repeat the sum three times.

"That's a lot of money," he said.

"Yes, I suppose."

"What's it for?"

"That is entirely none of your business."

He squirmed, struggling for a suitable quip, thoughts scrolling through a litany of glib responses. But this was no old-age pensioner, or shiftless used-car salesman, or teenage mother with a brace of under-fives and a robust heroin addiction. The woman's icy stare unnerved him.

He settled for, "I'll have to speak to the manager."

The teller slipped from his stool and Eeva thought he had fallen until his true height was revealed by the sight of his disheveled curly mop passing behind the counter like a clump of seaweed caught in a strong current.

Several minutes later, and to the relief of a growing line of impatient customers, Eeva accepted a sealed envelope of cash and departed. The cabbie had waited dutifully with two wheels breaching the curb in flagrant disregard of posted parking restrictions and was gratified further by the offer of a second crisp, twenty-pound note for his patience.

At another time, Beaufort Street would have been a classic Victorian thoroughfare - four-story, terraced dwellings stretching from the Fulham Road to Battersea Bridge, housing Chelsea's up-and-coming socialites and high-ranking government officials and London city traders. The exodus of affluent, post-war families to the leafy suburbs south of the river, and a decade of schizophrenic property values, left darkened windows on ever-darkening streets, and these once noble and groomed alleys of prosperity became prime hunting grounds for a legion of squatters. It always started with a broken window or a leaking gutter. Prospective dwellers would emerge from the undergrowth, quick and silent as vermin, peering through dusty panes and jiggling handles. Word would circulate and sooner or later, a back door would be forced by an inquisitive addict looking for trinkets to barter for cash or pills. They'd bring mattresses and portable televisions and camp stoves and record players and guitars and sets of drums. Neighbors would complain to an inner-city bureaucracy blinded and deafened by the skyrocketing onslaught of the homeless and the unemployed and *'For Sale'* signs would be erected like memorials to war heroes. And so, it spread. Like a virus. Communities of junkies and thieves and immigrants organizing in the underworld, goading and baiting authorities beyond the laws of the nation.

Heading towards the bridge, eight houses were plastered in neon green placards notifying the public of recent police evictions. Only one decrepit building had escaped the raids, a once-magnificent structure occupying the prized corner plot at the end of the street. The building displayed a staggering level of neglect. The fence surrounding the property was shredded with wood rot; the gate, suffering a similar fate, dangled from rusty hinges with screws ripped from their anchor points. A diseased Elm and an unkempt Holm Oak had entangled their branches from opposite sides of the footpath, becoming knitted together like a giant, green sweater, and grass and weeds consumed the modest garden to knee height.

"It's a little dodgy 'round 'ere," the cabbie said. "It's all those ne'er-do-wells from the King's Road. They pulled a driver out of his cab last Saturday night and stole his bleedin' shoes. I don't like waiting, but I'll keep circling if you like."

Eeva looked at him with tired eyes.

"Yes, I *would* like," she said.

The property had a commanding view of water traffic moving along the River Thames and for a moment, with the sun glinting off a slow-moving barge, Eeva was lost in the summer splendor of it all. A fresh, cool breeze whipped up from the gentle, sparkling chop and she had a sudden urge to go sailing. She'd take Beecher; she'd teach him the language of the sea and boats, and they would fish, and they would swim, and she would guide him away from Tomek's darkness. The suggestion prompted an immediate stabbing pain behind her eyes, as though Tomek was reading her mind. It was the first time she had contemplated such an obvious betrayal and a sudden and complete weight of loneliness pulled at her bones and tiny beads of sweat burst from her brow. She dug into her bag for a handkerchief and wiped at her forehead with such ferocity that snaking red tracks soon pulsed from under the deep Caribbean tan. Eeva stuffed the sodden square of cotton into the bag with shaking hands and looked about the street as nervous as a runaway adolescent.

From the street, the house showed every window as having been boarded with a graffiti-strewn sheet of plywood. The front door and sidelights had originally been framed under a beautiful, hand-carved porch that was set into the brick surround with much care and attention to detail. With cruel indifference, the majority of the surround had been hacked away for use as firewood and the ornate, crown glass and lead latticework chiseled out for pawning to any number of back-alley traders. Eeva stepped over an upturned baby's pram and two bicycle frames, sans wheels and handlebars, stood within the porch for a few seconds, listening for movement inside, and knocked lightly. The weight of her hand was enough to send the unlatched door into motion, opening hauntingly slow. With the accompaniment of several creaks and groans, daylight brushed a gloomy hallway that was empty but for furls of peeling wallpaper strewn over rotting floorboards. The smell of urine was immediate and pervasive, and rat feces trailed like black ants, becoming more concentrated at the door of what was once a sitting room, now a lavatory replete with open buckets of human waste. She ventured further in. Across the hall, with the door removed to serve as a tabletop, a second parlor was stuffed to the rafters with cardboard boxes brandishing the names and logos of global charities. Eeva noticed a collection of children's toys, still in their original packaging, spilling from one box. She lifted the lid of another and found several brand-new soccer balls and tennis rackets and cricket bats. A scale model of a WWII Spitfire peeked from crumpled cellophane, wingless and discarded. Eeva reached out and a bright, blue arc of static leaped from the toy, stinging her finger and she recoiled and massaged her hand. She reached again, tentative, her fingers brushing the surface to no startling effect. Without warning, she was overcome with a great weight of sadness, as if the mourning of thousands had been passed down through time. She knelt down and the waves of remorse kept coming, rolling in her stomach, pushing nausea through tensed muscles and clammy flesh so that it sat wet and shiny upon her skin. Cries of sorrow echoed loud and pitiful in her head and she covered her ears to quiet the assault. As if on cue, music filtered along the hall, like an antidote to poison. Melody and harmony consumed the sadness, and the weight abated. Eeva found purchase on a sealed box and brushed accumulated dirt from her knees. The toy sat harmless and abandoned and she retrieved it and placed it in her bag. A radio played at the back of the house and she picked her way toward the kitchen. The disc jockey came on, babbling in his caramelized, BBC-sanctioned voice, feigning syrupy enthusiasm as he sculled through fan mail and song requests:

> "We're gonna say, Hello, now to Mrs., or Miss, B. Stanfer, …I'm marrying you off, I'm sorry, …31 Noose Lane, Willenhall in the West Midlands, and I know you like Johnny Mathis. We don't actually have Johnny Mathis on the program today, but in the near future we may be able to satisfy you. (reads) …We are Vera, Linda, Barbara and Chris, we all work in the warehouse of a builder's hardware factory and we are unanimous in saying your program is great… you know how to chat me up don't you."

The hallway opened into a light and airy space, offering access to a private garden. A cloakroom, free from the detritus of the other rooms, presented coat pegs for the length of one wall; floor to ceiling closets on the other. Both were as empty as a new house.

> "…right, now who else have we got here… Mrs. Jean Irving, 32 Essex Street Longtown, in Carlisle, Cumbria. (reads)…could you be so kind as to play a record of your choice for my daughter Louise and her colleagues as they go about their work at Border Fine Arts, Middlehome Farm, Langholm, in Dumfriesshire…"

The kitchen was large and well-appointed and completely trashed. A cracked sink weeping brackish water into a puddle on the candy-striped linoleum was piled high with stained plates and empty food containers; the electric stove was slathered with grease and sported a crust of baked-on muck; open cupboards collected cereal boxes and a selection of empty jars - pickled onions, jam, marmite, lemon curd - and what drawers were still inserted, doubled as waste bins. The refrigerator, curiously, was untouched. In bygone days, the kitchen would have been the perfect space for conciliating petulant shrieks rising from vengeful tugs of hair or squabbles over seating assignments; for mentoring marathon homework sessions and consoling broken hearts over dying pets or cheating boyfriends.

A girl sat alone at a long, pine table, head resting on folded arms, a transistor radio inches from her ear.

"Hello," Eeva said.

The girl sat bolt upright, startled, eyes blinking into focus as if she'd been doused with ice water. The folds of her denim jacket had pressed deep grooves in her cheek, and she wiped at a line of spittle that was leaking from the corner of her mouth. After a spell, the girl focused on Eeva, said,

"Who are you? Are you in the top bedroom, 'cause you were supposed to get bread and milk?"

"No, I don't stay here. I'm looking for Derek."

"Are you a copper?"

From ten feet away, Eeva caught the heady perfume of last night's overindulgence evaporating from the girl's pores, laying a sheen of sweat thick as Vaseline on her face and neck.

"No," Eeva said. "Not the police."

"He comes and goes; not been here for a while."

The girl pressed the heel of her hands into her eye sockets and rubbed away the sleep. On the radio the DJ blathered on:

> "...they are ardent fans, and this will come as a complete surprise to them... so greetings to all of you and we shall move along with..."

A loping guitar riff introduced *T.Rex's, Hot Love.* The girl dropped her hands and stared at the speaker.

"Ah, I love this song," she said. "Do you like this song?"

"Yes," Eeva said, moving closer, taking a chair. "I do."

The girl mouthed along with the lyrics, said, "Reminds me of a family holiday. It rained every bleedin' day. We slept in a tent, all five of us, arguing about who was the coldest. This song takes me right back. Silly, eh?"

Eeva nodded and let the girl have her moment.

"Do you know Derek well?"

"Enough to know that he's a bloody thief and a fucking liar. What do you want him for?"

"Just a chat; a couple of questions."

"Last person that had a chat with him busted his bleedin' jaw."

"This is nothing like that."

"You got any money?"

Eeva said nothing, cocked her head, *huh?*

"Enough for a cuppa'?"

The Bluebird Café was a short stroll along the Embankment. It was still early; early enough for any of the past evening's litter, not having found a sodden gutter or dark culvert in which to begin decomposing, to be fanned into flight by rush hour traffic. Kebab and fish & chip wrappings, crisp packets, cellophane from cigarette packs, all gyrating about their legs as if they were participating in an earnest game of tag. The walk was also long enough to discover the girl's name, Claire, but she prefers Luna "...'cause, I don't know, I just feel like a Luna"; her age, twenty-two; how she knows Derek, turns out her roommate at college used to shag him; what she's doing in a squat, "got kicked out of me flat 'cause said roommate spent the rent money on drugs"; what her plans were, "no fucking idea, can't go home, probably gonna have to get a stupid job."

Luna dressed like a typical Chelsea girl - Doc Marten's, tartan skirt, and ripped T-shirt adorned with the silk-screened face of a fifties icon, as if bemoaning the relentless subjugation of a generation was somehow intrinsic to being catapulted to fame and fortune by overweight movie execs and squirrelly music publishing houses of that era. Thankfully, this teenage rebel acted anything but. Through the fading alcohol-induced haze, Eeva saw that behind the facade Luna was alert and educated, noting her affected inner-city meter was clipped and lazy and wavered in favor of a soft, Scottish brogue when challenged on topics outside of music, squats, thieves, drugs, and drunks.

"What college?"

"LSE," Luna said, with a smattering of dejection creeping in at the seams. "Political science and a dash of economics seemed like a good idea given the state of everything."

"It's a calling," Eeva said.

Luna spooned four helpings of sugar into her tea and took a cup-draining sip.

"I'll go back. When the time's right."

"Why not now?"

"Not much happening in the summer months. I'm supposed to be preparing my dissertation for September but not sure if I can be asked."

"What can you be asked?"

"Are you coming on to me? 'Cause I don't go that way."

Eeva smiled, wrinkled her brow, said,

"You don't realize how much you just told me without me having to ask."

Luna started to speak…paused, played with the tea spoon…. buying time. She looked at Eeva as if for the first time.

"Jesus, you're beautiful," she said. "You're fuckin' foreign-movie-star beautiful."

At the next table, a grizzled, lorry driver with ruddy cheeks and a bulbous schnozz that was blue with busted capillaries glanced up from the topless, tabloid tart he was savoring. Without saying a word, he weighed the gulf between imagined and reality, turned the newspaper over and checked the football results.

Luna rambled on, "Anyway, I haven't met anyone at college that doesn't want to do something else. Like be in a band, or make clothes, or just fuck off to France and hang out on the beach."

"Derek's in a band, isn't he?"

"Yeah, but he's a skinhead now, so I'm not sure what they play. He shaved off that lovely black mane. All it needed was a good wash."

She combed her fingers through fine and brittle, bleached locks.

"I'd give anything for hair that thick. Last time he was 'round, his new mates called him Nipple, 'cause of his weird shaped head. He looks a right twat."

Eeva poured more tea from the pot, said,

"You hungry?"

Two slices of fried bread, two eggs, a couple of rashers of bacon, a scoop of tomatoes and five rubbery mushrooms were soon reduced to a mahogany-brown and banana-yellow smear on a chipped china plate, with a sixpence-sized dollop of blood-red ketchup leaching into the tablecloth for good measure.

Eeva kept the conversation light while Luna slurped two more cuppas. She expanded on her interest in Derek, sharing her desire to check out new bands, saying she had money for demos.

"He used to drink in the Trafalgar but was barred for nicking fags from the machine," Luna said. "That's when he hooked up with the skins from Stamford Bridge. Got sucked right in; started handing out flyers for marches and meetings. And then him and a couple of lads started turning over charity shops and selling the stuff down the Portobello Road. He said it was money for the revolution; told me I had no idea what was coming. They mostly dump the gear in the squat, and he goes off and stays with the landlady at the *Prince and the Pauper* in Earl's Court."

Eeva was stone-faced.

"You think I'll find him there today?"

"Dunno. He does gigs in the pub every Sunday night, though. It's not a friendly place, even the hard-core punks give it a miss. There's always trouble; always someone gettin' stabbed. That's why everyone calls it the *Prince and the Slaughter*."

"Will you be there?"

"Are you joking? Haven't you heard of the World Cup? Scotland is playing the Netherlands. I'll be camped out in front of a telly as soon as I can find one that works."

Eeva paid for the breakfast, gave Luna the phone number of her residence, "*...just in case he shows up*".

She headed back to find the cabbie. The wind coming off the river had died and the glint on the water was no longer; the chop had settled, brown and mud-like. Halfway across Beaufort Street, she paused, mid-stride. On a whim, *"Of course!"* she wheeled around, returned to the café, found Luna staring at her hand, separating pennies from lint.

"What are you doing for the next few weeks?"

Several um's and aah's later, "How'd you like to make five hundred pounds a week, starting with a trip to New York City?"

"I fuckin' knew it; you *are* trying your luck, I told you…"

"Oh, settle down, girl. I want to hire you to look after a band's finances while they're on the road. I would have thought that someone attending the *London School of Economics* might be able to add and subtract sufficiently so that the guys don't get swindled."

"I don't have a passport."

"I'll take care of that."

Luna stuttered and fidgeted. The lorry driver looked up again, spoke through the fog of a No.6 that was burned down to the filter, said,

"If you don't go, I will."

The black cab lurched and bounced through a rutted section of abandoned roadworks abreast of Eaton Square, welded, apparently, to the backside of a milk float that rattled like a cage of castanet players. A slanting rain was assaulting this affluent sector of the city, scouring pedestrians from the sidewalks and emptying parks of nannies and nurses pushing wheeled charges with one hand, struggling with wind-tossed umbrellas in the other. Eeva lolled with bare feet on the seat, peering through misted windows, noticing how the blurred outlines of grand stone facades and the elegant glassed enclosures of resplendent Victorian homes had become dull and featureless shapes, able to be driven past with utter ambivalence. With this backdrop, the city seemed to groan under the weight of conflict. On this dreary summer's day, unity was found only in rebellion. Not like ten years ago; when explosions of vibrant color signaled a new generation coming of age in a perpetual carnival of vanity, arrogance and unshakable optimism, casting off the enduring cloak of war and donning polka-dot mini-dresses and flowery kaftans. Electricity in this context was more than science, it was an intangible atmosphere; it was an abundance of sex and rock 'n roll and insatiable curiosity, and young minds sparkled like pinpoints of laser light shining from bedrooms and darkened cellars. It was a time for authors and musicians and poets and filmmakers, and a true revolution of thought and behavior. It was also a point in time when Hans Tomek's desperation to connect to his world seemed more likely than ever to materialize. How could it not? As existential as his circumstance alleged, the world was aligning to a new era, and it was brave, and it was experimental. Miracles could happen, you just had to want them bad enough.

Eeva was met curbside at the Belgrave Place residence by a parade of doormen clutching umbrellas and she was annoyed by this. It was barely ten meters to the entrance, a few shallow puddles to kick through; some damp patches on the shoulders of her leather jacket, she would hardly be navigating the floodwaters of the Mississippi. Since meeting Beecher Stowe, she was becoming immune to status and privilege.

"Your humility is a contagious missile," she said. "Be careful where you aim that thing."

Talking with Beecher on the pier, bathed in the glow of a new day, Eeva found herself trying to defend her inherent pessimism.

"Society hands off its failings like the baton in a relay race. Each new generation takes hold and clubs its way to the inevitable finish line, only for it to begin all over again."

Beecher countered with, "What about the good stuff?"

"What do you mean, *good stuff*?"

"We came into the century flapping our arms like a demented bird trying to fly, and sixty odd years later we're walking on the moon."

"Science is not humanity. We don't take care of each other unless someone is getting paid. We sell success so well that it's become a way of life. Until it comes with a sacrifice. Then it's usually someone else's fault. If you had to choose between wanting clean water to drink or seeing a jet airplane circle the globe in record time, you'd think it would be an easy choice. The fact that it's not…"

Beecher interrupted.

"But I don't have to choose."

"And yet, millions do."

"I haven't seen what you've seen," Beecher said.

"Should we all have the same rights?"

"Of course."

"The right not to suffer?"

"I'm in. Where do I sign?"

"Right here," Eeva said, "...next to the addendum which says, ... *excluding royalty and celebrity; the wealthy and the political and the religious glitterati, who shall embrace fortune before function, one and all.*"

Eeva's greeting to the waiting doormen was brusque. She waved off the usual pleasantries and beelined for her apartment.

Two streets away, a human being was seeking shelter in the soggy confines of the discarded cardboard wrappings of a shiny, new refrigerator. It was a sturdy box, lined with acres of ruffled padding. And what's more, you could draw upon the walls to the ends of your imagination and your heart's content: windows, with sweeping views of the Serengeti; shelves piled high with cans of food and, *"oh look, over there, near the door, we have a new color television."*

Home sweet home.

Until it rained.

"No more darkness; no more pessimism," Eeva said aloud repeatedly, as she bathed in a cast-iron claw-foot, with bubbles spilling like creamy lava from every side of the tub. The mantra was echoed as she dressed and again as she sat before an expansive bay window with a steaming mug of coffee gripped between both hands. The thought of being out from under Tomek's wing had plagued her on the ride home and she flirted with visions of independence, and daydreamed of having a family of her own. The reality of growing old never crossed her mind.

"Time can be slowed," Tomek had said from the outset, *"...but you have to be in a very dark place to see it.*

She thought of Luna living in the squat; wondered if she should fetch her and coddle her. And then she laughed aloud, and it was a welcome sound; a hearty, soul-warming laugh. Like she'd laughed with Beecher.

"She'll really think I'm trying to get into her knickers!"

The telephone rang. It was five o'clock and it was expected. Repeated attempts to contact Tomek had proved fruitless, so messages were left, and assurances were made. And this would be him.

Hans Tomek bought a castle. It was a modest affair, no dungeon or spires, but it did have battlements. And a great hall with a walk-through fireplace. Two rooms heated for the price of one – if the price was burning an entire oak tree in a single sitting.

While touring the estate, he had toyed with a nagging question, *"How high of a flame is too high for one to vault safely to the other side?"*

It bugged him to the point that he was oblivious to the allure of the rest of the property. And so, soon after the final signatures on the deed of sale had been stamped with approval, a suitable blaze was set. The Outriders were in attendance, posted either side of the stone chimney, supplied with asbestos gloves and handheld fire extinguishers and strict instructions, *"...do not resuscitate..."* should the event take a turn for the unenvied - the wailing and screaming and blackening, sort. Tomek was the worse for one and a half bottles of *Rémy Martin* during the first two sorties, which amounted to nothing more than strolls across, first, a pile of glowing embers, and second, a knee-high flame that left the surrounding structure still cold to the touch. With a cigar chomped between his pearly whites, he contemplated his third dash. The lick of the flames was growing more excited. This would give him the chance to judge distance and speed while still being in a manageably-intoxicated state. He paced before the mantle. A pleasing sensation of heat was now spilling from its cavern and he decided no further exploration was required. He checked his watch, there was pressing business at hand. He'd gather his thoughts and make the call to Eeva.

Tomek left the tending of the fire to the Outriders, insisting that they stoke a blaze of such magnificence that it could raze the City of London, "good and proper."

The room Tomek had designated as the study housed two pieces of furniture - a ridiculously large pedestal desk and an accompanying chair. The desk was cleared of the usual clutter apart from a heavy, glass ashtray in which he crushed the cigar, leaving it smoldering like a campfire, and a telephone, black as coal and glossy as starlight, with a cord that was wound tight as a sleeping cobra. The objects rode the surface like a pair of cargo ships on a sea of green and gilded leather. Tomek settled into a wingback chair upholstered in a matching hue and rocked gently with eyes closed and hands clasped across his stomach. On his wrist, an LCD read three minutes to 5:00 p.m.

"Be prompt or be early, Eeva. It is the only way to conduct business. Heed this advice and you will never be uninformed or ill-prepared. Respect time as you would a lover."

A face appeared to him within the sanctuary of his closed eyes - a young boy, sand colored-hair and eyes that were green as emeralds. The boy smiled and beckoned. And then came his voice. It was the first time Tomek had been able to conjure up the sound of his son.

"Papa, come home to us; Papa, why don't you come home?"

Tomek answered, "I'm trying to get to you. Wait for me. Please, wait for me."

The boy mouthed more words, but there was no sound. It was the cruelty of the mind, goading and promising; bringing dreams to life; dangling intrigue and surprise. The face became obscured by clouds, thick and white as dollops of fresh cream, and they drifted over a bridge near Tomek's home, and there were stones missing from the span and the child walked upon it; played upon it, and one by one, the remaining stones were dislodged, and the bridge began to collapse and Tomek shouted himself awake, breathless and angry. He checked his watch. Thirty seconds had passed, time enough to lay a dull knife against the fabric of his soul, tearing another ugly scar into soft flesh that would remain open like a deep, scarlet valley.

At 4:59, he dialed. She answered at the third ring. His tone was somber; he needed the sound of a familiar voice more than ever.

"Eeva, my dear," Tomek said. "I hope you have some good news."

"There's a pub in Earls Court, *The Prince and the Pauper*. Seems to be a watering hole for National Front types; Sunday evenings, in particular."

"What do I need to know?"

"Most of the hardcore reprobates give the place a wide berth."

"Interesting," he said, "...too violent for the scum of the city."

"Look out for a chap called Derek Brinks. He's a new recruit; fancies himself as a musician; steals from charity shops on the side; seems to be looking for validation in all the wrong places."

The sarcasm in Tomek's voice was a bitter pill.

"Oh, good, a scholar and a leader of men."

Eeva said, "Do you want me to come along?"

"No, time is being squandered. Corral the band; get their adrenaline pumping."

Eeva began to speak and then faltered.

"What is it?" Tomek said.

"I worry about the innocents."

"If this place is what you say it is, do you honestly think that there are innocents amongst the trash?"

"No. Oh, I don't know. I met a young woman today; she's bright, and she's lost. I've hired her to look after the finances on the trip."

"She impressed you?"

Tomek let the question hang just long enough, said,

"A reflection of a girl from a different time, perhaps?"

Eeva wrestled with the weight of his words.

"It never occurred to me. But, yes, of course. I used to handle those affairs for my father."

Her eyes misted over, and she crossed the invisible barrier, and she was there, with her father, busy and excited. The smell of the concert halls and the train stations and the restaurants were rich and overpowering. Her father's hand wrapped around hers as they walked together down wide boulevards and ambled along cobbled streets, him drinking strong, black coffee and her eating sweet pastries in the cafés of Paris and Vienna and Berlin and Milan and Barcelona.

"You're a good judge of people. I'm sure she'll be a great help to you," Tomek said.

Another uncomfortable silence ensued.

Tomek felt her presence as if she was in the room.

"You have something you want to say."

Eeva chose her words carefully,

"I want this to be the last…"

Tomek interrupted,

"You want to go home."

"I know I can't."

The air in the study suddenly cooled and Tomek shifted in his chair. From out of nowhere, he felt a hand laid upon his shoulder and he was startled from his seat. He looked around, feeling foolish. He shivered reflexively. Eeva was still speaking,

"It's as though I'm not conscious when I'm with him."

Another sweep of cold air brushed Tomek's neck and he dropped the handset to the table. And then there was pressure, like fingers, tracing the peaks and valleys of his spine. He gripped the back of the chair, willing the sensation from his mind. The first time it had happened he was crazed with fear, convinced the embrace of insanity lurked behind every door. Over the decades, he had adapted, consigning prolonged bouts of flaring nerve and muscle to the over-indulgence of whiskey and pills - those little black beauties driving him to the edge of exhaustion so that he might sleep undisturbed. For the last year, the combatants of his chemical army had laid down their weapons, rising from the trenches to stand tall in surrender on the Western Front of loneliness; failing in their obligation to quiet the demons within. He pulled a vial from his pocket, upending its contents into his open mouth. The liquid trickled down the back of his throat and the dance beneath his flesh settled but did not disappear. This was a new experience for Hans Tomek, and this was unexpected, and it rocked his already erratic world.

Eeva's voice was small and scratchy through the earpiece. He picked up the handset and spoke through snatched breaths.

"When did you feel this?" he said. "When was the first time?"

"This morning," Eeva said. "I found a toy airplane, it was broken. I remembered the shape so well from skies above Vienna. I don't know how to describe it… there was electricity when I touched it."

Tomek used his free hand and rubbed his face, the scent of cigars and alcohol was strong on his palm. He thought of his son playing on the failing bridge and his voice registered his impatience.

"*Electricity?* What the hell does that even mean?"

Eeva recoiled from the challenge.

"I don't know… it was… it just happened…"

In the study, Tomek channeled his frustration away from Eeva, directed it at the pub bombing; a distraction to his work and in turn, his objective. Nothing else mattered. Calmer now, he said,

"I'm sorry. I know what you're feeling. The strength of recalling such events can seem like you are being suffocated, or shaken, or cut deep. It's different every time. You would do well to remember the shock and the pain when you think about stepping away from our world. Those who leave can pay a staggering price. You'll be vulnerable in ways that might harm you beyond your wildest dreams."

"I told you I wanted this to be the last one."

Eeva felt the wavering tones of pleading begin to surface and she backed off.

"Beecher Stowe is the best we have ever found," she said. "In this one, I believe."

"That may be years away."

"And it might not."

Tomek's pulse was steady and he breathed easier. Composed, with an even tone, he said,

"If Beecher Stowe is not who you think he is, will you stay with me until the end of our time?"

The street outside Eeva's residence flickered with the promise of sunlight as a final troupe of patchy clouds drifted across the capital city like mischievous children tugging shadows in their wake. She waited patiently until the band of sunlight filled her room, counting the seconds that it remained, tilting her head so that golden blanket caressed her creamy skin. Without hesitation, under the glare of the celestial spotlight, she agreed.

"You really *do* believe," Tomek said, feeling suddenly isolated. "I wish I was you."

In the great hall, the lick of orange flames topped out far into the black void of the chimney. The Outriders gathered about the fireplace, cajoling each other playfully with gentle laughter as sudden barks from damp wood sent hailstorms of embers to rebound off bared faces and arms. In all of the decades that fate had conspired to keep Tomek walking the earth in a time that was not his own, there had never been a day when he did not yearn for his former life. Until he discovered the six.

It had been after a day of tireless wandering, at the onset of dusk, that Hans Tomek was drawn to the grassy ridge of a steep hill to rest and bask in the muted majesty of a Spanish sunset. These were precious moments. Only when the day was at its ebb did he allow his memories to roam free, replaying them over and over again, always holding short of peering into an abyss that beckoned with the curled finger of depression and despair. As he approached the apex of the rise, the orange sky became obliterated with boiling clouds of thick, black smoke that swelled to the upper reaches of the atmosphere as if spat directly from the funnels of hell. The siege of San Sebastián had begun.

For seven days the city burned. Tomek watched the campaign of devastation consume houses and businesses, and he pressed his hands tight over his ears as the screams rose above the rooftops, and he tore strips of linen from his clothing to wrap his nose and mouth as the acrid stench of seared flesh coated his throat. Thousands of British and Portuguese troops ransacked and raped and engorged their bellies with wine and brandy, enacting a violent and riotous rampage as retribution for the loss of fallen comrades. In the lull of the battle, under cover of darkness; when the troops had collapsed upon each other with exhaustion and inebriation, Tomek descended into the town, trying to make sense of the chaos, coaxing the abused and the frightened from rat-infested cellars, loading his shoulders with the injured and the young and leading jittery processions to the relative sanctuary of the surrounding hills. Before the sun again reached its zenith; while a veil of deep shadow masked any number of discrete vantage points that afforded sweeping views of the city and the port entrance and the channel leading to the Bay of Biscay, Tomek would spend hours belly-crawling through tall grass and crouching amongst Juniper groves observing the movements of soldiers and supplies, mapping out routes amongst the buildings that had been overlooked or bypassed by the roving mobs, and later, with great stealth, pick his way through the rubble and carnage scavenging for water and food.

As dawn broke on the final morning of the siege, Tomek came across a stacked-stone barn with a thatched roof that smoldered like a scorned birthday cake. The main doors hung from frayed leather hinges and were canted and warped severely from weather and fire so as to prevent their opening. He was about to push on into the city when he noticed a grouping of deeply contoured footprints, an anomaly in the otherwise smooth and slimy red clay. The tracks led to the rear of the structure and in the murky, morning light, he followed the chaotic trail, clambering over hunks of chiseled granite that spilled from a break in the wall. He squeezed inside.

What he found would inform the rest of his life with the authority of a bible.

In a storeroom adjacent to the stables, by the light of a single candle, ghostly shadows danced to the soundtrack of drafts whistling through creaking timbers. Tomek's mind seized upon the imagined threats of multi-headed sea-monsters rising from a wild ocean. He stumbled against a pile of rusty, linked chain and the light was immediately extinguished, followed by a barely audible, "...*sssh.*" Tomek sank to his knees with adrenaline surging. He waited, with breath held and eyes fixed. The minutes ticked by and a profound silence pressed at his temples and he began to question his instinct and his sanity. His eyes adjusted to the gloom and curious, dark shapes came into soft focus, materializing as discarded hand tools and tangled bridles draped over wooden stalls and pitchforks resting against stacks of bundled straw.

A whisper floated from the stillness, confident and brave, and it was returned in short order. Tomek followed the path of the sound and made out a ragged, tangled shock of hair framing a filthy, cherubic face peering out from behind the storeroom door. The head was turned in profile and blooms of weak light piercing cracks in the stone wall illuminated darting eyes that glistened like raindrops on polished stone. It was a young girl, and she was joined by a boy, likely of the same age. They stared into the dim surround and saw and heard nothing. Bravado grew, as did the volume of their nervous chatter. Four more bodies were presented in various stages of crawling on all fours and scooting on bended knees from practiced hiding places and one began pantomiming the others' fears, encouraging contagious giggles as a welcome relief. At the height of their confidence, Tomek stood up, slowly, and with a gentle, unthreatening tone implored the children not to be frightened. Nevertheless, they scattered, going to ground, falling behind any object large enough to hide their frail bodies. A long moment passed, and again Tomek assured them of his intent.

"Little ones," he said, "I will not hurt you, I am helping others into the hills, away from the soldiers."

As orphans, the children knew the horror of isolation and cruelty and they knew loss and sadness. They also recognized the voice of betrayal. This man seemed different.

The girl emerged first, brushing at her soiled skirt and smoothing her hair. She must have been no more than eight-years-old, Tomek thought. Serving up a righteous stare, she said,

"We survive without help."

"Then maybe you can help me," Tomek said. "I am looking for scraps of food for the old people that rest upon the hillside watching their houses burn."

This statement made no dent in the armor of the orphan. She issued a response that was well beyond her years.

"Maybe they should have opened their homes to the unfortunate instead of locking them away for no other reason than having been abandoned in this filthy city."

The child wore a metal tag on her wrist secured with a coarse, twisted wire that gouged a weeping, crimson line into her milky-white flesh. Tomek gestured and said he could remove it if she let him. Her face registered a firm frown of denial, but her eyes softened, and she relented, hitching her skirt up between her legs and taking a seat on an upended water barrel, holding out her wrist in a determined challenge.

"Go on then, if you can."

Tomek set about scouring the barn for tools and returned with a metal chisel and a blacksmith's hammer. He wrestled slates of granite from the wall and fashioned a crude workbench, arranging the girl's arm with the delicate skin of her wrist raised vertically. She sat, with eyes darting around to the hiding places of her tribe. Tomek fed strips of cloth between the wire and her skin and set the chisel firmly in place. He raised the hammer to his shoulder, said,

"Don't move, *niña valiente.*"

Before she could react to his voice, the hammer came down with a single, resounding strike that sent sparks spitting like red rain across the dirt floor. The wire shackle fell into her lap and she grabbed at her wrist certain that it was going to come away in her hand. Tomek picked up the rusty tag and wiped at the crude inscription with his thumb. He read aloud...

"*Propiedad del orfanato de San Sebastián.*"

He looked at the girl for a long moment, savoring her fragile acceptance of freedom. He tossed the tag over his shoulder, said,

"*Ya no mas.*"

The remaining five children popped up into view as if by magic, eagerly offering up their shackles for removal, each receiving an avowal of bravery prior to Tomek's almighty strike.

"*...un valiente joven león!*"

"*...un valiente águila volando!*"

"*...un zorro valiente y astuto!*"

"*...un valiente toro elefante!*"

"*...un valiente y hermoso cisne!*"

The bond between Tomek and the castaways was instantaneous. In the ever-brightening interior of the barn, the children clambered over each other, physically and verbally, speaking defiantly of abusive treatment and isolation and abandonment. They sat in a circle, some with hands fidgeting, their nervousness apparent by the sweep of their eyes and the tight contours of their mouths. For others, the moment brought an opportunity to advertise individual personalities so cruelly quashed by the governors of the orphanage. Tomek was about to take his leave when the girl he had first encountered stood up and broadcast for the benefit of the group.

"We would like to accompany you away from this city."

Her statement was echoed by nodding heads. Three boys and three girls, bound by circumstance tighter than the skin of a drum.

Tomek studied a line of expectant faces.

"We are barely acquainted," he said, testing her assurance. "We are on different paths, little one. I do not need a band of followers to feed."

"Well, then it is our choice to walk alongside," she said, checking for her comrades' approval. "And when you are hungry, we will invite you to share our food. If you feel you cannot cope, we will understand."

Her challenge made Tomek burst out with laughter - the first time, he realized, in all these long years. He brushed the girl's tangled locks with his hand, said,

"*Mi pequeña rosa,* I believe with all my heart that I will not be able to cope, but when that time comes, I am certain you will guide me through."

The children stood before him, ready and eager, and before he knew what he was doing, Tomek said,

"We will go south, across the sea to Africa, and we will travel with the Bedouin tribes and we will undertake studies in many languages and cultures, and when you return to these shores, I guarantee you will never be looked down upon again."

Their education began immediately. As they awaited the coming dusk, Tomek used sticks of charred wood and drew maps upon stretched sackcloth. He outlined the continent and the countries, sharing knowledge far in advance of their understanding, and he spoke to them in terms that were relevant to their age, filling their eyes with the wonders of exotic lands and strange animals and great mountain ranges that blocked out the sun. At the failing of daylight, he gathered the troupe under his wing and together they roamed the city, scavenging from abandoned stores, finding shelves of stale bread and ruptured barrels of cured olives that spilled their contents like sandy pebbles dotting the earthen floors. And occasionally, whispered cheers pierced the haunting silence as several hunks of *queso de tronchón,* the aromatic cheese made from sheep's and goat's milk, were found wrapped and aging in dark and damp cupboards.

As they shuttled through the winding streets, red-coated raiding parties flanked them with aggressive shouts and reckless musket fire, but the children, with Tomek close at their heels, outpaced the soldiers, losing them easily in the tangled alleys, often bisecting endless drunken celebrations without provoking a second glance.

At the edge of the city, as they were pushing into the grasslands beneath a ridge of sandhills, the children stalled in their progress. An ominous-looking structure with weathered walls and gates projecting combs of sharp spikes stood proud against the purple blanket of dawn. It appeared from behind a screen of tumbling smoke seemingly at the will of gusting onshore winds and the children slowed and passed with heads bowed. A plaque carved from a slab of marble was set within wood slats and read:

Orfanato de San Sebastián.

The orphanage, even in its dilapidated state, drained the levity of their newfound freewill and wagging tongues and infectious giggles settled into stillness. Tomek sought to usher them onward, moving quickly into the hills before the rising sun announced their position, but he considered the abhorrent conditions and sadistic treatment these tender youths had experienced and decided this place had to be exorcised from their conscience by their own hands.

"Gather round," he said. "When a wound is exposed to the elements, we must cauterize it so that it might begin to heal."

The brave girl peered up with confusion in her eyes and the others drew tightly by her side. She had risked so much in steering her mates far away from this place and now she was unsure of this man's intent. Her mouth was dry and the command to scatter; to run for their lives, caught in her throat when Tomek said,

"Let us burn this place to the ground."

From the troupe's vantage point almost three miles distant, lounging upon cool, arctic-white sand, shrouded by tall wavering grasses, the flames from the burning orphanage licked the new day devoid of sound or smell. Tomek sat apart from the family of runaways. This was their moment of atonement and healing. In time, the brave girl broke from the pack and came to him.

"This was a good thing," she said, demurely. "Thank you."

Tomek studied her. Away from the oppression of the city, he noticed how frail she looked; how broken her spirit was, and he longed to repair the damage.

"If you had one wish," he said, "...what would it be?"

The ponderous moment was like sweets before supper. Her eyes widened so that the tiny, dark pupils were lost in an ivory sea, and when the words came, they fell from her lips barely above a whisper.

"I want to ride a horse," she said. "I want to ride a horse faster than the wind. And I never want to stop."

'So be it," Tomek said. "You shall ride for as long as you are able."

Across the decades, the unlikely band would become inseparable companions. Tomek would raise the children to be strong and proud and educated and within his presence, they would not age beyond the crest of their maturity. In time, and without prejudice, the young minds accepted Tomek's quest as their own and in turn, languished as he did, in a state of reluctant and isolated tranquility, with no disease to repel and no regrets to harbor, and with an agreed mission to dispel ignorance whenever and wherever the opportunity was afforded. And Tomek made good on his word - he taught the brave girl to ride; he taught the entire adopted clan to ride. Across grasslands and deserts, they rode as one entity, moving and thriving amongst indigenous tribes and cultures, sharing and absorbing. And in this harshest of environments, the children found purpose aiding Tomek, embracing their roles as seekers and protectors, clearing his path and safeguarding his possessions. For he was their mentor, and he was their answer, and the bond they shared was one of unbreakable loyalty, and it was a sacred and permanent way of life. It was, in time, a family.

Hans Tomek returned to the great hall with a narrow-eyed stare and a cold-blooded smirk. He poured, raised and gulped a glass of Cognac, removed his black, cashmere sweater, threw a "...*no more bets, please*" smile to the Outriders, sprinted across twenty meters of rough stone tile and launched himself headfirst into a wall of flames.

Chapter Twenty

Beecher paced the perimeter of the luggage carousel at New York's John F. Kennedy airport. He counted... again...for the tenth time.

"There should be six suitcases," he said. "I only count five. Whose is missing?"

No answers, just tired yawns and bloodshot eyes and hangover headaches. First Class meant free drinks, and so they drank. Everything. Miniature bottles of scotch, vodka, and gin; half carafes of wine, red and white; teeny-tiny cans of Coca-Cola, 7-Up, and ginger ale; coffee, tea, warm apple cider and a solitary glass of milk for Fez, who believed wholeheartedly, *"it'll line my stomach, nicely."*

Beecher probed further, "Harry?"

"Nope," Harry responded confidently, although he was completely distracted by a parade of stewardesses clad in pencil skirts that teased the tops of dark stockings, and candy-striped blouses that teased lacy bra straps, and the women had flawless skin and cartoon-red lipstick, and they sported jaunty hats pinned at exact angles to tight buns of lacquered hair, and when they gossiped and laughed, their teeth were perfectly white.

"Go on," Fez said, "...don't just stare, invite them to the gig."

"I don't know where it is, or when it is."

"Tell 'em 'bout the TV show then; tell 'em 'bout the song on the radio."

The stress was too much; the target too rich. Harry sighed and gave Fez a, *"never mind, there'll be others,"* shrug.

"Unbelievable," Fez said. "Un-fuckin'-believ..."

"Do you have your suitcase, Fez?"

Beecher was ratcheting up his concern, inch by inch. The cases were shiny, new *Samsonites,* delivered to the pub only minutes before the coach driver's pulse raced well into the three-digit danger zone of total exasperation as he contemplated further delays. Each case carried a leather fob with a personalized name tag stenciled in gold, a gift from Eeva to the band, which meant that transferring everyone's belongings from oddities of *hand-me-down, fortnight-in-Benidorm, Paella-stained,* holdalls, was an absolute necessity.

Beecher shouted, "Fez!"

"Yes, I have it right 'ere, boss," Fez said. "…haven't let it out of my sight since I took it off that twirling, slide-thing."

"Beech, I'm certain there was only ever five," Pengo said. "…one for each of us. Are you sure you're not counting the guitar case twice?"

"Maybe," Beecher said. "I must be losing my mind."

Settling on five cases meant everyone had a bag of clothes, and with the instruments accounted for: one road-worn Fender in a brand new case, lined with purple velvet no less; Snooze's trumpet, with its dented horn sticking from a battered, leather satchel like an antique vase, and, well… Fez's drum sticks - both of them - Beecher relaxed and took in the surroundings. He was envious of the crowd. People carried themselves with such certainty, he thought; they all seemed to know exactly where they were going. He noticed that Fez had wrapped each of his sticks with flesh-colored masking tape displaying a hasty *Magic Marker* scrawl,

Property of Fez Bramble. c/o The Railway Tavern, White City, London.

The telephone number of the lounge-bar payphone had been added, and subsequently scratched out, due to it now residing in the Shepherd's Bush rubbish tip having been summarily blown to smithereens. All in all, it was hardly the monster backline and laser-lighted stage rigging Beecher had envisioned in those private moments of ebullient ego-stroking. Snooze, as usual, stepped up and Beecher felt the familiar squeeze of his shoulder.

"From the pub cellar to a TV studio, to the fuckin' U.S.A.," Snooze said. "…*and* you survived having your ass blown off for good measure. Ride 'em hard and put 'em away wet, Beecher, my old son, we are off and running."

Snooze's wisdom often left those in earshot feeling like dogs doing math.

"Alright lads, listen up," Beecher said. "When we get outside, we're looking for some black limos. The plan is, they'll take us into Manhattan, straight to the hotel, and while you guys settle in, me and Snooze will scoot along and do the first radio interview."

"When are you getting back?" Harry said.

"Dunno. I'm hoping they'll have someone sorting that stuff out."

"Can we go out and have a look around?" Fez said.

"Just don't get lost," Pengo said, "...this ain't no bleedin' holiday."

The lads gathered up their belongings and stepped into the flow of humanity sauntering along the concourse. Here, they were swallowed whole; sucked into the universal melting pot. It was the habitat of the tall and the short and the wide, and the timid and the brave and the bold. Some were covered by turbans and keffiyeh and yarmulke, some strutted in suits, some in uniform. Without exception, all had their eyes wide open.

The London boys were a band of misfits, three-thousand miles from home, with absolutely nothing in common. Beecher clutched to Snooze's words like he was water skiing behind a 747: *"Never pet the tiger, Beech. When the lights go down, and the voices go quiet, and the angels come out to play, you could be standing under a blue moon, or a sailor's sky, or the bruised thunderheads of a raging winter storm - or, as it happens, a sixty-watt bulb in Pengo's cellar, - either way, it won't matter a jot, by our unified hand, you will be released."*

Pengo cradled a bundle of detective novels. Paperbacks. No-name authors writing no-plot pulp. But they were easy reads, and they had dames and goons and mobsters and roadhouses with blinking signs and endless midnight drives across cooling deserts.

"Twenty-five cents each," he said with such pride, you'd have thought he'd just made off with the crown jewels.

Snooze grabbed one off the pile. The blurb on the book's jacket spoke excitedly of, *"a faceless executioner - a mistress of disguise and the empress of pain."*

"Didn't know you were a reader, Pengo."

"I'm selective," he said. "...got a soft spot for a bit of whodunnit."

"Looks like you'll have your hands full with this lot."

Pengo took the book and tucked it safely back into the stack.

"Gotta be careful not to bend the pages too much. I'll make a killing down the market with these when we get home."

"Shrewd."

Beecher led his entourage through a set of automatic sliding doors, stepping from the icy, relatively composed confines of the terminal, with its looped musak and magazine racks and vending machines dispensing everything from candy bars and coffee to shoe polish and nail clippers, straight into a wall of heat and a barrage of sound. It felt like the world was pissed off - at everything. Cars puked dense clouds of exhaust fumes and belligerent cops blew shrill whistles and pushed fat fingers into fatter chests, and drivers leaned impatiently on brassy, tuneless horns, and all around, the air was shredded by the unyielding roar of jet engines as plane after plane sought the infinite calm of a crystal-clear Atlantic sky.

A couple of porters grabbing a smoke chuckled as the band members wiped at beading foreheads and peeled off layers of clothing.

One of them shouted across, "August in New York, it's like swimming with your clothes on."

"Is it always like this?" Fez was down to his T-shirt, wondering if he should go full Tarzan.

"Hell, no," the porter said, "…sometimes it gets hot, too."

"Limos," Harry cried, as if was spotting icebergs. "Three of 'em."

"That could be for us," Beecher said, craning his neck. "I don't see any others."

"Eh? Fat wood whore bus? What?" Harry shook his head and cupped his ear. It was like being in the stands at a QPR home game. The public address speakers spit an endless stream of departure and arrival information in accents only ever encountered through the magic of recorded sound. Hearing it up close left them all feeling a little dazed.

"I said, I don't see…"

And then she was there. Carving her way through the loiterers and the daydreamers and the panhandlers. Baggage carts stacked head high careened into each other as heads turned and bodies followed. Except for exposing a palm's width of tanned flesh around her midriff, she was resplendent in a white halter neck dress and knee-high boots.

Luna trailed a few steps behind. Wide-eyed and nervous. Gone was the King's Road ragamuffin; gone was the mistrust and the trepidation. The bleached locks were now cropped to shoulder length and tinted to a natural honey-blonde, hidden mostly by a simple red beret. She wore a leather jacket over a white shirt, cutting the air with just enough rebellion to suit her role as keeper of the cash.

"That's pretty rock 'n roll," Snooze said.

Beecher nodded and said,

"Yes, …it, …is."

He watched Eeva greet each member with an outstretched hand and a smile that would light up a runway at midnight.

"Welcome; Hello; How was your flight?"

Luna was introduced and received shuffles of nervous enthusiasm from the younger lads, while Pengo was the perfect gentleman, relishing in the opportunity to mock the boys' behavior.

Beecher was about to make another wry comment until he realized
Snooze had slinked away to gain a personal audience, regaling the
newcomers immediately with a tale of getting stuck in customs and
having to play his trumpet to prove it wasn't filled with drugs.

"I tried to tell them the good drugs were already here; that this place
was the envy of every stoner in Britain, and that only a moron would try
and smuggle in some shitty weed. Then I told the copper that it'd be like
him tellin' us how to make a good cup of tea. Didn't go down too well, so
I knocked out a rendition of the *Star-Spangled Banner*."

Eeva said, "You are quite the prodigy, Mr. Silver."

"It was either that or a blast of the Lone Ranger."

"Hi, Ho, Silver!" Fez shouted.

"Cheeky little bollocks."

Snooze's rebuke was lost in the take-off roll of an Eastern Airlines 727.
The group instinctively followed the plane's ascent as it rose above the
scalloped dome of the terminal, turning their attention back to the Queen
in their midst once they could be heard. All but one, that is. Harry's eyes
remained locked at the end of the platform. Two men stood in the bright
sunlight, binoculars raised, tracing the descent of another airliner and
nudging each other as if they'd spotted a rare bird. Harry wandered over,
stood behind the pair listening to their banter.

"*3:00 p.m. On the nose. Never late. It'll be unloaded and the cargo will be
put to bed within the hour.*"

"*You'll get the call?*"

"*Yeah, but later, when he gets off work…*"

"It's a wonder those things get off the ground, isn't it?"

Harry's voice was chipper, and the two men were startled and turned,
eyes glaring, immediately suspicious.

"Whaddya mean? Who the fuck asked you?"

"I just meant; they're so big. That one's German. Lufthansa. You can tell
it by the yellow dot on the tail."

He raised one hand, gave a pathetic wave.

"I'm Harry, from London."

The smaller of the two sported an orange vest under a cream suit
jacket. His neck was laced in gold chains and his mop was thick and
greying, hanging three inches past his collar and greased flat with what
had to be forty-weight oil. He set the binoculars in a sports bag at his feet,
said,

"Harry from London, *you's* need to mind your own fucking business.
This ain't Kansas."

Harry took a beat. So did the second guy who eventually said,
"Tommy, he's just being nice. So be nice."

And then to Harry…

"We like the planes," he said, and then with a laugh, "Makes a change from looking at cars."

"I guess," Harry said. "Your cars are as big as our planes."

Tommy was getting antsy.

"What the fuck is this kid talking about?"

"He's a tourist, ain't ya kid?"

"Nope, I'm here to play."

Guy #2 was a heavy-set black man with tired eyes.

"You a soccer player?"

"No, music. Piano. I'm in a band."

"No, kidding? Me, too. I sing blues, sometimes a little R&B."

Tommy was fit to be tied. Guy #2 shouldered in front.

"So, where you playin'?"

"Dunno, exactly. Somewhere in Manhattan, and then on the telly."

"Getting' around, huh?"

"Touring, mate. Keep your ears pinned to the radio. Listen out for *Supermassive Superstar*. It's killer."

Tommy didn't like the way Harry emphasized the word, *killer*.

"Were you listening to us?"

Harry finally clocked Tommy's stare. The stewardess's comment, *"You'll love New York, everyone's so friendly,"* obviously didn't include this bloke.

"Nah, mate, can't hear a bloody thing out here."

Tommy appeared pacified for the moment.

Guy #2 pointed at the sweating congregation surrounded by a low wall of matching suitcases, said, "Is that your band?"

"Yeah, everyone's pretty shagged. I think we're heading off soon." And then with chest-swelling pride, "We've got limos."

"Guy #2 picked out Eeva.

"She the singer?"

"Nah, she's…" he stalled, not really knowing what to call her. "She's our manager."

"Pity," Guy #2 said, "I'd buy her album just to look at the cover."

Tommy lit a smoke and coughed and spat.

"We done?" he said, more of a command than a request.

Guy #2 nodded, "Take it easy, kid. Good luck with everything." And then as an afterthought, "If you get a chance, check out Umberto's Clam

House in Little Italy. They've got a house band. I sit in sometimes. Food is great. Tell 'em Stacks sent ya. They'll take care of you and your friends."

"Are you Stacks?"

"Yeah, man."

"Cool," Harry said.

Stacks nodded his head, "Yeah, cool."

Harry left Parnell 'Stacks' Edwards and Tommy DeSimone to resume their overwatch. The pair would return to this very spot over the coming months, planning and plotting until, on December 11th, 1978, as part of a six-man crew, they would participate in the largest cash robbery on American soil when the Lufthansa cargo terminal at JFK was robbed of five million dollars of imported currency.

For Stacks, this would have been a sizable payday. He courted a robust heroin addiction that was hard to placate with a few random carjackings and some credit card fraud. Unfortunately, his assignment to ditch the getaway van was botched when he smoked a little celebratory weed and parked it in front of a fire hydrant in front of his girlfriend's apartment. The cops found it and Stacks went into hiding. But not from Tommy. When you have an addict as part of your crew, secrets are hard to keep. Seven days after the heist, Tommy DeSimone found Stacks and shot him in the head six times.

Three limos merged onto the Van Wyck Expressway. Eeva and Beecher rode in the first car, Luna and the luggage was stuffed into the second, and bringing up the rear, the remainder of the band lounged in regal comfort. The air conditioning was blowing arctic cold behind the glass partition and the vent in the center console blasted with such force that Snooze's long, blonde locks were upswept, swishing and swatting Fez and Harry about their faces as they sat on either side.

Having achieved the less than skin-peeling momentum of walking speed due to heavy traffic, the procession finally turned off the highway and inched along the twelve-lane expanse of Queens Blvd. with its litany of brick-built apartment blocks and concrete playgrounds, and neon-lit diners pushing fifty cent steaks, and tire shops with towering signs - usually of some prom queen in a pink tutu astride a stack of steel-belted radials, smiling with such fierce desperation, like she'd taken it so far up the ass her teeth were being forced out from their roots - and theaters with marquees featuring trios of single-syllable blockbusters, such as *Grease* and *Convoy* and *Coma*.

"We should definitely go to the movies while we're here," Fez said. "I hear they sell buckets of popcorn."

Pengo was irked.

"Why would you want a bucket?"

"I dunno, just sounds cool."

"But it's a bucket, who the fuck wants a bucket of anything?"

"Leave it out, Pengo," Snooze said, "He's just riffing," and then with a wink, "...thinking of ways to impress the girl."

Pengo turned his gaze outward again, mumbled,

"Sounds absurd."

The lads behaved like excited schoolchildren on a day trip. This was a fairground ride and it was pulsing and intimidating, rising from the spongy, heat-soaked tarmac with sights and sounds to match. On the radio, *"WPLJ, 95.5 FM, New York's best rock..."* belted Joe Walsh's, *Life's Been Good*, and every ten blocks or so, the brooding and mysterious Manhattan skyline was teased, carving a series of angular dark wedges from the blue horizon, eliciting a chorus of oohs and aahs and an occasional, *fuckin' 'ell*.

Pengo tired of the sights, he leaned back in the seat, decided to play Dad.

"You can't just roll up and start talking to strangers, Harry. You're liable to get your head kicked in."

"I don't believe that for a minute," Harry said.

"Tell 'im, Fez. He'll listen to you."

Fez was busy spitting a tangle of Snooze's hair from his mouth, said, "He's a big boy."

"You can't come this far and ignore everyone," Harry said. "I wanna go back to London with a few memories. Anyway, one bloke told me about a great place for us to eat in Italy."

"Little Italy," Snooze said.

"Yeah, whatever. He said they have live music. He sings the blues."

Harry switched his attention to the cavernous jungle of steel and concrete that was the 59th street bridge.

"Good blokes," Harry said.

"Fellas," Snooze added. "This is New York, they're fellas."

"Yeah, Good fellas," Harry said.

Beecher had never romanticized the new world; he'd never craved crossing an open prairie or basking in the purple mountains' majesty; he'd never imagined his face on the silver screen or even on a box of cereal. In fact, he'd never wished to be something out of the ordinary to anyone, let alone a nation of strangers. Making art was so different from being art, and he felt a sense of inevitable dread creep along his spine. He wanted to stop the car and get out and run. No direction; no destination, just run to exhaustion. He breathed in, deep, and the aroma of Eeva's perfume filled his head and his thoughts and dreams and desires collided like meteors.

One hundred and thirty feet below, the East River showed no current, just a brown glaze, as though a highway of mud ringed the entire city.

Beecher recalled Hans Tomek's ominous address as they stood at the departure gate:

"Travel the world as much as you like; see the seven wonders, take high tea at the Raffles hotel, ski the Matterhorn, race an open-wheeler around the Brickyard, or dive the Great Barrier Reef, but nothing prepares a soul for the overwhelming feeling of inadequacy pressed upon it during their first sortie into the canyons of Manhattan. It's not a long-lasting effect, but it's enough to change a mind forever. No matter the scope or depth of your prejudices on the way in, they'll be uniquely warped by the time you leave. That is, if you've experienced it right; if you haven't just nibbled around the edges. You'll think differently of money and power and hopelessness and anger and humor and food and ironically, peace and tranquility."

The lead limo flashed its blinker and hooked a left coming off the bridge at 2nd Ave and carved its way into midtown and the glass of the city caught the late afternoon sun and flashed through angled girders like frames of celluloid running through a projector. One structure stood apart, stately and stoic against the surrounding cascade of featureless walls and flat roofs. Beecher locked onto the Empire State Building and all at once, the structure validated his journey and shredded his nerves.

It wasn't supposed to be like this.

Next to him, Eeva checked her watch for the tenth time in as many minutes.

"Are we late?" Beecher asked as another tender nerve twanged.

She shook her head, leaned forward and twirled the radio dial. Alien voices tumbled over each other in waves of static. Her hand settled on one station and she frowned, listening impatiently to a child's voice spout a ringing endorsement for some washing powder. The station identifier blurted from the speakers with a suitably brash rock undertone and before it was finished, she inched the dial to the left. Another commercial, this time, *Folgers* coffee,

"Gee, honey, your coffee sure tastes great."

"Hallelujah, it's a special blend and it's mountain-grown for the best taste."

For a fleeting moment, Beecher was lured by the ad man's snake-charming patter, wondering if it really did taste great. The car slowed for a red light and came to a stop. A sliver of sunlight cut through the buildings and burned the sidewalk, highlighting a man pissing against a wall. A woman stood close by, yapping into a payphone with three pint-sized dogs in hand, all straining at their leashes, losing their minds in a caterwaul of barks and yelps. The woman was oblivious of the stream of urine pooling at her feet. Was it his, or theirs, Beecher wondered? Or hers? This was New York City, after all. The car set off again. Another jingle aired, followed by a rich baritone announcing the time and temperature. The billboard jungle at Time's Square loomed, filling every window with its shallow indifference for artistic restraint. Eeva sat back in her seat, said nothing, waited for Beecher's eyes to complete their scan.

The avenue bled puddles of oil and grime, and sodden trash papered the sidewalk, and two-dollar sex shows lined the intersection, and all the while, sirens echoed with the wails of birds of prey.

"I didn't believe it was real," Beecher said.

"Real?"

"Well, yeah, …I mean, I knew it was a place. I just never expected it to be so, obvious."

"Too much?"

"A part of me says, yeah. Another part says I want in. It looks so raw."

"I think that's a healthy reaction to seeing it for the first time."

The limo slowed and two black women in short skirts and high heels scuttled from a doorway. They kept pace with the vehicle, tapping on the darkened windows with chipped and chewed fingernails, and their lips were painted green and gold with glittering eyeliner to match, and they worked the sale, hard; fearfully. Pleading for something; anything.

"Forty dollars will get you five of their best minutes," Eeva said. "Or, rather, it used to. It's probably gone up."

"When were you last here?"

"It's been a few years. Tomek lived here for a while when this part of town was habitable. I was young…" Eeva paused, took a beat, and then said, "…it was different, always crowded and always rowdy, especially when sailors were on leave, but it never felt hostile."

She took an extended gaze out of the window, said,

"I wouldn't care to stroll around here after dark nowadays."

Twenty yards ahead and fifty feet up, the *Coca-Cola* sign blinked to life, dominating the limo's windscreen like a giant, satanic mural; painting all within its reach with the pallor of anger and fear. All eyes were immediately upturned, drawn to the primal intensity of heat and light.

Hanging directly above, a canvas tarp fluttered, obscuring the face of a newly erected billboard. A brace of workers dangled from ropes either side, passing the time, smoking and chatting as they awaited further instructions.

A minute later, the drab covering fell, revealing the face of Beecher Stowe, three stories high, emblazoned with the title of his song.

In the rear limo, with heads shoved through the retractable sunroof, taking snapshots of the endless parade of hookers and junkies and peep shows and sleazy bars, Fez and Harry clocked it first. A lit cigarette fell from Fez's mouth, spiraling down into the cabin, singeing the hairs on Pengo's arm.

"Fucking 'ell, Fez, what the fuck are you playin' at?"

Fez said nothing, dropped his hand below the roofline and pointed forward. Snooze followed the directive, adding insult to injury as he slapped Pengo directly on his charred flesh.

"Ah, Jesus fuckin' Christ, Snooze, what the fuck..?"

"Look," Snooze said. "Look. Up there."

Pengo continued rubbing his arm as he shuffled and twisted in his seat. "What? What?" And then, "Oh, fuuuck…"

There was a moment of reverence as the band paid homage. There he was; their mate, born within shouting distance of the Westway, singer of songs in rowdy pubs and working men's clubs, server of brews and shorts; a scrapper, a strummer, and a biker, with his thirty-foot high, cheeky-as-fuck mug now hanging God-like on a hotel wall in New York City.

"How do you think he's takin' it?" Harry said.

"Wonder, amazement, a few questions, and then a long, hard wank."

"All class you are, Fez Bramble," Snooze said. "All fuckin' class."

"You don't see that too many times in your life."

Beecher sat on his hands, trying to stifle their shaking.

"Hans thought it would be a good way to generate a buzz," Eeva said. "We blew up one of the promo shots. I think it looks magnificent."

'It's gonna be hard to live up to."

"Nonsense, business is business, and this is show business. Everything is just that little bit bigger."

"Imagine getting used to that; to seeing yourself like that."

"Some folks can't handle it. But that's not you. You'll see."

Scrawled beneath the poster, the words:

He set London on fire; now he's heading to New York.
Make a date tonight with,
Beecher Stowe
The Down Beat, New York

Sponsored by Aeon Records

"Tonight? I mean today, tonight? Are we playing tonight?"

"We thought you could knock out a quick set. Just a song, maybe two. You'll have time to get some rest. Tomek's invited some journalists. The venue is a small, grubby place. Lots of character. As far as new music in New York goes, it's the place where it all happens."

Eeva sold the event like she was shifting a used car. All that was missing was a bow tie and a quart of *Brut* cologne.

"I better tell the lads that they're gonna be performing."

"Plenty of time for that. We'll be at the hotel soon. You can get checked in and sort it all out then. Just take a minute, look up there. Isn't that what you've been dreaming about for all these years?"

Words failed him. Before today, he believed the expression, *'my mind went blank,'* to be an alien concept. A blank mind was a dead mind. Surely, this was a concern that did not apply to him. And yet, try as he might, he couldn't so much as dribble out a single profitable thought from a brain that only moments before could have recited the entire back catalog of Beatles lyrics, in order of release. He craved a snappy comeback or a juvenile slight, or indeed for a wave of elation to consume his body, or for the red mist of irrational anger to descend so he could lose his shit and launch into some sort of nonsensical tirade. But none came.

"Maybe this is death; maybe this is what we do when we die, we finally see ourselves for who we really are, and then shut off every tactile connection to the world and peer out of empty, soulless skulls."

As if the heavens were attuned to his turmoil, the opening bars of his song swelled from the limo's speakers with all the subtlety of a television preacher clutching a tax bill. Tomek had bought time on practically every station in New York to advertise the song and the artist and the gig and Beecher fell to the snake charm of the Ad-man once more, this time the slithering viper sank its teeth to the bone.

Fez led the lads at a run. He banged on the lead limo's window, shouting,

"C'mon, Beecher, we gotta get a group photo. You, me, Harry, Snooze, and Pengo first, and then one with the ladies."

They mugged for the camera with Luna handling the majority of the photographic duties. She shot them in pairs, as a band, as an entourage, the works. Exhausted with laughter and making their way back to the cars, Luna pulled them up sharply.

"Hang on. Beecher, Eeva. I forgot to get just the two of you, together."

And so, they posed, side-by-side.

"Closer," Luna shouted, down on her knees, clicking away madly with Fez's scratched and dented Nikon.

The sun fell upon their faces in thick, orange bars as it streamed through the great stone avenues.

"C'mon. you can do better than that," Luna's call came again. "I've only got a few frames left."

Beecher put his hand around Eeva's waist and pulled her close. He shook like a schoolboy on a first date. She responded, melding her curves with his.

Click.

She turned her face, lifted her chin.

Click.

Beecher stared into her eyes, saw for the first time that her suffering was timeless.

"It can all be real again, I can give that to you," he said. "I can give you that life."

"Can you?" she said. "I don't even know what that means anymore."

"It'll mean more than words, and it'll mean you can go back to the place you know."

"That's a lot of catching up."

Her smile settled and her eyes closed, and her lips found his.

Click.

Luna brushed grit from her knees and walked to the rear limo. She wiped at her eyes with the sleeve of her jacket. She tossed the camera to Fez without looking up, said,

"That film's going to be worth a fortune someday."

And then,

"Can I ride with you lot for a while? Your suitcases don't have so much to say for themselves."

"It'd be an honor," Pengo said. "Move over lads, and mind your manners, there's a lady present."

Chapter Twenty-One

The *Down Beat* took its name seriously. At the far end of a brick-lined alley, one bare sixty-watt bulb dangled from a strand of wire over a metal door heavy enough to repel a Viking horde. A semi-functioning neon sign the size of a cereal box announced the location as *The Do_ _ _eat*.

Beecher and Eeva arrived first. She exited the limo and headed into the club; he retrieved his guitar and remained by the car. Lining one side of the alley, six black motorcycles were parked with riders astride, engines purring. Beecher moved along the line of machines, slowly, studying the tinted visors for any sign of life. Halfway along, he threw caution to the wind, raised a hand in a meek, "Hello."

Immediately, all of the riders returned the wave, raising gloved hands, lifting visors, revealing glinting eyes staring out of dark shadows. Engines were shut off and helmets were removed. Beecher felt underdressed. He hadn't seen this much black leather since Snooze had roped him into doing a few weekends worth of bouncing at Coco's Basement, an after-hours retreat in SoHo for the, *"more extravagant amongst us."* The clientele was friendly enough, no real trouble. Never anything more than a few drunken tirades from the chicks, and some pulled hair and smeared lipstick from the blokes. Money was good, drinks were free, but ventilation for the tiny dance venue consisted of a battery-powered wall fan that spun so slow you could count the blades. The place reeked of post-copulation. It oozed from the gyrating bodies and the flaking walls and especially the floor. Snooze's only instructions to Beecher were, "Don't inhale too deeply, and never, ever, turn on the light."

The rider facing Beecher was a man of similar age, darker-skinned, with sharp features, hair falling past his shoulders.

"Buenos noches," he said.

Beecher nodded with a half-smile, said nothing.

"Good evening," the rider repeated.

FUCK. "Yes, of course, …hello, good evening," Beecher said.

The rider set the motorcycle on its stand and walked over with his right hand extended.

"It's good to finally meet you."

"I've seen you all before, on the road out of London," Beecher said.

"Hans likes us to keep an eye on his investments," the rider said.

"He's here?"

"Inside."

"And I'm an investment?"

"If you're Beecher Stowe, then, yes," he said. "I am Amelio…"

He spread his arms.

"…and this is my family."

One by one, they approached. An equal divide of men and women, offering names and a greeting reminiscent of an old friend. The males shook Beecher's hand.

"I'm Ceasar. Hola."

"Carlo. Welcome."

The females leaned in for a light embrace and a kiss on either cheek.

"Alma. Hi."

"Chavela. I like your song."

"Fidelia. Welcome to our world."

This last comment struck Beecher as odd.

In the dimly lit alley, Fidelia's skin was smooth as coffee-colored silk and she stood proud and confident at the pinnacle of her youth. She carried herself with more authority than the other women which made Beecher look deeper. Her eyes were black and perfect and dotted with reflected neon light, evoking the serenity and stillness of a forest lake at sunrise. Fidelia was the brave one. The savior. She had protected the innocent ones and herded them to safety. She had scavenged for scraps of food and clothing, securing her charges under piles of debris as fighting raged all around. She had whispered words of hope and sent babies to sleep with stories of knights and princesses and warm beds and hot food.

"Hans Tomek's world," Beecher corrected her.

"It is all our world," Fidelia said. "We journey together."

"I'm still learning just how much I don't know."

"He thinks you are capable of great things."

"It wasn't supposed to be like this," Beecher said. "I don't mean it's not a good thing, just not like I imagined."

"Time will tell," she said.

Beecher realized their hands were clasped together and her grip was firm and warm.

The riders returned to their motorcycles and with a roar of exhaust, filed from the alley, filtering into traffic, consumed within the perpetual flow of a steel river.

Beecher stood for a moment, opening his eyes and ears to the city. He imagined lone flower buds bursting from cracks in concrete, spreading delicate, colorful petals within the sanctuary of a hidden park or on a private rooftop, where sirens and screams go to die. Doubt was slowly receding, but he wasn't quite sure what it was being replaced with.

At the mouth of the alley, a gouge in the road surface ate the nearside tires of every speeding vehicle, covering the sidewalk with murky water that had pooled after a late afternoon shower, eliciting angry, mechanical protests as springs bottomed out and wheel struts clawed fresh pebbles of tarmac from the deepening hole. He sparked up a *Marlboro* and watched for another minute. The rhythm of the street set his mind awhirl. There was a song out there, whispering from the shadows, innocent and scared, and it had a pulse, like a heartbeat. And he didn't want it to die. He knelt on the ground, fumbled with the latches of the guitar case, pulled his journal from the innards and started writing:

> *When there's a road you can fight in;*
> *There's no point in communicating;*
> *From the church to the people;*
> *Hear the high winds blow;*
> *Make it easy, be the same;*
> *Fight it on the streets forever.*

Beecher was shaking as he wrote. The words were coming unbidden and unburdened, and he let it all out, scribbling, misspelling, scratching out phrases as better lines emerged from nowhere. He couldn't write fast enough:

> *At the mid-point of confusion;*
> *Hear those hound dogs scream;*
> *And in the soaring light of your fantasy;*
> *Find your destination means more than meditation;*
> *Just breathe.*

He stared up at the night sky, saw the ghostly shapes of skyscrapers disappearing into a haze of reflected light like the legs of giants obscured by a rolling fog. And with face upturned, he bellowed a mighty, "Thank You," to the city.

A block away, with cheeks full of pepperoni pizza, Harry said, "Did you hear that?"

Fez, Snooze, and Pengo were likewise engorged mid-slice. In unison, with their muffled voices indistinguishable, said,

"What?" "Hear what?" "Huh?"

"Sounded like Beecher, shouting."

"Oh, fuck off, Harry," Fez said. "You've been watching too many movies. If anyone's shoutin' round here, they've probably just been shot."

Pengo dragged a paper napkin across his mouth leaving a pink stain of tomato sauce from cheek to chin, uttering,

"Now who's been watching too many movies."

Fez shrugged a, *just sayin'*, and took another mouthful of cheese and grease and pitched the last piece of burnt crust into the gutter.

"We should keep moving, gents," Luna said.

The pace was slow, and she'd been charged with getting the lads to the venue on time. Around her neck hung a spanking-new leather satchel, complete with a combination lock, and in her fist, she clutched a bouquet of crumpled receipts. As the group meandered, she made notes in a little black book.

"What's the deal with keepin' those?" Fez pushed his nose closer only to have the pages slapped shut.

"It's my job," Luna said, "…keeping the money straight."

"How much 'ave we got?"

"You…'*ave got*… nothing. I am the keeper of the cash. You'll get your wages when you get back to London."

"What if I want to buy somethin', like a jacket, or a new camera?"

"Then you'll come to me and put in a request and if it's within budget, I'll purchase it and deduct it from what you're owed."

"Why can't I just get the cash?"

"Because you'll spend it."

"So?"

"You'll spend it too quickly."

"Says who?"

"The history of rock 'n roll. Read a book, why don't ya?"

"She's right," Snooze said. "The Who spent fuckin' years in debt. Didn't have a penny to their name 'cause they lived it up too much."

"I thought that was the point."

"The point is that you're paid to do a job," Luna said. "…and until you've done the job, you don't get paid."

"What if I wanted to buy you a drink?"

"Then I'd tell you to fuck off."

Harry launched a sludge of chewed pizza simultaneously out of his mouth and down his nose, choking like a baboon swallowing a giraffe, receiving several hearty slaps on the back from Pengo.

"No, listen, right…" Fez was disturbed. He changed tack, "What if I need to buy something personal?"

Snooze waded in, "Ah, have you run out of lotion, Fez, me ol' mate?"

"Funny. Just 'cause she's a bird, don't mean you have to act the fuckin' clown."

"You're allowed walking around money," Luna said. "The record company gives each of you twenty dollars per day, in cash, for food and necessities."

Snooze turned his back to Luna, made a sly, wanking motion.

Fez winced, asked, "Do we have to pay that back as well?"

"Of, course."

"Fuck." And then, "So, when do we get it?"

"We just landed. I haven't been to the bank to change any money yet."

"C'mon, Fez, you'll get what your due," Snooze said, twirling his trumpet. "Look around, you're in New York City on a hot, summer night, walking to a venue to play your first American gig. How fuckin' cool is that?"

To emphasize his point, he stepped to the curb, faced the oncoming traffic and blew a few lines of Gershwin's *'Rhapsody in Blue.'*

This was the first time Luna had experienced the full force of what the lads referred to as, *"a spot of Snooze-ology."* She was taken aback by his charm and his talent. It all seemed so right - five Euro-transplants, rocking down a Manhattan avenue, seemingly without a care in the world; hearts and minds in tune, hopes and dreams simmering on an open flame. She stopped writing and stood amongst the others and fell under the spell of Snooze's solo symphony.

"Play it, brother," Pengo shouted, "…play it loud!"

The venue wasn't a venue, it was a toilet with a bar.

"There's shit in the bog," Harry said. "A long, coiling, thick rope of shit. And there's no door on the bog. And the bog's in the dressing room. And the dressing room has no walls. And the dressing room is next to the stage. So, …right, get this, …someone could've sat there and shat while watching a band."

Snooze, Pengo and Fez peered into the bowl. Luna was pressed against the wall twenty feet away, her face contorted in horror.

"I'd make sure your keyboard is facing the other way mate," Fez said, pointing to flecks of brown matter coloring the floor around the toilet. "I don't think they've finished."

An electrical buzz and crackle from the stage announced a guitar being plugged in.

"We've only got time for one run through lads, so, quick as you like, Beecher said. "I wanna try something a little different while we soundcheck, something I just put together. Run the desk will you, Pengo. You know how I like it, plenty of bottom end. Nice and easy, Fez, this one's a little hypnotic, play it pretty straight until you get my nod, then you can loosen up."

Beecher walked Harry and Snooze through the changes and then took his place at the mic. He doubled Harry with an ambient bass line until Fez found his way in. Pengo shot a thumbs up from the back of the room, riding the faders with one hand, nursing a large whisky with the other. The band's unified creation was immediately at odds with the club's décor as the delicate sounds were more in tune with an infinite cosmos than a hole in the wall in the Bowery. The melodies rebounded off scribblings of perverse graffiti and swatches of crumbling plaster and they seeped into the yellowing foam innards of shabby bar stools and clammy booths.

Hans Tomek sat with Eeva, his brow was furrowed as deep as a plowed field. His protégé was straying from the brief.

"Let him be," she said. "If he were a puppet, you'd have walked away weeks ago."

Tomek grunted.

"Every step is important," he said.

"He knows what's at stake."

"You told him? I'm surprised. It's never gone well before."

"Well, it's hardly logical."

"A little frosty today?"

"Nervous, I think. It feels different."

Eeva sipped steaming black coffee from a paper cup.

"I called the Glitter Boys. Beecher said he wanted to fill out the sound with more brass. Earl said they'd be down sometime tonight."

On the small stage, Beecher had the band locked into the tempo of a new song and he relaxed into his own space. The first line out of his mouth caught her by surprise.

"When there's a road you can fight in, there's no point in communicating."

The powerful and derisive lyric loosed the bonds of time and the streets of Vienna swelled from the ether, and Eeva watched as field-gray uniforms marched in step, and a legion of black boots stomped upon bloodied streets, and the dead eyes of brainwashed soldiers were trained toward a dark horizon. And she saw vermin crawling through the wreckage of stores and over the smashed furnishings of houses, and they scurried across contorted bodies that lay naked and abandoned and it was biting cold and the world was freshly dusted with the first snows of winter.

And Beecher sang:

"From the church to the people;
Hear the high winds blow."

Hans Tomek was equally arrested. He tried to resist peering into the void but his will faltered under the spell of the song and his white-knuckled grip on the cane revealed his effort to be pathetic and futile. And he was rendered helpless as the melancholy descended.

In the span of a single beat of his heart, he was cresting a hill with his son's hand, so small and trusting, enclosed by his own. They were breathless with laughter and they sucked down gulps of fresh, alpine air and they collapsed onto boulders that were weathered smooth as varnished wood. And far below, in a valley encased by towering cliffs, a settlement sparkled like a lone diamond resting on a sea of green silk. Tomek pulled the boy onto his knee and they shared hunks of bread still warm from the oven, and they crunched into juicy apples, red as rubies, and they spoke in hushed tones as a herd of deer grazed nearby, oblivious to their presence.

Together they studied the tumbling clouds and the snaking stone walls and the tilled lands, and they belly-crawled to the edge of a cliff and peered over, and their faces were caressed by warm air ascending from the valley floor, and here they lay in a patch of soft grass smothered by the blanket of summer. And from here they heard echoes of voices raised in worship; raised in song.

And it was from here that Hans Tomek would be taken.

In this moment of incalculable serenity, he would slip from the overhang and he would fall, gentle as an autumn leaf. And he would evade the state of ultimate nothingness, released from its grasp as though a single granule of sand tumbled from an overloaded fist. He would awaken upon an immense plateau, grounded in another time, destined to remain ageless and defiant for the span of eternity.

Tomek struggled as the pages of his memory were being drawn anew. He hid from the daylight, succumbing to a vicious unrequited suspension of thought. But no matter what he did, from that moment on, Tomek could not remember with any degree of clarity where he had come from. Sporadic visions intruded his thoughts in the moments after dark and in the stillness of waking, and they would manifest, burning phosphorous-bright, for a fleeting second, searing nerve endings and driving imaginary fists hard into his gut. But they would pass into vapor just as quickly. And so, he prevailed. And the decades passed. And he wandered unfamiliar lands, and he set up a home wherever made sense. But he could not settle, for he did not grow older. And he found no purpose. Until he encountered the orphans. And as the youths reached the crest of their vitality, he confessed to them of his fate, and in doing so forestalled for each of them the invisible embrace of time.

And Beecher sang:

> "And you stayed for me; A silence I'd never seen;
> This is the coldest day; When wise men just walk away."

Coaxing soul from a plank of wood and a few steel wires was no gift. The Gods had never allocated Beecher Stowe with a free ride. He wasn't a prodigy; this was the result of hard work. The instrument was a tool used to expose the underground stream; the nutrient-rich waters of curiosity and confusion and pain and suffering. Here, the reservoirs overflowed with empathy that was denied to his conscious form. The signpost said, PERSEVERE, so he did. The signpost said, DO NOT YIELD, and so he complied. And where others fell by the wayside, he stayed the course, navigating, calculating, moving ever upward in search of an answer. He didn't crave adulation, nor the treasures of kings. And for that, he often felt alone. Instead, he sought a connection to a time or a place or a feeling that resounded so perfectly alive and so utterly invisible. And he chased it like a drug, blowing up a thousand relationships in the course of the pursuit. Psychologists align happiness with the ability to live looking forward; Beecher found the effort to be nothing less than a vacuum. His mantra, *"the present is what you do; the past is what you are."* There lay the fertile turf worthy of mining. Beneath that soil and under those rocks was the answer. Eeva had risen from that world. And Hans Tomek. And...

BANG!

Blackness.

"FUCK!" Pengo shouted. "Power's gone out."

The narrow white beam of a flashlight bounced behind the bar, strafing liquor bottles and confused faces. The disembodied voice of a janitor said,

"It happens a 'couple time's a' night."

Beecher had been mid-solo. Lost in the netherworld. Released from its grasp so sudden made him irritable. He'd been swimming deep and the flesh of his lover was soft and warm and had been pushed into the curves of his body and now the only sound he heard was Pengo bemoaning the fact that he'd spilled his drink.

"Is this how it's gonna be later on?" Beecher wailed into the dark. "'Cause this is bollocks..."

"We'll sort it out," Hans Tomek's voice was velvet smooth and calm. He was close. At the edge of the stage.

"Everything will be alright, I promise."

Beecher stepped outside for a smoke. It was as warm as a tropical jungle and a light rain was falling, granting the sky a silver veil pierced with effervescent stars. A young couple stood close together, taking shelter by the door, hands pushed into pockets, the wayfarers' curiosity painted across their faces. Beecher took to the shelter and offered up a cigarette. It was the English way. The guy accepted; the girl declined. The uniform of the day was present and correct - beaten up leather jackets, T-shirts and blue jeans. Both had shaggy hair, dark and matted from the wet. They looked barely out of school, Beecher thought.

"You 'ere for the band?" he asked.

"We don't know who's playing, we just heard about this place from some kids at the Port Authority. Said it was the only place worth going."

"Where you from," Beecher asked, feeling, more than knowing, that he was talking to some fellow out-of-towners.

"Me, the southwest," the guy said, and then nodding in her direction, "...she's from your neck of the woods."

"Cornwall," she said, shyly, her eyes were wells of honey and molasses. She jabbed the guy in the ribs. "We don't sound a bit alike."

"Travelers?" Beecher inquired.

"Of sorts," the guy said. "Heading up north, neither of us have been to New York. Couldn't pass it by without having a look."

"What's up north?"

"Work. On a trawler. Trying to get enough money together to buy a small plane and start a charter service in the islands. She's gonna find some work in a diner or something."

The girl grimaced like she'd swallowed something sour.

"I'm studying political history," she said. "...well, taking a break and studying."

"Remember that face," the guy said, pointing, "...the next President of the U.S.A."

"Cool," Beecher said. "It's a shame I can't vote."

The guy nodded up at the dim neon sign that hissed like a stuck rattlesnake.

"When does the club open?"

"An hour or so," Beecher said.

'You work here?"

"No, we're playing tonight. It's our first time in New York, too."

"It doesn't look so great from the outside."

Beecher let out a hearty laugh, "Mate, wait 'til you see what's inside. Imagine a derelict building that was infested with rats, and then the rats decided they could do better."

"Do they charge to get in?"

"Yeah, a few dollars I think..."

The couple exchanged looks that said, *"Food or music, we can't do both."* Beecher stepped up.

"...but you'll be my guests." He looked directly at the girl, "I can do with a little homegrown support." And then with a wink, "Even though Cornwall is virtually another country."

Beecher flicked the butt of the half-smoked cigarette into the night, heard a faint fizz as it found soggy ground. He moved toward the door, said,

"Hey, what's your name? I'll let 'em know inside."

"Muir," the guy said, "Thomas Muir."

The crowds started building about half an hour later. The rain had no dominion over the congregation assembling in the alley. Junkies, bikers, trannys, teen queens, preppies, goons looking to get laid, hookers from the Port Authority looking to get paid. The line was a rowdy, irreverent dragon's tail winding out of the alley and splintering onto the avenue.

Harry and Fez wandered through the tribes. Each held a can of beer inside a brown paper bag for no other reason than they'd seen it done in a movie.

A pirouetting teenager, pierced and chained beyond all consideration of sterility, pranced breathless in their path. A pair of welding goggles were strapped across his forehead, pushing matted strands of yellow hair vertical, and he flounced and minced with tassels from a suede western jacket whipping at Fez's face like riverbank flies.

Harry tensed. Fez had no patience for cunts.

The teenager said, "What's in the bag, man?"

He was a wobbling bag of acne, laughing hysterically one second, slobbering with wide-eyed aggression the next.

"I'm gonna drop this toilet-brush," Fez said.

Harry tugged his mate's arm, "Leave it out, he's messed up."

The kid was relentless. He'd found a new plaything in Fez.

"A bevy," said Harry.

The teenager sang, "A whaaat?"

Fez was a little more direct.

"A tin."

"A what?"

"A can."

"Of what?"

"Brew."

"Boo..? What? You got any weed?"

Fez stepped closer and stared at the kid. He saw bare toes pushing out of carefully distressed Chuck Taylors; he saw soft hands and manicured nails; he saw golden highlights painted into golden hair, and he saw shiny buckles and polished leather.

"He's a fraud, this one," Fez said as if he was considering the authenticity of a museum exhibit. "He's a fuckin' posing, pin cushion, dolled up for a night on the town. He's a little spikey Nureyev hanging out with the rough boys."

"Don't judge me, man." The kid fronted up and balled his fists, "This is who I am."

"Fuck," Harry said, knowing what was coming.

Fez's forehead smashed onto the bridge of the kid's nose.

Nureyev's eyes crossed, sinking into his skull like fish bait cast into a still pond. Fez stepped back quickly with arms spread wide, the indignant expression of, *"I didn't do anything, honest,"* scrawled across his angelic face. The kid threw his hands up, probing his blindness, wailing like a newborn awaiting a feed, sinking to his knees as rancid spit and salty tears and blood that was coal-black under phosphorous streetlights, was ejected with the force of a firehose.

"Alright, settle down," Harry said, patting the kid on the shoulder. "You'll be alright."

The kid was apoplectic. He wriggled out of his jacket, flung it to the ground in a tantrum and started to shred an already ripped T-shirt, spouting something about the taking of his yearbook photo. He wobbled to his feet and took off down the avenue, and was last seen stumbling amongst the flow of the midnight traffic accompanied by a chorus of honks and angry shouts. The lads looked about as if they'd just mistakenly taken a whizz on a sacred landmark. Not one of the other passing freaks paid a blind bit of notice.

"I don't think that boy's ever had a slap," Harry said.

"Seems that way," Fez mumbled, retrieving the jacket and trying it on, pleased with the fit.

"You're not?" Harry shook his head.

"I fuckin' am," Fez said. "I've always wanted one of these. I think it gives me a little *Sundance Kid* vibe, don't you?"

"You'll fit right in down the *Railway* on a Friday night. With you in that, and Pengo in his vest, you can be *Butch Crass-idy* and the *Sundance Knob*."

The lads ambled down the alley kicking through mounds of litter strewn ankle-deep and it was saturated and stinking. They elbowed their way past more members of the suburban uprising. This time it was a gaggle of square-jawed quarterbacks and bubble-blowing cheerleaders, nervous as stray mutts, clearly out of sorts having mistaken *The Down Beat* for a similarly branded, lite-beer-swilling disco bar.

Harry threw a good-natured nod in the direction of a bushy-haired girl that was the spitting image of one of *Charlie's Angels*. The brunette. The one with big tits. He received a smug scowl and a flex of biceps from her stooge in tow.

"I dunno if these folks are gonna like what we play," he said.

"Ah, they'll love it," Fez said, slightly distracted by the jacket's dancing tassels, "…'cause they've heard nothing like it."

"Doesn't mean they have open minds."

"It doesn't matter, we're not from here. We have an edge."

"What's that?"

"We've got nothing to prove."

"How'd you work that out?"

"Americans don't discover things, they react to things that are advertised to them."

"And we've been advertised?"

"Absolutely. These people had never 'eard of Beecher Stowe. And yet…"

Fez pointed to the gallery of rogues propped against the alley wall like human graffiti.

"Look at 'em, lined up like disciples for Jesus. It'll be the immaculate concert-*tion*."

"And I suppose we're wise men?"

Fez wrinkled his brow and supped from the bag.

"Truly hadn't thought of it that way, but, …yeah, …why not?"

"Still think it's a long shot."

They gathered under the blinking neon sign. As usual, Pengo was waxing loudly about some philosophical shite and Snooze was in rare form.

"*Roll on up, see the main attraction…* Ahoy, lads. What are you like, Fez? Where'd you get that? You look like Buffalo fuckin' Bill."

"Found it, Fez said. "Worth a fortune, this is."

Glances were exchanged, followed by shakes of heads.

Snooze changed tack. He had news.

"This is the biggest small gig you'll ever play," he said. "I just heard, if this goes well, we might push on and do a few dates out West. You know what that means?"

Pengo's question regarding Fez not being alone in looking like a "*complete fuckin' twat*" sent fits of laughter echoing into the night, while Snooze was sent into fits of frustration.

"Ca, Ca, Cal - i - fuckin' - forn - ia!" he stammered for effect.

Beecher was standing to the side, enjoying the privacy of the shadows.

He moved towards the group and sodium light draped his shoulders and for a moment he appeared to float inches above the ground.

"It's not confirmed," he said.

Snooze and the lads were caught off guard.

"Jesus, you're gonna give us a fuckin' heart attack, Beech."

"Just sayin'. Let's wait 'til after the gig before we break out the buckets and spades."

The band sparked up, one after the other, and a minute later, a contagion of cigarette smoke hung about their heads. They were lost to the conclave. A locked world. No entry for the uninitiated.

A deep baritone intruded; *'Ol Man River,* deep. The group turned to see a man, standing as still as a marble statue, resplendent in a white linen suit, lemon shirt, and white tie. His pants were cuffed over leather loafers that were polished to an atomic shine, and the ensemble was topped off with a white fedora wrapped with a yellow band. He held a ratty saxophone case by the handle.

Again, the deep voice rattled, "You the band?"

Snooze's mouth started flapping before his brain engaged. He tried to match the man's weighty charisma.

"We are the band…"

The attempt to make his voice deeper was met with raised eyebrows and there was a moment's silence as Snooze hacked up a lungful of *Pall Mall* phlegm and spat a walnut-sized ball of nastiness into a glassy puddle.

Beecher moved forward wearing a grimace of apology.

"Sorry," he said, …yes, we're the band. You on tonight as well?"

"That depends on what you're paying."

"Oh, shit, Snooze shouted, "The Glitter Boys. I mean, …a Glitter Boy. Fuck, I'm sorry mate, I didn't expect…"

"An old black man?"

"No, uh, …yeah, …you know… Eeva didn't say…"

"She was fucking with you. She does that."

Snooze slinked over with his hand extended and it was suddenly lost in a grip that made his eyes water.

He squeaked out, "Snooze Silver, trumpet. And, this is Beecher Stowe. It's his band, …his songs, you know, it's his…."

"I get it," the man said. "I'm Earl. Eddie's parking the car."

Earl scanned the lads, trained his eye on Fez and Harry.

"Damn, y'all are puppies."

The lads each raised a brown paper bag in the air.

Earl chuckled.

"Welcome to our little family," Beecher said. "And if you have any wisdom for us, don't be shy. It's our first time here."

Earl gave Beecher the once over. Eeva had been understating the boy's appeal. "Just keep it in your pants," he said. "There's some nasty shit goin' 'round this city."

"Cool." Beecher made eye contact with Fez and Harry. "Got it, lads?"

"It's Pengo you've gotta watch," Fez said. "If he whips off his jacket and reveals that waistcoat, it's game over."

"Fuck you, Fez. The sight of your hairless balls would send Helga the East German shot putter reaching for a sick bag."

Earl grinned wide as the brim of his hat.

"Happy family. I like it."

Eddie rolled up. Same suit; same hat. The sky had resumed its drizzle and he flipped his collar and crystals of water shot from the jacket.

"Twins," Pengo stated.

"Not even related," Earl said.

"But you look so much…"

Beecher clapped his hands and cut him off with a *"what the fuck,"* look.

"Where'd the name come from?" he asked.

"Made it easier to book sessions back when black folks couldn't sit up front."

"Not like that now then, eh?" Beecher said, wryly.

"So they say," Eddie said, doing a round of handshakes and hellos. "I guess you'd better show us what you got in store, we been hearing good things."

"Snooze'll gonna walk you through the chart," Beecher said, and he was immediately pulled up by some deep sighs.

"We don't do charts," Earl said. "We like to feel our way in."

Eddie picked up the ball, "Don't worry, we won't step on anyone's toes."

"So who we got here?" Earl said. "I know, you is the *geetar* player and…" nodding at Snooze, "…I know you blow the horn."

"Harry 'ere, is on keys," Beecher said, "…and Fez is our resident caveman."

Earl looked at Pengo, "You take care of the bottom?"

"No," Pengo said, "I take care of everyone."

"Harry's left hand," Beecher said. "It's a miracle of modern science. He does double duty."

"That can work, but just so's you know, we got a guy that'll fit in pretty good if you need him."

Harry perked up, "How good?" And then, "Beech, I'd love to stretch out a bit and not have to carry the bass line. Maybe we could give it a go?"

"Cutting it a bit fine," Beecher said. "By the time he gets here, we'll be back at the hotel."

"Doubt that," Eddie said. "He works here, cleaning up."

"That guy?" Pengo said. "I was just chattin', to him, lovely fellow, says he's seen everybody, Miles, Jimi, Aretha, Sam Cooke, Otis..; says they've all played here; says he jammed with Stevie when he was still Little Stevie."

"That's Rosy," Eddie said. "He's got more soul in his floor mop than any of those long-hairs struttin' around on TV with gold-plated geetars."

As if on cue, the rickety fire escape clinging nervously to the apartment complex opposite clattered like it was coming loose from the brickwork. In the darkness above, the sound of glass smashing came ahead of a stern rebuke, followed by an enraged screech. The air was still for a moment, and the gathering at the club's entrance exchanged bemused looks that said, *"another night in the city."*

And then, from the night it came.

A deadweight slammed directly onto Pengo's back, buckling his knees. He went down like an accordion tossed under a bus. A siren of screams immediately rang out. One was from a sodden cat, black as deep space; the other was Pengo's, topping out a few octaves above high 'C' - a sound Fez would later smugly remark that was so loud, and so intense, that he felt a quiver in his back fillings. Pengo would follow suit by whipping a brand-new ride cymbal twenty feet across the room with such surgical precision that, had he not fallen off his stool in abject fear, Fez would have submitted to a clean decapitation.

The pissed off feline flailed and spun in ever-maddening circles with fully protracted claws puncturing Pengo's delicate, white flesh. The hairy, whirling dervish somehow found purchase enough to spring from his groveling, fetal form and sprint away down the alley like a rabid, ebony missile.

Eddie said, "That's Satan, Rosy's cat."

He shouted up, "Rosy? You fancy a play?"

A perfectly-spherical afro leaned out of a window three stories up. The owner of the magnificent mane was backlit by a string of colored bulbs.

"Who's that?"

"Eddie. Hey man, you wanna play tonight?"

"With you?"

"Yeah. And Earl. We're helping out these English fellas."

"Oh, lordy, lordy," Rosy said. "They sho' need a little spice in their chili."

Beecher looked confused. He appealed to the brothers for some sort of confirmation.

"What's that mean?"

Earl winked, started to make his way into the club, said, "Yup, he's in."

"I must be insane," Beecher said. "I'm adding three new members to my band ten minutes before we play live."

The band, all except for Luna, stepped over and around Pengo who was still on his knees bemoaning the loss of three buttons from his waistcoat.

"I'm feelin' this," Snooze said, draping his arm around Beecher's shoulder. "Three white guys and three black guys, and you out front like a rock 'n roll unicorn. It's like a ride on a multicolored magic carpet."

"I don't get it," Beecher said.

"We're an international rainbow."

"A black and white rainbow?"

"Clarity, mate," Snooze said, "That's what this band is. We are monochromatic clarity."

Chapter Twenty-Two

Beecher didn't bother with a greeting. He took the stage before the others and stood at the microphone, looking down contemptuously at a flock of shopping mall braggarts preoccupied with preening and parading and tweaking homemade outfits and back-combing sink-dyed hair, and adding the final touches to garish make-up that had been slathered on by the lackluster glow of dashboard lights. On the tiny stage, the band settled into their positions, rubbing shoulders in the stifling heat, sharing their first-night nerves like winter blankets. At the back of the room, Eeva was easily picked out. Her poise and grace were obvious and perfect and Beecher chose to believe her smile radiated for him alone. Hans Tomek stood on the other side of the room, propped against the door frame, deep in conversation with two guys sporting shaggy haircuts, porno mustaches, collared suits and neckties as wide as pant legs. *"They're TV execs,"* Eeva had shared earlier. *"Along for the ride. Looking for a taste of those advertising dollars that Tomek has been spreading around town like grass seed. He's betting everything,"* she said, *"…all on you, but don't let that make you nervous."* The smile was inevitable; the laughter that bloomed, unexpected. She said they'd talk later; said he looked amazing and then planted a warm kiss on his cheek. As he walked away, he thought he heard the words, *"I love you,"* and he turned quickly, but a troupe of transvestites had pushed between them and Beecher's vision was filled with lacy bras stuffed with athletic socks and leopard-skin mini skirts short enough for flaccid cocks to be seen dangling through ripped fishnets. He echoed Harry's thoughts, *"Not sure if this is our crowd."*

Now Beecher looked at Eeva from the stage and he saw his life unfold like a flower seeking the light of the sun. And that was a good thing.

Pengo raised his hand and spread his fingers and Beecher matched his count. *5, 4, 3..,* the house lights were cut to black. *2, 1..,* Fez slammed the band into gear, sculpting rhythm from thin air, rejoicing in the concussive counterpunch rebounding off the piss-damp brick walls as he engineered a riotous, relentless groove. Rosy stood over Harry, following his hands, feeling the pulse propel his fingers high up the neck into a virtual solo.

Beecher played to the crowd as if he was exorcising the enemy within.

"This is for you," he shouted into the microphone, "...for all of you fuckin' freaks with your pierced tits and your empty heads and your studded dog collars trailing silver chains that you cling desperately to as you get dragged deeper and deeper into boiling oceans of misery and regret!"

With every slight and with every insult landing like a Muhammed Ali right cross, a roar of approval exploded, sending a tidal wave of applause toward the stage.

"If you think you're nobody; if you think life is running over you like trash on the highway; if you think the world has fucked you into oblivion, then pay attention, 'cause I've got some fuckin' advice for you all!"

The Glitter Boys found their way in, just like they said they would. But it wasn't easy. The four white guys from London weren't puppets and this was no 12-bar blues. These boys didn't pander to the crowd or shake their hips or smile like electrocuted chimpanzees. They played like they didn't care. Which means they did care, way fucking more than was expected. They cared about pace and they cared about phrasing and they cared about each other.

Rosy caught the dumbfounded stares from the Glitter Boys acknowledging that they were the only ones playing with their eyes open. This was a foot race and the soul brothers were having trouble keeping up.

"Hold the fuck up..." Rosy felt the bile rise in his throat, "...white boys can't teach black men about soul. It's in the rules. Your great granddaddies weren't ripped from their homeland, shoved into a hell hole, chained like animals, puking and shitting and dying. This is our thing, you honky little fucks."

But the song grew like a virus in his belly. And it wouldn't let him go. And it was warm and he drank from the cursed chalice in great gulps, and it spilled from his pores in bullets of sweat and rivers of guilt.

Beecher brought the tempo down, strumming softer and softer until only the faintest of his whispers colored the air. Pengo ignited a single spotlight and picked out Beecher's face, painting his shadow indelibly onto a wall pasted with hand-drawn flyers and screen-printed posters. Beecher signaled to Harry and the heavy reggae downbeat of the new tune resonated like a ghostly heartbeat in the tiny club. He raised the

Fender to shoulder height and peered along its neck, swaying slowly, lost in the void of the empty music. In profile, the shadow on the wall came to life, belying its earthly form. Beecher sighted the weapon, scoping the audience, settling on a young woman transfixed by what she saw. He started to sing and she started to move. She sank into the melody, breathless and quivering. Her bared breasts glistened in the reflected light and Beecher gestured to her and she was suddenly vulnerable and exposed. She felt the weight of his stare as he motioned for her to cover herself. And she did. And he answered with the first bars of a solo that would fold her into his journey. And together they soared ever higher, reaching for that elusive inner light that would guide them through every living fear.

Behind him, Fez and Rosy had found a home. They were locked together, inseparable against Harry's delicate touch and the Glitter Boys' dual saxophones that colored the room with shades of violet and blue. And riding high, on a languid, ethereal cloud, Snooze Silver sprinkled diamonds onto a glimmering ocean.

When Beecher finally brought the song to a close, Pengo held off with bringing the lights up. In time, he and Luna raised the faders, one by one, illuminating a crowd exhausted of their emotions, caught between the byways of beating hearts and rebellious minds.

Beecher Stowe had arrived at the club as a stranger. He left the stage that night as a fucking prophet.

Chapter Twenty-Three

A midnight talk in an all-night diner.

"They will have died thinking of me as the man that left them all alone when they needed me most."

Hans Tomek drifted, his thoughts tumbling with practiced guilt.

"Could you live with that?"

Beecher answered when he should have remained silent and his regret was immediate.

"I don't have a family. I don't have children."

"You don't need to have children, a dose of empathy will suffice."

"Yeah, you're right. I'm sorry, that was stupid."

Beecher upended a sugar dispenser and a stream of white granules plunged beneath the surface of his black coffee.

Tomek lightened the mood, "I've seen folks do that with cocaine."

Beecher grinned, recalling, "Fez was so busy with his bullshit the other night, he mistook the salt shaker for sugar. We all saw him do it, but he was being such a little princess about a lumpy motel bed, we let him get on with it."

"And?"

"The Glitter Boys loved it. Our senior-citizen brothers laughed so hard I thought at one point we were gonna have to call an ambulance."

"Rosy's a good addition, fits right in."

"All three of 'em do. I've never played so well. It's like knowing whatever you do, there's someone there to catch you if you fall."

"They're having a good time then?"

"Everyone is. It's Disneyland out there. Every city's a movie set without a single reminder of home. Do you know what that's like? Cars, currency, food, clothes, television, weather… If it weren't for the language, we'd be on another planet."

"You've played thirty-five cities in forty-five days, and that includes the two trips back home for TV appearances. That's a lot of traveling even for someone that's been at this game for a while."

Beecher lit a cigarette, the smoke bothered Tomek.

"You want me to put it out?"

"Do you mind? Gets in my eyes lately, just lays there like a fog."

Through the window of the diner, a gang of youths circled the car park on bicycles. The boys hung back in the shadows; the girls were braver, taking it in turns to come close, cup their hands to the glass and sneak a peek past sunbaked posters declaring $1.49 meatloaf specials - including dessert.

Tomek studied the fans' bare-faced compulsion. On the strength of one single, they'd swallowed Beecher for the Rock God the press had ordained him to be. The boy from Shepherd's Bush had touched a nation's nerve, just as Eeva had promised.

Beecher caught the action outside, too.

"It won't last, will it?"

A statement more than a question.

"You're turning a lot of heads that normally don't pay attention. That's a good thing."

"For you?"

"Absolutely," Tomek grinned, a rare, warm smile. "It's all about me."

Beecher searched Tomek's eyes for any sign of sarcasm.

Found none.

Tomek said, "You still don't believe, do you?"

The response was wordless - a hand pushed through thick, black hair; a heavy sigh; a reflexive pull on a dead cigarette; an *"I don't fucking know,"* shrug.

"Well, I'm here," Beecher said. "I gotta believe in that."

"None of this works if you don't believe."

"For me?"

"I just got through saying, it's all about me."

Beecher forked a piece of cherry pie into his mouth, licked his lips, said,

"What happens next… if it all goes to shit?"

"Nothing. We move on."

"Move on to where?"

"Somewhere else; someone else."

"You mean everything goes back to how it was?"

"Correct."

"Would any of this count?"

"This?"

"The success," he said, nodding at one of the young girls cruising shakily past on a gleaming Schwinn Sting-Ray. She was so nervous, she dumped the front wheel in a drain and nearly toppled over.

"The folks out there are really into it," Beecher said. "Naturally, they'll want more."

"My dear boy, you are putting yourself on entirely too high of a pedestal. If the Pope dies, they get a new Pope, simple as that. Where do you think you fall in the consciousness of society?"

"Hey, I'm just echoing the will of the American people."

Tomek took a beat, maybe he'd misjudged the humility of this young man. The stillness between the two men was electric with anticipation, but Beecher cracked too soon, should have held his laughter at bay for a minute longer.

"Mate," he said, "...for a man of your age, you gotta be careful, I think I just etched in a few unnecessary worry lines."

"Guilty," Tomek said. "I can only take the U.S.A. in small doses. I find it to be the geographic equivalent of a petulant child."

"What.., like tantrums at Christmas?"

"Exactly. A complete lack of gratitude."

A waitress appeared, silent as a snake. She refilled the coffee mugs from a fresh pot and cleared away the empty plates. Her hands betrayed a nervous shake.

She cleared her throat, "Get you anything else, sir?"

She was high-school young, and her voice was small and pure and tinged with the warmth of the Spanish language. The request was directed at Beecher. Hans Tomek might as well have been invisible.

He chuckled, said to Beecher, "Get you anything else, sir?"

"Beecher smiled up at the girl, 'No, thanks, all good."

She slid the check under his cup and then reached into her apron and added another piece of paper and darted away.

"Let's hope it's not her phone number," Tomek said, with raised eyebrows, "...otherwise you'll be finishing out the tour from the county jail."

Beecher unfolded the scrap. The diner's name was printed at the top in bold cursive lettering and underneath, a scrawl had been made with a pen on its last ounce of ink.

Knight Out Diner
52222 US Hwy 160
South Fork, Colorado.

*My name is Marisol and I am sixteen-years old. This Friday is our
homecoming party and I would be very happy to have you autograph the
check for your meal as it will help me convince my friends that I did not
make it up. Also, if you had a picture it would be great to have and I would
put it in a frame and hang it on my wall.*
Thank you,
Marisol Garcia

Beecher slid the note into his pocket, said, "She'd like a photograph."

Tomek reclined in the booth and supped from the steaming mug. He
watched the girl go about her chores.

"What kind of future do you think she has? How much time has to pass
before she walks the streets without a single thought of where she came
from?"

Beecher followed suit, putting his back to the window, stretching out
his legs, careful to keep muddied boots off the upholstery.

"Maybe she's proud of where she comes from. Maybe she comes from
here, so it'll never cross her mind."

"Unlikely. This is a country made up of immigrants that nurture their
forefathers' prejudices as if they were born of the very same suffering.
Blacks oppressed by whites; whites oblivious to blacks; Jews and Asians
equally suspicious and contemptuous of everyone; Hispanics quietly
swarming through the borders and breeding like their lives depend on it,
and the American Indian wondering how the hell this all came to be. I've
yet to find a single sentiment that's shared unconditionally by the entire
nation."

"Except for music," Beecher said.

"Not even that," Tomek said. "Independent radio stations are being
bought up by the dozen and the first order of business is to cut their balls
off. The age of a disc jockey breaking an artist is long gone. Song sales
against advertising sales, that's the new game."

"From payola to peanut butter," Beecher said.

"The youth of America doesn't give a shit; they're bought and paid for.
It's on you and your British brethren to fuck it up again, give it back to the
kids."

"Punk was dead coming out of the gate."

Tomek was intrigued by the statement.

"How so? Because the kids are impatient?"

"No, because there's only ever one emotion in play."

"And that is?"

"Apathy. The only way to live up to it is to do less and less. I don't see many anthems coming out of that."

"What about anger?"

"Punk isn't about anger, it just wears the costume. At best, it's a distraction; at worst it's a corruption that preys on the weak."

"What about its energy?"

"Loud isn't energy, loud is just loud. Elvis had energy; Little Richard had energy, and he was banging on an upright piano with no amplifier. For fuck's sake, Dylan has energy enough to blow your mind if you approach it right."

"So that's how the mistakes are made."

"That's a good line, *mistakes are made.* I'm gonna use that."

"Great, I'll take the royalty."

"I thought you already did."

Tomek winked a, *"you bet your ass I do."*

He thought for a moment, "In a rocker or ballad?"

"For you, a ballad; a sparse, ethereal, production; solo guitar and voice, maybe a little string section in the middle. It'll be a great closer to an album side."

Tomek felt the pull of the ages.

"I met a girl, a long time ago," he said. "She was an artist. In Paris. I found her wandering the streets after having been arrested for inciting debauchery. She had to bribe her way out and lost everything she had."

"Debauchery?" Beecher asked.

"She'd been searching for her sister whom she believed to be lost amongst the prostitutes in the sex market at the Palais-Royal. 'Incite to debauchery' was a charge that was tossed at any woman standing in a public place. It was an attempt to clear the streets during the French Revolution. Didn't work, though; no way to police it effectively, what with so many wars breaking out all over the continent and manpower being scarce. Anyway, this woman was distraught; inconsolable. She had had her portfolio confiscated. Turns out her life's work was now sitting on some bureaucrat's bookshelf. Imagine that, everything you had brought to life under the stroke of a brush, suddenly gone; out of your life, forever."

"Sounds like it would be impossible to even consider."

"What's worse, the two men that had picked her up hadn't banked on her fighting so hard to keep hold of her work. By her admission, she clawed one of the men, scarred his face. They made sure she'd never draw or paint again. They stole her precious gift by laying the tips of blacksmith's irons on her palms and binding her hands until the metal cooled."

Tomek sat up. He spoke with a singular ache, lost in the memory.

"When I found her she was about to take her own life. I talked her into retribution. Sometimes I think I was so insistent because it gave reason to my anger. If she chose revenge, I had a purpose; I could help her with that."

"And you did," Beecher said.

"Oh, yes. They were easy to find, running the same scams in the same location, picking up anybody that looked the part. I told them about a barge on the river; told them I'd been robbed by a few prostitutes running an illegal bordello. It was a gift for them. They were juvenile, joking about fucking all of the girls and then arresting them and coming back and cleaning out the barge of anything valuable. I told them it happened below deck, down near the boiler. So, down they went into the dark, like lambs to the slaughter."

Tomek leaned back again. He spoke clearer now; very matter of fact.

"You're wondering what happened?"

"Of course."

"Eye for an eye," he said. "With a few extra eyes."

"You did that?"

"She did. It was her fight. I learned that night that revenge is necessary. It's what makes us human. The aspiration for a person to attain some sort of higher moral standing is a solid value, and I believe we all need to evolve in that direction, but it gets wielded so smugly in the aftermath of someone else's misfortune. Not much gets said about not committing the crime in the first place. For me, what comes next is warranted. The song you played at the *Down Beat* on that first night, it reminded me of her, that innocent flower; that beautiful, gentle artist. She led me here. The *mistake I made,* was that I did not bring her along with me."

Marisol-the-waitress approached the table with a filled coffee pot in hand and Tomek waved her off. Beecher offered her his half-empty mug.

"Careful, it's really hot. I keep telling the cook that something's wrong with the percolator and that someone's gonna get burned and then sue him, but he just ignores me. I've got decaf in the other pot and that one works way better."

"No, this is good, thanks," he said, "I will have another piece of pie, though."

Marisol couldn't help herself, she whispered, "God, I love your accent." She quickly reverted.

"My mother makes it fresh every day," she said. "You can take a whole one with you if you want."

"Nah, just one piece'll do."

Beecher blew the steam from the boiling brew and took a sip.

Tomek had observed the exchange and felt the warmth of the girl's words.

"I think you've made a lifelong friend there."

"Speaking of that," Beecher said. "I can't help but notice that your escorts have been absent this past couple of days."

"They're taking care of some business for me. Overseas."

"All of them?"

Tomek avoided the specifics.

"It took longer than expected. They'll be arriving tomorrow and we'll head out to Los Angeles ahead of the tour."

He stretched and yawned.

"Last stop on the schedule. We'll make it a party to remember, eh?"

He popped the latches on a black briefcase, removed a plain folder containing a few of Beecher's latest headshots and some images of the band in full flight. He retrieved a copy of *The Times* and pushed the bundle across the table. The newspaper was dated three days previously.

"Here are a few snaps for your new friend, and you might want to have a read of this."

Tomek tapped a headline that read: *West London Pub Bombers Identified Among Warehouse Fire Casualties.*

The article was illustrated with graphic photos of bodies being stretchered from a blackened structure. A line of stationary ambulances filled the foreground, lending the picture the appearance of an unlikely funeral procession.

"Mistakes are made," Tomek said.

> *Tuesday, 28th November 1978 - - - A known National Front meeting venue was the sight of a stand-off with armed police in the early hours of Monday morning. Pursuant to the event, the Metropolitan Police yesterday released photographic evidence of military incendiary devices stockpiled at the warehouse and believe*

these devices to be the cause of the fire that has resulted in the death of 27 people.

The chief constable for West London, Mr. Clarence Wood, stated that when challenged by an armed police unit the individuals within the structure began preparing the devices for deployment against the officers.

"To have allowed such an attack could have been catastrophic to all concerned - to the armed officers following strict rules of engagement, and innocent bystanders in the surrounding community."

Mr. Wood also stated that the discovery of the warehouse and its illegal cache of weapons had been the result of an anonymous tip.

"We have been led to believe that a member or members of the general public have been engaged in independent surveillance of the premises for quite some time. And while I cannot condone vigilantism in any capacity, I am grateful that no further loss of life due to rampant domestic terrorism has occurred."

Among the dead is Derek Brinks, of Earls Court, London. A warrant for the arrest of Mr. Brinks had been outstanding following substantiated police inquiries into the August bombing of the Railway Tavern in White City, London. In conjunction with the bombing investigation, two accomplices of Mr. Brinks were also believed killed in the fire although police refused to release their names prior to further identification. They did, however, suggest foul play is suspected as the three individuals were bound together with what looked to be musical instrument wire.

Beecher choked a little cherry pie onto the checkered tablecloth. He read the last line, over and over, *"with what looked to be musical instrument wire..,"* the last time, out loud.

Hans Tomek leaned across the table and whispered, "Do not mourn those that would see you buried and forgotten without losing a wink of sleep. The only way to navigate this world with any degree of dignity is to fix whatever you can, whenever you can." He straightened up and sat back in his seat, adding, "No matter what the outcome."

They were silent for a while. Outside, the empty parking lot shimmered from a recent deluge of Rocky Mountain rain. Two tiny dots of silver light appeared, dancing upon pathetic puddles, becoming fixed and evident as the headlights of a container truck lumbering along the highway. As the beast neared, it growled as it throttled down through the gears, showing a coat of amber running lights around her skirt. The road curved and the ground shook and a pair of intense scarlet eyes drew their stares before being sucked into the black oblivion.

"What was it like?"

Hans Tomek saw his face returned in the window as a ghostly apparition and he felt the composite of his fears pushing to the surface, and it was dense as lava, scalding his gut, searing the events of the past into a cavern of charred flesh. He'd gone through the motions of an explanation many times before. In different centuries. With different charges that he'd embraced as close as family. They never understood. It was expected. He filtered the touchstones of Beecher's generation, auditioning and collating, filing anything that might register as not being entirely absurd.

"What's it like? I'm not sure I've ever put it successfully into words. You'd think to have all this time…"

The waitress clicked on a radio and messed with the volume. A panicked housewife was mid-rant, something about soap suds not performing well. The dial was fiddled with and Beecher and Tomek subconsciously waited for the static to clear. It did. Beautifully. *Love, Reign O'er Me.*

"Imagine being on a fairground ride that becomes disconnected from the earth. You might feel like you were dying. Maybe it *is* death?" he said. "All I felt were the elements - warm wind; cool water; the smell of damp earth; the lick of a flame. And there was color everywhere. And then there was no more color, only the sensation of falling. But somehow, through all of this, you know, without a doubt, that somewhere in this world a great event tore a planet-sized hole in time, and only a great event can close it. Until then, all there is is the journey."

"Is that why you drugged me the first time we met? To give me a little peek behind the curtain?"

"A little stress is a great diviner. You were just another face in the crowd."

Beecher tilted his coffee cup and studied the tarry grounds.

Tomek laughed.

"Don't worry, it was just the once. You proved your mettle."

The check was settled and the pair took their leave with Beecher filling his pocket with free butterscotch candies from a bowl by the register.

"Fez and Harry can't get over all the free stuff. The bus looks like they robbed a candy store."

The wind had turned since they entered the diner. Colder now, brushing the mountain dwellings with the first snowflakes of late autumn, fine as granules of salt, kissing the ground and vanishing without a trace.

"Phoenix tomorrow," Tomek said. "It was 105 degrees down there today. Let's walk a while; up to the crest. I hear there's quite the view."

They tramped across the car park toward a hulking-eighteen wheeler with the mass of a cargo ship. Emblazoned in zany, colorful fonts for the length of its trailer were the words *BEECHER STOWE ON TOUR*.

A honey-glow burned from behind thin curtains and Beecher paused alongside when he heard muffled laughter. *Fez, playing the fool, entertaining the troops.* He placed his hand on the vehicle and the mechanical hum of the onboard generator vibrated like a tuning fork against his skin and in a flash, he considered that his entire world was shut up inside - warm and drunk on free scotch. He was overcome with a sense of fatherly pride as he jogged away to catch up to the man that was paying for it all.

A full moon cast long shadows of pine trees along the lane, like black coffins on a parade ground, and the dirt underfoot was cold-hardened and rutted with the tread of logging trucks.

"I grew up in weather just like this," Tomek said. "Winter for six months of the year. The snow was as much a part of our lives as breathing. When it wasn't falling, it was freezing; when it wasn't freezing, it was melting and flooding. You could set your clock by the turn of the seasons."

The lane ended abruptly at a wide, shallow stream that dissected their path flowing silent as an arrow in flight. The embankment on the opposite side rose to a steep, rocky grade and continued for a half-mile until they broke from the tree line onto a meadow tinted purple and silver. Beecher struggled to catch his breath. Hot air plumed from his mouth and for a full minute, the altitude left him giddy and off balance as he focused on the erratic swaying of grasses that moved like wavelets atop a vast ocean.

Hans Tomek was soon a silhouette, moving easily through sparse thickets of juniper, raspberry and wild rose, and dodging the clutches of Alpine Firs with their limbs of dead bark striking monstrous shapes. And he jogged through grassland dotted with snow buttercups and pink primrose flowers that darkness had rendered black as drops of motor oil, and then scrambled up onto a rock formation that had been weathered tabletop-smooth. He had not faltered in his climb and his breathing was unlabored, and he picked his way across the crest roused by memories that reached through the ages triggering a bout of precious euphoria.

Beecher joined him in staring out over a vast expanse of inky-black forest that cut the violet-blue horizon with the precision of a surgeon's scalpel. Humankind was irrelevant. Not a single flare of electric light drew their eyes to distraction; nor was there the faintest intrusion of wandering industrial noise. There was only the sedate, end-of-summer harmony created by Mother nature as she brushed curious fingers across the land.

"You can be the most successful human to have ever lived," Tomek said, spreading his arms to encompass the grand vista at their feet, "...but you'll never be able to own this because you're part of it. Every molecule in your body is in tune with the ebb and flow of the seasons, making you sweat and shiver; making you restless and making you fearful of behavior and consequence; making you steal and mistrust and lie. And making you seek love and affection. Time on this planet has shown me that being human is most certainly a tragic experiment. Of course, how *you* deal with it is another matter."

"It makes me want to write," Beecher said.

"Writing serves only you."

"I can reflect what others might have difficulty expressing."

"So you become the catalyst?"

"I'd prefer to be regarded as an inspiration. I don't want others to adopt my belief."

There was a lightness in Tomek's voice as he batted around Beecher's comment.

"You just want others to absorb your thoughts and then go on about their business as if it was their own idea."

"Isn't that what we all do?"

Tomek removed his Fedora and jacket and laid them on the ground. He wiped at tufts of damp moss and brushed loose dirt from the face of a boulder and sat down. Beecher marveled at how Tomek's clothes were pressed and clean while his own boots and jeans were muddied to the calf and his sweater draped ill-fitting across his body, and the white cotton T-shirt felt clammy and cold as it leeched perspiration from his skin.

Tomek switched his attention from the grand vista and studied Beecher to the point of being uncomfortable.

"I think you might have developed an infatuation."

"I was thinking it might be love."

"And you would know what this feels like?"

"Breathless in her presence; mindful of every word I say; quivering like a wet puppy if we should accidentally touch; adoring her looks and the smell of the sun on her skin; wanting to be alone with her, always."

"An adequate description of a deep attraction," Tomek said, his tone now cut with the weight of his apathy.

"Love isn't what the other person gives you or how they make you feel, it's the measure of your sacrifice for them. People paint love as a rose-colored emotion; history has proven everything but. Love is suffering and nothing more. There is no boundary to cross; no finish line. True love is an enduring force as powerful as gravity."

Beecher heeled the mud under his boot, feeling lost and inadequate.

"I could turn everything you just said into a song that would connect with millions."

"I have no doubt," Tomek said. "But would you surrender that gift to cure her pain?"

The sky above was alive with shooting stars and their trails remained as imaginary white lines long after they had disappeared.

Tomek said, "When I was young I used to lay on a mountainside much like this and imagine faces amongst the stars. I knew nothing of the constellations but the shapes would speak to me, and from them I would draw answers to every question I could conjure up. All except for one. And I always feared the coming dawn, deluding myself into thinking that if the daylight could be repressed for one more hour, I would prevail; the answer would be mine. But daylight always comes. No matter what is occurring."

Beecher wavered, he wanted to press for the elusive question but Tomek was not given to such obvious clarity. The aged man was a hunter at heart. He respected the stealthy pursuit as a mark of respect for the prey and Beecher was growing accustomed to his way. Instead, he said,

"It's getting cold, we should light a fire."

Together they set a ring of stones and gathered dry grass and twigs for kindling. Tomek picked through several fallen branches and piled them next to the pit. A single match brought a ruddy glow to their faces as the grass took to the flame and in short order, a crackling blaze was sending orange sparks into the freezing air.

A visit from God.

Hans Tomek and Beecher Stowe were engrossed in conversation. They talked openly and at ease of childhood antics (Beecher), to first encounters with women (Beecher, again), to the collapse of the British Empire (Hans Tomek, entirely). On no account did Beecher feel he had a firm grasp on any of Tomek's educated theories. He was a boy from Shepherd's Bush who probably couldn't pick out a real shepherd from an imposter. His burgeoning curiosity for the world at large had been stymied, ironically, by his education. Inside the classroom, such matters that would now pique his interest were delivered so dully and so dryly as to absorb every molecule of fluid in his brain, meaning that what little he did know of world affairs had been studiously ingested by way of dog-eared biographies pulled from Pengo's bookshelf. Such was their subjects' impact on history, they could be identified by surname alone: Roosevelt, Churchill, Darwin, Presley, Lindbergh, Twain, Dickens, Kennedy and King. These bible-sized tomes detailed the journeys of curious men; men that brought light and color and hope to lives of blindness and uncertainty; men who willingly suffered exploits worthy of great fiction, leaving a young and impressionable mind invigorated and inspired to do the same.

Tomek was about to expound on humanity's indifference to the act of forgiveness when Beecher stirred the fire and began the telling of an incident from his youth that evolved quickly into the darkest of confessions. So intent and so lost to his thoughts was he, that a disturbance at the tree line went entirely unnoticed.

Not so for Hans Tomek.

Something heavy crashed through the undergrowth, heading their way, growing louder and more obtrusive, announcing its presence with a series of deep, guttural huffs - in anger or from exertion, it was hard to tell. The sound of branches snapping with the crack of electricity and thick foliage bending like river reeds threatened to eclipse Beecher's tale but the young artist did not falter.

"I was fourteen. Kinda small for my age. Didn't shoot up in height for another year or so. Looking back, it seems like an age when your life should be filled with wonder instead of confusion."

Tomek turned fully toward the sound. A shape with the mass of a boulder sucked light from the full moon into the darkest of voids. He scanned the ground for anything that might serve as a weapon.

Beecher said, "Anyway, it was late spring. I know that because school was about to break for the summer and the talk around the house had been largely focused on me getting a job, something to pass the time. Pumping gas, as it turned out. Could've been worse."

A brown bear moved from the tree line, padding slowly across the soft grass, its nose raised high taking the air.

"It was a Saturday morning and as usual I had found myself with an abundance of energy and no way to expend it. I wandered the house, doing what kids do, a little provoking; a little bellyaching. I settled into my Dad's chair. A rocker. My mother was ironing - a chore she set to with a scowl. She had a cigarette burning in the ashtray. I'm sure I said something derogatory about that. I don't remember. Something Freudian there, maybe. It probably explains why I never iron anything, and I smoke way too much."

The animal was mooing and slapping his gums and ejected streams of saliva that hung like fresh viscera, and it was undeterred by the crackle of fire or the sound of Beecher's voice.

"I don't know what brought it on but I uttered a phrase that haunts me to this day. I said, *I wonder what it's like to be in prison?* Harmless enough, eh? A bored teenager saying stupid shit. Not exactly groundbreaking news. Trouble is, I said it just as my father walked in. I felt the air change like every positive ion had been sucked from the room. There was immediate tension, worthy of having just admitted to stealing a car or robbing a bank. I had no concept of what was in play between my parents if indeed anything was. That's what being a kid is all about, isn't it? Being joyfully oblivious."

Tomek's fingers brushed the dirt, feeling nothing more than a few rocks and a few sticks. All the while, the bear circled the men, pawing and pounding the ground.

"My father had been violent before. I was used to it; I got quite good at dodging it. Fear makes you noticeably more aware but I missed this one coming. I was too wrapped up in being, well.., fourteen. Anyway, the ol' man grabbed me by the hair and yanked me to my feet and dragged me through the kitchen, upending a chair or two, and out into the garden. He threw me down and told me to stay - like a dog. And I did, with my heart racing like a motherfucker. He disappeared into the garage and I heard the drawers of his toolbox opening and subsequently being slammed shut. He came out and I remember I was cowering, hands at the ready to protect my face. He said, *"So you wanna know what it's like to be in prison."* I went to stand up and he kicked me in the stomach, told me to, *"stay down."* He rolled me over and put his boot on my chest. He had the scissors in his left hand, and he punched me in the face twice with his right. Then he kneeled next to me, got up close with hate spilling from his eyes and pushed the scissors into my hand. He told me to cut the grass. I didn't at first and he grabbed my head and slammed my face into the dirt, yelling, *"Cut it."*

The bear moved upwind and its musk filled the air with the smell of wet leaves and rotting bark. In the flickering light, its matted fur rippled like an ocean set on fire and its hide was torn and scarred by an age of contests.

"I started to snip away. I couldn't see a thing for the tears and bloody snot running down my face. Bizarrely, I can still feel the resistance of those scissors in my fingers, cutting blades of green grass, inch by inch. This went on until I had cleared a patch about two-feet square and then he stood up. I saw that as my chance; the only chance I would have to run. When he turned his back, I flung the scissors away and ran for the fence. I scrambled over and took off. I didn't say a word. I just ran as fast as I could. Away from the hate; and from the embarrassment; and from the guilt."

At that moment, the night became perfectly still and the bear rose on its hind legs and summoned a call straight from the depths of hell. Tomek froze with his head bowed and the bear slammed to the earth and

217

charged with eyes wide and mouth agape. The beast came as swift as a bullet and with the force of a bulldozer razing a brick house. The fire pit collapsed and blackened branches exploded, sending a shower of sparks to singe the surrounding grass, ringing the area with small, golden fires.

"I was gone for the entire day. Lost to my fear. Planning and plotting on how I was gonna get the fuck outta there. I walked for miles into the center of town. Hung out in doorways and at bus stops. I had no money for food, only had the shirt on my back. It didn't seem important. The world was moving all around me, going about its business like I didn't matter. Because right then, at that precise moment, I was invisible and I didn't matter. To anyone. Running was all that made sense."

The bear slid to a halt spitting hot, corrupt air into Beecher's face but an invisible chasm had opened, impossible to cross. Beecher was lost to another time. The man had become a boy. The demons of the past had taken him by the hand and were leading him down a windowless corridor that echoed with the racking sobs of the abused and the forgotten. The bear's eyes reflected the shimmer of hot coals that burned blood-red and its nose glistened shiny, like polished ebony, and its coarse, pink tongue slapped and slurped as it tasted the scent of the unyielding creature.

"Evening came and I started walking back toward home, toying with some harebrained notion of getting my bicycle. I thought I could claw back a shred of dignity if I had my own wheels. Another step toward independence. By this time, I must've been gone for eight hours or so, and I was walking along a busy road when I heard the sound of his motorcycle. I knew instinctively it was him, and then I saw him across the street. Even then, after what he'd done, I was conflicted about running away. I know now it's because no kid wants to run; no kid wants to live with disappointing their parents. He bumped up on the sidewalk and shut the engine down. He said he'd been looking for me, even had a spare helmet. He coaxed me onto the back and we rode out of town and he pulled over on a patch of dirt. I don't remember too much of what he said, only that he never apologized. That was too much for him. It's funny, the most frightened I was over the whole encounter was when he got off his motorcycle and he started walking toward me, asking me not to run. When he got me back home and I walked into the house, my mother was standing in the kitchen, smoking; contempt spilling from every pore. She said my dinner had grown cold, and that she had thrown it away."

The bear backed away, no longer huffing; no longer threatened. It lumbered away, cutting a new path through dense foliage. Tomek watched from the corner of his eye. The bear turned back and stared; unmoving but for the swell of its lungs, and Hans Tomek unwittingly matched its breath, shivering against the strengthening breeze as it returned icy cool and erratic. The bear took the air again, swaying from the shoulders, slowly rocking, flattening the earth. Finally, the great, brown animal lowered its head and was absorbed back into the tree line, soundless as a shadow.

Beecher raised his head, looked at Tomek, said, "We're imperfect creatures because forgiveness is a weight we are not able to carry. It doesn't matter if it's given or received, we can't handle it. When someone drives you to your knees they might as well have staked you to the ground, because it is from there you have to summon the strength to get up. My childhood ended that day; I am defined by that day. So to say I can forgive those actions would be a lie, no matter how much I wish I could."

Chapter Twenty-Four

"Oh, the Phoenix is rising…"

Pengo was up with the lark and in rare form for six o'clock in the morning. He leaned over the bus driver's shoulder and blagged a Marlboro jutting from a pack wedged under the visor.

"Get you back at the next stop, Lester," he promised.

The driver recoiled with eyes watering and put his hand over his nose.

"You might wanna wash the dog shit outta your mouth before you go sayin' too much. Damn, that's raw."

Pengo sorted through a sea of discarded paper cups, found one with what looked like orange juice, upended it into his mouth, swished the contents around, slid open a window and spat out the dregs. He sparked up the cigarette and lurched down the length of the bus, coming up on a bunk piled high with dirty clothes and cassette tapes. He made a meal out of crawling aboard, prompting groans from Harry, below and Fez, up top and across the aisle.

The lads had been magnanimous regarding Luna, suggesting she take the double bed at the rear of the bus for privacy, where she could get a good night's sleep behind a latched door.

Pengo shook his head at their pathetic attempt at seduction, "So, the thought of one of you buffoons worming your way into her affections, and by that I mean, *bed*, didn't cross your minds?"

Their affronted expressions were immediate and worthy of its own framed photo.

The horn section traveled separately. They took motels every night and motored along in the Glitter Boys' 1974 Cadillac El Dorado Convertible - white on white, with spanking new whitewalls. Snooze had been officially adopted by the elder statesmen and was afforded the supreme honor of being their driver.

Beecher pulled him aside at a truck stop south of Flagstaff.

"You know they're fuckin' with you; gettin' you to do the hard work up front while they slumber in the back?"

"I know, I know, but c'mon, I get to drive this beauty across America listening to the story of the blues from folks that actually lived it."

"When you put it that way, I guess I'm kinda envious," Beecher mused.

"There are a few drawbacks," Snooze said. "Feet and ass. Like you wouldn't believe. Rosy slipped off his shoes going across the continental divide. It was sheeting rain outside, freezing as fuck, so the windows were wound tight, heater full on. And then there was this smell. Like pickled skunk. Forget about tasting it, I could see it. I thought it was coming out of the vents so I shut 'em all off. Jesus, mate, I thought I was gonna fuckin' die. The Glitters didn't bat an eyelid. Said forty years of cocaine had destroyed their nasal passages. Earl offered me a hit, but I didn't do it 'cause I remember Pengo going on about how it made his senses so acute and how he could see people walking on the moon or some shite, and how everything was brighter and more colorful. If that had happened in there, with that stench, I would have probably driven off the nearest cliff."

Snooze was pacing. He dragged on his cigarette, hard. He made to exhale and instead sucked down some more.

"And Earl's got a condition. That's what he calls it, *a condition*."

Snooze's eyebrows raised to the point of detaching from his forehead.

"I call it a fuckin' lethal weapon. When his ass goes off, there is volume and there is vapor. If I get to Phoenix without puking in my lap, or needing counseling, this car ride will represent an entire chapter in the life of Snooze Silver."

"What about the desert?" Beecher was doubled over with laughter. "We're due in Los Angeles the day after tomorrow and that means hauling our backsides across the Mojave in the middle of the day. Tomek said it was 120 degrees out there. You got air conditioning?"

"Way ahead of you, brother."

Snooze had an evil glint.

"I sold Fez and Harry a bunch of bullshit about Jack Kerouac and John Steinbeck and Marlon Brando and James Dean, and they got all misty-eyed for the open road and posing with their sunglasses and cruisin' with their elbows perched on the door like they were in *American Grafitti*. So, I said if they slipped me a few bucks I'd have a word with the Glitter Boys and see if they could chauffeur the last leg."

"How much?"

"A hundred. Each."

"Brutal."

"Think of the stories they'll have for their grandkids."

"We need photos for sure. Maybe you can get the Glitters to snap a few off from the back seat?"

"Done."

"Tomek is leaving us in Phoenix, so I'll be joining you lot back on the bus. It'll be good to have some time together. I'm cooking up a new tune; having a little trouble with the middle."

"Beauty. What is it?"

"It's for all of us. I'm calling it, *Roam*. Seems to fit. It's a slow burner in the beginning; gets a little rousing later on."

"Anything to do with your lady?"

"What lady?"

"Eeva."

"Does it show?"

"Only to those amongst us that have known you since you were five years old."

"I didn't want it to be confusing for the lads."

"They wouldn't notice if you hoisted her on your shoulder and carried her off into the woods. The pair of 'em have got it pretty bad for a certain tour accountant."

"No? Really? She'd eat the pair of 'em alive."

"Not to worry, though. Pengo is playing papa to all. It's funny, it's the first time I've seen him out of his element and, strangely enough, he seems absolutely in his element."

"I've said for years there are hidden depths to ol' Pengo. He's not as weird as he makes out. Heart a' gold…"

Snooze capped it off, "...and pubic hair to match."

Pengo was wedged into the skinny bunk like a recumbent praying mantis. He slapped his bare belly, announcing,

"It's middle-fucking-America, man, where everybody wears their conscience on their sleeve and their weight over their belt. Have you seen what's out there trucking along the interstate? Hearts are being crushed faster than old Toyotas. Mealtime is cholesterol and fat with a chaser of salt and sugar. It's corporate America's final assault on the sad fuckers that think having stuff, regardless of its value, is a fucking birthright; like somehow being intolerant of weakness in any form is a sign of strength. I know it sounds weird but I used to love this country."

"That's what the telly will do to ya."

Harry's disembodied voice was small and muffled, rattling hoarse with cheap whisky and cheaper cigars from behind a pair of curtains imprinted with colorful caricatures of *Pony Express* riders fleeing from marauding Indians. A few sprigs of bleached hair was all that was visible from the cocoon of his goose-down sleeping bag.

"What the fuck are you on about?" Fez dangled his white as snow stork legs over the bunk. He pushed off and landed with a thud, naked as the day he was born.

"Jesus, Fez," Pengo said, "What if Luna comes out?"

"Nothing to hide here boys. I am a man in his prime and I am poised to make a move toward those double doors any day now."

Pengo stubbed out his cigarette in a silver ashtray screwed to the bulkhead. The lid was missing and the receptacle was overflowing with broken peanut shells and spent matchsticks and he started a little fire in the process.

"Well, you've got until tomorrow night," he said, a little distracted as he shuffled about in the confines of the bunk. "I heard she's going off with Eeva to sort out some business."

His words carried a sense of alarm as he resorted to slapping at tiny flames with his hand. "They're flying back to London in a private jet."

"So be it," Fez said, slipping into a cubicle the size of an upright bathtub for a piss. "Time to crank it up a notch."

"What's that even mean? Harry said, "...and what's that smell?"

"My sheets are on fire," Pengo was matter-of-fact.

"Fez sang out from the toilet, "You'll go blind, Pengo."

"No, on fire. Really."

Pengo toppled from the bunk in a heap.

Harry peeked out, couldn't quite register what he was seeing. And then...

"FUCK!"

He kicked his feet inside the sleeping bag like a channel swimmer being chased by sharks.

"The zip," he yelled. "The fucking zip's stuck."

Fez leaned his head out, saw Pengo racing up front, heard his frantic pleas to stop the bus, and immediately showered the cubicle with piss.

"LESTER! FIRE! STOP!"

The bus was ambling along at the speed limit. 55 mph. Lester mouthed the words to Charlie Rich's, *Behind Closed Doors*, all the while slurping and sucking on a grape *Tootsie Pop*. His eyes were fixed on a shiny-red hauler at his ten o'clock and he was deep in fantasy land, lost to the eighteen-wheeler's allure, imagining how he'd decorate the sleeping cab.

Dark brown shag pile carpet; built-in stereo speakers; two refrigerators, one for Budweiser and one for the staples - bologna, cheese, pickles, mayonnaise, and mustard.

"LESTER! I'M NOT FUCKING KIDDING!"

A 600 horsepower diesel would make this tub of shit feel like a skateboard.

"LESTER! LESTER! PULL THE FUCK OVER!"

The chick that takes the money at that truck wash in Tallahassee, I know she'd appreciate a little on-board, Lester-time."

Pengo saw headphones bulging from the underside of Lester's woolen hat. He reached up, ripped the cord from the eight-track's socket and screamed into the driver's ear,

"LESTER...FIRE!"

Lester bolted upright and spat a stream of purple saliva from pursed lips. He lost his balance and flung himself onto the steering wheel, causing driver-induced oscillations that swung the back end of the vehicle around like the business end of a cheerleader's baton. Lester let out a piercing scream and slammed both feet onto the brake pedal and Pengo mashed the dash with his face, slicing a deep gouge across his cheek, narrowly missing his left eye.

At the back of the bus, Harry was sent tumbling down the aisle with arms and legs cartwheeling in such perfect symmetry as to make a gaggle of synchronized swimmers pee in the pool with envy. At each revolution, the wind was pushed from his lungs with a thin, squealing wheeze.

The bus cut across two lanes of the highway and careened onto the shoulder, kissed a sea of loose gravel whereby the front suspension collapsed, bringing the shuddering locomotion to a sudden halt and sending the rear of the vehicle airborne through 180 degrees in a painfully-slow, vertical arc.

Calamity befell every loose item within the crumpled metal shell. Into the tumble dryer went the human cargo, greasy pizza boxes, splintered drum sticks, empty beer bottles, full beer bottles, Pengo's extensive collection of books and cassette tapes, Lester's extensive collection of porn, Harry's baseball bat, Harry's football helmet, Harry's cowboy boots and cowboy hat, and twenty-two boxes of *Cap'n Crunch* breakfast cereal. Also, Fez's fondness for deodorant sticks meant that fifty or so scented missiles shot the length of the carriage in a scene befitting the Vietnam conflict.

An eerie silence washed over the smoke-filled interior. Pengo roused first, with face and hands slathered red and sticky. He was on his back, staring at a ceiling that looked remarkably like a floor. His legs were cocked at an odd angle. He ran his hands over each limb, probing for breaks and the sensation of touch was missing.

"I think I'm fucking paralyzed," he shouted, at a volume that brought Harry conscious, coughing and wheezing and wondering why Pengo was squeezing his legs like he was testing melons for ripeness.

"Pengo, that's my leg, you fuckin' idiot."

Harry looked down the passage, saw the fire grabbing hold of some discarded towels, screamed a predictable, "Fuuuccckkkk!"

Above them, Lester's body was jammed between the steering wheel and the floor. His head lolled at a weird angle and his eyes were fixed and sightless, and they were dark and wide, like those you'd stick on a sock puppet. Harry pulled himself upright. *He's dead. He's dead.* The terror had taken hold. He leaned in, inches from Lester's open mouth. When it spoke, he shat. Just a little.

"Push on the damn door," Lester said, "...it'll open out."

Lester squirmed, unwinding his overweight form from the seat belt. He didn't think, just unclicked the buckle. And Pengo was in his flight path. And Pengo saw it coming. Tried to shout, *"no!"* but the words never came. What did come, was three hundred and fifty pounds of cheeseburgers and fries with a spot of gout, a handful of *Brylcreem* and an ocean of *Aqua Velva*.

"*Now* I'm fucking paralyzed," he shouted.

Lester pawed Pengo's face like a fat cheetah.

"Out," he screamed, "...get out now."

Three bodies tumbled from the coach, landing in a patch of roadside scrub in an untidy heap. Harry wasted no time yelling for Fez and Luna. He raced the length of the upturned vehicle banging and wailing like a banshee.

"Fez, Luna, you there! Shout out, c'mon, shout out!"

Fez's feeble voice called back. But it came from behind Harry.

"What the fuck?"

"I'm out mate, got chucked through the fuckin' window."

Harry did a double-take.

"What the fuck?"

Fez was still stark bollock naked.

"Luna?" was all he could say. And he repeated her name, over and over.

"Luna, Luna, Luna!"

Lester and Pengo gathered with the lads at the back of the bus. The rest of the coach was now completely engulfed by flames and the misshapen body panels succumb to the intense heat with a sonic assault of metallic pops and groans.

Covering the width of Luna's room, the emergency exit window was cracked and blackened by smoke and there was still no response to their repeated calls.

"She's dead," Lester said. "Move back, get out of the way before this thing blows up."

"Shut your fuckin' mouth," Fez snapped, "...and help us pull this fucker open."

The exit latches were collapsed and contorted into fists of pitted chrome. In twos and threes, they heaved, singeing hands on scorching metal and opening deep wounds on shards of cracked glass.

"Lester continued with his panicked pleas, "Get back, man, you're gonna get yourself killed."

"Fuck you, she's still in there," Fez screamed.

A caustic, primal sound built in his stomach and poured from his mouth through strings of milky-white saliva. Fez bellowed like a wounded animal, settling both hands either side of the catches. Adrenaline pumped through his veins like a firehose. He squatted, took a breath and stood straight up. The catches blew from their hinges like they'd been shot out by a cannon. The entire back window came free and Luna's fractured, smiling face peered up at a sky of infinite blue, and at a legion of marching clouds, white and fluffy as marshmallows, and she bathed warmly in the life-giving sun, shining down like a golden pearl, and when focus returned and the light was no longer regarded as an enemy, she realized with mixed emotions that she had a face full of Fez Bramble's dusty and dangling cock and balls.

Chapter Twenty-Five

"Out of all of the shit that was flying around, no one was hit except me? It makes no sense whatsoever."

Pengo was beside himself. Again. Ten days had passed since the accident and this was the fiftieth time he'd mentioned his ill-fortune. It came in waves of self-righteous grief, starting small, with a brief whine or an offhand comment, and built into a full-blown hurricane of condemnation. And it always coincided with the placement of an ice pack on a bruised rib or an abundant scoff of pain pills.

The lads lounged poolside on a line of sunbeds, alternately roasting and cooling their creamy flesh at the mercy of a palm frond's windblown shade. Mad dogs and Englishmen, and all that. They were enjoying the sanctuary of the *Rose Bowl Motor Hotel,* a fifteen unit survivor from the heydays of Route 66. For a handful of London boys experiencing cowboy country for the first time, this was no bad thing - the temperature was a steady ninety-five degrees, the entire facility had been booked out for the group, they each had an air-conditioned room with a color T.V. and a refrigerator, and best of all, the complex nuzzled up to Phoenix's premier topless steak house. A relaxing holiday in the sun, albeit adjacent to an interstate that proclaimed itself to be a *'Gateway to the Southwest'.* In reality, this meant the beds shook round the clock from the steady procession of big rigs. Strangely, this far from home, it felt like home; like a row of terraced houses, except without the damp and the rain and the cold, and striking workers and dole queues, and soggy mash and boiled cabbage. Actually, it was nothing like home.

Luna had been the deciding vote. She'd floated the financial incentives with a tentative smile, due to the cuts and scrapes painting her cheeks and forehead, fronting up to the lads dressed as they all were, in varying shades of hospital scrubs.

"It's not the *Ritz*," she said, "but we can save a heap of our earnings if we hunker down here, and there are clothes shops nearby. I saw something called *Blue Jean Bonanza* and there's a shopping plaza that's a short taxi ride. And until a new bus can be found, the tour's ground to a halt."

"Subtle, it ain't," Snooze said, gazing up at a thirty-foot tall, neon sign depicting a smiling waitress with the outline of two ribeye's glowing with atomic ferocity in place of her breasts. The sign read: *Pinkies Grill*.

"…but I'm suddenly feeling a little peckish."

Harry pacified Pengo in between slathering spurts of suntan lotion onto his peeling skin.

"It's your gravitas, mate," he said, "It's your natural attraction."

"Or, it's just bad fucking luck," Fez offered. "Put it this way, how many times have you been knocked out by some wanker in the pub?"

"None, never," Pengo said, "What's that got to do with anything?"

"None, you say; my point exactly," Fez said. "You were due for a little mishap."

Fez pounded Harry's shoulders.

"Look at Harry, this lad's had a lifetime of grief."

"No I haven't," Harry chimed in.

Fez carried on as if Harry were invisible.

"This little chap has been run over by a car…"

"It was just my foot."

"He's been tipped off his bicycle, four times that I know of…"

"Three, and those laundry bags are heavy."

"He was chased the length of the Goldhawk Road, and that weren't that long ago."

"Last year, and I didn't know those dogs could smell wrapped sausages."

"And we all remember that tumble he took gettin' off the bus a few weeks ago."

"You dared me," Harry said. "You bet me ten quid that I couldn't step off the platform while it was still moving and not lose my balance."

Fez's eyes streamed with tears.

"Someone needs to invent a movie camera that I can carry in my pocket. The look on your face as you tried to keep pace at twenty miles an hour was fuckin' priceless."

Pengo sniffed and raged on, "None of that bears any comparison to being burned and speared and fucking squashed."

He rolled onto his stomach and his newly acquired swim trunks cut into his ass crack like they were afraid of the light. Snooze's suggestion that *Little Mister's* might not be the best place to shop for clothing had fallen on deaf ears. Pengo was having none of it. *"It's different here,"* he challenged, *"...people in America have bigger bones."*

"Maybe he hit his head," Harry whispered, genuinely concerned, "and something's goin' on inside that we don't know about?"

"You're serious?" Fez was perplexed. "He's fine, he's just a sulky bastard. He'd have no sympathy for you, mark my words."

"Still," Harry said, resorting to his time-honored thousand-yard stare, "...he is a mate."

Harry was soon lost in a world of delusion and daydreaming, and Fez saw it as a perfect opportunity to go for a swim.

As soon as word filtered out regarding the crash, stock in Beecher Stowe and the band had increased a hundredfold. *Supermassive Superstar* had solidified its place at the top of the Billboard charts, outselling its nearest rival by three million copies.

"The pub bombing exposed you to the masses in the U.K.," Eeva said. "Seems something similar is happening here with the band's bus crash."

Beecher was a little glum. It was 4:40 p.m. It said so on his recently acquired Mickey Mouse watch, although the ambiguity of the position of the white-gloved finger could have put the time off by as much as an hour. They'd been strolling the same three aisles of the county's largest *Museum of the Old West* for two hours. Eeva had selected the location as it seemed best suited for greeting members of the local media. She'd flashed a mischievous grin when offering, *"...think of it as you paying tribute to pioneers and the exploration of new territories. A little existential but I think people will pick up on it."* For Beecher, the juxtaposition of a British rock 'n roller posed against the likenesses of Billy the Kid and General Custer plumbed a number of psychological depths only Pengo Crane could sort through. In its favor, this house of dummies was situated only one block from the motel.

"I'm not sure I want to be known as the rock star who's always on the verge of death."

"The public wouldn't buy your music if they didn't like it, no matter how much you suffer."

"Good to know, I guess. How many more interviews do we have today?"

Beecher tested the rope on a makeshift gallows and was shocked to feel how sturdy and usable the rig was.

Eeva sifted through a folder of papers, "One T.V; two radio, and then we're done for the day."

"Swell."

"Picking up a little lingo?"

"Not meaning to. But it does get under your skin."

The open front door was indeed like a gateway to the southwest. An invisible wall of refrigerated air separated the darkened interior from the skin-peeling sunlight and Beecher wondered for a moment if the real Apache chief whose effigy he gazed upon, now depicted by a hastily-lacquered clothes store mannequin with mop-head wig, a beaded loincloth and makeup befitting a blind transvestite, might've found it a bit chilly.

As the next video crew assembled their gear, Eeva snuck in a little food for thought:

"Hans suggested that we make use of the down time and get away for a few days, see a bit of Arizona."

"When?"

"Next week."

"So, we're not finishing the bus tour?"

"He doesn't think it'll be necessary, what with all this media coverage."

"But it's just one side of the story," Beecher said. "The other being, oh, I don't know, …the music."

Eeva ran her tongue across already succulent lips and Beecher regretted coming off like an *ungrateful fuck* - Snooze's words of admonishment just yesterday - so he quickly made amends.

"I'm sorry, that wasn't called for. It's just…"

She finished his sentence, mocking, with a flick of hair and a wiggle of hips, "…it wasn't supposed to be this way."

Beecher was speechless. And a little embarrassed. He'd never spoken those words aloud. Well, not in the company of anyone he knew. Those were his thoughts, from the deepest recesses of his quiet ambition. And there were rules. There was a way to live life, and a way not to. It was the *act* of living that mattered; it was the journey that made sense. The road might be bumpy or intolerable or downright impassable but you must exhibit decorum, always. And you were most certainly excluded from active duty if you were incompetent, or lazy, or bereft of passion, or allergic to the struggle, or a cunt. And above all, life worked best when it was presented in technicolor, on a widescreen, and in quadrophonic sound.

"I started out as a struggling artist; I'll end up as a reluctant hero."

"Then maybe you should've written something a little less motivating."

"I don't know how to do that."

Eeva spread her arms like a ringmaster, "And, we're back. Ladies and gentlemen, after one complete cycle of the Beecher Stowe planetary system, I am proud to announce absolutely nothing has changed. Please feel free to help yourselves to as much popcorn as you can eat."

"You've been spending too much time talking to that Snooze Silver fella."

She winked, "He does have a way with words."

The interviews wrapped without any drama and Beecher and Eeva strolled the block back to the motel at a snail's pace, window shopping for turquoise jewelry (her); leather belts with buckles the size of dinner plates (him). The sun had dipped below the surrounding hills, the thermometer had fallen to a bearable eighty-nine degrees, and Beecher's lengthy consideration to rest his hand within hers was shattered by frantic yelling up ahead.

"Beech, he's gone fucking crazy."

Fez and Harry bounded up, the pair of them wearing stripes of sunburn like crimson zebra crossings.

"Settle down, Harry, who's gone crazy?"

Fez was out with it first.

"Pengo. He's got the maid locked in his room. She kept tapping on his door; she's been trying to clean the room. It's bedlam. Fuckin' shouting in Spanish or Klingon or some fuckin' language. We dunno what to do. Everybody's watching. All standing 'round. The manager said he's gonna call the police."

"Is he stoned? Or drunk?"

"No, he's completely sober. He's been saying for a week how she taps on his door like a fuckin' demented woodpecker. Really loud. And he's told her to stop. And she laughs at him and taps again. Louder. She's been fuckin' with his head and now he's lost it. He was waiting for her. He kept saying,

"I'm gonna have her. I'm gonna get the bitch, tomorrow. You fuckin' see if I don't. I'm gonna fuckin' drown the bitch."

"We thought he was just winding us up," Harry said. "...having a laugh, you know. And he wasn't! And now he's got her locked in the bathroom and he's tied the door shut with towels. He says she's being hoisted with her own fuckin' petard. And we don't know what a fuckin' petard is."

Beecher broke into a run.

Fez shouted after him, "Is it a rope? Or a crane?"

"I told you, it's not a fuckin' crane," Harry insisted.

The lads took off in pursuit. Beecher was way ahead, cutting through *Pinkies* car park, clearing a waist-high cement block wall that ringed the property without slowing. Pengo's room was at the end of the block. No.10; the red door. *"Luck, happiness and joy, that's my room,"* he'd boasted.

A fraternal order of wailing cleaners pressed against the curtained window, cupping hands against the late afternoon glare, seeing nothing except their own contorted reflections. Snooze stood apart from the crowd doing his best to appease the motel's day-manager. In typical Snooze-worthy fashion, he calmed and reassured a man for whom severe and unrelenting diabetes must have been a birthright. Overweight to the point of giving a grand piano a run for its money, the caretaker sank his bulk between the collapsable arms of a triple-strung lawn chair he'd brought along especially for the proceedings as standing for even the duration of a single *Kool King Size* would've sent his heart into jungle-drumming spasms. The man was a cartoon, with thin, pink lips pursed like a cat's asshole flowered with flakes of chapped skin. When the ribbons of salami-colored flesh were pulled apart they exposed a gap in his front teeth wide enough to siphon grape juice through a garden hose. He wore a white singlet with bitch tits spilling hairy brown nipples at the armholes. He nursed a half-emptied bottle of Tequila and nibbled on a turkey leg that he waved around like a toy bat. And he repeatedly mopped his face and neck with a grubby hand towel, pasting clumps of straggly ginger hair to freckled flesh, grumbling constantly about not being paid overtime for such, *"stupid bullshit."*

Snooze paced in circles, placating the fat fuck; making light of the scene, stopping short of pleading for a little understanding. But the language barrier was too great, the manager spoke moron. Snooze abandoned his efforts as Beecher came running up. He greeted him with a desperate *"shit's gone crazy"* embrace.

"What's tipped him over?"

"He was fine, well, …fine for Pengo, considering his ailments. The girl from the reception came out to the pool, said he had a phone call, and he skipped off with a smile. He's been waitin' for word from the insurance company about the repairs to the pub. Ten minutes later, it's like a scene from *The Alamo*. Fuckin' cleaners bursting out of rooms, all shoutin' and running around like they were on fire. Can't understand a bleedin' word, of course."

"How long's he been locked in there?"

"About forty minutes. The manager called the police a while ago, but he reckons they don't exactly crank the sirens or set the red lights a' flashin' on account of the reputation of the place."

Beecher screwed up his face, *"Huh?"*.

"Apparently, they do a lot of renting the rooms by the hour," Snooze said.

"Well, maybe we can get Pengo put straight before they get here. I'll go see if there's a window open 'round back. See if you can get him to the door."

Beecher legged it into the alley. A line of air conditioning units hummed like metallic beehives, dripping steady streams of condensation, cultivating nests of weeds with stems as thick as his wrist. Pengo's room was first up. The back door hadn't seen a coat of paint since it had been installed twenty years previously, and most likely hadn't been opened for as long. Only one window was set within the cinder block wall. Hard to tell if it was a bathroom or a bedroom. The sill was more than six feet off the ground so Beecher upended a rusty, metal trash can, spilling out a few pounds of garbage and one ambivalent pot-bellied lizard that remained a blinking statue. Pengo's voice rang out from inside,

"Is that you, Beecher?"

"Yes, mate."

Beecher clambered onto the can and felt his way up the wall, craning his neck. A wire screen covering the window was holed in several places and Beecher nearly tumbled to the ground when Pengo put his head through an opening.

"She's gone," Pengo said, over and over.

"Who's gone?" Beecher regained his balance. "Everybody's here."

"Not here, Beecher. Nana's gone. My mum's died. I don't know what I'm gonna do. She's all I had."

"Oh, shit, Pengo, I'm so sorry. When; how?"

"This morning, they reckon. Arch had the doctor out to the pub last night 'cause he said she weren't right and she kept asking 'bout me as if she thought I was working behind the bar. But the bar is nothing but a jumble of firewood 'cause the insurance hasn't been sorted. Doc said she was a little warm; had a slight fever, that she was right as rain otherwise. But Arch said it didn't feel right, and he should know 'cause he goes right back with her. They went to school together, those two."

Beecher felt the sides of the trash can give a little under his weight.

"I know," he said, "they were pretty good mates."

"Anyway," Pengo said, with his eyes filling, "Arch settled her back upstairs in bed and gave her some aspirin and he stayed back for a while, reading from the book she had on the go, some romance bollocks, she loved those, couldn't get enough of 'em."

"And the Doc had gone?"

"Yeah, said he couldn't stay 'cause it wasn't an emergency."

Beecher jerked sideways as the metal beneath his foot crumpled. He grabbed for the window surround with his full weight bearing on the edge of the can.

Pengo carried on regardless, "Arch said he locked up downstairs and went across to Lola's, but he couldn't sleep, felt something was amiss. So he went back, early, around five a.m., and he found her downstairs, sitting in one of the burned-out booths, fully-dressed, eyes staring blindly into space, nursing a packet of fags and a vodka and orange..."

Beecher convulsed like a rag doll in a dog's mouth, and he was gone. The trash can concertinaed and rock 'n roll's newly ordained prince was sent sprawling onto the dirt with a handful of wire screen mashed into a tight ball in his right palm. He felt a tingle, saw the shredded ends of the screen spearing his flesh and gently plucked them free. Pink depressions darkened with shiny new blood. *Fuck.*

Pengo hadn't even noticed he was gone.

"...she loved her vodka and orange, not as much as *Pernod* with a splash of blackcurrant, but ever since she'd had those headaches, she'd been on the *Smirnoff.*"

A muted whine crept past a fluffy white gag and drifted over Pengo's shoulder. A simple utterance of *"Please"* and *"Help,"* defying the barrier of language, like the call of the wild, or the tears of grief, or the lust of humankind.

Beecher brushed dirt from his ass and knees, "You gotta let the woman out, Pengo."

His plea fell on deaf ears.

"PENGO!" he shouted, seeing focus return to his friend's glassy eyes.

"You gotta let her out of that room, mate. It don't matter how much she was fuckin' with your head, no good's gonna come of this if the police roll in and she's still tied up. They don't fuck around over here."

Pengo looked down at Beecher, and then back at the cleaning woman lying on a bed of crumpled linen. He disappeared from the window and Beecher heard his soft atonement - Nana's name; a heartfelt apology mixed in with a little residual irritation, and then, finally, compliance. The girl was released of her bonds and she bolted, somersaulting over the single bed, chipping several fingernails as she yanked at a flimsy chain and a rattling deadbolt, finally bursting from the room with a piercing, primal screech.

Beecher jogged back around and found the door open. He waited a few moments for his eyes to adjust to the darkened innards.

"You in here, mate?"

Pengo's fetal form was curled into blankets on the floor. He was an empty shell. A shirtless, empty shell.

"We're gonna get you home, sharpish," Beecher said. "Snooze is getting word to Eeva and she'll book you a flight out. You cool with that?"

"Who's gonna do the lights and the sound?"

"That's the least of your worries, we'll muddle through. You switch your thoughts to giving Nana a good send-off."

"Death seems like such a fucking waste of time," Pengo mused.

"Who's time?"

"Mine. Yours. Everyone's."

"Mate, this is not the time to be going deep. Your Mum loved life, so don't dwell on the dark stuff. There was no brighter star in the room when she was standing next to you. We all saw that. She was so proud of her little boy, raising you all on her own, seeing you take charge of the pub when all of the other blokes in her life had fucked off."

"Feels pointless."

"Now you sound like a spoiled child."

"It's alright for you, think of everything you've done and everything you can still do."

The words were out before Beecher could stop them, "That's why we have to make each moment count."

"Oh, fuck off, I give you passion and you give me a sermon."

"I'm just saying."

"I do make every moment count, but I want more. I need more time. Nana needed more time. Give me that and I'll shut up."

Another trite comment tripped from Beecher's lips, "A man's got to know his limitations."

Pengo lifted his head and eyed Beecher, "Oh, fuck you and your existential bullshit. If limitations defined a man, we'd all be living in caves. Beethoven was deaf, in the fucking 1700's! If he took your advice he might as well have curled up in a corner and waited for the Grim Reaper to come knocking."

Beecher toed Pengo's ribs, "Curled up in a corner?"

"You know what I mean."

"No, I don't," Beecher said. "Your Mum died in a place that she loved."

The air-conditioner's thermostat clicked on. The open window had sucked in warm air along with a legion of flies and the room was now stifling and thick with bugs.

"My mother loved the seaside," Pengo challenged. She wanted to retire in Bournemouth or Brighton, own a guest house, or something. She was saving for it. See, there was no fucking use in saving all that cash. She coulda been spending all of her money on new clothes and a new car and…"

"Maybe she wanted to save all that cash so that she could leave her son a wedge big enough that he might be able to buy his very own business 'cause she knew she was dying?"

The words hung in the air like moths flapping around a bulb. Beecher didn't know if he'd gone too far. Pengo floundered, the concept of being excluded from anything concerning his mother was working its way through fields of grief and uncertainty.

Finally, "What do you mean, she knew?"

"She did, mate, she told me. And she told Snooze. She said that her world would stop turning before she'd see another summer."

"And you didn't think to share that with me?"

"She made us promise; said we had to be strong for you; said that if you knew then you'd be fussing around her all the time, and no one wants to live with that reminder every day."

Pengo brought up his knees and sank his head onto folded arms and the swim trunks were drawn tighter, neatly separating two hairy balls that surfaced like weather buoys riding out a storm.

Beecher shuddered, knelt beside his friend and said,

"Mate, you are the glue. You are the reason we're all together; you're the reason we're a family. Nana saw that. We're all lost in some form or another, and she knew you'd keep us straight."

Pengo reached out and his friend was there. The tears flowed, wetting Beecher's shirt to the skin. And then the tears stopped and there was silence and there was reminiscing, and then there were smiles and there were laughs.

And then there were shots fired.

Beecher raced from the room directly into the strafing glare of red and blue lights sitting atop a police cruiser. The vehicle sat empty, doors wide open, abandoned. The crowd that had gathered and gawked so openly were now cowering in the shadows or scattering across the car park like olympic sprinters wearing frilly aprons.

Another round was fired. It came from the pool area. A single blip of white against the purple dusk. The blinding array on the police cruiser sucked the depth perception from Beecher's vision and he stumbled over the day manager's chair, shoving a boot through the narrow folds of frayed webbing and dragging the clumsy obstacle thirty feet before shaking it free. Twenty paces further and Snooze tackled him from behind.

"It's the motel manager, he's gone mental. The cleaner that Pengo tied up saw him laughing. She went fuckin' berserk, launched at him and chewed his fuckin' ear to a pulp. Cops arrived as it was going off and the fat bloke lifted a gun from one of their holsters and started bangin' away."

"Where are the lads?"

"Scarpered. I think Fez is over by the wall and Harry's in the pool with his snorkel."

"And Eeva and Luna?"

"They're good, they left a while ago. The Glitter Boys took them to sort out flights for Pengo."

"Rosy, too?"

"Haven't seen him. In his room, maybe?"

Sirens, distant and hysterical, pushed through the confused ranting coming from poolside. Beecher and Snooze belly-crawled along the perimeter of the chain link fence that enclosed the commotion. The fat man reclined on the diving board. He raged at the sky, popping off a random bullet or two, shooting at the stars. The side of his head was a molten mess of sticky blood and collapsed flesh. A flashlight flicked on and a gun barrel was trained. *Bang. Bang.* Gunpowder flashes served and returned. The fat man was unscathed but from behind the comparative safety of a *Coke* machine, one of the police officers let out a sharp squeal. His shrill protest cut the night as another bullet shattered the *Colgate* smile of the sun-drenched, bikini-clad reveler adorning the lighted front panel. The shot pierced an orderly formation of cans of *Mountain Dew* and turned the loose change receptacle into thirty bucks of shrapnel made up of nickels, dimes and quarters. The fat man howled with delight, saw the officer dive for cover and took aim. His chubby index finger wrapped around the trigger and he pulled. Click. *Shit.* The weapon was lobbed and splashed into the deep end. The cops came out of hiding and rushed towards the fat man. He stayed on the diving board, bouncing his girth up and down like a gelatinous yo-yo.

"Get him," one of the officers said, brandishing his weapon. The second cop skipped around like a lost puppy.

"Huh? How?"

"Go out, on the board."

"It'll break. It's touching the water now."

The fat man stood up and pulled a pack of smokes from his jeans and sparked up. Still bouncing, the top of the board submerging on every downstroke. The cops shouted; fatty ignored them, choosing to drop his pants instead. He fumbled under his belly, released his cock from folds of sweaty flesh and pissed a perfectly-yellow, glistening arc. Beecher and Snooze caught the whole show from twenty feet away. They suppressed giggles as the officers strutted and huffed.

"Shoot him," they heard the unarmed one say.

"For taking a piss?"

"No, for shooting at us."

"But he doesn't have a gun no more."

"But he did. No one will know. Do it now. I'll back you up."

"Are you sure?"

The fat man turned his back to the water and faced the officers, still clutching his groin. His head was tilted back and he grinned madly. Beecher immediately caught his breath; Snooze took a second to realize the man's hand was pumping like a windmill in a hurricane.

"Oh, Jesus," Snooze said, partly impressed, mostly disgusted. "He's rubbin' one out."

The cops' faces were drained white as ghosts and the fat man let out a roar that filled the sky, and the armed officer succumbed to reflexes of fear and confusion and contempt and together, he and the fat man shot their loads. Both chambers were emptied. The fat man's seed spilled over his knuckles, and the cop's bullet exited the .38 handgun at just shy of 500 mph, whistling between the fat man's legs, scorching his scrotum and singeing bulbous ass cheeks, enjoying unimpeded flight for the span of *Pinkie's* car park, defying the heavy swing door that kept lecherous teens from catching sight of bare-breasted waitresses hoisting trays of rare T-bones and foil-wrapped baked potatoes over the heads of sales managers and truckers, and buried itself in the heavy mahogany surround of the greeter's podium.

Fifteen squad cars arrived on scene to cordon off the area and sequester witnesses and it was only when the headcount was taken that Beecher and the gang realized Harry was missing.

"No way, he can't still be under?" Snooze was appalled at their oversight.

Fez was astounded, and quite impressed.

"Nothing by halves," he said. "Harold Floom does nothing by halves."

The band inched their way to the side of the pool. Reflected light had turned the water black as ink. Fez stooped down and slapped the surface, shouted,

"Harry, c'mon lad, it's all over."

On the other side of the pool, a hand broke the surface and Harry's goggled face came clear of the water. He pulled the snorkel from between his lips with a slurping, smacking sound and flashed a wide, toothy grin. He dog-paddled over and was lifted shivering into the warm air.

"Gets fuckin' cold when you stay down a while," he said.

Statements were provided and contact details were taken and assurances were made that none of the band members would be expected to appear before the local courts. The fat man's ensuing testimony, protesting that he'd been the subject of attempted murder by the police, was summarily dismissed owing to the absence of any physical evidence and he would be duly sentenced to fifteen years in the state penitentiary for aggravated assault with a deadly weapon. Curiously, the charge of having a wank on a diving board in a public place while intoxicated was omitted by the prosecution. Having his ear chewed off by a rabid member of the janitorial staff seemed punishment enough.

Fortunately, Pengo's situation was never mentioned as none of the cleaning staff had hung around.

"Undocumented workers," Snooze said. "I think Nana was looking out for you, Pengo. How 'bout a toast?"

The lads gathered poolside. Fez floated on a rubber whale. Harry massaged pruned ridges of peach-colored flesh. Pengo had donned his favorite vest and Snooze twirled his trumpet and beer cans were popped.

"To a mother to us all," Beecher said.

"To the most gracious lady White City has ever known," Harry said.

"To the best steak and kidney pie.., ever," Fez added.

"To the heart and soul of our wee little family," Snooze offered.

Pengo had the last word.

"God bless you, Mum, I love you, wherever you are."

Chapter Twenty-Six

El Gran Cañón

Sunrise, red as lava, kissed the desert good morning, brushing the face of the earth, nudging sleepy creatures awake to stretch and to groom and to hunt.

At the edge of a ruler-straight horizon, a cloud of dust ballooned from the surface. It was a cavalry charge of riders, leather-clad, with faces hidden under helmets with blackened visors. Beecher Stowe stood alone on a moonscape that was at once featureless and breathtaking. He was small here. He was a child here. He imagined the ground shuddering against the mechanical roar of the riders. They commanded chariots of steel, careening through patches of scrub and across stony furrows packed hard as concrete by wind and ice and time. Time was everything, and it was nothing. It was the ambivalence of the universe, scorning reflections of life and death. Time passes. Time slips by. Time to go.

Beecher walked over to a pick-up and the ground was chalk-white with frost. He slid behind the steering wheel, noticed that a thermometer taped to the sun visor read thirty-one degrees Fahrenheit. The engine ticked over and the heater vents streamed warm air, and together the sound was that of a purring lion. Music spilled from a dashboard speaker. It was a refrain; a fade buried in a wash of reverb, *I Can See For Miles.* He ejected the cassette, thumbed the latch of a leather case and filed it amongst orderly rows of annotated plastic. He selected a freshly recorded C90, popped the cover and fed the tape into the mouth of the player. *Click,* Rewind; *Click,* Play. "*On the first part of the journey....*"

He'd brought along precisely 1825 songs. Essential listening; classics, honed from the borderless songbook that is rock 'n roll and jazz and soul and blues. Alphabetized by artist, of course. Only a chump would do it by song. If the histrionics of a few time travelers were to dictate his future, he figured that before it all went completely pear-shaped, he'd season the passing of the seasons, as it were, with a soundtrack; a daily appreciation of who he might have been, or may still be. A year's worth should do it. It seemed like a good way to exhaust every emotion. Listening to five of the greatest songs ever written, every day, for precisely 365 days, was suitably intimidating. It was, he thought, medicine for insanity. After that, he'd be famous or shunned or back working in the pub. Either way, the muse would be well nourished. Fate, he'd argue with a seductive wink, was being severely lubed.

He looked through the dusty back window, checked the bed of the truck. Eeva slept, curled and still, wrapped in thick Navajo blankets. Her feet were exposed, brown and delicate. A sky-blue summer dress lay crumpled on the tailgate, kicked free, shed like armor after a battle.

"...'cause there ain't no one for to give you no pain."

Within the span of the state, on a drive that took no more than four hours, the temperature had dropped sixty degrees, calling for the roadside purchase of sweaters and jackets.

Beecher stepped down from the cab and stoked life back into a small campfire. Embers burned like rubies and soon a metal coffee pot was burbling like a forest brook, with clouds of steam puffing from the spout, vanishing quickly against the strengthening light of the day. He set out two cups and poured. By the time he had put the pot back on the flame, there were murmurs from the bed of the truck.

Eeva sat up and her hair was tousled like white straw and he thought his heart might break.

"Cold," she announced through clenched teeth, "...and don't look at me. I'm hideous."

"You are many things," Beecher said, handing her the coffee. "Hideous is not even close."

"You were talking and I fell asleep."

"That was seven hours ago."

"Did you sleep?"

"A little," Beecher said, with a nod to a bedroll next to the fire. "It was a long night. I dreamed I was out here with you, staring at the half-erected rigging of a sound stage the size of a Hollywood studio. On the horizon, over there," he pointed. "From a quarter-mile distant, there was a ragged structure scraping the sky with crooked fingers of black steel and cranes were hoisting giant orbs of glass onto platforms that ringed a stadium-sized field lined with seating and concessions and..."

"You're a dreamer," she said. "That's good for business."

"Maybe, but it was too real. And to top it off, two hundred thousand people were all singing the same song; my song, at the top of their lungs, and the sky erupted purple and blue and…"

The mechanical signature of the approaching caravan filtered through the air.

"Anyway," he sighed, "…it doesn't matter." He nodded in the direction of the road, "They're a few minutes away."

Eeva pulled a heavy wool sweater from a shopping bag, made to slip it over her head, said,

"I'm afraid I had no such adventure, the only other place I've had such a dreamless sleep is in my little one-room house on the beach."

"Do you spend a lot of time there?"

"As much as I can. It's perfect. No people; no noise other than the sound of breakers smashing into the shore. I drive into town once a week, leave it longer if it rains and the roads wash out, stock up on food and books."

"Books?"

"*Books*, he says, as if they were written by the devil's hand."

"No, I mean, *just* books? No music?"

"Not there. That place is just for me. No work allowed."

Beecher focused on the vehicles approaching.

"You and Tomek, you're a pretty good team considering all the time you've spent together."

"You don't think it should be that way?"

"Just sayin'. Me and Pengo are bound to get on each others' nerves if we're stuck together for more than a few hours."

"There's been a lot of moving around. Reinvention has been necessary for all of us."

"All of us?"

"The Outriders. We're family, our fates are intertwined."

"I promised myself I wouldn't dwell on it," Beecher said, "It's kinda hard not to…"

He stalled. Again. He always stalled. Right here; right when he needed to be articulate and smart and insightful, not dumb as a bag of hammers.

"…flesh and blood are too real to ignore, 'cause there's you, and them, and him. All from another world."

"Same world; another time."

"I realized last night that I've been stuck on the question, *how?* Last night, watching you drift off to sleep, it struck me that I should be asking, *why?*"

"Hans would say you were starting to accept the unacceptable, and that's a good thing. It means your mind is opening beyond what you thought was expected."

Beecher shrugged an eternally confused, *"I dunno,"* said, "Where's this beach house?"

She smirked, "On an island, in the Caribbean."

"Of course it is."

He walked back to the fire.

"Oh, and by the way," he said, shoulders raised in a defiant shrug. "I know it's not your thing," but here's wishing you a very, Merry Christmas."

The Outriders flanked Hans Tomek's 4x4. They arrived at speed, skidding to an abrupt stop and raising a curtain of sand and dust. When the air cleared, Beecher and Eeva were there. He brushed dirt from his T-shirt and jeans and wiped at watering eyes. She was resplendent; untouched by nature, wearing the dress that was as blue as the morning sky.

"How does this happen?" Beecher was dumbfounded.

"How does what happen?"

"This," he said, batting at his clothes, "Look at this, I'm covered. You look as though you've just walked out of a beauty salon."

"It's there, I just don't fuss with it."

Tomek's entourage dismounted and gathered in a group. Greetings and embraces were exchanged. Beecher was immediately taken with the latest renditions of their motorcycles - black BMWs, kitted out for desert warfare, he joked, with knobby tires, high fenders, supplemental fuel and water bottles bolted to the frame. And aerials. Each bike sported a radio antenna that whipped gently in the breeze. Amelio gave him the guided tour.

"Now we're connected even more than we were before."

He showed Beecher how the riders communicated with two-way radios hard-wired into the electrical system.

"Hans believes that the more we share, the happier we will be."

"He's one persuasive bloke."

Beecher let the comment hang, like bait, hoping for an easy bite.

"Yes, he's quite the master," Amelio said.

Time for a little rattling of the rod.

"That's it?"

Amelio raised an eyebrow, *"Huh?"*

"What's his power? How's he get what he gets, or do what he does? What's in the secret sauce?

Amelio was stone-faced.

"When you've seen everything, it's hard to be impressed. His power is his patience. And for those that try to impress him the most, he simply suggests that whatever it is they care about is no longer relevant. It might be warmongering, it might be smoking, or driving without seatbelts, or love or sex or food. What you once craved; what you thought you couldn't live without suddenly becomes tasteless and unappealing. I saw him stand with a billionaire; a total stranger. They spoke for two minutes and then he walked away. Over the next year, the rich man liquidated his entire fortune, gave it all away to the needy."

"So, he's a mystery?" Beecher offered.

"Yes. A mystery."

They walked a little way off, conversing at ease, unafraid to nurture the inevitable periods of silence.

Amelio gestured to a line of low trees a few miles away.

"Have you seen, El Gran Cañón?

The inflections of his native tongue ran the words together quickly, so he added, "…the big hole."

"Not yet. I've heard about it, seen pictures. We came out here last night to sleep under the stars. Eeva said it was vital that I felt the tranquility of the desert before I witnessed such beauty."

"And did you?"

"I felt lost. Like I was drowning under the sky. Does that sound crazy?"

"A little. But I have been to London and the sky is always a gray blanket, so I can imagine you must feel like you are flying through space out here."

The mention of London ignited a sudden flash of memory; a violent explosion. Time compressed and Beecher swayed on his feet. Amelio reached out and grabbed him by the shoulder.

"Steady, my friend. Do you need to sit down?"

"No, I'm fine," Beecher said, and then he took a knee.

The other riders joined, forming a circle around him. Beecher stared through their legs, caught sight of Tomek and Eeva, standing side-by-side, watching intently.

"I'm sorry," Beecher said. "I don't know what's come over me."

Fidelia, the brave one, stooped to meet his gaze.

"You are traveling," she said. "When the memories come we can let them wash over us, or we can return to the time and place. Only the special ones have this gift."

She stood and rejoined the circle and Beecher surveyed the group, twisting his head, squinting at flares of blinding sunlight as he passed between their expressions.

"It was the blast in the pub," he said. "It was so real, like I was there again, watching from across the street, and then I was inside the bar, and then close to the crush of bodies. I saw Herbie. He was laughing and then he was a mangled mess. I felt the rumbling of the beams as they collapsed and the lick of flames and Herbie's screams came from all around, like banks of air raid sirens."

Beecher stood, spoke with confidence, "Yeah, that's it, it was like the beginning of a war, a barrage of shellfire. And then I was walking through the rubble, across the car park. I saw some skinheads slapping each other on the back as though they'd just scored a goal or won the pools or something. I saw it, clear as day. One of 'em had on a green flying jacket and black drainpipes cuffed at the ankle."

"We've seen this too," Fidelia said. "We know this one, we know what he did." And then, in almost a whisper, "We protect the investment."

"Ride with us," Amelio said. "I think it's time for you to see the world fall away at your feet."

He guided Beecher to where his motorcycle was parked. The others mounted up, dispensing with helmets and jackets in the building heat. Engines whirred into life with the press of thumbs and the twist of wrists. Amelio and Fidelia rode pillion.

The group abandoned any sense of formation in favor of racing across the open desert. The loose ground was alien to Beecher. His grip was too tight and he careened the bike sideways, losing his front wheel to a running depression, tumbling over the handlebars, face-planting in the exposed roots of a patch of salt-brush.

Fidelia came alongside and killed her engine.

"Ride like you are holding your lover," she said, and then with a cheeky grin, "...like you are holding Eeva."

Before Beecher could protest, she had spun up the revs and was skillfully carving a channel in the earth, rooster-tailing a stream of sand and shale in her wake.

Beecher pulled the bike upright and thumbed the starter. The engine hesitated and then caught with a gleeful roar and he muscled the machine's bulk clear in a clamorous and chaotic display of determination that was applauded by the entire group. He was soon within the pack, fighting tooth and nail to regain his pride. Bent almost double in a jockey's stance, with eyes streaming salty tears, he misunderstood the gradual deceleration of the other bikes as a celebration of his dignity-fueled accomplishment. The ground was a blur of multicolored sand and vast as an ocean. To his left and right, the Outriders fell away and his elation evaporated when he recognized the line of scrub growing quickly in scale. Gnarled branches reached for daylight, clawing at his arms like wizened old men brandishing wooden canes, and gaps in fat bushes hinted at the canyon's edge as rays of morning sun speared the thickets with shafts of blinding light.

FUCK! Beecher backed off and the mechanical roar dissolved. He slammed on the rear brake and locked up the back wheel, raising a shower of dirt and gouging a narrow, wavering valley in his wake. The distance halved and then halved again and still, he was racing to the edge of the earth. He dragged his left foot and filled his boot with desert scrub, and he flung his weight across the gas tank, pulling on the handlebars with all of his strength. The machine was petulant and combative, resistant to any detour. Beecher heeled the mass of steel over, and his knee dragged along the baked and broken soil, shredding denim and lining the innards with streaks of new blood. Slowly, the bike veered, falling into a languid turn, coming reluctantly to a stop inches from a two thousand foot drop.

Beecher killed the engine, He stepped from the machine and let it fall into the dirt. Sticky sweat cascaded from every pore and coursing adrenaline filled his racing heart. Before him, stretched an expanse that filled the extremities of his vision and arrested his breath as if a fist had been buried in his gut. The world had ended at his feet and he couldn't string together a single, rational thought. With the rising wind pushing at his body, steady and strong, he beheld layers of rock painted all the colors of the rainbow, and plateaus, flat as a blacksmith's anvil, stepped with deep gashes of inky blackness, and valleys of rising mist and falling water, and sheer cliff faces and fields of lumbering boulders, and a winding river, thin as the stroke of a pen.

"A new morning is begun," Tomek said. "What memories will you build upon this day of days, Beecher Stowe?"

The voice startled Beecher. He turned, found a vision in black. Out of place in the environment, pressed and polished, the suede Fedora was being toyed with by his hands. Thirty paces further back, Eeva's silhouette was visible through a dust-laden windscreen.

Beecher made to extend a hand in greeting and it shook and he withdrew it, plunging it into the safety of his jeans pocket. Tomek noticed, said nothing. He turned their attention to the magnificent expanse. The morning sun was cutting the crater in half. Day and night in plain sight. The horizon was visible as a jagged rim, fourteen miles distant as the heat haze had yet to manifest and obscure precious details, and the floor of the canyon was impossibly serene.

"I remember the first time I saw this place," he said. "It had been unknown to me, in writing or pictures. Until I stood as you do now, I never would have believed the world could be swallowed. My everlasting memory will be the absurdly deafening silence."

Beecher struggled to engage but he did not have the words. He wanted to be profound at this moment; he wanted to meet the challenge of this moment. Instead, he nodded, and smiled, like a mute child.

The Outriders returned. They came at speed, arriving in the turbulence of exhaust and roaring engines and there were laughs and lighthearted parodies and Beecher took them on the chin, in good humor.

To Hans Tomek, he said, "The prospect of my body ending up splattered like roadkill seems to have given your entourage a bloody good laugh."

Amelio cut in, bending over his bruised and battered motorcycle, "Ah, this machine would never let such a tragedy occur. She is a loyal conveyance, sound of mind and strong of pistons."

He laughed and it was infectious.

"She was instructed to shepherd you like a lost lamb in this vast desert."

"Well, extend my thanks, in whatever language she understands. I'll be over here counting my blessings."

Tomek beckoned Beecher and they moved away from the pack. They walked for half a mile, following a path of awkward switchbacks that had been cut into the cliff face many centuries ago. Loose stones clattered underfoot and were silenced only as they were ejected out into the void. They halted at a point where the path elbowed the abyss and they took to the shade of a petrified tree that protruded from the limestone plate, lonely as a prairie church.

"The canyon sleeps now," Tomek said. "People come here in droves, looking for postcards and T-shirts and they gawk like fools with their mouths open for only minutes, then stand with their backs to this wonder, preening and posing for photos that will end up in shoeboxes under beds. They look but they do not see that there's a pulse here. And a temper. This is a cradle awaiting a birth."

He pointed to a discoloration forming against the aqua blue sky, a smear of darkness bringing a squall to wash the soil, and to fill rock pools, and to seep into cracks where drops of crystal clear water will settle cool and still.

"This place creates its own weather. That disturbance, that massive force of nature that looks so distant can be on you in no time, and you'll never hear it coming."

Tomek was silent for a moment, toeing the ground, testing the strength of a bough, leaning forward with head tilted, scanning the darkness of the emptiness below. Beecher looked on, holding an unlit cigarette between his fingers, settling into a state of reverential stillness. He thought the moment warranted being photographed - the man in black, poised precariously next to the tree; the backdrop of the weathered canyon providing subjective context; the approaching storm pressing into the frame like an unwelcome intruder.

Tomek quizzed, "Do you remember your first kiss?"

"I do. I messed it up, royally," Beecher said. "She was a year older and a foot taller but when I held her hand it was like pulling on a silk glove. It was the first time I felt powerless."

"What does it take to spark that memory?"

"Well, it happened in the alley behind Franklin's chip shop down by the river, so I'd guess just being around that area, or maybe hearing a song from that time. To be honest, ever since then the smell of a battered Cod has made me a little jittery. Pengo says I get too sentimental about stuff like that."

"But how does it make you feel, now?"

"I dunno, a little sad; a little envious."

"Go on, tell me why."

"I guess because it can never happen again. It can only happen differently."

Tomek focused on one area of the canyon wall. The rising sun was drawing back a line of shadows that seemed to shiver their way across the cliff face revealing a craggy descent of jagged sandstone plunging 5,000 feet to an isolated grass meadow carpeting the valley floor.

"Look there," he said, distracted. "Have you ever seen such a sight?"

Beecher crept closer to the edge and he felt the first waves of vertigo force tiny beads of sweat to his brow. He gripped the tree roots with both hands and looked over. Layers of crystals buried within granite outcrops surrounded the meadow and burned like fires blazing within a village settlement, and they twinkled in hues of amber and crimson.

Tomek continued, "Okay, now imagine that the recollection of your first fumbling encounter isn't just a brief distraction, that it is, in fact, a source of energy that when multiplied would be capable of transporting you wholly back through time."

The remark hung in the air like an eagle spiraling aimlessly through a summer thermal.

"In isolation, that memory demonstrates no physical power, but when you expand it to the consciousness of every sentient being on the planet, don't you think that the forces of time and space might have a little trouble reconciling the past from the present? That maybe these emotional touchstones could engender some sort of tear in the fabric of time? A tear through which an unwilling soul might plunge?"

"Sounds like science fiction," Beecher said. "The boundaries of language and culture would make that impossible. And then there's free will. You can't even get people in the same room to agree on what's for dinner."

"It's not a question of agreement," Tomek said. "It's all about emotion - anger, love, hate, pain - these amorphous weights we harbor; it's as if we're hauling monstrous sacks of coal on our backs just in case we feel the need to build a fire. The secret is setting the stage, so to speak, and tapping into the quieter recesses of the human brain and triggering a few of those unwilling sentiments. No one cries because they want to. It's a reflex. It's the same with memories, good, bad, and indifferent. They're all there waiting to be upset by some sort of pressure."

"Eeva's told you that I'm struggling with all of this."

"Of course, and it's why we're here. If you don't believe, it'll be like an anchor around your neck, and when the dust clears you'll never commit fully to anything. I know this because I've seen it."

Beecher shuffled back and stared up at the slow dissolution of a solitary cloud. He reeled like a drunk; like an icy wave was bowling his body through a monstrous surf.

"You can't just believe in the unbelievable," he said. "Faced with the impossibility of reason, how do you form an opinion on something that is... well, impossible."

"People do it every day, with no proof whatsoever," Tomek said. "Legend has it that centuries ago, a child was born on this day. A simple story that has upended history with such fantastic and unquantifiable suffering for as long as humankind has recorded their celebrations and their struggles. And yet, hearsay is enough. I don't think humanity realizes what power it holds."

"Or how gullible we are."

Tomek was animated; like he held the answer to the impossible question.

"Why can't music literally be time travel if anytime I hear it, I go there?"

Beecher shook his head in stern refusal.

"A memory isn't time travel."

"Of course it is."

"Not literally."

"Yes, literally." And then, "You just can't do it alone."

Tomek's voice adopted a tone of serenity that was unfamiliar to Beecher.

"I can't go home without you," he said. "You are my ticket out of here. There's nothing more powerful than memories, and that's what you have created, for millions of people. These thoughts don't just live in the past, they're the reason for our future. We need them like fuel; we burn them, and they're contagious, like laughter or sadness, and they can be set off like wildfires. It's why we tell stories of what's been and what may be. It's why we cultivate friendships and romances. We're marking time. The music you write; the stories we share, they're catalysts; they're sparks."

"What about the stuff that hasn't happened; stuff I haven't done or want to do?"

"Time holds no prejudice. Aspirations are simply memories that happen in the present."

Tomek removed his tailored leather jacket and folded it carefully, placing it at his feet. He unclipped the pocket watch from his vest and slid the timepiece into the lining of the coat. With boots kicked off and the Fedora topping off the bundle, Beecher saw that Hans Tomek was dressed in black dungarees gathered at the waist with a drawstring, and he was cloaked in a simple tunic of white cotton, bound at the wrists with a thin, leather cord, knotted as though by a child's hand. He gathered up a handful of rocks and climbed barefoot onto the bough, shuffling along its length until he was aligned with the edge of the path. He raised and sat with his back to the trunk, dangling his legs in the open air. The horizon was now muted with hazy colors and with dancing heat and somehow appeared less cruel.

Beecher said, "Why are we here? What is it with this place?"

"Well," Tomek said, "...best as I can explain, it's all about falling."

He winked and glanced down, saw a pair of falcons gliding through light and shade.

"Living as a castaway is like being injected with anesthetic," he said. "Your muscles are numbed but the brain ticks on and on and on. So you end up walking through life like you're on a conveyor belt. And life drifts past in slow motion. That's what I want to end. I want explosions of laughter and passion and sex and sadness. I want to feel all that I cannot feel. This huge rift in the earth's crust is the perfect sanctuary for our memories, a place of peace and solitude and majesty."

He pitched a single stone into the canyon.

"There goes one," he said. "That's the moment I met my true love."

He dropped another.

"...and that's the birth of my son by the firelight in our home. I can still see his mother's eyes, sparkling like stars, wet with tears of joy. It was just the three of us, snowbound for weeks at a time, surviving on game I had hunted through the summer and fall."

He was silent for a spell, lost to the past.

"I never had the time to teach my son to hunt," he said, in barely a whisper.

"And today, I would like to teach my son to hunt."

Beecher said, "Why is today so important?"

"Because today is his birthday."

Beecher felt a sudden lightness about his being. He met Tomek's gaze, level and expressionless.

"Today is also my birthday," he said.

"I know."

"In my coat pocket," Tomek said. "...there's a radio, take it out, will you?"

Beecher reached down and sorted through the pockets. The radio was a shortwave unit, capable of transmitting about ten miles in line of sight. Any obstructions, hills or trees, would reduce that drastically. The handset also received A.M. radio stations, a feature Tomek had insisted upon.

"The Outriders each have a unit," he said. "...so that we might enjoy a very special event."

Beecher frowned, clearly not following.

"You're up," Tomek said. "Tomorrow night, Hollywood Bowl, Los Angeles. 17,000 seats, completely sold out."

"You're having me on."

"Hardly. This is what we've been working toward. At roughly 10:30 P.M. tomorrow, the ascendance of Beecher Stowe and his band of misfits will be complete."

Beecher was breathless from the magnitude of the thought.

"In my wildest dreams…" he said, trailing off into silence.

Hans Tomek climbed down from the bough. He offered his hand to Beecher.

"Go now, young man. Be with your family; be with Eeva, she will guide you the rest of the way. I have instructed her to tell you all of what she knows."

"You're not coming?"

"No, I will be here, with my own family."

Beecher began the trek back up the cliff and when he'd navigated the first switchback he caught Tomek's eye.

"You dreamed and I answered, Beecher Stowe," Tomek shouted. "Don't ever forget, you dreamed and I answered."

When Beecher made it back to the campsite, Eeva was reclining in the front seat of the pickup. The radio played low. Christmas songs painted mental pictures of sweet candy canes and jingling bells and winter wonderlands. He was breathless from the hike and confused and he spilled his thoughts quickly in the hope she would do the same.

"Let's talk on the drive back," she said. "We have a bus to catch."

Meanwhile:

Rosy and the Glitter Boys were deep into their lunch.

"Corn on the cob," Rosy said, "…it's like gnawing on a bone, except that it tastes like pussy."

Snooze gagged a little.

"C'mon, man, have some."

Snooze checked the buttery slime oozing from Rosy's mouth and felt bile rise in his throat.

"No thanks. Listen, one of you needs to drive back out to the airport and pick up Fez and Harry. Pengo got off okay but the lads have lost the money I gave 'em for the taxi."

Earl was mentally counting dollar signs, said,

"What's it worth?"

"I'll suck undigested corn niblets out of your pert little asshole."

"Oooh, you want this pretty bad."

Eddie piped up,

"100 bucks, and you fill-up the car."

"50 dollars. And I thought Luna already gave you guys gas money."

The trio gave up greasy smiles, gestured at the spread on the table.

"Man's gotta eat."

Rosy vacuumed the last of the corn from his plate with lips pursed like a camel sucking a lemon.

Snooze countered with, "So what happened to the food money?"

Earl fingered a slimy rack of barbecue ribs. He ripped one free and set to work.

"Lost it last night…(slurp)… in a card game… (slurp). Strip poker. This chick was unbelievable, man. Tits worthy of a brass sculpture. She let me touch 'em."

Snooze checked out the room: upended chairs; ripped bedsheets; wall art askew.

"What the fuck else happened in here? Oh, I don't care, just don't get another speeding ticket. We could've toured Europe for the fines we already owe."

Snooze moped about for a bit. The motel was a ghost town. He went out to the pool. Luna was sitting under the shade of a tatty umbrella. The bikini Eeva had loaned her was too big everywhere it counted. *Not big enough,* according to Fez. Her hair was damp from a swim and she combed through its length while studying her prized tour ledger.

Snooze announced his presence with enough time and distance for her to cover up.

She didn't.

Yes.

"The Glitters are gonna get the lads," he said. "Need anything else while they're out?"

"No, all good. Did you have lunch?"

"Not yet. I thought Pengo was never gonna get off. He insisted on wrapping all of his souvenirs in newspaper which trebled the size of the case he needed, which set into motion another round of stress."

"But he was alright?"

"A few more tears. No doubt whoever sits next to him on the way home will get an earful and a few soggy hankies to boot."

"Did you know his Mum?"

"Nana? Yeah, she was like the matron in those *Carry On* movies. Larger than life, always in charge; always falling for the wrong bloke. Pengo was constantly having to cheer her up and get her motivated again. And like clockwork, she'd swear off the fellas, throw herself into her work. Then one night she'd get a little tipsy and cozy up to some wanker with a sports car who'd jangle his keys and promise the landlady a better life. As soon as they found out she didn't own the pub, they were off, leaving Pengo to mop up the mess. So, around and around it goes."

Snooze pulled up one of the sun loungers and squatted on the edge. Not too close, but he could smell the coconut lotion slathered on her peachy skin.

"When she took ill, it all changed. She took to her bed like a duck takes to water. Hardly ever got up, even if she weren't too bad. Pengo and Beecher did a fine job with running the pub. We reckon she just lost the will to carry on."

"So, what's next? What's the plan?"

Luna's soft Scottish brogue made the hairs on Snooze's arms stand on end and he ran his hands down their length.

"We're waiting on Beecher and Eeva…"

"No, your plan. In life?"

Snooze flashed a goofy smile and pressed his hands to his cheeks lest they showed too red.

"Living day-to-day, playing anywhere I can. Trying to take in all of this craziness."

"And when it's over?"

"Do you know something I don't?"

"No, but everything ends."

"I run a cafe most days; for an old friend of the family; they hit some hard times what with all the strikes."

"Married? Engaged? Girlfriend?"

Snooze laughed, "The bright lights of fry-ups and cups of tea."

"Well, you've got this now."

"Yeah, not sure if it's all it's cracked up to be."

"I guess the girl of your dreams is still out there."

"The girl of my dreams would never look my way."

Snooze recoiled from his accidental honesty.

"Where the fuck did that come from?"

His usual, ice-breaking snippet of Snooze-ology failed him.

"Come on, say something funny, a throwaway line; anything."

He chewed his lip like a Christmas toffee and his cheeks shone like two stoplights at midnight.

Luna seemed oblivious to his anxiety. She thumbed the ledger, said,

"I think I can find ten bucks for a couple of sandwiches. Fancy that?"

"Where shall we go? We don't have any wheels."

She pointed across the highway to the glass-fronted edifice plastered with garish posters advertising everything from tinned ham to boxes of soap powder, all at low, low prices. Luna mimicked perfectly the southern drawl of the T.V. commercial that had been running five times an hour, every hour, since they'd checked in.

"My mama taught me how to shop at *Piggly Wiggly*; there's savings in every aisle; it's about friends serving friends; down-home is down the street."

Snooze rightly applauded.

She tossed the book on the table, kicked her legs to the side of the lounger and that's when Snooze Silver's world changed. Forever. Luna stood up and arranged the loose-fitting lycra bottoms, seemingly unconcerned that he was less than two feet from the most exquisitely wrapped dimpled buttocks the Gods had ever created.

"C'mon," she instructed, "...I'm gonna whip us up a couple of masterpieces."

Snooze coughed, "Maybe you'd better change first? The folks in *Piggly Wiggly* might not be ready for… that."

"Ah," she said, "finally, a man that wants me to put my clothes on."

The supermarket was huge and cool and clean. Musak dripped from the ceiling, covers of pop hits, usually by warbling lounge singers. Occasionally an original version surfaced inspiring a few raised-eyebrow acknowledgments from bored checkout girls.

"I've never seen so much food," Luna said.

Snooze fondled a few watermelons.

"Wonder what they do with it when they throw it out. They can't sell it all, can they?"

"Dunno, maybe they give it to charity."

"Or pigs," Snooze said. "That's what they do at home. I've seen it, mountains of rotting vegetables. Pigs fuckin' love it."

He grabbed a basket and they strolled the lanes, pausing every now and then to study brightly colored labels. The breakfast cereal aisle brought the pair to a standstill.

"I want it all, Snooze said. "I want to try it all."

He began counting, inching his way along the selection.

"*Sugar Smacks, Count Chocula, Froot Loops, Cheerios, Capn' Crunch, Sir Grapefellow, Baron Von Redberry, Pink Panther Flakes, Crazy Cow,*

Klondike Pete's Crunchy Nuggets, Twinkles, Punch Crunch, Wackies, Moonstones, Lucky Charms..."

After eyeballing the fifty-eighth brand, an alarmingly ambiguous cereal called *Most*, he gave up.

"A seat by the pool, a bag of Fez's stash and I might just retire here."

"What're you gonna do for money?"

"I'll look after the motel, keep out the riff-raff..."

Luna finished his thought.

"And play a little jazz in the topless steakhouse of an evening," she said.

"Exactly."

Her laughter tripped across gloriously-moist lips and Snooze melted at both the sight and the sound. She'd dressed down for the first time - a blue T-shirt emblazoned with Saint Andrews' white cross, butt-hugging blue jeans, and scuffed tennis shoes.

"All nationalities will be welcome," he said with a wink. "Even Scotland."

She smoothed the wrinkles in her shirt by brushing her hands across her breasts, "Gotta represent."

They wandered the surgically-lit aisles, singing Christmas carols, playing word games with food labels, courting the obvious innuendo. *Hubba Bubba* gum was easy; *Cheese Balls*, even easier; *Pudding Pops*, was creative; a TV dinner called *Beans and Franks* made Snooze howl and blow a sheet of snot out of his nose. When Luna went to bat with a description of how *Swiss Cheese* was so named, he thought he might need to be resuscitated. Preferably by her.

They gathered ingredients, all packaged in thick cellophane - white bread, which looked like bread but had the consistency of a rubber doormat; some round meat dotted with red and green peppers that looked like astronaut food; squares of sliced cheese sporting a radioactive-yellow hue, Snooze noted, that exactly matched the color of his old Ford Capri; some ketchup and mustard; a head of lettuce the size of a soccer ball; a tin of baked beans; a literal sack of potato chips; a box of powdered donuts; some plastic forks and knives, and bag of napkins. The total cost was $9.49.

"Under budget," Luna said. "That's the way we shop in Scotland."

"Clearly, this country is wasted on you," Snooze said.

Fez and Harry were waiting by the pool. Luna ripped them both a new asshole for losing the cash. They floated a rehearsed defense but it was lame and she cut them down, threatening to dock their wages. Fez fell out of love with her on the spot.

"Fuckin' bitch, she can't talk to us like that. I pulled her skinny backside out of that bus. She would've cooked like a fuckin' Sunday roast."

Harry was more compliant, "She's just doing her job; just like you, doing the best for the boss."

"Yeah, but you can't speak to a member of the band that way," he huffed. "What if I fuckin' left?"

"They'd get someone else."

This sudden awareness of his fractious existence was sobering. He sulked for an hour and then all was good.

The Glitter Boys produced three bottles of Rum and a case of beer and sun loungers were set into a circle and an impromptu Christmas party took flight. Rosy toasted Snooze and the lads and the Glitters separately. He preached long and loud of the Lord's hand in bringing Beecher Stowe to the world, and he spent a full five minutes taking a misty-eyed stroll down memory lane, *My Papa was a great ol' man...* Luna got a bear hug that left her panting for breath and then he downed a Dixie cup brimmed with Rum, chased by a few cans of beer. He belched and swayed a little, and then he sang like an angel, just shy of a full soprano, *Let It Snow...*

Under a canopy of colored bulbs strung around the pool deck, the temperature was a balmy 84 degrees and the laughs and songs flowed smooth and easy. As dusk fell, thoughts turned to home and drunken promises tripped from slurring mouths. Fez, Snooze, and Harry pried open the lock on the manager's office and dialed Arch Pudding in London.

"Whatchya, mate!"

The line crackled like a Sunday broadsheet.

"Who the fuck is this?"

Arch's voice was so very small.

"It's Fez, we're here, we're all here. Where are you?"

"Home, you just called me, you twat."

"Merry Christmas, Pudding," Harry dribbled into the mouthpiece. "Get it?"

"Yes, yes, ha bleedin' ha! Did Pengo get off okay?"

Snooze took the receiver, "Arch, it's Snooze, yeah, he arrives tomorrow midday. Will you be able to pick him up?"

"Alright, Snoozy, yeah, we'll get him, don't worry. How's Beecher? Is he there?"

"Not right now. He's out in the desert with his bird. He's back later."

"When you comin' home?"

"Soon, mate, we'll have a few bevvys and fill you in."

Snooze swore he heard Arch's voice crack a little, but couldn't be sure.

"You give him my best and say Happy Christmas for me, won't you? Tell him I miss him; tell him I never meant any harm; tell him I love him, won't you?"

"Of course, mate. You fuckin' take care. We love you too!"

Snooze rang off.

"I think Arch is gettin' soft in his old age."

Five thousand two hundred and sixty-seven miles away, Arch Pudding laid the phone back in its cradle. On a transistor radio, *Little Drummer Boy* played. His cheeks were wet with tears. He sobbed until bile scorched his throat and his sleeves were sodden. On the bed, a leather belt was looped into a noose. In the middle of the room, a chair sat beneath the light fixture. Pinned to the door, a note was scribbled in barely legible handwriting. Arch toyed with the belt for a few minutes, let out a deep sigh and undid the noose.

"Probably wouldn't have held anyway," he said.

Chapter Twenty-Seven

Beecher fretted. He marched along a line of bags. Counting again.

Post-Christmas blues; post-Christmas hangover. He'd arrived at the high point of the poolside celebration. Nothing else to do except catch up. Eeva broke Luna off from the pack. She needed at least one clear head to help with the arrangements for their departure.

"There's either too many or not enough," Beecher moaned. "Who's missing?"

His skull pounded from the inside, a persistent ache above his left eye. He squinted like a pirate without a patch.

"That's everyone's," Snooze said. "No one's left anything behind."

"Where's the big yellow one; the one with stickers from Marbella on it?"

"Long gone, mate. Pengo took it."

Beecher made a note in his little black book.

"Leave all this for Luna," Snooze said. "She's got it covered."

"What about the Glitter Boys?"

"They went shopping for Indian jewelry; reckon they can make a mint flogging that turquoise stuff back in New York."

Beecher's ear lobes turned the color of a baboon's ass.

"We're supposed to be on the fuckin' road by now."

"They're gonna make their own way; said they'd probably beat us to the venue 'cause you were so busy with your thumb up your ass counting bags."

Beecher was about to sound off when a loud honk announced the tour bus turning into the motel car park.

Fez and Harry scrambled aboard as soon as the door opened, testing bunks, rifling through cupboards, jostling each other for the right to christen the bog.

"We're not sleeping on it," Snooze said. "It's only a six-hour drive."

The lads wore cowboy hats and suede vests. Fez had gone all in and strapped on a pair of leather chaps.

"Nice to see you're wearing trousers underneath that lot," Beecher said. "We've got female company on this trip so best behavior, right?"

Bags and gear were loaded and the premises were scouted for leftovers one last time. Beecher ducked into Pengo's old room. The window screen flapped open and the hum of flies was industrial. A six-pack sat on the dresser. Beecher took a can and popped the tab. Eeva's shadow fell across the doorway.

"Hair of the dog?"

He nodded and then drained the brew.

She looked about the room, felt its emptiness, said, "He'll be landing soon; he'll be happier being back at home."

"Death is so fucking inconvenient," Beecher scoffed.

"For the dead? Or you?"

"For the living…"

Eeva perched on the arm of an easy chair that looked like it had been pulled from a trash pile.

"…it changes everything."

"It requires an adjustment."

"It requires abandonment," Beecher said. "Pengo's never gonna be the same, his world's been upended; his routine's gonna be fucked."

"In time, after he grieves, don't you think he might be freed up to see what else is out there, …in life, that is?"

"He's not that sorta bloke."

"You mean, he wasn't that sorta bloke."

"See, it changes everything."

"All I see is you being a little bit scared of what it means for you."

"I'm tired of making plans around everyone else. *It wasn't supposed to be this way.*"

"Let go of the reins," Eeva said, "…you might find the reward is a little sweeter when it's unexpected."

"Some of us don't have unlimited time."

The remark wasn't intended as a slight, but it wasn't retracted either. He studied her face. Beneath faded blue jeans and a *Deep Purple* T-shirt, she was a statue of ivory. He should've tried it on with her in the desert; injected a little equilibrium into their relationship. No more of the teacher and student bullshit. He'd seen the way women looked at him when he was with her. They knew. It didn't matter what century they were born in, women knew women. They knew she wore the trousers, that he was an adoring puppy. It didn't matter that his name was on the marquee, she paid the bills. The Snow Queen and the Black King, the fucking dynamic duo, from a time when there was no such thing as a dynamic duo. He was suddenly disgusted with his train of thought and fell backward onto the bed, hands covering his eyes. Beecher stared at her through interlocked fingers, wondered what it would take to get her to lash out. Insult Hans Tomek? Or her family? Or her religion? Maybe she'd learned to avoid conflict. *If age equated to wisdom then she was a fucking guru.*

He said, "Why the fuck do I drink? I'm such a lightweight."

"It won't work," she said.

"What?"

"You, being pissed off and hungover and looking for a punching bag. Be thankful for the time you have and what you're doing."

"Popularity isn't all it's cracked up to be."

"Beats obscurity."

Beecher sat up and reached over and checked the bedside table drawer. He found Gideon's bible, some chewing gum wrappers, and Pengo's crossword book and pen - liquid hula momma was reclined, showing naked. He pulled out the book and flipped through the pages. All the puzzles were complete.

Beecher was the last to board. He scanned the car park once more and then tapped the driver on the shoulder.

"That's everyone, mate. Whenever you're ready."

The driver was Alfonse the Mexican. It's how he referred to himself. Like William the Conqueror or Alexander the Great. He was born in Sinaloa and raised in Los Angeles. He dressed like James Dean and spoke like everything was a secret.

"Hey," he said, checking out Beecher from head to toe. "I been drivin' for twenty years. I seen all of you guys…"

Alfonse eyed Luna in the rearview mirror. She was chatting and laughing with Eeva, pointing to her wavy scrawls in the margins of the ledger.

"…you go ahead, do what you gotta do; fuck who you want to fuck. I forgot more shit than you'll ever see."

Beecher shook off the remark, "Today, all I care about is getting to the Hollywood Bowl before five o'clock. Sound good to you?"

"That's why you pay me the big money, you get the best. I seen so much shit, it'd make your ball hair turn gray."

"Well, let's see if we can make this the fastest, most uneventful ride across the desert you've ever had."

"If you pay the speeding tickets, I'll get you there before you can shoot a load in your pants."

Alfonse clocked Luna again.

"That one looks like a groupie I used to know that got her nipples burned off. She was spilling whisky on her titties and getting dudes to lick it off, and then one guy had a joint and got too close. Started a little titty fire."

Beecher caught Luna's eye. She was focusing a dark, frosty glare onto the back of the driver's head. She pulled a folding knife from her pocket and held it up for Alfonse to see. She flicked out the silver blade and pointed it in his direction for a few seconds, the scowl never left her face.

"Yeah, yeah," Alfonse said, with his beady eyes wide and excited in the tinted mirror, "I seen some shit, man."

The storm kissed the canyon walls with bombast and thunder, washing all traces of footprints from dirt paths and river beaches, and the Outriders sheltered together under a rocky overhang, feeding dry brush onto smoldering coals, enticing petals of orange flame to dance and grow. The banter between the family was subdued. Fidelia, the brave one, stood and offered Tomek her hand.

"I will go first," she said. "You know that I have always been first. So I will say goodbye to you, first."

Hans Tomek stood and wrapped his arms around the woman. For she was now a woman, tall and fine-boned and strong and breathtakingly beautiful.

Tomek said, "It is my greatest dream that you will have your own family to raise and to teach the ways of the world."

"And to ride," Fidelia said.

"Yes, and to ride."

Tomek was transported to a time when six orphans were hoisted in turn onto the back of a blind mule. Here they learned to coax the animal from the confines of a familiar pasture with gentle, playful whispers and soft touches of tiny hands and feet. He remembered the spills and scrapes, and the tears and the rivalry. And he remembered the triumph and the pride, and how they had learned to command all of their mounts. *"Time can never be halted,"* he had instilled within their impressionable minds,

"...but it can be harnessed if you move with the wind. You have to keep moving, or the sands of time will see you wither on your bones."

He held each of them in turn with the crushing embrace of a father. And he welcomed their tears and he absorbed their grief.

"Our voyage has not been without purpose, we have crossed the universe together, and now we will pause and we will claim back our lives and we will bask in these memories. We are lucky, you and I, we have lived so many lives without remorse or regret. I want you all to feel excited about what awaits you because, without the unknown, we are deprived of enlightenment. And I have seen it in your faces, that sense of wonder when new horizons greet you like a cascade of shooting stars."

Tomek moved amongst his family, recalling anecdotes, brushing hair from nervous faces and wiping away the shining tracks of salty tears.

"I remember your grubby little faces, spooked by a stranger in that cold, stone barn."

He stoked the fire and damp wood crackled and splintered.

"War babies," he said. "...that is what you are. You are all war babies. No one has seen or overcome as much as you. It is a wonder your minds do not explode from the sensation."

He looked at them with his own tears welling.

"I wonder how much more you can tolerate."

The erratic drumming of rain on shiny rock stopped abruptly and the party stepped away from the overhang to be greeted by a turbulent sky smeared with washes of blue and violet, and fractured clouds were pierced by several arcing rainbows that plunged into the blackness of the canyon.

The Outriders assisted one another in the donning of heavy backpacks, adjusting straps and brushing away puddles of water that had gathered in the folds of the material. Only when they sat astride their machines, still and in silence, did tears break from Tomek's eyelids.

He said, "We are united as a family because we draw from a common source. Through the decades we have seen that humanity is flawed and fragile, and in its desperate pursuit of unity will bow to the words of the preacher and the charlatan alike. When Beecher Stowe takes to the stage on this day, you will each have completed a task of peculiar importance, and in that respect, you are pioneers. The equipment you carry will amplify radio waves transmitted from stations at all points of the compass. You know the mountain you must climb, only from there will the signals be accessible. Stay together. The music will come through you and be sent on to me, and the atmosphere will be saturated with thoughts of love, and fears of loss, and fleeting moments of joy and tenderness, and with our belief intact, we will host the forging of a memory; we will shape the course of this river as though a magnet was drawn over iron filings, and it will flow into the canyon and press against the curtain of time."

Hans Tomek paused, his grandiosity becoming an honest confession.

"And then I will see my son."

He searched for judgment in their expressions and found none.

"I lied when I said I was building an event," he said. "I was creating a God."

Chapter Twenty-Eight

Beecher Stowe tried to sleep. The rutted road was an irregular heartbeat and he searched for a steady rhythm to quiet the raging voices within. He turned onto his side and a shaft of sunlight spiked the parted curtain and left him sweating and annoyed. He sat up and found Eeva staring at him from across the bed. Her back was to the bulkhead in the cramped room at the back of the bus.

"Sleeping is impossible," he said.

"I'd say you've had about four hours of impossible sleep."

"No way!"

"Afraid so. You should count yourself lucky, the gathering up front has been full tilt on downing as much of the alcohol on board as they can before we hit the California border. The driver's got them believing they can't take booze across the state line; something about being arrested and sent to jail for a very long time."

"He's kidding, right."

"Of course. Well, there is a limit, but nothing you need to worry about."

"That's all we need," he joked. "...a band of drunken misfits. The tabloids will have a field day."

He reached for a smoke and caught that pained, *"do you have to?"* expression on her face. He made to adjust the curtain instead.

Eeva had changed clothes. The blue jeans and T-shirt had been cast off in favor of a yellow dress - noonday, height of summer, yellow. Her lips were red as cherries and she toyed with strands of her hair. She smoothed the material over her curled legs and Beecher saw she was barefoot.

"Hans told you he is leaving; going home."

"I'd be lying if I said I understood," Beecher said.

"My time, too, is coming to an end."

Beecher sat up. He felt the shiver of impending loss come awake, crawling under his skin like a virus taking hold.

"But we've only just met, I mean..."

"I know," she said.

The rattle and bounce of the bus heightened and then settled.

Beecher said, "Maybe his theory is wrong."

Eeva stared out of the window. They moved along an arrow-straight road through an expanse of tedious desert. *"Nothing romantic about this place,"* she thought. The only descriptive words that came to mind were, *brown* and *empty.*

She said, "Tomek believed he did not age simply because he did not belong here; that he was constantly out of sync, like a cog in an engine, spinning but never engaging. He was an actual *ghost in the machine.* And because of this, those he held dear fell under the same spell. Sometimes he'd say that he could hold back physical time by convincing your brain of a memory so vivid it forgets to age you; that your mind would become so distracted, it would do everything in its power to maintain the sense of euphoria connected with a particular time and place, and that once your body starts to decline, it slows to a virtual crawl. The Outriders grew up naturally enough, with no ill effects. Once they reached maturity, they just…stopped."

Beecher was settling into full, *what about me?* mode.

"So what's going to happen? To you? To us?"

"I have an idea, and I don't want to be around if I'm right."

"I can handle whatever it is," he said. "I can be there, no matter what happens. I've never met anyone like you,…doubt I ever will."

"You have an extraordinary talent, Beecher, you're doing what you have always wanted to do. You're loved by the people that matter. Don't wish for anything more."

"That's your way of telling me time's up?"

"Cute turn of phrase."

"I didn't mean…" He shrugged, changed course. "I haven't done anything that wasn't for you. I'm not sure it makes sense if it's not for you."

"But this was your dream," Eeva said.

"Actually, you were my dream, long before I met you. Snooze used to call you my rock n' roll delusion."

"I'm sure fate would have intervened either way."

She sensed his confusion and nodded at the pack of cigarettes.

"Just open a window."

Beecher dug a kitschy, silver Zippo emblazoned with a relief map of the Grand Canyon from his jeans pocket but it was out of fuel, so he struck a match and the bedroom was instantly filled with its sulfurous odor. Eeva covered her nose and mouth with his discarded T-shirt.

"Have you written anything new?"

"A couple of things. One of them has real potential."

"What's it about, or is that prying?"

"I'm sure they're all about the same thing. We need a new word in the English language. Just one word that describes heartache, loss, redemption, and serenity. 'Cause that's what it's about."

"In one three-minute song? That's pretty inspiring."

"I agree, it would be, only this little ditty stretches to just over seven minutes."

"Ooh, taking a stroll down introspective lane. I hope I get to hear it."

"I'm closing with it tonight."

The smile on Eeva's face disappeared and Beecher's heart sank. They were silent for a moment and then he pulled back the curtains, said with a wink,

"There must be a crossroads around here somewhere. Maybe I can strike up a deal with the devil."

Eeva said, "Oh, you silly, beautiful fool. You don't have to sell your soul…"

She leaned forward, set her hands on either side of his face and then smoothed his brow, whispering,

"…I've already sold mine."

Alfonse cruised the tour bus across the state line at fifteen miles per hour over the speed limit. Two cop cars were parked hood-to-trunk; officers sharing bullshit when they should've been breaking balls. His smug plan failed. No traffic stop. He trained his beady eyes on the rearview mirror, saw the band's apprehension dissolve, watched the false bravado swell in their chests.

Under his breath, he spat, *"Ricos cabrones."*

Fez was having none of it. He'd recently discovered whisky sours and he sidled up to the front and rattled his beaker at the driver and drops of golden liquor sprinkled to the floor.

He slurred, "Don't fuck wiv da west end boys, right?"

Alfonse waved off the challenge, "I seen it all, man. I seen it all."

The bus was jarred by broken tarmac, the perils of living on a fault line. The suspension jumped and crashed along the chassis and Fez lost his footing. He dropped the glass and reached for the handrail with both hands. He caught himself but the sudden, violent movement set the whisky in his belly into motion. It wanted out, and it didn't want to wait. Fez choked back a little bile and it slithered back down his gullet inspiring a little false confidence. *Steady, boy, steady.* In his time, he had staved off any number of eruptions. This time, he might as well have dropped a grenade in a gas tank. His cheeks instantly filled with liquid and though he fought it bravely for a good two seconds, dribbling strings of saliva from the corners of his mouth like yellow shoelaces, his body was now on autopilot. His stomach lurched with the power of an exorcism, spraying the devil's own cocktail of stinging alcohol into the driver's right ear with the force of a dropped firehouse. Alfonse was blinded and let out a girlish screech. He swerved the vehicle across two lanes of blacktop, shunting Fez onto his knees and into the stairwell where he completed the evacuation of his system.

In the main cabin, Harry let out a pathetic and wearisome, "Not again." Thankfully, this time the wheels of the bus never left the road and Alfonse was able to clear his vision with the damp tail of his shirt.

A moment later, Fez popped his head up, looking startlingly refreshed; as if he'd just had a good sleep.

"Bet you've never seen that...*man!*"

The soiled tour bus pulled into a roadside gas station for clean up. Beecher spent almost half an hour smoothing things over with Alfonse, finally convincing him to finish up the last thirty miles whereupon he would receive a bonus that would effectively treble his salary.

Where ordinarily, Beecher would have lost his shit with the lads, he was strangely distracted.

"Something's goin' down," Harry said.

"It's a big gig," Fez said. "He probably just wants it to be over."

Snooze was shaking off the effects of his indulgence. "And we're going to help him out best we can, eh, fellas?"

"I'm good, now," Fez said. "It was like being pissed for half an hour. Look how straight I am."

He stepped off, heel against toe, for twenty yards, his leather chaps flapping in the desert breeze like dragons' wings.

"Well, done," Harry shouted, "Now come back on your hands."

A raised middle finger signaled that the message had been received.

Eeva spent the duration of the unplanned stop on a payphone that stood outside of the men's bathroom. Two offset concrete walls made up a hamster maze entrance that did nothing to withhold the stench of stale urine and floating turds that wafted from the innards every time the wind picked up. She was unfazed, preoccupied with making arrangements, clutching a fistful of dimes and quarters with the sun shining through her hair setting the dress ablaze with mirage-inducing splendor.

The lads passed the time prepping for a little post-puke brunch. Harry ordered cheeseburgers and fries from a kiosk window; Fez hit the general store for cookies and candy; Snooze was in charge of restocking the beverages. On Beecher's instructions, nothing harder than Dr. Pepper was allowed on the bus.

Alfonse took care of his vomit-infested clothing by running through a coin-op car wash, rinsing and shaking and wringing as he passed through the spray stations. At one point, he was encased in soap suds so dense that Fez bestowed upon him the name, *Snowman,* to which Alfonse was utterly chuffed. He took it entirely to heart that the lads thought he might be a drug-cartel kingpin and showed his forgiveness and affection with uncomfortably-long hugs and kisses to both cheeks.

"Funny what a little upchuck can do," Snooze said, heaving three cases of soda up the newly scrubbed steps. "I might try that back home if those skinheads think to invade Maureen's restaurant again."

Chapter Twenty-Nine

The Days Before

Hans Tomek had spared no expense in bringing the Beecher Stowe experience to the consciousness of nations. From the sidewalks of cities that never sleep to mid-size college towns, to one-stoplight map dots, celebrations on par with the ending of a war were breaking out with a sense of bygone euphoria long since absent from the predictably self-serving season of avarice and religious convenience. Beecher's face was, as Snooze Silver so delicately put it, *"as profitably ubiquitous as a sugary soft drink."* In the U.S.A., it was *his* two-dimensional pout lining every major thoroughfare in the country, staring down from billboards normally reserved for some vacuous model shilling for a cosmetics company. Tomek had carefully selected an empathetic pose for the artwork. With overbearing confidence, he insisted that the public would relate; that they would recognize that Beecher Stowe understood his audience. He was with them in unemployment, and through divorces, and when fires raged and when floods breached. And his was the soundtrack of weddings and graduations and births, and it would be his sweet, consoling tenor that would echo through the long nights when frightened soldiers embarked on the long voyage home, or grieving mothers and heartsick fathers were cast adrift at a dying child's bedside.

Satellites sweeping across the northern latitudes witnessed snow parties dotting the continents, blazing like new cities as hundreds of thousands of bonfires erupted with constellations of sparks that painted rosy cheeks and runny noses orange as a Caribbean sunset. And further south, the temperate climates embraced carnivals and parades that were routed into city parks and sports arenas with whistles and cheers, setting into motion ripples of effusive humanity, bringing together young and old to huddle in the shadow of huge screens erected solely for the purpose of projecting a rock n' roll concert, live.

Where television reception was compromised, FM receivers and stacks of speakers, standing tall as Easter island statues, rose from baseball diamonds and soccer pitches, and they were constructed on rocky hillsides and in open pastures, and on beaches and on the banks of rivers.

"The whole world in one shot," was Hans Tomek's wish. *"No matter what the cost. I want the eyes and ears of the world, regardless of race, culture, skin color or religion. I want a moment of their attention, even if I have to buy it."*

And, he did. He unleashed a gut punch to financial markets from London to Singapore, liquidating assets like he was scattering confetti. He bought media where the penetration was greatest, saturating every network in every country with Beecher's sound and Beecher's face. The rules no longer applied. Payola's legacy of the fifty dollar handshake was eviscerated in favor of sleek briefcases containing simple *'thank you'* cards upon which were printed access numbers to discreet Cayman Island bank accounts. From shore to shore and sea to shining sea, *Aeon Records* enlisted the services of a thousand cutthroat promotions executives willing to sell their own grandmothers to close a deal. And word spread like a blistering rash, and it dredged the murky realm of the bottom feeders, and over a thousand more applied. And Hans Tomek hired them all.

His brief was simple: find the program director; lock him or her into a set of *Supermassive*-shackles. If civilized persuasion failed, *"...get creative,"* he said, *"...twist the knife a little, everyone's got a funky polaroid or two taped to the bottom of their desk. Air time is the engine that drives awareness and song rotation is the fuel."* He held up two fistfuls of one hundred dollar bills. *"And I'm providing the spark."*

For the sleaze-balls and the shylocks and the grifters alike, the cries rang out, *"Cocaine or cash, weed or pills; hookers or rent boys, we got all the thrills."*

Case in point: one particularly stubborn station manager parked his morals a little too close to the ethical flame and found his ass canned and kicked to the curb within five minutes of denying a promoter's rather pointed request with what he referred to as, *"an egregious betrayal of the public's interest."* In short order, Houston's, *KTOS*, segued from a playlist consisting of easy-listening jazz to hourly rotations of, *"all Beecher, all the time."* As expected, the switchboard lit up like mission control during a moonshot, leaving operators to read from a prepared statement: *"...at this time, KTOS is honoring a nationwide spirit of sonic unity..."* - a message clearly taken to heart by the station's owner who, with an impressionable young secretary pulled straight from the typing pool, was last seen speeding toward a Corpus Christi beach cottage in a brand new, sea-foam green Lincoln Continental.

"Twenty-eight days to go," Eeva said. "When will you inform the headliner that he's going to stand before the entire world?"

"I'll not say a word. For Beecher Stowe, it'll be just another venue. A grand one, of course, but that's all he needs to know."

"With all of this publicity, how do you propose to keep him in the dark?"

"I'll leave that up to you, I know his innocence can only be guarded for so long. Show him another side of America; give him a few stories to tell his grandkids."

Eeva picked up a slight shift in his tone; as if a whisper of doubt had drawn an unintended pause in his thoughts.

"You know, the magic we create is not entirely of our own doing," he said. "I'm not inventing anything new here. We are all troubled. We all carry burdens across centuries and hand them down to each new generation, insisting that vengeance or prejudice is somehow timeless. It's as if by not doing so, we will be forgotten."

Eeva watched and listened. When Hans Tomek spoke he became very still, as if time itself were slowed by his words. She observed the moment of silence that passed between them and then tapped the newspaper she was holding, underlining the headline with her finger.

"You made the front page," she said.

"I'm guessing the article speaks of an eccentric act undertaken by an eccentric fool."

"You read it?"

"No need, I'd probably write the same."

"Actually, it's not all criticism. If you close one eye and hold it upside down you can just make out a sense of excitement building."

"Christ, it must be so tiresome for those journalists to be so jaded."

Tomek stretched out fully on a leather sofa in his Manhattan apartment. The room was wood-paneled and warmly lit, with minimal furnishings, chosen for comfort, not aesthetics. A series of original paintings by old masters lined the walls. Not a single work was known to the general public. These were all paid commissions, painted by the artists in their prime. Some illustrated windswept oceans, others were cityscapes at the birth of industry. One portrait hung isolated from the rest of the collection. It was a rendering in oils of the photograph Eeva carried everywhere - the picture of her family and Hans Tomek outside the music store in Vienna. She had realized for some time that Tomek's couch was positioned to view this painting to the detriment of all the others. A question danced on her tongue for the thousandth time but failed to leap. A line would be crossed. And it was comforting to know there was a line.

The penthouse was on the fifty-second floor and muted sirens from the chaotic streets below blended with the howl of wind driving sleet against the windowpane. Tomek smoothed the shaft of a thin, black cheroot and sparked it up and inhaled deep.

"I haven't decided if Beecher Stowe is complex, or just innocent. He seems impervious to wealth. And in that, I am envious. Imagine living for the sake of living. I'm not suggesting that's what he's doing, but I am curious."

"After all this time, you're still not convinced."

"I think that is how it should be."

"What do you mean?"

"Blind conviction is for fools."

"Perhaps there's a happy medium?"

"Doubtful. Not knowing is a gift," he said.

Eeva perched on the window sill, looking down at the dots of light inching along Fifth Avenue. She imagined the squinting faces of pedestrians as they hustled and bustled against a biting north wind.

"Come sit with me," Tomek said.

And she did.

"I have provided for you; you will want for nothing."

He stroked her face with the back of his hand, the way a father would caress his child.

"I appreciate that," she said. "But I did not ask for it."

"Nevertheless, it's there if you feel the urge to purchase a small country."

The levity was welcome and they sat together, confronted by the painting as if for the first time. They traveled back together. The smells and the sounds were shared.

"There was a woman that lived nearby," Eeva said. "Do you remember the wife of the shoemaker? A tall woman; taller than her husband by a foot or more."

"I do. She was always berating him for not dressing well."

"That's the one," Eeva said. "One day she made it known that my father had left a bill unpaid for having new soles stitched on a pair of boots. She showed up on our doorstep with her husband in tow, meek as a puppy.

My father worried for the little man's well being so much he settled the bill on the spot. It left us without money for food."

Tomek was aware that Eeva's eyes were softening.

"It was the day you came and sat at our table," she said. "And we had nothing to serve you."

"I recollect that we ate very well that first night."

"Because of you. You provided the meal. I will never forget that."

"What of this woman? Why has she come into your thoughts?"

"Because as I look at this image of my father I remember that he never owned a pair of boots."

Hans Tomek was drawn into her melancholy. They sat in silence, her hand resting in his.

"I am afraid," Eeva said.

"You feel you are in the eye of the hurricane," he said. "Keep the wind at your back; move in the direction of your rising pulse. Your heart will not steer you wrong."

Chapter Thirty

For the benefit of his sanity and focus, Beecher was oblivious to the wheels of corruption turning so universally in his favor. He and Eeva and the band were met at the outskirts of Los Angeles by three limousines and a police escort - this modern-day savior of rock n' roll was hardly going to arrive at the Hollywood Bowl in a converted Greyhound bus.

The broad boulevards that stretch the length of the San Fernando Valley were lined with banners commemorating the young Londoner's meteoric rise to fame, and miles of lights danced along power lines, twinkling red, white and blue, evoking the color palette of the flags of the USA and the UK respectively.

Fez and Harry felt like traitors in their cowboy get-ups. The Union Jack seemed more appropriate right now. They dug through their bags pulling out a series of wrinkled T-shirts, holding them across skinny chests, seeking mutual approval. Fez struck gold first: a sky-blue sweatshirt with a charcoal drawing of Marc Bolan's snake-like physique in full thrust behind a Gibson Les Paul.

"You're gonna sweat your balls off in that," Snooze offered with professorial candor. "This is Los Angeles. It's eighty-five degrees outside."

"I've got nothing else clean. If it gets too hot, I'll take it off," Fez said.

"With that rib cage, you'll look like the poster child for an end to animal testing."

"How's this?" Harry held up an off-white T-shirt dotted with holes and sporting a faded map of the London underground.

"Fine," Snooze said. "But you might want to keep your arms down by your side. Those pit stains look like a cat pissed on a doily."

The driver lowered the partition glass, cast a glance over at Snooze.

"So's you know, there's a complete wardrobe waiting for you guys at the venue."

"Yeah, cheers mate, Snooze said. "It's a good job there is. See what I have to put up with, these clowns have trouble dressing for bedtime."

The driver chuckled, "Yeah, I got kids. Three girls. Tried to settle 'em down. No use."

Snooze poked his head through the divide.

"So how do you handle it?"

"I bought me some fancy headphones, the kind that gets the radio. I put 'em on and go about my day."

The driver checked his watch.

"Should be about another twenty minutes," he said. "So you guys are that rock group, huh?"

"Yeah, the main guy is in the lead car. You know about us?"

"You'd have to have your head up your ass not to know 'bout that song. It's everywhere. I bet I can switch on the radio and turn the dial and hit it ten times."

"No way!"

"Wanna bet?"

"How much?"

"Thirty bucks."

"You're on."

Snooze patted his pockets and found a few crumpled bills that amounted to ten dollars. He ducked back in the cabin.

"Gimme ten dollars each."

"Fuck off. Why?"

"Doing a bet with the driver. He reckons he can find ten radio stations that are playing our song."

"I only have twelve dollars left," Harry said.

Fez was suspiciously mute.

"C'mon, you tight bastards," Snooze said. "I can't lose this one."

He popped his head back through.

"I'm coming up front."

Like a drunken spider, Snooze slipped into the passenger seat clutching a wad of bills.

"Let's do this."

The driver stuck out a mahogany-brown hand the size of a coal shovel.

"Louis," he said.

"Snooze Silver, at your service."

Louis laid three crisp ten dollar bills on the seat, said,

"Go ahead. Switch it on."

"Ten stations, that's the deal?"

"C'mon," Louis said, "…you're wasting time. Gotta get it in before the top of the hour otherwise they'll start spouting the news and weather."

Harry and Fez pushed their heads into the front compartment like two anxious puppies. Snooze reached out and…*Click,* a crackle of static and the volume grew louder. And then,

…*Superstar your life…*

"No fuckin' way!" Fez blurted.

"That's one," Louis said.

Snooze turned the dial. He hadn't gone but an eighth of an inch when the syrupy sounds of Doris Day singing, *Secret Love,* filled the car. Harry began to mouth the words and Fez frowned, "Next!"

Another quarter turn, "…*mmm, take us back, to the places we know…*"

Louis was stone-faced, "That's two."

The next three stations were running commercials, two of them in Spanish. Snooze kept turning and a confusing burble of unintelligible nonsense spat from the speakers.

Louis said, "Ahem, go back please."

"What? It's just noise."

"Humor me."

Louis reached out and reversed the dial and an excited Hispanic voice was mid-sentence,

"…sentado en la parte superior de las listas, superestrella supermasiva…"

The song's fairground-like intro began.

Louis craned his neck backward and clocked Fez.

"That's three. Next!"

Snooze scanned the dial, never going more than two stations before hitting their song in full flight. He went up and down the waveband two more times for a total of nine plays.

"Sorry, mate," he said, "… don't fuck wiv ol' Snoozy when it comes to bettin' cash."

Snooze reached out for the dollar bills and again Louis cleared his throat.

"What? A bet's a bet," Snooze said.

Louis calmly reached out his right hand and depressed a button labeled, FM.

"Oh, we've only just begun."

Like magic, Fez's raucous drumming, Harry's delicate, ethereal keyboards and Snooze's angelic horn were swirling about in leather-bound luxury.

"That's ten. Nice doing business with ya.., Snoozy."

Harry turned Snooze's peculiar brand of psychology on its head.

"Ne'er mind, Snooze, that's probably the best bet you'll ever lose."

A light bulb went off over Fez's bleached roots.

"'Ere' do we get paid every time it's on the radio?"

"Beecher does," Snooze said while clambering back over the seat. "You get a wage and the chance to see the world in style. If you want any more than that, I'd get writing."

"Yeah, but we played on it."

"Which is why you got paid."

"But there wouldn't be a song unless we played on it?"

"Moron."

In the front seat, Louis smiled and shoved a cassette into the player. He cranked the volume on B.B. King's rendition of, *The Thrill Is Gone,* and shouted into the back, "Love this song, you guys know this?"

Harry was immediately alert and scooted along the seat that ran the length of the car.

"Oh, hell, yeah," he said.

"Did you know that B.B. couldn't talk so good, had a wicked stutter when he was a kid?"

Harry shook his head, *"No."*

"I used to drive him when he came out to L.A. He joked that if he had to give himself an alibi for a crime he'd be in some serious shit. They'd think he was guilty long before he got out one sentence. Music became his voice and he gave himself over to it like his life depended on it. Because it did. He said a man has to come to a reckoning on his own; has to risk everything if he ever wants to be true to himself, no matter what he chooses to do."

Fez and Snooze had stopped their bickering and crawled nearer to the partition. The music dripped from the speakers like vintage wine.

Louis directed his words at Harry, "Maybe you wanna tell your friend that if wants to get paid, he needs to stick his neck *all* the way out."

Oh I'm free, free, free now;
I'm free from your spell;
And now that it's all over;
All I can do is wish you well.

The trio of limousines eased off a steadily moving freeway into gridlock.

Not of cars.

Of people.

Walking.

Shuffling.

All facing the same way.

On the road to confession.

Five hundred yards and a half-hour later, the lead car turned off Cahuenga Blvd., filtered through a car park and accessed a private area, backstage at the Hollywood Bowl. The vehicles were received like a presidential convoy - multiple hands grabbing at door handles and men with aviator sunglasses, dark suits and walkie talkies squawking orders and excuses.

Beecher stepped out and excited whispers turned to raucous cheers. Eeva stayed back. She listened to the adulation echo around the complex. A savior was in the house. She waited until the clamor died down and then alighted with the aid of Beecher's hand.

Louis looked on, digging out a pack of smokes from the center console.

"Man, that's some woman. Is she a movie star?"

"Nah, mate, that's our manager."

"Makes me feel old when I see young ones doing so well for themselves."

"It's been a strange few months," Snooze said.

"That's all it's been?"

"Yeah. This time last year the band didn't exist. She's the reason it does."

"You be nice to her," Louis said.

"I think Beecher's taking care of that for all of us."

And then, as if prodded by an electric poker, Snooze turned to the lads and said,

"So whaddya reckon, lads? Whaddya say we do something nice for Beecher, seeing as it's the last gig an' all?"

"We should get 'im a cake," Fez said.

Snooze hung his head and smashed his eyes shut.

"Why do I fuckin' bother with you two? I mean we should do something profound; something suited to the occasion."

"Sky banners," Harry enthused. "A message towed behind an airplane like they do at the seaside."

"Nice one, Harry. I like it," Snooze said. "Maybe they can fly over the Hollywood sign? That'd be brilliant. We could say something cosmic, something like:

Beecher Stowe Rocks The Universe. Love From The Earthlings of Shepherd's Bush.

"Yeah 'cause that folds in everyone back home," Fez said. "It'll put our manor on the map."

Harry smirked, "It's already on the map, Einstein, it's where *The Who* comes from."

"I know, but that was ages ago."

"Alright, alright," Snooze said. "Let's collar Eeva when we get inside and see if she knows how to make it happen."

"Cool," Fez said. "We're earthlings." And then reassuringly, "Feels good."

Snooze and Harry shrugged a begrudging, *"Yeah, suppose it does."*

Chapter Thirty-One

It was twenty minutes to 9:00 pm.

Arizona time.

An hour ahead of Beecher and the lads.

The concert would kick off at 8:00 pm.

Los Angeles time.

Hans Tomek was alone. He had time to kill.

It was fully dark and the sky was clear as new glass. The temperature had fallen dramatically and a north wind blew strong and steady, brushing the rocks and grasses underfoot with sugary frost. Over the last day, he had traipsed a well-worn path from his tent to the edge of the cliff. Now he followed the snaking route lighted only by the soft, blue blanket of moon glow, and each of his steps found its place and his movement was silent as shadows. Where the earth stopped, he was confronted by a vast, dark animal and he felt swirling eddies and powerful gusts rising from its belly and push against his body. He considered the emptiness to be a clean slate; a fresh start, and he wondered if the memories he carried would be his undoing. He had come forward in time, open to learning; gathering the baggage of lessons learned. Now its weight was impossible to bear.

"How do you unlearn? How do you eradicate knowledge of phones and cars and airplanes and gas pumps and gas ovens? And the Outriders? And Eeva? And this catalyst called, Beecher Stowe? If the weight of memory is the product of life, then that's all we are - memories and a few aching bones and torn muscles. Maybe these thoughts will corrode slowly, like scrap metal? Or dissolve like salt under snow?"

Tomek returned to the tent and rummaged through a duffel. At one minute before the hour, he would conduct the final radio check. He switched the unit on and off again and realized his hands were shaking. He laid the handset down and rubbed his palms together, bringing fresh blood to the surface. The tremors persisted.

In his isolation, the questions infected his thoughts like a plague. But as his time drew near and his longing became all-consuming, the answers did not matter. What mattered was a world united by the birth of a single thought. Only then, in its most precious state, could the passage of time be arrested for the blink of an eye. And only then would he get a chance to be whole again.

Tomek wrote in a heavy, leather-bound journal, lost in the story that tumbled from his pen in an untidy, meandering scribe. He closed out the lengthy letter with, *"What would you do for love?"*

The delicate chime of a small alarm clock sounded.

Five minutes to go.

As he closed the journal, a photograph jutted from between two pages. A picture, taken a few days previously, given to him by Beecher.

"Harry took it," he had said. *"Me, you and Eeva. I made three copies, one for each of us. Next time I see you, you better have grown older."*

He stuffed the image inside of his tunic and packed away his belongings. All except for the radio. He thumbed the circular dial and found the agreed wavelength. He set his bag in the middle of the tent and looked at it as if he had just cast Moses adrift in a basket. The bag contained the story of his life, in thirty-five volumes. Eeva would retrieve it. Or the ravages of weather would see it scattered to the winds. Either way, it no longer mattered.

He stepped from the tent and the alarm sounded again and he immediately switched on the handset. The display bloomed vivid green and he invited contact from the Outriders. Fidelia was first to communicate. She shared their progress and her state of wellness and they swapped informal banter knowing that the entire group was listening. Hans Tomek addressed each of the Outriders in turn. He welcomed their warmth and their spirit and their laughter, even after such a short time alone.

"To be regarded as part of a family is the richest prize a person may receive," he said. "Bless you all, my love for you is timeless."

Amelio took the lead, adjusting the wavelength on the handset and with only a slight delay, the radio in his hand became a fragile beacon in the wilderness. An exuberant announcer was heard, and behind the machine-gunned repartee swelled the murmurs of an expectant audience. Tomek picked up the signal. He imagined the venue's lights dimming and the curious stares and the smell of beer and cigarettes. He felt Beecher's nerves tightening as he too was departing from the conscious world. They would journey on this last voyage together.

Tomek made his way along the path for the last time. He crawled the last few feet, feeling with his hands, finding the rim's ragged edge. He leaned over and felt the air shift violently and it was warm as the Sahara and wild as an Antarctic storm. A purple fog covered the canyon floor, giving dimension and form to rock walls rising sheer as skyscrapers into impenetrable darkness. Tomek's eyes watered against the wind and he shuffled back and patted them dry with his sleeve.

He depressed the call button on the handset, said, "Let us make a memory."

And so, the Outriders huddled together on a rocky, featureless escarpment, channeling radio signals from all around the world. The satellite delay was evident as soaring voices and jubilant cheers and crashing drumbeats collided out of time and as the abyss sucked the cacophony from the jeweled sky, the ground trembled as though an artillery barrage held forth with phosphorous white flashes, rolling and forking and glazing the earth below.

Hans Tomek felt the muted reverberations of the music as they were consumed within the fog, and his mind gave birth to shimmering visions of multi-colored columns that swelled and writhed and surged higher and higher, dispatching bursts of incandescence like great, fiery wings. He saw the tops of rainbows rising from the canyon floor like boiling geysers, carrying the unity of saints and sinners, blasting the cliff face, and punching the sky, and soaring into the upper reaches of the atmosphere.

Tomek rolled onto his back and watched the rainbows sprout and curl, dipping uniformly to every horizon. And the music waned, and Beecher's voice filled the emptiness of the canyon, and the tears of a child poured from Tomek's eyes. And when the music resolved, his body was dappled by a crystal shower. He felt drunk and confused, and he pressed his hands against the bedrock that he lay upon, and with a ferocious howl, a violent gust slammed into the cliff face and a cannon-fire of hail stones gouged deep depressions from the aged quartz, gypsum, and clay. Tomek felt the overhang give under his weight and he raised to his knees, sheltering his eyes, peering into the depths once more. The fog filled the canyon like an ocean, and the radio waves that speared his consciousness were becoming erratic and abrasive, and the ice storm unleashed its fury and a crack snaked across the rocks at Tomek's feet and he curled into a ball and covered his head.

On the radio, the crescendo was within reach.

Chapter Thirty-Two

"Twenty minutes, Mr. Stowe…"

An officious stagehand accorded Beecher with respect, which in turn, sent the lads into fits of belly laughter.

"La, de, fuckin' da," Snooze sang. "I hope you're not gettin' used to that, 'cause you got more chance of seeing a brace of pork pies fly out of Harry's ass than getting me to call you, *sir*."

Beecher was tuning his guitar for the twentieth time. He paused, looked Snooze up and down, missing the gag completely, "You know, I haven't had a pork pie or a sausage roll in over three months. Sad, eh?"

The stagehand wasn't done, "…and that's fifteen minutes for you, Mr. Silver. We need you and the rest of the band in place before the lights go up."

Fez piped up, "Well, la, de, fuckin' da yourself, *Mr. Silver!*"

"I dunno," Snooze said, "…on me it sounds kinda regal; sorta like it was meant for a man of my stature. *Silver* has a ring to it, you see. Stowe just sounds, well, common."

Beecher caught on and smiled at the lighthearted snub.

"You mean like I'm from the rough and tumble streets of West London?"

"Yeah."

"Then so be it. From now on, I am to be acknowledged as Mr. Stowe, a man of the people, and you shall be known as Princess Snooze."

Snooze shot Fez and Harry a look that said, *"He can make that joke, you fuckers just mind your mouths."*

Message received; subject changed.

"How's about a quick warm-up?" Snooze said.

Harry went back to tinkling softly on the ivories of a battered upright, settling into a daydream. Fez shrugged off the invite, choosing to lounge on a lighting case and sort through a box of cassettes. He settled a pair of shiny, new *Walkman* headphones awkwardly onto sunburned ears and began to nod in time to *The Stranglers'* muffled optimism as they extolled the virtues of, *"Walking on the beaches, looking at the peaches."*

Snooze's nerves were showing. He paced the length of the band room, checked his look in the mirror a few times, adjusted the collar of his jacket and smoothed the creases forming in his crotch.

The band's image had been transformed by the clothes Eeva had provided. A collision of the sixties and the seventies. Tailor-made paisley jackets, each showcasing a section of the rainbow spectrum; white T-shirts; matching drainpipe trousers, and white Chelsea boots. A perfect compliment to Beecher's black velvet ensemble.

"Makes me wanna dance like the Temptations," Harry had said, at which point the Glitters and Rosy performed a step-for-step rendition of *My Girl* that would make angels weep.

Snooze loped off into an adjoining room leaving a, *"Fuckin' unbelievable,"* hanging in the air.

He crossed the international divide, hoping for better luck, or else just more sense. He found neither. Rosy and the Glitter Boys were sipping Jamaican rum from a flask, passing it between themselves as if it was a Native American talking stick. Which it was - with every swig, a funny anecdote or a startling confession found its way to air.

Snooze caught the tail end of one of Earl's encounters with the head of some record company.

"...paid for the whole album in hookers; five-a-day, for eight weeks. We hadn't even got the drums down before we had to start taking motherfuckin' rain-checks..."

"Here," Earl said, offering up the flask to Snooze. "It does wonders for your nerves; makes you see real good when the lights go up."

Rosy reached over, grabbed the container and shook it as if he was mixing a Martini. *Almost empty.*

"Damn, we gonna see clear to the back row tonight."

The trio let go with chuckles more suited to an inside joke.

"Come on, Snooze, you'll be amongst it soon enough," Eddie said, beckoning with an athletic wave. "Come and tell us your troubles."

Snooze pulled up a chair.

"No troubles. Guess everyone's in their own world."

"It happens at big gigs," Eddie said. "Some folks want to talk, others want to hide."

Earl added, "And some just quietly crap their pants. Remember that backing singer on that, *Motown in the Movies,* gig?"

Eddie screwed up his face and shivered.

"Nice guy," Earl said. "He didn't say much of anything to anyone. He was cool the entire tour until we gots to Madison Square Garden. He starts shaking like Jell-O straight outta the icebox. He woulda skipped the gig altogether except he weren't gettin paid 'til after. Those singers was all wearing these fancy white suits, and they was doing their stuff in front of us, and man, he let loose like he'd sat in a bowl of spaghetti. I could taste the stink every time I put the reed in my mouth. An' every time they'd do a twirl, a little more stuff would slip from his pant leg onto the stage. Motherfucker ended up slipping in his own shit. He brought all the singers down, fuckin' microphones started feedin' back like a truck full of pigs squealin'. God, that was a mess."

"I'm not nervous," Snooze said. "Well, not like that; not shit-my-pants nervous."

"You got no need for anything other than being excited," Eddie said. "You boys come a helluva long way in such a short time. Keep that train movin' forward. That's how you get people to stay on board."

That was Rosy's cue. He jumped up and busted out with, *"People all over the world, join hands, start a love train, love train."*

The Glitter Boys picked up their horns, found the melody and slipped right in, punching out little solos along the way.

Snooze bathed in the music with a smile as wide as the Mississippi.

"That's what I'm talking about."

Backstage, the Hollywood Bowl was a ghost town. Hans Tomek had left explicit instructions that no celebrities or journalists or record company executives were to be allowed within five miles of his band. Ordinarily, he'd have stuffed the place to the rafters with industry types and the associated throng of self-righteous scum - anything to gain publicity. But not today. This wasn't a concert, this was a baptism.

Beecher took a peek through the stage curtain. He sipped from a bottle of beer. Good stuff; an ale with body. Not American. The front row was studious. Older faces turned out in their finery. Black tie for the men, flowing gowns for the ladies. Everybody was paying attention to everything. As the rows progressed further back, so did the behavior. Backward, that is. A scan across the back row showcased shirtless dudes swigging from styrofoam cups and brown paper bags, and they were necking on chicks in tank tops with nipples that stood out like tire valves. *"Welcome to the cheap seats."*

The crash of a cymbal from center stage resounded like breaking glass. A stagehand was out front replacing some gear on Fez's new kit. Red and white tom-toms, and two blue kick drums. Eeva had promised the lads a special Christmas present. Needless to say, expectations were shattered -

in a good way. Fez spent the first hour circling the kit like a lioness assessing her kill. Every so often he'd stroke a drumhead or marvel at the paintwork. The first hits were tentative and Snooze goaded him with, *"Is that all you've got?"* Rosy and the Glitter Boys gave him a groove and he set off like a 747 taking flight.

For Harry, the scene was ripped straight from a romance novel. A giant red bow sat atop a grand piano. Months ago, he had joked that a Steinway was in his future. It was safe to say that the tears rolling down his cheeks when he was called from backstage were entirely sincere. He even offered to pay for it.

"You couldn't afford the seat," Fez said.

"Installments. I'd do it in installments."

"No need to," Eeva said. "It's yours. We'll send it wherever you want."

Snooze dropped a little reason and common sense into the bargain.

"You're gonna need a bigger shed," he said.

Harry heard none of it.

The afternoon wore on with lighting and sound checks, and gorging on catered food, and pacifying a few lucky reporters' mindless questions with equally mindless answers:

Circus Magazine: *"With such a sudden rise to fame, how are you coping with all of the attention?"*

Snooze: *"We're hiding behind stacks of pancakes."*

The Times of London: *"Supermassive Superstar has taken the world by storm. People are hailing it as one of the greatest rock anthems of all time. How are you going to follow it up?"*

Beecher Stowe: *"We're not."*

Melody Maker: *"If you had to choose between global success and fantastic wealth, or a long, quiet life, what would you choose?"*

Harry: *"Quiet success."*

Fez: *"You twat, one or the other."*

Harry: *"It's one of each. What's wrong with that?"*

Fez: *"It's not what he asked."*

Harry: *"He don't mind, do you?"*

Melody Maker: *"Is Beecher going to be free soon?"*

And then there was the reluctant chore of dousing the band's inevitable nervous squabbles.

Snooze: "I should be closer to Beecher."

A Glitter Boy: "You's can stick your dick in his ass, for all I care. But if you want the brass section to sound like it knows what it's doing, you's better pull out, wipe off and come be part of the band."

Around two hours before showtime, Eeva and Luna corralled Snooze, Harry and Fez and delicately informed them of a slight mishap at Van Nuys airport. The aged Piper Cub assigned to tow their sky banner had strayed from the runway and snagged its 100ft long tail.

"They lost some letters. I don't exactly know what that means but the folks on the ground say there's no time to get back and fix whatever happened and be airborne again before the light goes. They said it was okay to cancel the fly-by and do it some other time."

"It's now or never," Snooze said, looking for support from the other lads. "Unless their gonna fly alongside a fuckin' British Airways jumbo, 'cause that's where we'll be tomorrow."

"Alright," Eeva said. "I told them to carry on unless they heard otherwise."

She took a step back, checking out their stage outfits. The transformation was complete, the image now fit the sound.

"Looking sharp, gentlemen. It's going to be quite a night."

Harry shrugged an, *"Aw, shucks."*

Fez ran his fingers down the lapels.

"Never worn nothing like it," he said. "Can we keep 'em?"

"Of course," Eeva said, "They were tailor made for the occasion."

Snooze pulled his shoulders back, nodded a humble, *"thank you."*

Eeva caught the exchange as it was intended for Luna. She felt a sharp jolt of envy. Hans Tomek's words intruded: *"This is not our time."* She checked her watch and suggested they take Beecher out to the car park. The plane would be along soon.

It started as a dot, hanging in the sky, like an abandoned star. A light blinking at its belly, agonizingly small. But it was moving.

Beecher was losing his patience.

"Lots to do lads, ain't got time for watching UFO's or whatever the fuck this is."

Rosy and the Glitter Boys planted themselves on the hood of the Cadillac and kicked up their feet. They started guessing as to what the fuss was all about.

"A missile," Ernie said, pointing east. "From Russia."

"Russia's the other way," Rosy mused.

Eddie backed up his brother, "Coulda come the long way 'round."

"There!" Snooze yelled. "I see it."

Beecher looked at his band as if they were possessed, his eyes settled on Fez.

"You been skinning up something I should know about?"

Fez's protests of innocence were loudly interrupted.

"There!" Snooze was a broken record. "Now can you see it?"

Beecher obeyed, shielding his eyes.

A single prop airplane canted through ninety degrees, rocking its wings against updrafts tumbling over the Hollywood Hills. Behind the tiny craft, a banner dutifully snaked in the warm air, shredded in places, like an abused fishing net.

"This is for you, mate," Snooze announced, as if he was granting a magic wish. He rested a hand on his lifelong friend's shoulder and his eyes welled as the gravity of the moment took hold.

"What you've done for us is immeasurable," he said. "You've changed our lives in so many ways that saying *thank-you* just isn't enough."

Beecher twisted away from Snooze's impending embrace, his expression was wiped of emotion. In the cloudless, indigo sky, soaring a mere few hundred meters above one of the most iconic scenes in the western world, like a proclamation from God trailed the words:

Beecher Stowe   *Love*   *Bush*

The silence throughout the venue was eternal.

"I knew there was a reason I liked that boy," Rosy said.

Chapter Thirty-Three

At ten minutes before showtime, Eeva appeared in the doorway of the band room dressed in the soft earth tones of her youth. A simple jacket and a long skirt. Her hair hung straight, gathering on her shoulders like mounds of fresh snow. Beecher was sitting in silence, his guitar resting on his lap. Whereas the rest of the band were bathing in the jubilation of the coming event, Beecher surrounded himself with a somber atmosphere. The lights were dimmed and his personal effects were packed and the cases neatly arranged by the door.

"Not sticking around?"

He looked up at her with a bright, gentle smile.

"Seems like a good time to make tracks."

"To where?"

"Dunno, just not here."

Beecher rattled a pack of cigarettes and found it empty. He toyed with the lighter.

"Maybe I'll find a desert. A warm one. Find a suitable rock and sit down for a long while."

"Sounds uncomfortable, and lonely."

"You can come with me," he said.

Eeva shuffled her feet and crossed her arms.

"I don't know…"

Beecher cut her off.

"Bad joke, sorry."

"Nothing is certain," she said.

Beecher laid the guitar on the chair and rooted through a gear bag. He pulled out his journal and opened it to the last entry.

"Hans said something to me, the last time we met."

He read from the page: "*You can't just expect to be great, you have to bleed to live.*"

"What do you think he meant by that?"

"I'd say he meant that hard work pays off."

"No, I get that part. But this, *bleed to live..?* What's that all about?"

"Suffering is part of life," she said.

Beecher shook his head. He dug in the bag again, found another empty pack of smokes. He balled up the wrapper and threw it in the trash.

"Suffering is the result of loss and cruelty and sickness," he said. "That stuff's unavoidable. I think he means we need to cut ourselves on purpose; we have to deny ourselves that which would make us complete. And I've just figured out why he said it - this moment of unity and reminiscing he's been banging on about are one and the same. It's like a first kiss, you miss it already while it's happening."

Eeva was tentative.

"So what now?"

"All I know is that if I do my bit, give him what he craves, I lose."

"Bringing joy to millions of people is hardly losing."

"It wasn't supposed to be this way."

"Again with all of that? See it as a blessing," she said. "So you craved an apple and you got an orchard."

"That sounds like something Snooze would say."

"Gratitude isn't wisdom," she said, picking her words carefully, settling on, "I think you're scared. You've set your expectations in stone and every time they aren't met, it breaks as surely as someone took a sledgehammer to your heart."

Beecher shot her the vacant look of someone that had been ceremoniously exposed. He struggled for a witty comeback but none came.

Instead, he said, "Well, anyway, ...it doesn't matter, none of this has been about me."

"It's your name on the posters; it's your song that's stirring up all of this emotion; it's your friends that are standing beside you through it all. Nice try, I'd say it's absolutely all about you."

"I've known you for nine months. I've gone from nowhere to everywhere. It's unheard of."

"Most miracles are."

"I don't believe in miracles," Beecher spat with disgust.

"You don't have to believe, that's why they're called miracles."

He wandered the room, lifting seat cushions, opening drawers.

"I had a carton full of cigarettes in here this afternoon," he said.

A knock at the door preceded a stagehand announcing, "Five minutes, Mr. Stowe."

Beecher shouted an acknowledgment and sat back down on the chair. He packed away his journal and pulled his guitar onto his lap, said,

"So, you're off then?"

"I think it's best."

"And I don't get a say?"

"Not in this."

Beecher strummed the guitar aimlessly, wiped a few smudges from the neck.

Eeva was conciliatory, "It may all be for nothing…"

He completed her thought, "…but it's not a risk you're willing to take."

"It wasn't supposed to be this way," she said.

Beecher felt the humor and granted it a half-smile. He spied his jacket hanging in a closet, remembered a pack of smokes from the bus ride. He set the guitar down, went over and rifled the pockets.

"Don't be angry," she said.

"I'll try," he said, with his back to her. "Snooze says you don't remember the toothache, you just remember the coins under your pillow."

There was no response. He sensed the sudden emptiness and his pulse quickened and he turned his head toward the door. Eeva was gone. The scent of her perfume lingered. He ran through his options: cancel the gig; go after her; go on with the show. He replayed the first sighting of her under the Great Oak. He remembered how the light cut through the branches and cloaked her like a golden fleece. A lifetime had passed in the blink of an eye.

A knock on the door.

"Time to go, Mr. Stowe."

Chapter Thirty-Four

Beecher gathered with his band, his friends. They shared a few nervous jokes; shared the wish that Pengo's wiry frame should be behind the sound desk. The Glitter Boys and Rosy stepped aside, leaving the young ones to their banter.

"Packed house out there," Snooze said. "There's a boat load of celebrities in the front rows, so don't focus on the faces."

Fez and Harry spoke in unison, "Come on, who'd you see?"

"Don't worry about that now," Beecher said. "Keep your eyes on each other, watch for the changes. Think of the crowds back home looking for us to do good."

"Arch sends his best wishes," Snooze said. "He's only gone and got the Odeon to show the concert live. It sold out as soon as it was announced. I told him to take plenty of photos."

"God, I'd love to be there," Harry said.

Fez rolled his eyes.

"But you're here!"

"I know, I know," Harry said. "But imagine being there, seeing yourself up on that huge screen."

A trio of roadies hurried from the far side of the stage, each with flashlight beams strafing a floor strewn with cables. Last-minute hugs and handshakes were exchanged and Fez and Harry were led away, closely followed by Snooze, Rosy and the Glitter Boys. Beecher stood with the last stagehand feeling like a lost child in a department store. He listened. The air was filled with restless murmurs rising and falling in concert with the wandering breeze. The punters were consumers, one and all, some here for self-gratification, others to celebrate, with heads upturned in prayer to their chosen God, or simply to drain a bottle of beer.

Seated before the cavernous dome, the crowd sensed movement from within and responded accordingly, and but for a few errant wolf whistles, an eerie stillness fell across the venue. Pinpoints of light bathed the faces of television cameramen in a haunting glow, and Beecher watched as their bulky cameras came to bear on the spot where he would make his first appearance.

"A great opening shot," the director had said. "You, standing here, against a wall of light, you'll be isolated from the others."

Wanker.

"This is a band," Beecher said, "...not a fucking cabaret. Keep us all in the picture."

The director huffed a little disappointment so Eeva took him aside. A little pre-show diplomacy was annoyingly necessary to the success of the show.

With dignity restored, the director said, "We'll make history with this telecast."

If you only knew.

Snooze was busting to know the details.

"How'd you sort that out?"

Eeva flicked her eyes from side-to-side and flashed a cheeky smile.

"I made promises I won't keep," she said.

Beecher realized he'd been white-knuckling the neck of his guitar. He swapped hands, wiping the sweat from his palm. He noticed two televisions at the entrance to the stage. He moved closer. Commercial time. The set on the left showed some shirtless guy ridding himself of a serious case of dandruff; on the right, a bunch of kids dancing with an animated jug of lemonade.

America the Beautiful.

The network cut from dandruff guy in mid-shampoo. The screen was filled with streaks of red and white lights crisscrossed on a black canvas. The sound had been muted and it was a long moment before Beecher realized he was staring at an aerial view of the Hollywood freeway. Lanes of traffic were backed up for miles. The other TV cut from the commercial to a stock picture of his face superimposed over footage of exuberant fans carrying coolers and picnic baskets. He looked anemic and ghostlike staring out from the screen.

It wasn't supposed to be...

He caught himself. Eeva's words were tripping down the backstairs of his thoughts.

Maybe I am scared?

"Fear isn't always fright," she had said backstage. "I've been living in fear for forty years." She dropped her eyes. "I've only ever been frightened once."

Beecher had resisted the snarky comeback, bit his lip and tasted blood inside his mouth.

Fuck it, say what's on your mind.

He asked, "When was that?"

"Right now," she said.

The stagehand responded to a garbled request on his walkie talkie. He touched Beecher's sleeve.

"We're ready," he said. "I'll show you to your spot."

They skirted a towering row of speaker cabinets in pitch blackness as the first rumble of Rosy's bass and Harry's keyboards swelled up and out into the night. Soft purple lights bloomed at Beecher's feet and he found his mark and grabbed the microphone stand to steady his vertigo. He swiveled his head in search of a familiar face but found none. Power was fed to another bank of lights and a three-dimensional rendition of the known universe projected onto the curved superstructure brought the audience to their feet with ecstatic cheers and applause. Standing proud before it all, Beecher's band cast their shadows across galaxies and solar systems. And still, the volume grew, with Harry and Rosy layering and amplifying subsonic frequencies until the air pulsed with the force of a stampeding herd.

When the break came it was as though a meteor had crashed upon the land. Columns of fire streaked skyward and blinding lights washed the audience of all color and form. And then, he was there. The anointed hero of the day had been cut from the pack, wild and free.

Beecher Stowe played the extended intro with his back to the crowd, teasing the desires of the broken, and of the lonely, and of the virtuous, and of the failed. He turned and faced his audience as a man cast adrift by his own hand, and he fought to stifle the acid rising in his throat.

She made me, and now she has abandoned me.

The songs coursed from the stage to the world, and the people responded with a riotous fervor; with fists punching the stifling air.

Beecher strode before his band, tearing off lines of hypnotic melodies that cut through the night with the precision of a surgeon's scalpel. He enticed Harry and Snooze into trading phrases that were mournful, romantic, and triumphant, and challenged Fez to match his every step, pushing the boundaries of the groove to its thunderous limit. Nothing was off-limits today. He sparred with Rosy through every musical measure and was elated when ribbons of sweat dripped from the big man's face. Rosy had nearly forty years and a million miles on Beecher but he locked into the young star's rhythm as if they had been conceived by the same mother.

Song after song, the band drew tighter.

Harry shouted across to his bandmates, "I could do this forever," receiving, in essence, a "*me too,*" from all except Fez Bramble. His soul brother was not given to such brevity. The bombastic drummer issued an inarticulate stream of jubilant profanity that was picked up by every open microphone, flooding the airwaves with what he referred to as, "*the universal language.*" His burst of rock 'n roll enthusiasm sent sound engineers scrabbling for mute and delay buttons across a complex network of satellite transmissions, all the while rattling the nerves of cash-counting corporate suits. Correspondingly, the outburst was singularly responsible for educating the English-speaking world as to Fez's imminent servicing of the Rose and Crown's resident buxom barmaid. Henceforth, Sharon Godwin, of #13 South Africa Road, White City, London, would be immortalized on T-shirts with the slogan, *Shaggin' Sharon: Superstar.* They would become one of the more cherished collector items from the event.

The Last Song.

Beecher stood before the frenzied mob and called for silence. He wanted to speak, and he wanted to be heard. His voice echoed around the venue, folding back to the stage pitched lower than he expected. There was depth and there was warmth. It was the sound of someone he had yet to come to terms with.

"You are expecting to hear a song, a song that has meant a great deal to all of us. Somehow; someway, our desire to strive for more love, more connection, and more dignity, has been reflected in this coupling of words and music. I'd like to say I planned it all, but even I'm not that arrogant."

Beecher shot a sly wink at Snooze, who started a ripple of laughter amongst the band. He turned back to the audience and searched the faces for the one he loved most. A reserved seat bearing her name remained empty. He struggled for a moment to recall her face. He felt the quickening of his pulse. *What have I done?* The knife twisted in his belly. *Run, you fool.* In his head, sadistic voices mocked and screamed, "*You'll never be anything, you'll never be anyone.*" Beecher felt suddenly lifeless; felt his soul drift up and away, leaving his body pathetic and motionless. And with the hypnotic allure of a mirage, she was there - taking her seat, smoothing her skirts, smiling bright as the North Star. She nodded encouragingly, *"Finish this."*

Beecher snapped back, feeling an electric charge coursing through the microphone stand. He yanked his hand away and saw the soft, scarlet track across his palm. Snooze caught his eye, poised to sprint across the stage, *"You alright?"* Beecher saluted, showing off the burn.

He went on.

"When we come together like this, we are preparing each other for forgiveness; for the time when our strength and our character lies broken; for the time when we will depend on the compassion of others to see us through our many struggles. Today we are giving birth to a powerful memory. And this memory can heal those of us that are in need. We can look back and raise our voices in song and we'll be transported to a time when love filled our hearts; when the final words of goodbye to a friend were the truest you had ever spoken; and when you decided to place your fears second to the welfare of others, no matter where you stand."

Beecher was emphatic now. His voice was controlled and direct and he was speaking to one person.

"...because life is about standing for something bigger than you. So, I ask you now, will you stand?"

The crowd erupted with applause. They stood, row after row. From the coddled luxury of the millionaires down front to the cradle of hardscrabble hope and cheap after-shave beyond the reach of the lights. An air of confession had descended on the arena and Beecher milked it like a mid-western preacher.

He goaded the crowd, demanding over and over, "Will You Stand? Will You Stand?"

The people lapped it up, oblivious to their commitment, resolute to their desire. Fez caught Beecher's eye and began to hammer out the tempo for the final song and the chants fell into time, echoing from speakers large and small the world over. Harry and Snooze and Rosy and The Glitter Boys fought their way into the mix, obliging with ethereal, melodic runs befitting the opening of a classical aria.

And in a single, blinding flash, Beecher Stowe reached out and grabbed the microphone and gave himself to the world.

Chapter Thirty-Five

Eeva stepped aboard Hans Tomek's private Learjet 35 as Fez's first drumbeats landed with characteristic grandeur. She settled into the cool confines of the cabin, matching the click of her seat belt with the clunk of the aircraft's main door closing. Wheels were up less than five minutes later.

She stared out of the window, nursing a vodka and tonic, sipping delicately, wiping lipstick residue from the rim of the glass with her thumb. The ground shifted hues quickly as green, heavily-irrigated fields gave way to the featureless, brown desert. The dissolution of civilization was, in this way, poetic. She felt comfortable knowing the frontier had never been completely absorbed; that the magnitude of nature was ever-present. One only had to journey a few miles from the city to be swallowed by its expanse and to submit mind and body to the harshest of climates. It was a satisfying choice. This would be a fitting place to say goodbye.

Once the aircraft had reached cruising altitude, the co-pilot came into the rear cabin.

"Flight time is one hour and fifteen minutes," he said. "We will set down at a private airstrip about twenty-five miles from your final destination. A 4x4 will be waiting, she's been topped off and there are two extra Jerry cans filled with gas. And it's been fully stocked with water and provisions, as you requested."

"Thank you," she said. "Do you have any news on the weather in the area?"

"Last report was light winds out of the southwest and few scattered clouds at 6,000 feet, temperature was 67 degrees Fahrenheit. It'll be a nice night for stargazing."

"I look forward to it."

She refilled her glass with ice and tonic water and swirled the contents until the popping and cracking sounds subsided. A radio set was built into the bulkhead and she made to switch it on, then paused.

Is it better to know when the end is coming?

Her thoughts danced through the many hours of intimate conversations between her and the protege, Beecher Stowe. She allowed herself to wallow in thoughts of failure and remorse and rejection. Her love could no longer be held at bay. She did not belong to this age, and yet she craved his companionship and his trust. Hans Tomek had been the paternal figure she knew she would one day lose. In this regard, the passage of time has no sentiment or compassion. Loss is loss.

And love is love.

The aircraft dipped its port wing, changing course, heading northeast.

There was static at first. She turned the dial, searching for the best signal. Beecher Stowe and his band commanded the airwaves this winter's night, weaving sublime melodies into works of art that wrestled fear from the downtrodden and breathed new leases of life into the hopeless. Those magnificent misfits had come of age in her time.

And on their wings, I will return.

The pressure in the cabin changed. The descent had begun.

The Learjet touched down on the abandoned runway and rolled to a stop. The co-pilot ducked into the main cabin and opened the door, inviting warm, desert air to fill the interior with the scent of wild sagebrush. He escorted Eeva to the 4x4 and made sure the engine started with no difficulty.

He shouted above the roar of the turbines, "Are you sure you will be okay?"

She answered with a thumbs-up, *"Yes, all good."*

He shook her hand goodbye and re-boarded. The jet made an about-face and taxied back for the entire length of the runway. By the time the aircraft nosed up into the Arizona night, Eeva was almost five miles away.

Racing across the desert plain, the Jeep's headlights carved vibrant, yellow tunnels through the inky blackness. Eeva paid no mind to the smaller patches of scrub, she plowed through them, hands loose on the wheel. On the radio, Beecher Stowe was in full flight. By her reckoning, the half-way point of the concert had been reached. There had been high energy and soft refrains and stirring solos and moments of levity between lifelong friends. She wanted nothing more than to be by his side, finding it difficult to dismiss a persistent sense of longing, relegating it to the pit of her stomach where it paced like a caged animal. Her answer was to press her foot harder to the floor, finding the rush of speed to be intoxicating.

Ten miles from her destination, Eeva ran into a wall of weather. From out of nowhere, sheets of driving rain ringed the canyon rim, muddying the ground with scattered ponds of axle-deep water. She drove on with wipers beating in time to the rhythm pouring from the speakers. Mile after mile, squinting through the deluge, Eeva drove entombed within a wall of water that draped across the vehicle like heavy, translucent flags stirred by a steady wind. She eased off the gas and slowed the vehicle to a crawl. Familiar landmarks appeared - a rock formation here; a clump of bushes there. She was close.

The speakers went silent. She turned the volume knob to its stop. There was only the white noise of the anxious crowd. And then there was his voice. A stir of emotion rippled through the audience. Beecher was talking.

"When we come together like this, we are preparing each other for forgiveness; for the time when our strength and our character lies broken; for the time when we will depend on the compassion of others..."

A movement to her left drew Eeva's eye. The first rainbow ascended through a cloud of purple fog, bright as daybreak, saturated with color and vibrant as a child's painting. The ambient light spread like wildfire and through the rain, Tomek's camp rose from the scrub like a lost temple.

Eeva slammed the accelerator to the floor and raced forward.

"Today we are giving birth to a powerful memory. And this memory can heal those of us that are in need."

She stepped from the vehicle, shielding herself against needles of ice moving across the landscape in thick sheets. She shouted Tomek's name again, and again. In these final moments, she realized that there was still more to say; thoughts and feelings unexplored.

"...because life is about standing for something bigger than you. So, I ask you now, will you stand?"

The final song pulsed from the car radio, projecting louder and louder, and Eeva ran towards the canyon's edge; toward a thousand rainbows rising to kiss the sky, arcing to every horizon.

"Hans!" she screamed. "Hans, wait!"

The passage of decades had not been in vain, nor had they been exhausted. But now the endless blanket of time was being pulled away and she was suddenly lost and alone.

"Supermassive Superstar your life, let me see those super magic eyes..."

She found Tomek, sodden, curled small as a child. The recognition of her role in his life came upon her in an instant - this man had never wanted to be alone. He had sheltered her as he had the orphans. And now he faced the eternal void once more.

"...*and I felt the same desire. Mmm, take us back, to the places we know; take a little piece of freedom and you fly...*"

Hans Tomek lifted his palm.

"No," he said, wearing a mask of acceptance and resolve. "You will find your place."

She hesitated, staring at the widening crack that separated their bodies like an irreparable wound setting continents adrift.

And Beecher Stowe's symphony expired.

And together they bathed in the silence of nature. The ground faltered underfoot and Eeva was thrown backward. She pressed her hands to her face and wept. And as the final onslaught of the squall moved away, she heard the reassurance of Tomek's voice, and it was rich and smooth as aged scotch.

"Take care of my family," he said.

And through laced fingers, she answered.

"I will."

The slab of granite separated without a sound. Hans Tomek's body fell slowly, with arms outstretched, spinning weightless, dissolving from sight within the rolling, retreating fog bank, soon becoming as insignificant as a raindrop on the surface of the winding Colorado River.

Eeva turned away from the canyon, blinking away dirt and tears. She did not look back. She walked the moonlit trail for hours but could not find any sign of the camp or her vehicle. She slept in the shelter of a small dune, awakening at first light to the sound of wood being chopped nearby. An old truck was parked at the edge of a ravine and a man was clearing brush with pick and ax. Eeva approached him, straightening her hair, adjusting her clothing.

"Fancy you being out here all alone," the man said.

"I seem to have lost my way back to my 4x4."

"Your what?"

"My vehicle, it was parked..."

Eeva turned through 360 degrees and did not recognize the landmarks.

The man was wary, "Never heard of any woman spending time out here alone."

His cheek was stuffed with tobacco and a thin, golden stain cut his beard like dried honey. The man hooked a grubby finger between his lips and flicked the juicy wad onto the dirt.

"You sure you ain't in trouble?"

Eeva caught the slight and ignored it, "I must have wandered further than I thought. Can you give me a ride into the nearest town?"

"Might'n you give me a few minutes to finish up here and I'd be happy to get you some help. I've got a supervisor that is gonna jump all over me if I don't get these markers placed."

"What are they for?"

"Some new road they're buildin'. They say them tourists don't wanna take the train no more. You can go on and wait in the truck if you like. I got some sandwiches and a few apples packed under the seat if you're hungry."

She thanked the man and made her way up to the lip of the ravine. The pick-up was a tired old rig. In places, the kiss of the desert sun had bleached the paint back to bare metal.

Eeva was ten paces from the driver's door when her heart kicked off a few irregular beats and her knees buckled. Her vision wavered and she struggled for breath, with fists clawing and clenching in loose sand.

The license plate showed an embossed black number, *W466,* on a yellow background. The notation across the top read, *ARIZONA 38.*

The man saw her fall and hurried over.

"You need some help, missy?"

"The year," she said, pointing at the truck. "What year is it?"

"I got her in the summer of '31. She's my workhorse, never lets me down. You think maybe you're in need of some water? Let's get ya..."

Eeva's voice cracked hoarse and insistent, "Not the truck, the date. What's the fucking year?"

The man was affronted and immediately hostile.

"I ain't never been spoken to like that by a woman," he said. "You mind your mouth if you expect my hospitality."

He stared down at Eeva, saw the desperation in her face and his anger softened.

He said, "Well, it's 1938, don't ya know?"

Chapter Thirty-Six

Harry woke first. He lobbed a shoe across the room, knocking Fez upside the head.

"On your bike, matey, we gotta be out of the room in twenty minutes or else they'll charge for another day."

The hangover had started at Fez's toes and was working its way north, perilously slow. He'd felt it coming on all night. At one point, he got all transcendental, willing it into the shape of a cloud, visualizing it dissipating like early morning mist on the Thames Embankment. That didn't work, so he got up and drank a gallon of water. That didn't work, either. So, it was time for the magic fingers. Two should do it. Shove and hold; gag and puke. In the dark, he missed the bowl by a foot or more. He also got more than he bargained for as, under exertion, a well-lubed turd shot from his ass onto the bare floor. Worse still, he didn't notice; too busy clambering back to the bed with the room spinning like a Sopwith Camel's prop. He traipsed fresh shit across the carpet, through Harry's bundle of discarded clothes and tucked his feet back under the sheets and fell sound asleep.

That was three hours ago.

Harry yawned, smacked his lips, said,

"We should open a window, smells a bit ripe in here."

Snooze and the Glitter Boys were down first, bags packed, anxious for the coming round of goodbyes to be over.

"Rosy's getting the car, he'll be along in a minute," Earl said. "What about Beecher?"

"He's gone, mate," Snooze said. "Don't worry about it."

Eddie said, "You not flying back with him?"

"Nah, I don't think so," Snooze said.

"How come you don't go with him?"

"I offered," he said, "…but it's best I look out for the lads, see they get on the plane okay."

As if on cue, Fez and Harry wandered into the reception area looking like two recently unearthed mummies.

"Here they are," Snooze said. "England's answer to abstinence."

"I'm starving," Fez said.

"You've not an ounce of respect for the parting of ways, Fez. Take a minute and…"

"I can't help it if I'm hungry."

Snooze shrugged him off, turned to Harry, "More goodbyes, mate."

Harry choked back a tear and squeaked out his fondness for the brothers.

"I hope it isn't goodbye, …you know, like not forever."

Eddie and Earl wrapped Harry in consecutive bear hugs, extending only a nervous hand in Fez's direction.

"I love you, Fez," Earl said, "…but I ain't never seen no one drink that much beer. I'm sure I don't want that all over my shoes."

"Too late, "Harry said. "The cleaning woman screamed when she saw the bog."

Fez felt the tickle of rancid scotch coat the back of his throat but managed a quick smile.

Rosy rolled the Cadillac to a stop under the vast awning that served as the front entrance. He parked a few yards away. He wasn't alone. From the rear, two Afro's competed for stature. The passenger's won out for its immaculate sheen. The car door opened and a pair of nuclear-orange platform soles hit the driveway, followed by a shimmering silver jumpsuit. Rosy heaved his own bulk from the driver's seat and yelled,

"Look who I found up on Sunset."

The man was known by the Glitter Boys and a great deal of whooping and hollering ensued, with the smack of skin on skin echoing like summertime firecrackers.

Snooze took Harry and Fez aside and left Rosy and the Glitters to meet and greet without the need for any awkward introductions.

"Pancakes," Snooze said. "I think we've got time for one more go at the big stack. Whaddya say?"

"Sound idea," Fez piped up.

"I can't believe we're going home," Harry said, the melancholy alive and well in his tone.

"All good things…," Snooze said. "Anyway, think of the stories you'll have for the girls back home. You won't be able to buy a drink for months."

"Like anything's changed on that front," Fez said. "Short arms, deep pockets, that's what this boy has."

The mutual needling survived through breakfast and well into their third cup of coffee, right up until Luna parked herself next to Snooze and announced all was settled with hotel bills and taxis and..,

"...this lot," she said, waving her arm over stacks of plates smeared with maple syrup and egg yolk residue. "I'm down to a few notes and some coins, so from here on out it's every man for himself."

With Eeva off the scene, Luna had reverted to black jeans, ox-blood Doc Marten's and a baggy Ziggy Stardust T-shirt tied at the waist. Clearly, dear old Snooze was smitten.

The four sat in the booth, killing time with small talk, always with one eye on the clock. Deep down they were shell-shocked and silent and lost. The waitress cleared away the dirty plates and put a fresh ashtray on the table.

"Oh, shit, that reminds me," Luna exclaimed. "I was supposed to give something to Harry."

She stood and rustled through her jeans pocket, piling up crumpled dollar bills on the table and shaking off strands of lint. She finally came up with a matchbook.

"I don't smoke," Harry said, "...well, not fags."

"I know," Luna said. "Rosy gave it to me. There's a name and number on the inside cover. He said if you're ever back in Los Angeles you should give this bloke a call because he saw the gig and freaked out; he loved your playing."

Harry flipped the matchbook open. The handwriting was barely legible. It read:

Harry, you got style, man!
Gimme a call, let's hang.
L. R.

Fez nosed over his shoulder, screwed up his face, "Who the fuck is L.R.?"

Harry felt nine pancakes, two fried eggs and eight rashers of bacon begin to dance the Meringue.

Luna was quick to respond, "Lionel Richie."

Harry sighed, said quietly, "Mate, I think I'm gonna spew."

Chapter Thirty-Seven

Beecher Stowe drove for most of the day. Heading east, exchanging coastal fog and a cool ocean breeze for slate blue, cloudless skies and the steady assault of a southern tempest that milked the water from his soul. His ride was a 1953 Jaguar XK120 Drophead Coupe. Midnight black, with a red leather interior. Hans Tomek said memories were made for this.

He gassed up the car three times before he decided to stop for food. A handwritten placard tacked to a telephone pole at the side of the highway announced, *Last chance for home cooking*. It sealed the deal.

The notice pointed to a dull and dusty Airstream with a tattered awning that threatened more shade than it delivered. Spirals of smoke rose from three portable grills tended to by a heavy-set woman whose face was hidden by a wide, flowery scarf. Beecher tapped the menu, ordered barbecued chicken and rice and beans. He ate alone at a picnic bench, mopping his platter with fresh tortillas and sipping a cold beer. The table was gouged with graffiti such as badly drawn heart shapes with names scored beneath, and allegiances to sports teams, and crude scratchings of cocks and balls, and a particular work of art that struck Beecher as soundly ironic - a pair of Superman's iconic symbols used as capital letters for the title of his very own song. He drained the beer, set the empty aside and opened a second. In America, it takes two to get a buzz.

A station wagon pulled into the dirt car park with kids hanging from the open windows like panting dogs. They clambered from the innards of the car before the resulting dust cloud had settled, stretching, running and shouting. The mother herded them away from the man nursing the six-pack; the father looked longingly at the man sitting alone supping a brew.

Two more cars came and went before Beecher decided to move on. He thanked the woman and overpaid, refusing to take any change for the hundred dollar bill. He cast a pensive glance at his classic ride. The Jaguar wore a beige skirt of road dirt for the length of her body and thick layers of sand covered the red interior like a second skin. He used wadded napkins to wipe the seats and dash clean before raising the roof and squeezing his six-foot frame behind the oversized steering wheel. He unfolded a map of the American southwest and stared at a vast emptiness. Nothing but thousands of square miles of brown dirt scarred with thin, black lines connecting small, white dots. He noted a couple of the towns from the old music hall standard, *Route 66* - Amarillo, Texas; Gallup, New Mexico. His heart skipped a beat when he traced the road west and saw Flagstaff, Arizona. He marked his position at some two hundred and fifty miles south, hugging the border of Mexico. He thought about heading north but the car was aimed east.

In his memory, Eeva's face was translucent against the vast sky and her voice was soft and wise, "No point turning into the past," she said. "Your life is over there." She nodded at the horizon. "Don't be consumed by reminiscing. Trust me, it's heartache, 24 hours-a-day, seven-days-a-week."

"Sometimes it's hard not to dwell on the past," Beecher said.

"That would be guilt or shame talking. You'd do best to free your mind of all of that nonsense, and trust me, it is fucking nonsense."

"Ooh, that's a little salty. I don't think I've ever heard you talk like that."

"I can hold my own when I want to."

Beecher was startled by the sound of a diesel generator. He'd been lost in a daydream, eyes closed, head bowed in half-sleep. The Airstream was suddenly awash in light. Strings of tiny, yellow bulbs swayed in the breeze like hanging sunflowers. In the failing dusk, the old woman stared in his direction, trying to make out if anyone was sitting in the darkened interior. He flicked on the headlights. She looked straight through him and went on about her business.

Beecher rubbed his eyes and checked the map. He settled on a town thirty miles distant to stop for the night. He eased back onto the lonely highway, the sole occupant of the two-lane blacktop. The Jaguar spun up effortlessly, quickly exceeding the stated speed limit. The beer buzz was a warm blanket around Beecher's shoulders and he lowered the window, luxuriating in the feel of the night air swirling around the tiny cabin. The scent of Italian leather and the feel of English walnut and the stark beauty of the desert exploded within his senses and for a fleeting moment, he thought nothing of the past nine months.

THE BUENA VISTA MOTEL.

A sign bragged in violet neon the words, *VACANCY* and *COLOR TV.* They were laid out in crooked letters, as was the creatively misspelled, *H..ATED POOL.*

Beecher turned off the highway and pulled up in front of a door marked, OFFICE. He opened the car door and listened to the Jaguar burbling away for a moment before turning the key. The silence was complete except for the tinkling sounds of the engine and exhaust cooling and an occasional burst of canned laughter filtering through net curtains that hung straight and still in the airless night.

"Rooms are fifteen dollars."

The clerk was a middle-aged woman. She had a kind face and was soft-spoken.

Pretty at some point in her life.

"You'll be in room seven."

"As luck would have it," Beecher said.

"I guess so, seeing as all the other rooms are flooded. We had a rainstorm last night that wouldn't quit. Stretched all the way up to the Nevada border."

"I'm just passing through," he said. "The weather seems kinda perfect now."

"Oh, you're from out East or somewhere, ain't ya?"

"London is about as East as I've been, so yeah, I suppose I am."

The woman studied Beecher's face.

"You look so familiar. Then again, I say that to every person that comes through that door. We had a blonde woman stop by a while back and I coulda swore we'd been at the same high school. I called her Betty and gave her a hug and everything until she started talking all strange. My Jimmy says it was Russian or Polish or something, and that I must be an idiot 'cause she don't look nothing like the real Betty who didn't even have blonde hair."

Such was life in a town where the population numbered 167 souls and the average summertime temperature was 106 degrees Fahrenheit.

"We see it up near 120 degrees some days," the woman said, wrapping her arms around a bundle of clean towels. "Jimmy says he don't feel much difference, but then again, he don't venture too far from the TV, if you know what I mean."

Her laugh was all her own. It started as a chuckle, developed into a snort and ended with a small hiccup.

"If you're looking for nightlife, there's a bar at the other end of town," she said. "Pay no mind to the lights being turned off out front. Charlie the owner is having a tussle with the power company. He's got his beer in coolers out back and he's put some candles on the tables. I think it's kinda quaint. Just watch out for the Indians."

Beecher's expression was enough.

"The Indians," she repeated, as if it was an everyday annoyance, like mosquitoes or cloudbursts or taxes. "Some of them wander around the town when it's dark. They don't say much, they mostly just look around."

Confused and wary, Beecher unlocked the door to unit number seven. It was a predictable square of white walls and brown shag-pile carpet. A double bed took center stage, with an easy chair and a four-drawer dresser in supporting roles. The TV had rabbit ears formed out of bent coat hangers and the bathroom presented a decor that was best described as being sympathetic to the dismembering of wayward travelers. With every detail of the room burning into his mind and overwhelming his sense of smell, he thought this might be a good place to write songs or a novel. Left alone to fend for himself he wouldn't miss the memories. She had an island; he might as well have a room.

Beecher locked up and went exploring. There was a grim beauty about the town. And everything was warm to the touch - the road, the walls, the pavement. The heat rising underfoot made his body feel positively buoyant. He walked the length of Main Street which, as it turned out, was the only street. Eight shiny parking meters stood like obedient soldiers before angled spaces. They lined only one side of the street, as did a drugstore and a lumber depot. All signs of active commerce faced off against a row of derelict brick buildings wearing skins of sun-bleached plywood. The street was dark enough to map the stars; light enough to pick out patches of grass sprouting like pleading fingers from cracks in the asphalt - the optimistic beneficiaries of pooled groundwater. The sidewalk ended at a vacant lot strewn with piles of gravel and concrete rubble and picked up again at a cluster of single-story shacks, isolated and darkened but for the lick of flames coming from a fire pit set a ways out back. Voices, animated with laughter and chatter, and the deep, dominating growl of an obvious blowhard, carried through the stillness and Beecher stopped, thrust his hands in his pockets and wondered if his racing thoughts could be quieted long enough for making the requisite small talk. He checked his watch, saw the time as only 9:30 pm, and decided that a beer was in order.

"…fourth down," the giant said, "…on fourth down, you gotta go for it."

The words landed as a directive, rather than part of a conversation. He caught Beecher's entrance to the circle.

"Go on, ask the long hair."

The shadows of five cowboy hats atop bodies hunkered down in lawn chairs danced along the side of the building. Heads turned, eyes trained on the newcomer.

"Just here for a beer," Beecher said.

"Pay no mind to Lucas," a voice from the shadows said. "There's cans of Budweiser on ice in the trough, and I've got bottles of Coors over there in the coolers. They's all a buck-a-piece. Make a tick on the sheet, we'll settle up later."

Beecher rolled up a sleeve and dunked his arm up to the elbow in the trough and chased a few cans around. He snagged one, popped the top and brought it to his lips. The water dripping from his hand had a strong odor.

The voice from the shadows piped up again, "Sorry 'bout the whiff, it's harmless. Had to wrestle the damn thing out of the barn yesterday. Don't think I got it washed out too good."

The giant said, "A little snake piss'll put hairs on your chest."

He howled at his own joke and the air shook. Beecher shoved the thought aside.

The voice went on, "Them sons-a-bitches cut my electricity off. Says I didn't pay the full amount on my bill. I told 'em, I don't pay for blackouts, which is what we get around here every other week. The whole town was out last night. Strangest storm I ever saw."

Beecher asked, "Are you Charlie?"

The voice became a fully-rounded face as a hat was tilted back and the fire glow lit up craggy cheeks and ebony eyes and a toothless smile.

"That'll be me. You holed up at the *Buena Vista*?"

"Yeah, seemed like a good place to stop for the night."

"If you can swim, that is," the giant said. "I heard the whole place was flooded out."

"Oh, hush up, Lucas. Irene and Jimmy will have the place dried out soon enough."

Charlie waved Beecher over to an empty chair.

"What brings you out to these parts?"

"Just driving through, taking the long way home. Back to England."

"That sure is a pretty place."

"Oh, come on, you ain't been further west than Albuquerque," Lucas was clearly craving some attention.

'Fuck you, I ain't," Charlie shot back. "I's was out there on my honeymoon back in '65."

"Which one?"

"Dolores Soffit. Knew her in school. She had a couple of divorces under her belt, too. But we's married in Phoenix and flew out the next day. Went to New York on the ways there, and on the ways back. Her parents paid for the whole thing. Rained every damn day. They gots more history over in them parts than you'd ever believe."

Lucas fumbled with trying to better the story. All that came out was a frustrated grumble. Beecher felt suddenly sorry for the big man, said,

"Yeah, but out here you have this amazing scenery on your doorstep. I've only ever seen places like this in the movies."

A gentle murmur of acknowledgment spread throughout the group.

Beecher finished his beer, bypassed the trough and stepped up to one of the coolers.

"Anyone else?"

All quiet, except for Lucas.

"You buying?"

"Absolutely."

"Then that's a yes."

Lucas came across and took the bottle in a fist big enough to hide a small child. He was dressed in paint-stained overalls and sported a shock of hair that rimmed his bald dome like a whitewashed fence.

Beecher couldn't resist, "How tall are you?"

"Just shy of seven feet."

"Been that way since before he was a teenager," Charlie said, laughing. "Someone must've filled his boots with pig shit in first grade."

"Are you all family?"

"Might'n as well be," Charlie said. "Small town like this, you kinda get to be in each other's business whether you like it or not."

There were more good-natured grumbles of agreement. Charlie coughed, hacking long and hard. He brought up something thick and slimy and dispatched it into the flames like it had been fired from a gun. He knocked out a pipe on the sole of his boot and began to stuff it with fresh tobacco from a leather pouch. That's when Beecher realized Charlie only had one hand. He gripped the pouch with the stump of his right arm, scooped it full and packed it tight with one finger. He brought out a

Zippo, wheeled the flint and sucked on the rich, aromatic blend until it burned fiery red.

Charlie let out a thin trail of blue smoke from the side of his mouth, said, "What about you, you got any family?"

The question seemed harmless enough; the answer, even more so. But something in Charlie's tone set Beecher on edge. Hans Tomek's last words were, *"Take care of your family."* A spark of anger flared in his gut. The concept of family seemed suddenly disposable. Family wasn't friendship or bandmates. Family was bloodlines and organ donations. Boozing with your mates down at The Railway Tavern wasn't the definition of family. Putting up with a shedload of inherited bullshit, that's family. Getting punched in the face repeatedly, just for being a kid, that's family. He didn't have a family. Fuck family. Beecher clenched his hands together to stop the shaking.

"Not for a while," he said.

A perfectly acceptable moment of silence passed and then Beecher raised the empty beer bottle, said,

"Got anything stronger?"

"What, like whisky?"

"That'll do."

"I got some firewater, the stuff they brew on the reservation. Ain't legal, but it gets the job done."

"Just like the movies," Beecher said.

"Charlie can't handle it," Lucas said. "Gives him the pukes and the shits."

Charlie put up a weak defense, "It does not."

The bottle was fetched and when held up to the firelight it was cloudy and brown.

"Don't look at it boy," Lucas said. "Get it poured and get it down your neck."

Beecher took a shot and felt the burn rise from his stomach and shoot up his throat. His eyes misted over for a spell and a line of sweat broke out across his upper lip. When he wiped at it with his fingers he found the skin around his mouth to be numb.

One of the other cowboy hats perked up, "Lemme get a taste of that, Lucas."

Lucy Doherty was the motel manager's big sister. Beecher would soon come to know she had fucked every guy in the town, married or not. And what's more, no one seemed to mind. She was pleasant; she was part of the scenery and actually kinda cute in a certain light. She despised the thought of marriage, and she couldn't bear children, so she posed no threat to the other women. She was only a whore if you counted food and shelter, for which she was passed around like a bread basket at dinner time. Other than that, she took no money.

"Lucy, you know the doctor said you gotta ease off the hard stuff," Charlie said.

She removed her hat and ran thin, bony fingers through silver hair, shaking off the loose strands as if touched by plague. Beecher reckoned she had an aging Bond-girl thing going on. He'd seen off a few like her during his stint bouncing at Coco's Basement - divorced, on the prowl, dressed up to the nines, reeking of Brandy and Coke, slathered with enough make-up to mount a West End production of *Cabaret*, and absolutely gagging for it. The prey, on any given night, would start off as the bloke that bought her a round or two, might even extend to the barman if he wasn't too much of a gargoyle. Most likely, it would be the bouncer of an after-hours club (him), or the cabbie that dropped her off. A Lucy from Arizona could easily have been a Sheila from Tottenham or a Brenda from Tooting.

The reservation whisky wove its spell. The campfire was now a confessional. The big man was the first to fall to its lubricated charms.

"...she was my best friend's girl, but it weren't like we knew each other that good. Only saw her a few times growing up. We just made each other laugh. Ain't known any other woman been able to do that."

"God moves in strange ways," Lucy said. "He mighta been testin' you both to see if you'd sin."

Charlie said, "You can't help who you love."

The old man's words were drenched with melancholy and Beecher was unsettled. He drank more and his pulse spiked liked fingers drumming on his chest, biding their time, keeping pace with the faltering rhythm, waiting for the moment when they'd reach in and wring his heart empty of the last drops of tainted blood.

Lucy poured another shot.

"You love her, Lucas?"

"I do. I did. But she never knew."

"She's not around no more?"

"She passed last spring. Cancer ate her down to the bone."

"That why you were back east?"

"Yeah, I helped clear out the house, she didn't have much."

All eyes were focused on the scarlet embers scattered within the fire pit. Charlie got up and walked into the dark, came back with an armload of wood. He dropped them from waist height and dribbled on a little whisky from the bottle and jumped back.

"Jesus, Charlie!" Lucy shouted, brushing sparks from her clothes. "These are my best blue jeans. I lost the last pair from sitting around this damn fire."

"There's a sale on over in Bisbee," Lucas said. "...saw it on the TV."

"I ain't driving no fifty miles for a stupid sale."

Charlie said, "What would you drive it for?"

She laughed, "A hot bath and a steak dinner."

"I'd drive it for ice cream," Lucas said. "They got that place that serves thirty-one flavors."

"What about you, young man? What would you drive fifty miles for?"

"Back home, fifty miles would put me either in the middle of the country or in the ocean. So I'm gonna choose the ocean. I'd drive fifty miles to sit on the beach and stare at the waves."

"I ain't never seen the ocean," Lucy said. "Maybe you'll take me with you?"

"Whoa there, Bessie," Charlie said. "This fella don't need your old bones slowing him down."

Charlie leaned forward and spat into the flames. He's got a secret a mile long and two miles high. You can see it in his eyes. It's eatin' him up. You in love or something, young man?"

As sure as a spotlight was aimed, all faces turned in Beecher's direction. This was sport for the locals; something to gossip on when the stranger left town. They had a million stories to chew on but fresh meat tasted best.

Beecher drained his glass and picked up and shook the empty bottle. "Got any more?"

"I think we got another one around here somewhere," Charlie said.

"Go get it and I'll tell you a story that'll blow your fucking mind."

And so, by the light of a Mesquite fire and a billion stars, a few expectant strangers sipped rot-gut and heard told the tale of time travelers and music and friendship, and abandonment.

Lucy was soured.

"Where's the happy ending?"

"It ain't ended yet," Lucas said. "Has it ended?"

Beecher was slurring now. They were all slurring now.

Charlie was wearing his booze like a suit of armor.

"You believe all this shit? I'm alive for sixty-five years and I don't believe any of this shit."

Lucy wore the drink like a precious fur coat.

"Some story, huh? I don't care if it ain't real."

"If you can remember it sober, it's real," Lucas said. "My ol' man told me that."

"Your ol' man was a drunk," Charlie said.

"Party's over, boys," Lucy said.

She hooked an arm under Charlie's elbow and hoisted him to his feet.

"Sure as eggs is eggs," she said. "You can set your watch by his temper."

Beecher stood and took a few uneasy steps, found his balance and walked out into the dark.

"Other way," Lucy shouted.

He about-faced, lifted his hand in a playful wave, snorted out a laugh. He got as far as the drug store and ran out of steam. A wooden bench facing the derelict buildings beckoned and there he rested with the night draping over him warm as a wool sweater. He smoked his last cigarette and flicked the butt into the street and mind and body folded in concert and he closed his eyes and slept.

Eeva's face was everywhere - on the boarded windows and doors; in the constellations overhead. And she was drawn angry and scowling within the wide, tarry seams of broken asphalt.

"Such a chance we gave you," she hissed, "...such a stage upon which to speak your truth."

"I did what I needed to," Beecher said.

"You are such a little boy. When will you walk like a man and cast your spear into the flesh of a raging lion? What bravery will you muster to earn your crown?"

Beecher's sleeping conscience sparred with the dream girl.

"What's with all the theatrics? Why're you acting weird?"

Eeva lay on a bed of summer grass and laughed at him.

"You can't handle normal."

"Says who?"

"Why didn't you fuck me?"

Continents have collided with less of an impact. Beecher reached for her. He clawed at the air but she floated clear, mocking his frantic efforts.

"I didn't because..."

HEY!!!

A bellow that could've toppled trees and the distant sound of shattering glass sent Beecher rigid as a week-old corpse. His eyes flew open, and he was blinded by a fist of morning sun pounding into his brain like George Foreman wailing on a heavy bag.

"Now go and pick all that shit up!"

Lucas the Giant was screaming at three teenage boys. They each had a slingshot dangling from their left hand, and each let go of a golf ball-sized rock from their right. The boys were tearaways from the reservation. They'd exhausted pocket loads of ammunition on rabbits and birds and a lone coyote. The town was a new and fertile hunting ground.

Lucas tore out of the drugstore's front door letting go with another tirade and the boys took off like roadrunners.

Lucas's bluster dissipated quickly. He stepped from the sidewalk onto the street. Turned to Beecher, said,

"You gotta be impressed, that's one helluva shot. Must be fifty yards or more."

Truth is, the boys had loosed their unified firepower simultaneously in a beautifully choreographed display of native brotherhood. For whom the honor should be bestowed upon for connecting with such incredible accuracy, they would never know.

Lucas sauntered his bulk over to where Beecher slouched.

"You get up with the dawn, or you been here all night?"

"All night," he said, with no degree of certainty.

"Man, we told some lies last night, eh?"

"Did we?"

"Sure. Once the hooch gets passed around, the evening starts gettin' good."

In the glow of the new sun, Lucas was a mountain with legs. A more powerful-looking man Beecher had never laid eyes upon. Chest as wide and square as a refrigerator, and forearms like Christmas hams. If anything, his size was the only aspect of his presence Beecher had nailed. Where he had taken Lucas for being mostly bald, his hair was merely tightly cropped - *fully carpeted*, as Snooze would say.

"You wanna use the facilities, go ahead," he said. "There's coffee on the hotplate. I gots to go and chase these brats down otherwise they'll think it's open season on every sheet of glass in the county."

Lucas bounded down the street decked out in a fresh pair of pressed overalls and white sneakers the size of canoes. He moved like he'd just had a soothing massage rather than three hours sleep. Beecher staggered to his feet, found a sweet spot of balance to calm the bells ringing in his head, and attempted to suck it up and ease his aching body back to the motel. The aroma of the coffee pot changed his mind.

The drugstore sold more than drugs. It was like stepping onto a movie set from the fifties - part general mercantile, part diner. A stainless steel lunch counter with red vinyl stools commanded the floor, with racks of comics and pulp fiction fixed to the wall at either end. Stands of witches brooms and string mops guarded other household wares, and plumbing supplies, shovels, hoes and axes hung from iron hooks like an executioner's armory.

Beecher let himself behind the counter, found two pots of coffee. He avoided the decaf, poured a cup of the regular and ladled in three spoons of sugar. He held the cup to his lips, bathing tired eyes in the rising steam. There was a ceremony in the act of hangover cures. This was his. Behind sealed eyelids the regret was complete.

"Tied one on, didn't we?"

Lucas came back, panting a little. He reached over the counter and grabbed a half gallon of milk and upended the jug until it was empty.

"Did you catch 'em?"

It was all Beecher could muster.

"Yeah, down past Charlie's bar. They're good kids. Bored out of their minds. We did the same thing at their age. What about you? Get into much trouble?"

"Had the coppers 'round a few times. Just little things. Probably not as serious as here?"

"What do you mean?"

"You lot carry guns; we just got a belt 'round the ear."

"Our Sheriff carried a rifle in his car," Lucas said. "Never saw him take it out. He'd lock us up, though. Throw us in with the drunks for a few hours. We'd end up playing cards for most of the day until the ol' man would come get us after he got off work. He'd always wait until after dinner was cleared away before he took the strap to me and my brother."

"That must've been a tense meal."

"Got outta hand a couple of times. Once, when he was drunk, he ended up on his ass and we laughed. That didn't go down too well."

Beecher came around and took a stool.

"And the other?"

"Ah, you know, there comes a time when you don't want to take it anymore. I got bigger than him pretty quick, told him I'd had enough if you know what I mean."

"I'm guessing that that didn't smooth things over."

Lucas nodded up at a framed photo hanging on the wall over by the coffee pots.

"Fathers and sons, what are ya gonna do?"

Beecher walked back around the counter and stared up at the photo of a man in shirt sleeves leaning next to a truck parked in front of what appeared to be a half-built house. He was slighter than Lucas, but the features were unmistakable. The man had an arm draped around the shoulders of a woman, her face was hidden by wind-tousled hair and harsh, midday shadows. *Click; one frame exposed.* The man and woman dressed alike - work clothes, muddied and baggy. Her mouth was set and unsmiling; her body was rigid and so very thin.

Beecher turned, studied Lucas, pegged him to be about forty, maybe a little older.

On the photo again, "Is that your mother?"

"No, Mom was taken while giving birth to my brother. That's our stepmother. Well, sort of. They never married. The ol' man helped her out at some point and she settled close by. After Mom's passing, she raised us best she could."

"She doesn't seem too happy to have her picture taken."

"Probably more to do with him. He worked us like dogs building that house."

"You live there?"

"I did 'til a few years back. Couldn't find anyone willing to help out with the farm. Sun and storms beat those old wooden homes up pretty good, so I was spending all my time on repairs."

Lucas pointed to a set of black and white photographs hanging over the door frame. Landscapes showing the changing seasons - cracked windows filtering sunlight with cosmic brilliance; the house alone on the wide desert plain engulfed by an ethereal mist; the roofline cutting into a boiling range of cumulus clouds.

"That's the house, such as it is now."

Beecher was lost in the images' artistry and grace.

"You do this for a living?"

"Used to. It was a great way to see the world."

The bellowing stranger he'd encountered the previous night was a fraud.

"I took you for something else."

"Such as?"

Beecher didn't own up.

"Just not this."

Lucas smiled, "I tends to fuck with strangers until they show some spirit."

"And what is my spirit, exactly?"

"Your story was honest. That's spirit enough."

"No one believed me."

"Oh, I dunno, small-town folks got their own peculiar way of listening."

"I could live here," Beecher said.

"It's December. Wait til August comes around."

Beecher stayed at the drugstore and ordered breakfast. He found a perch at the end of the counter facing the door and watched the town roll in. Every stool was filled. Tables, too. There was a stranger in town. A little spice for the syrup. Lucas drafted Irene and Jimmy from the motel as waitress and busboy respectively, and the clatter of plates and cups and chatter scored a sweet and captivating soundtrack. The menu said pancakes and bacon. Beecher asked Irene for eggs and toast. She patted his shoulder and whispered that the menu said pancakes and bacon.

"Sounds good," Beecher said. "I'll have pancakes and bacon."

The golden-brown stacks came six high with two rafts of foil-wrapped butter and a jug of Vermont's finest. Everyone was served the same. Beecher was amazed by one lady. She was ninety if she was a day. She shuffled into the drugstore, accepted the *"Hi's,"* and, *"Mornin, Lizzie's,"* from the patrons with an expressionless nod, sat down, laid a napkin on her lap, pulled out her false teeth, deposited them on the side of the plate, and proceeded to suck down every morsel she was served. He was particularly enamored with how she gummed and slurped on the last rasher of bacon with her eyes tightly shut.

Thankfully, by his own sugary indulgence, with a fork in one hand and a steaming black brew in the other, the hangover waned. He cleared away his own plate, which was met with unanimous nods of approval. He sat back down to nurse his coffee and the inquisition came soon after.

"Whattya doing in these parts?"

"Are you traveling alone?"

"How's that traffic up there on the 10? I heard there was a helluva snarl up comin' across the ridge."

"What do you do for a livin' there young fella?"

"Is England near France? I've always wanted to go to France."

Lucas bid the last of the breakfast crowd a hearty goodbye around 8:30 a.m.

"Most of these folks carpool out to the shopping malls. Only place they can get work these days. That damn highway took the chance to make a decent living in their own town right out from under their feet."

"Happens where I live, too. Supermarkets undercutting family-owned shops that have been in business for generations."

Lucas wiped down the counter, bringing the stainless steel to a mirror shine.

"I normally close up now, until around eleven."

He gestured toward the black and white photos.

"I gots to run an errand out to the old property. You're welcome to tag along if you like. I'd be glad of the company."

"I'd like that," Beecher said.

"Good, I'll pick you up at the motel in a half-hour or so."

Beecher strolled slowly down the abandoned sidewalk. The sun was cresting the buildings opposite, kissing the concrete at his feet, sending insects scuttling for shade.

In broad daylight, the *Buena Vista* wore its colors like a ragged flag. Up close, the paintwork of pinks and greens, once vibrant and glossy, now faded by age and weather, hung in flakes from dry wood. From a distance, the bleached and blasted fascia was a soothing collage of pastel colors courtesy of time's weary hand.

Beecher thought again, *"I could live here."*

The Jaguar was quietly suffocating under a blanket of dirt that sprinkled from the door handle when upset. There was no sign of Irene or Jimmy, only the clank and growl of a generator pumping water from Unit #3. Beecher stepped over a sodden carpet that had been rolled out in the yard and poked his head around the door. Empty, but for a few framed photographs, the room had been stripped of anything that would hold the damp. He ventured further inside. Slats of morning sun fell across the pictures. They were earlier variations of those in the drugstore. Before the rot set in. Same property; different angles. One picture showed the reflection of a pick-up's side mirror. Two boys wrestled in a yard bordered by flowers in bloom. A woman stood in shadow. The same woman. Beecher shielded his eyes and stepped forward out of the window glare. His foot slipped into a puddle, wetting his boot through the sole.

"Fuck."

Beecher went to his own room, set the key in the lock and the door swung open. Irene faced him. She let out a startled yelp, like a puppy with a trodden foot. Towels fell to the ground.

"I came to change these but the others ain't been used. You didn't say you'd stayed out all night."

"Yes, sorry. Seemed rude."

"Honey, when you're paying, you can do whatever you want."

"I'm thinking of staying another night."

"Well, that's great. Try the bed tonight, she's a soft one."

Irene noticed his soggy boot.

"I need some dry socks," he said. "Going for a drive with Lucas."

She moved aside.

"The sun hits the side window around noon," she said. "Great for drying any wet clothes."

She took her leave across the yard, waving to Lucas as he pulled up.

"He's changing his socks," she said. "Where y'all going?"

"Out to the farm," Lucas said, "...see if the storm dealt me any damage."

"Jimmy'll give you a fair price for seeing to that roof, you know he will."

"Seems hardly worth it for three days of rain a year."

Irene set the towels on the hood of his truck.

"Don't be surprised if you're under three feet of water," she said. "This roof was fine two days ago, now look at it."

"Tell Jimmy to give *Let's Make Deal* a miss and you'll have it dried out by suppertime."

She hooked her neck toward Beecher's room.

"You find anything out about the boy?"

"Oh, you missed out last night. That right there is a bonafide rock and roller," he said. "You know all that fuss that was on the TV and radio, that Hollywood concert? Well, that's what the fuss was all about."

"He's that guy?"

Irene got all flustered, smoothed her hair and straightened her shirt.

"I don't believe it," she said.

Lucas winked.

"I'm tellin' ya straight. He really tied one on last night, told a helluva tale."

"Did Charlie get out that Indian moonshine again?"

Lucas laughed hard.

"Lucy didn't get in his face, did she? Oh, God, what must the poor boy think of us?"

"Your sister was the one that kept the peace. She jumped square in Charlie's ass when he started gettin' ornery. I bet the boy don't remember nothing about anything. Though he did seem to be taking a shine to Lucy there for a minute."

"Last thing she needs is a traveling musician making promises he won't keep."

"I think the boy's heart is elsewhere. He strikes me as kinda lost."

Beecher pulled the door to his room shut, twisted the key, made his way over.

"She's a beauty," he said, casting his eyes over Lucas's truck. "Old one, eh?"

Irene struck a strong southern twang, "Look at you two with your *vintage ve-hi-cles*. By the way, the pair of ya are gonna fry in there with no air conditioning. It's gonna be a hot one."

Beecher climbed into the passenger seat. Irene gathered up her towels.

"We'll be back before opening," Lucas said. "If I get held up, can you start lunch? Meatloaf's cooked, just needs heatin' up."

Irene nodded a subtle, *"yes."* She watched with a glint in her eye as Lucas backed up and turned out of the yard. As soon as he was out of sight, she ran into the office, hollering,

"Jimmy, you'll never guess who we got staying here."

The ride out to Lucas's property headed away from town on a dusty road paralleling a lonely, black ribbon of highway. A wall of scrub hid all but the tops of big rigs trundling along in single-file, and the stutter of diesel engines downshifting for the approaching grade preceded plumes of inky smoke spiraling from silver stacks.

The old pick-up turned away from the industrial grime and with the constant squeak of rusty springs, scattered nervous cottontails and routed fat prairie dogs from cramped burrows.

Beecher was transfixed by the environment as they labored along a bumpy, dirt track that wound between imposing profiles of Saguaro cactus, and soon enough cut a path between desert willows posing like palace guards. For twenty miles, they skirted the south side of a rise that finally opened out onto a fertile, green plain, barren except for a few farm buildings and a solitary tree that was rooted within a ring of rocks a hundred yards or so distant.

"The mountain acts as a catch and filter for any rain we get," Lucas said. "All of the water gets channeled into an underground lake that feeds a few springs at either end of the property. It's cool and sweet by the time it gets to the surface. Wildlife around here goes crazy for it. There's nothing else like this in the state. The ol' man used to grow stuff out here as good as anything you'd get up north."

Beecher recognized the setting from the photographs, except now, the outlying buildings were rubbled, wiped from the earth of any form or structure. He saw the stone piles as incongruous shapes littering the plain, resting silent and awkward as canted grave markers.

The main house was intact, coddled and protected beyond its worth, like a bottle of vintage wine. A wide, freshly-painted wood veranda wrapped walls of stone that showed original mortar patched in many places with new cement.

Lucas parked and shut off the engine. He surveyed the property at a distance, a habit refined over time. The house presented its entrance through double doors leading to a modest receiving area. A family room and a kitchen opposed each other and were beneficiaries of strong, morning light. Lucas left Beecher to explore while he checked for signs of flooding or intrusion by insistent critters.

The family room was empty but for a tattered easy chair and a small table that was set by a window that held a commanding view of the valley, and bookshelves lined the walls, filled with first editions of notable works, all yellowed with age. The wide planks underfoot were scarred with the passage of generations.

"You keep a lot of books," Beecher said.

"I come up here and read when it's too damn hot down in town. This place hasn't seen a single volt of electricity since it was built so the sun becomes your lord and master, lets you know when it's time to slip back into the present."

"Any damage?"

"None so far. I wanna check out back."

Lucas busied himself while Beecher found his way to the kitchen. He pulled open a few cupboards and drawers. In one he found a length of silk ribbon. Canary yellow. Wound tight and sealed in a clear plastic bag.

The daylight dimmed as Lucas filled the doorway.

"The ol' man wouldn't throw that away," he said. "It lived in that drawer so I thought I might as well leave it there. Come on, come out back."

They walked to the fence line separating a square of lawn from the fields beyond.

"This pace is vast," Beecher said.

"Almost nine hundred acres. We only ever farmed the front half. He liked to wander the back lot, said it felt like his own piece of heaven. We spread his ashes out there. I think he would've liked that."

Lucas stood with his arms interlocked, resting on a gate. He looked out at the land, lost in its past; lost in his past.

"Had almost a thousand head of sheep out here when I was a kid. After the war, wool was so damn expensive, and this grassland was so lush, that for a while there we was punching our own ticket. My father even threatened to buy a new truck, but that never happened."

The wind picked up and raked the knee-high grass into an obedient bow, and its warm breath spilled the aroma of creosote bush across the open plain.

"How old were you when he died?"

"Just turned sixteen. We were out here seeding the last few acres. He was over there by the brush, went down on his knees with his hands balled up in the dirt. He never got up. Doctor said it was his age. I know different. He died from a broken heart. It was written all over his face. She'd let out a week or so before Christmas that year. The ol' man beat on about there being someone else. She never denied it, but I don't think there was. She was always distant. I think she stayed around for all those years out of gratitude but I never said that to him, would've been more than he could bear. Before he passed, there was an emptiness about him I ain't never seen before, nor since. It was like the sun and the moon had been plucked from his sky. Maybe if he was a younger man he'd have held on …I don't know."

As if drawn by an invisible thread, they started walking. The closer they got to the place where his father fell, the calmer the air became.

"She saved this stand of sagebrush from being plowed under, ringed it with stones, said it would bring the farm luck one day; said that it would stand for something. I guess I'm still waiting to see if she was right. The sheep used to gather around it for shade. Him and her spent a lot of time over here with the dogs cutting out the ewes that were getting close to lambing. Got some pictures somewhere."

Beecher wandered away, while Lucas stared up at the infinite blue of the Arizona sky and then back at the bush, trying to rekindle an old memory.

He thought aloud, "What the hell did she call it? Oh yeah, *arbusto de pastor*, yeah, that's it, *arbusto de pastor*."

Beecher shouted back, "Whatchya say?"

"Nothing, no matter."

Beecher and Lucas padded around the field for another few minutes before heading back to the truck.

"Well, she still stands," Lucas said. "Something to be said for that."

They were silent for a moment.

"You gonna stay on for a bit?"

"I planned on it. But something about all this and how you all get on with each other, it's making me miss my home."

"Then I'd say we've done you some good," Lucas said. "Home doesn't leave us, we leave it." He cocked his head, cast a glance at the main house. "It's good to go home."

They talked across the hood of the pick-up, arms folded on the warm fender.

Beecher said, "You ever had a dream come true, and then not wanted it?"

"My dream was always to get as far away from this place as possible. And I did. And then all I wanted to do was come home. I beat myself up pretty good about it, but folks understood. They'd all been through their own hell. All I know is, the soul wants what it wants, and there ain't no telling it what to do."

"Mine's telling me to go home."

Chapter Thirty-Eight

A black cab cruised by the Railway Tavern; the clickety-clack of its diesel engine was lost amid the deafening concert of construction clatter. Beecher asked the driver to slow down. He repeated the request twice. The cabbie had been incessant with all manner of current events and needless tour-guide babble.

"I think opening time is a ways off."

He laughed at his own joke, hacking up half a lung in the process.

The pub was adjusting itself nicely to its new frontage. The roof was on, the walls were framed and clad in new brick. The only reminder of tragedies past was the gaping depression in the middle of the car park. Beecher was drawn to the macabre stain, feeling a little queasy seeing its funeral-black innards and the detritus of wind-blown trash lining its core. He urged the driver onward.

What would have been a ten-minute walk took nearly half-an-hour by car. The cabbie renewed his mundane babbling as he navigated abandoned roadworks and a borough-wide gridlock caused by a double-decker bus ejecting vital lubricants onto the Goldhawk Road.

Beecher retreated, lost to his thoughts, mindful of his whereabouts only when the cab lurched to a halt at the bus stop outside of Maureen's cafe. He handed over a five-pound note. Predictably, the driver struggled to make change.

"Got anything smaller?"

Beecher asked, "Slow day?"

The cabbie sneered, upended a leather purse, counting coppers.

Beecher got out and stood at the passenger window.

"Warm for January," the cabbie said, stalling and rattling coins. "Fella on the telly says it's set in like this for a week or so and then we're gonna get hammered with snow."

The outcome was inevitable.

"Keep the change," Beecher said.

"Ah, you're a gentleman."

The cabbie made eye contact, apparently for the first time. He did a double-take.

"Ere, are you that musician bloke?"

"One of 'em."

"Of course, the pub and all that. Well, I never. The papers said you'd seen the bright lights of America and had enough; said show business weren't for you."

"I don't know if anyone gets to decide things like that."

"Well, it was good while it lasted, eh?"

Beecher smiled, picked up his bags and walked to the window of the cafe and peered in between a sun-bleached menu and a 1976 poster for a pantomime, Goldilocks and the Three Bears at the London Palladium.

He felt a little nervous, something didn't seem right. This was his place, these were his people. The smell of fried everything bled from the skin of the building and raised voices and radio songs seeped from cracked window panes. He thought of putting the meet and greet off, walking for a bit, easing back into the pace of things, when…

"You can't place your order from out here."

Arch Pudding shuffled his own nervous dance from twenty feet away.

"Look at you," he said. "The prodigal son returns."

Beecher looked down at his single overnight bag and a battered guitar case. From the scuffed boots on up, it was the same blue jeans, same leather jacket. The only concession was a new black sweatshirt that was one size too big.

"Not exactly dressed for a parade down Whitehall, am I?"

"And home cooking isn't Gordon blue *(cordon bleu)*, but I know what I'd rather have for Sunday dinner."

They shared a moment of silence, then the smiles came fast and easy, and the years compressed. Hardship and companionship, walking hand-in-hand. The exchange might've lasted all day had a cloud of exhaust fumes from the No. 88 bound for Ladbroke Grove and Oxford Circus not turned the special moment into a choking, eye-watering, High Street evacuation. They fell through the door of the cafe like a pair of wheezing old age pensioners, meeting a barrage of astonished and immediately excited gasps of delight. Snooze came across the counter like a gold medal hurdler, careening into Fez and Harry whose own collision sent Maureen's collection of silver jubilee mugs and plates spinning across the floor in a travesty of royal magnitude. The Queen's ambivalent grin bounded about the scuffed linoleum, immediately sending her dutiful subjects to their knees to gather up shards of broken china.

"Never mind all that," Snooze said. "We've got boxes of that rubbish upstairs gathering dust."

He took a breath.

"Now what do you call this, Beecher Stowe? We've been racking our brains for days on how to receive your Highness back from the colonies. And here you are, showing up like you own the place."

"Home sweet home," Beecher said, with arms spread. "I couldn't stay away."

"Well, that settles it," Snooze said, looking at Fez and Harry. Tell Pengo that we'll christen the pub with a few bottles come opening time, even if he's still two months from the actual event. Arch you'll fetch Lola, and I'll try and drag Maureen and Freddie down. Now, let's get some tea brewing."

Within the breezy confines of the Railway Tavern's new bar, Pengo officiated. Separated from the world by a flap of soiled canvas covering the gaping window frames, glasses were raised in honor of Beecher's return and Nana's passing.

"The times we knew within these walls," Pengo said. "Sometimes I feel they don't bear mentioning for worry that they might disappear forever. I know how wrong that is, of course. We are a family, and family doesn't disappear. I think that in so many ways, we've become ingrained deeper into each other's hearts."

"Here, here," Fez said.

"Don't be a wanker, Fez," said everyone else.

"Nana's soul is here," Beecher said. "I feel it, mate. I do."

"Speaking of I do's," Snooze said, stepping forward gingerly, his face scrunched into a bashful smirk. "I know it's only been a few weeks but I've got some news."

Fez let out a dismayed sigh, "You haven't?"

"I have, dear boy, and what's more, she's only gone and said, yes."

Beecher scanned the room, confused and alarmed.

"What? What did I miss?"

"Luna has agreed to be my wife."

"No, I haven't," Lola said with a disgruntled huff. She was mid-suck on a cherry bon-bon and the fruity marble popped free of her lips and fell into the dark recess of her cleavage. The lads leaned forward reflexively for a closer look and were quickly screened as Arch rescued the moment. And the candy.

"Not you, you deaf old bat," he said, with fingers plunging deep into the neckline of her faux leopard-skin jumper. "*LUNA*, not *LOLA*. The young one."

"The thin one," Fez said.

"The one that's not a slag," Harry whispered.

"Alright, you two," Arch said, with his index fingering wagging like the tail of a ravenous puppy. "That's enough of that."

"Snooze, you old dog," Beecher said. "How did..? I mean, when did..? I mean... congratulations. Where's the lucky bride-to-be?"

"Preparing her parents for the inaugural visit. I'm going up to Scotland at the weekend. Nervous as fuck? Why, yes I am."

"Don't be. They'll love you. Play them a tune."

Beecher's turn to toast.

"Here's to us all..."

Beecher took a beat. His shoulders sagged a touch, and the levity waned.

"...what a ride. From nothing to everything. A journal full of encounters, some burns, some scars, some losses..."

He danced around Hans Tomek's and Eeva's disappearance as best he could.

"It seems our benefactors had other plans, and unfortunately those plans didn't include us, ...well, ...me, specifically. We've still got some juice from the song and the tour. You'll all get paid what you're owed, and then some. Buy a house; buy a car. Buy your future. Further than that, there's no more financial backing. The company no longer exists. All of that might seem a little, doom and gloom..."

"That's because it is," Fez said.

Beecher relented with a sigh.

"Yeah, I guess it is. Here's the thing," he said. "I've realized this life isn't for me and I'm compelled to apologize for all of this getting so out of hand."

A rustle of polite disagreement spread from chair to chair.

He went on.

"I always said it wasn't supposed to be this way. But I was wrong. It was absolutely supposed to be this way. I was supposed to give the world a reason to raise their voices to the sky; I was supposed to receive love and support from those I care for the most; I was supposed to discover that to continue being celebrated on such a massive scale makes a mockery of our potential because we would never be allowed to make another mistake."

The faces he addressed were no longer innocent. The passage of miles and events and the gift of time spent sharing in a common warmth had etched memories deep as oceans.

"And, I was supposed to be taken by the hand and shown that anything can be rendered as divine if enough people say it is. That a single sentiment, as expressed in my song; our song, galvanized so many to acknowledge one another in a positive light is at once a magnificent and humbling event, but it is also an incredibly sad reflection of how misguided we are. I don't mean to suggest that we are forever broken and don't let anyone tell you otherwise. I believe our unified strength is an incalculable force. Which is why the world's repair has to come from each of us, in infinitesimally small doses. That's the only way our message prevails. Supermassive Superstar *your* life," he said emphatically, "...and then let me see those super magic eyes."

Beecher scanned the gathering of his friends. He saw that Arch's hand was interlocked with Lola's and that both of their faces were shiny with tears. He saw that Harry and Fez were sharing a chair, bonded together, tight as brothers. And he saw Snooze and Pengo, mirrored, with elbows resting on the bar, as mentors and coaches, and friends for life.

"Whatever you do, from here on out," he said, "...will be off your own backs. And that's the way it should be."

The group digested his words, numb to the extent of their meaning. The past was a burned city. Home was here. It was safe here.

"I'm here for you Beecher," Arch said.

"And I'm happy to have you around. Couldn't have done any of this without you, mate."

Arch beamed at the room. Behind his back, he signaled Harry and Fez with a moist and pudgy, nail-bitten, *fuck you,* middle finger.

Pengo plugged in the new jukebox and dropped a fistful of coins into Harry's hand.

"Choose us some suitable tunes, eh?"

Fez came off his stool like he'd been electrocuted, "How come he gets to choose?"

"Because I'm better with money," Harry said.

Fez was indifferent.

"You still owe me a quid from last week."

Heads turned, curious.

Fez announced to whoever was listening, "He wanted a box of Durex, said he wanted to practice."

"And, I'm back," Beecher said.

Pengo left the lads barking at each other and pulled Beecher aside.

"We've got a bit of a surprise for you," he said, catching Snooze's eye. "Something a little cosmic happened here the other day. I've only told Snooze 'bout it, 'cause it's all a little freaky."

Pengo retrieved a small, metal box, hinged, with a rusty padlock. He set it atop the newly installed bar.

"The builders found it when they were redoing the floor under the bay window. It's a wonder it survived the fire."

Beecher brushed off some dirt and his fingers followed the contour of a large dent in the lid.

"Why haven't you opened it?"

"It's not mine to open," Pengo said.

"Well, who's is it?"

"Yours, apparently."

Beecher sipped his beer, felt a cascade of shivers trickle down his spine. The canvas sheet covering the window rippled and grew taut as a sail, flexing with a sharp crackle, and then rested with the soft patter of rain oiling its skin.

Pengo turned and tilted the box to face Beecher. He thumbed clean a blackened plaque engraved with Beecher's name. The letters had been softened by the flames, thinned where beveled edges had succumb to intense heat.

Beecher felt as though the universe were folding in on itself. A vacuum was drawing breath from his body.

"It's a joke," he said, the only words available.

"I swear it's not." Pengo was stone-faced. "They dug it out from under the floorboards. It was deep. Deep as the foundation. It could only have been put there before the place was built."

"And when was that?"

"1954. The year..."

"...I was born," Beecher said.

Beecher turned the box upside down, sideways, back upright. The tips of his fingers were reddened with lines of rust and his palms quickly blackened with soot and grime.

"I think the lock will pop off pretty easy," Snooze said. "It looks rusty as fuck."

Pengo reached behind the bar, pulled out a screwdriver, two pairs of pliers and a hacksaw.

"If not, these should do the job."

Beecher's eyes pleaded, *"Are you sure you're not fucking with me?"*
Snooze and Pengo slapped their hands across their hearts.
"Mate," Snooze said, "A year ago this would've been a serious windup. Now, after these last few months, I wouldn't be surprised if there was a note in there from King Arthur telling you where he'd put his sword."
Pengo tapped the bar with the screwdriver.
"In your own time, gents," he said, impatiently.
They moved to the back lounge, now completely refurbished.
"What a difference a car bomb makes," Beecher said. "It's lost something, though. It's missing a little of that lived-in character."
"Yes," Snooze said, "It doesn't smell like a room full of sweaty ball bags."

Beecher set the box on a table and worked the padlock with the screwdriver. It released from its catch easily and fell to the floor like a lost earring. Snooze gathered it up, played with the mechanism.
"The only thing holding this together was dirt," he said.
Beecher placed his hands on the lid and then hesitated.
"It's like going on stage," he said. "Before you go on, there's hope. When you come off, there's just reality."
"If you don't open the lid soon enough, there's going to be a fucking aneurysm," Pengo said. "Mine."
Beecher made a show of opening the lid gracefully. A moment passed. He adjusted his grip, the whites of his knuckles showing bright as steamed scallops. Another few seconds ticked by.
"Trouble, Princess?" Snooze said.
"It's stuck," Beecher said. "I mean, really stuck; rusted shut."
"Give us a go," Pengo said, snatching it from Beecher's hands.
He grunted with the box shoved between his knees for a full ten seconds. With breath held and mouth twisted into a tortuous smile, he exerted such force that a line of snot shot unexpectedly from his nose. Beecher and Snooze fell back in disgust, wiping atomized residue from their hands and faces.
"Jesus, Pengo," Snooze squealed. "A little warning next time."
Pengo set the box on the table and dabbed at the translucent smear glistening on his upper lip.
"Use the pliers," he muffled from beneath a handkerchief.
They worked for another half-an-hour, prying, bending and banging.
"You gotta cut it open, Snooze said. "You gotta take the lid off with the hacksaw."

Beecher wasn't convinced, "What if there's something valuable in there and we damage it?"

They drew chairs up to the table, staring at the inanimate object as if it was a rare, religious artifact.

Beecher was forthcoming, "Maybe I'm not supposed to open it? Maybe it's a test of my character?"

Pengo was more deliberate, "I think you might be taking the mystical, hocus-pocus thing a little far. Maybe it's a prank by someone none of us know?"

"A reporter," Snooze said. "Someone looking for a story."

"Or someone trying to make you look like an arrogant, self-righteous wanker," Pengo added.

Beecher raised an eyebrow.

"Seems a little excessive."

"You can't trust the fucking newspapers," Pengo said. "They'll stroke you on the way up, and fuck you hard on the way down."

"I hadn't thought of myself as on the way down," Beecher said.

"No, I'm just sayin', that's what they do."

"You say you found it under the floorboards, by the bay window?"

"The builders brought it to me, I didn't find it."

"What builders? Do you know them?"

"Not really. There's been so many of 'em, coming and going. They're just builders. They do a bit, and then they drink tea and read the paper."

"I think I want to live with it for a while. Let's leave it as it is for now."

"Absolutely," Snooze said, with a knowing wink. "Let it percolate for a bit. Let's not destroy a perfectly good biscuit tin."

Beecher caught the good-natured slight and threw one straight back.

"How the hell did she ever agree to marry you?"

"She accepted my personal guarantee that there would be a substantial lack of money and fame," Snooze said. "She deplores wealth of any sort. I assured her I would comply."

"Is your bike running?"

"It is. You know, you *can* buy one of your own."

Beecher's eyes lit up.

"You know, that never occurred to me. I suppose I can get my own place, too. Maybe stay in a posh hotel for a bit."

"Well, that's just as well," Pengo said. "…seeing as your room was deposited over most of West London."

Pengo led the way out front. Beecher gathered up the box and stuffed it into a rucksack. He noticed a scorch mark on the table similar to its shape. He brushed the pattern with his fingers and it was warm to the touch. He worried about Pengo's anxiety over the new furniture and decided to keep that to himself.

Chapter Thirty-Nine

Boris Flattley hadn't sold a single motorcycle in three weeks, and only one in the preceding two. It was winter; it was always that way. The last sale had been to an American wanting a weighty souvenir of England; a sentimental token bearing the Union Jack. He had informed Flattley, in a grating, southern drawl, "It will be a permanent reminder of your glorious country."

Flattley assured him that the Triumph model he was buying was imbued with the very best of British craftsmanship and would indeed, last a lifetime. What the man ultimately received was a remnant of an ailing industry that upon arrival at his Texas home, refused to start. And when it did start, it failed to run. And when it did run for any length of time, it stopped. And so the world turns.

Flattley was up to his elbows in a plate of pie and mash when the jingle of the doorbell rang out. He yanked at the tea-towel tucked into his shirt, wiped away flakes of Cornish Pasty from cheeks and chin, trolled his tongue through the residue of thick, brown gravy coating the top of his mouth, and bolted into the showroom. He pulled up as he caught sight of a lone, shaggy-haired gentleman strolling the aisle dividing a sea of brightwork and glossy paint.

As the establishment was housed in the heart of Mayfair, Flattley was quietly confident of the visitor's intent to part with some cash. Along an avenue that counted agents for Ferrari, Rolls Royce and Bentley as neighbors, once a punter crossed the threshold, a marriage, of sorts, was implied.

"Can I be of assistance, sir?"

The verbal address was plummy and practiced, almost royal in its elocution. The fact that the customer was dressed like a mechanic fresh off the assembly line had no bearing.

"I want one of these," the man said, adjusting a rucksack on his leather-clad shoulder, gesturing to a line of handlebars that intertwined like chromed antlers. "Preferably in black. What do you have that can be ridden away today?"

Beecher was certain that the salesman squirted a little piss down his trouser leg.

Indeed, Flattley did feel the stirring of a sale warm his loins, but he hesitated.

"I'm afraid the majority of our merchandise requires advance notice for delivery. We are an exclusive boutique. Our inventory is for show only. The factory prepares a unit to a customer's specifications and we coordinate payment and delivery."

Fuck. Sod's law.

"The only time in my life I've had the cash…"

"There *are* a few things," Flattley said, "…depending on your, uh, requirements. They're not bespoke machines as we advertise, you understand."

"I understand," Beecher said. "All I require is that it looks the business and runs even better. Now, where do you keep 'em?"

Flattley led Beecher through to a dark and brooding storage facility that virtually screamed of a previous life as a Victorian workhouse. Several aged and sturdy oaks had suffered for the building of the door as great slabs of the wood were bound together with iron slats and heavy gauge carriage bolts. A bunch of keys was extracted on a zip line attached to Flattley's belt and he set to work detaching padlocks and loosening catches and finally inching the great slab open so that a sliver of daylight knifed the gloom like daybreak on the moon. The half-light gave rise to odd, demonic shapes and the odor of gasoline and oil was heady and inviting.

Flattley fumbled in the dark, letting go with a few errant curse words as shins were knocked and knuckles scraped, and when the lights came fully on, Beecher saw him on the opposite side of the facility as a thin, pale figure wallowing in a corral of glinting muscle.

"All used, I'm afraid," Flattley shouted. "An estimable collection, for sure. Traded-in by impatient owners eager to flaunt the latest model."

"This is heaven," Beecher said. "Or a mass grave, I can't be sure which."

He stood amongst vintage examples of Triumph, Brough and Harley Davidson and BMW, resting his hand lightly on their controls, paying homage to the Gods of the internal combustion engine.

"Okay," Beecher said, "What's for sale?"

Flattley shot him a blank, forlorn stare, looking very much like a poor, young waif made to work for food and shelter.

"All of it," he said.

Most of the machines on exhibit had been toyed with and discarded like unwanted pets; pets that no doubt had sunk their teeth into soft, peachy flesh on more than one occasion.

The chosen machine called to Beecher from an unlighted, forgotten corner of the warehouse. Flattley tried to dissuade his interest, said the machine had no obvious pedigree beyond its brand.

"This one came to us as part of a consignment. Anyone that's ridden it says it's tried to kill them; that it has a mind of its own."

"You ever try it?" Beecher asked of Flattley. "Laying flat on the tank, with the wind ripping at your skin, in one hundred-degree heat?"

"I'm not sure the backwaters of England quite conjure up that spirit," Flattley said. "Although, T.E. Lawrence went out pretty spectacularly."

Together they wheeled the motorcycle into the open, whereby Flattley attacked it with a duster first, and hose and wash rag second.

Beecher paid in wads of ten-pound notes, banded together in stacks of one hundreds. The agreed price was settled without question and for his patronage, he was assured that any dissatisfaction would be met with absolute understanding and every effort would be made to rectify his complaint.

The machine was rolled through the showroom to the squeal of new rubber on polished tile and it was set upon its stand against the curb on Park Lane. Beecher sat on the bike, dressing for the ride, and agreed with Flattley that the balmy nature of the day would make for an excellent journey down to the coast.

The key was turned and Beecher put his scuffed boot to the kickstarter and the chassis trembled and the exhaust bellowed to life with a rumble that plucked at vivid boyhood memories like starlings unearthing bloodworms from plowed soil. With one hand settled on the throttle, Beecher's fingertips absorbed the vibrations of the motorcycle as though he'd been relieved of the power of sight. Every stutter of the engine played like music to his ear; a mechanical symphony teasing anxiety and aspiration from his wayward soul.

Flattley hovered close by, anxious to return to his office and gloat by telephone of his accomplishment. He gathered up Beecher's rucksack from the pavement, felt the rectangular bulk of the object within, and quickly altered his grip, snatching the strap, waving his hand as though he had drawn it across the cooking element of an electric stove.

"You got a flask of tea or something in here?"

Beecher flipped open the helmet's visor.

339

"What?"

Flattley raised his voice against the unyielding white noise of cars and buses, "There's something scalding hot leaking from your bag."

Beecher took the bag, unhooked the catch and rummaged inside. His first thoughts had gone to Fez and his tendency toward practical jokes.

"I'll kill the little bastard."

All he found was the mysterious metal box resting in the folds of an Aran sweater.

"Can't feel anything."

Flattley watched Beecher settle the straps on his shoulders. The sensation of heat resonated clammy and insistent on his palm, and with it came a cloying odor that resisted multiple wipes on his trouser leg. He masked his troubled expression and with matey bravado, dispensed with the need for handshakes, bidding his goodbye from the showroom door, observing Beecher from the opposite side of the glass. The exchange had left the habitually arrogant salesman confused and troubled and he stood rooted to the spot for a long moment after Beecher departed.

In time, Flattley returned to his desk but he did not make boastful phone calls. Instead, he pushed aside his dirty lunch plate, retrieved a phone directory and called a florist in the vicinity of his home in St. John's Wood. When he spoke, his accent was no longer affected by class or implied stature:

> *"I'd like to order a bouquet for delivery;*
> *White roses if possible;*
> *You do?*
> *Oh, good;*
> *Yes, a dozen, please;*
> *A card?*
> *To my darling wife, … Yours forever, …Boris."*

Beecher roared into Hyde Park Corner with his ass welded to the saddle of a bike that was black as burned coal and streaked with war paint in lines of shimmering gold. His plan was to agitate a few pram-pushing nannies along the pillared avenues of Belgravia and Knightsbridge, and then cruise past Maureen's cafe and give Snooze a look-see before heading full tilt for the coast.

Brighton.

A week at The Grand Hotel.

A sea-view suite, no less.
A winter vacation.
An English vacation.
Read, drink and walk.
And think.
Of her.
No bands would play.
No flowers would bloom.
Salt spray glistening in the frigid air.
Like diamonds.
She didn't wear diamonds.

"Now you're just fuckin' showin' off."
Snooze stood in the back alley of the café, bare shins poking out from under a terry cloth bathrobe. Ships wheels and symmetrical anchors were dotted about his person at odd angles. He had a mug of tea and a cigarette on the go. Smoke and steam. Central heating for grown-ups.
"It's used," Beecher said.
"Doesn't look it. You did well."
He took a drag and coughed until his eyes watered, said,
"Opened it up yet?"
"A little burn down the King's Road."
"I meant the box," Snooze said.
Beecher patted the rucksack, shook his head.
"Later."
Snooze did a circuit around the bike.
"Look at this thing. New tires, too. She needs a name."
"Don't fuckin' start."
He played dumb, "What?"
Beecher sipped from Snooze's tea, dragged on his cigarette.
"Feels good," Beecher said. "No gigs, no guitar. It's like being reborn."
"You're on hiatus," Snooze said, sounding a little pissed off. "That load of bollocks you told the others last night, I know you needed to say it but we both know that you won't be able to keep away from it. You've wanted it for too long. It's fuel for your soul."
"I dunno. I like to be in control and I wasn't. But I went along with it, drank from the cup. Big gulps, the kind that takes your breath away."
"Sounds like love," Snooze said.

"It feels more like an encounter with a really big lie. The kind of lie that follows you around like a stray dog. You know it's there, but every time you look for it, it hides."

"Definitely, sounds like love," Snooze said.

They stood side by side before an altar of chrome. Maureen was busy as evident by the clatter of dishes coming from the kitchen. She hollered a, *"Hello, darlin',"* through the window and went off singing high and clear, *"Hit me with your rhythm stick, hit me, hit me…"*

"She was way older than me, you know," Beecher said.

"I know."

"I mean, way older."

"I know," Snooze said.

Beecher just nodded, pulled on his helmet.

"Wish me luck."

"With what?"

"Being me."

Snooze broke out an ear-to-ear grin.

"You don't need luck, you need…"

Beecher put his foot to the starter and the engine caught and filled the air with Italian thunder.

"I said," Snooze shouted, "You need…"

Beecher blipped the throttle, saw his friend mouthing, *"…a monumental shag."*

He pulled away from the cafe, sedate and unhurried. In the mirror, Snooze, in robe and slippers, stepped into the middle of the road. Maureen was by his side. He watched them for as long as he could.

Chelsea Bridge was empty and Beecher was suspicious. He thought he might have missed a roadblock. He slowed right down, sat upright, kept looking back and forward as if his head was on a spring. The crossing of the river seemed to take forever. At the midpoint, the bike stuttered, and then caught again.

"You don't like slowing down, do you?"

He felt a rumble manifesting beyond the machine's own resounding battle cry. The sound grew louder, more insistent. He glanced down at the engine as if enlightenment lay there. On the road, white lines flashed bright and hypnotic. He fought to return his gaze to the other end of the bridge.

No traffic approached.

He whipped his head around again.

That's when he saw the pack descending upon him at speed.

Masked faces, tucked behind blackened screens. Soldiers and devils.

Beecher twisted the throttle but it spun without resistance.

Looking forward again, the opposite bank remained distant, unattainable. He tilted his head to either side, confused and angry. The white lines blurred as they do at speed and yet he felt his momentum tethered. He tempted fate, put one foot to the tarmac. He found purchase and balance.

And then the shadows were upon him.

And they were riders.

And they glided to a standstill, silent as falling leaves.

The lead rider's face was caressed with age and his skin was brushed pale by milky light.

"Hello, Mr. Beecher Stowe."

Amelio reached out, rested his hand on Beecher's shoulder.

"How far you have come," he said.

"Oh, my, God," Beecher was ecstatic.

"It's you," he said. "Do you have news? Is Eeva alright? Can I see her?"

Amelio did not answer. Another rider joined.

Fidelia.

The passage of time had etched the lines of her smile deep into her complexion and her eyes smoldered, dark as pellets of coal.

"We have been following you," she said. "You have been lost to your freedom and we have come to tell you that everything is as it should be."

"I have been traveling," Beecher said. "I'm due a vacation, or so my friends tell me."

"You have good friends," Amelio said. "They love you and they miss you."

"Well, it won't be for long. Just a week, a little longer if the weather holds. I thought I might do some writing. A book, maybe."

The surface of the river mirrored the flat sky and winter's silvery cast returned and fell across the city.

"I've been thinking," Beecher said. "We found a box. They say it had to have been buried when the foundation was laid in 1954. Can you believe that? I was born in 1954. Hans or Eeva or …you, someone I've met must've put it there. But I can't open it. Not yet, anyway. I've tried but I don't want to damage it."

Fidelia said, "Do you remember that Hans promised to share with you the problem he could not solve? This object you hold will satisfy that promise."

"I don't know what's in there."

"I can tell you it is everything you were. It is your accomplishments and it is your potential. You don't lose it when you die."

Beecher felt the cool breath of the river fill his lungs. He walked to the rail and listened to its song. The surface ripples were orderly and he saw fish drifting motionless against the current. He dropped the rucksack from his shoulder and fetched out the box, running his fingers lightly across the rusted latch. The clasp let go with a soft click and the lid opened. He removed a leather-bound journal embossed with gold lettering.

He read aloud,

"Beecher Stowe, that is my name, and this is my band."

Fidelia moved closer. She pressed her face into his collar and whispered, "Awaken your wound."

The wind backed to the north and flakes of snow grazed the river banks platinum white and the music of the water settled into an equable rhythm.

"I'm in need of new dreams," Beecher said. "The ones I had all came true."

The End

EPILOGUE

Austrian News Service, Present Day.

Hallstatt, Austria.....

What is claimed to be one of the most sensational archeological discoveries of the century has today been announced in the village of Hallstatt, Austria.

A series of subterranean burial chambers lying beneath the ruins of a Roman-era village amongst the picturesque foothills of the Salzkammergut Mountains has been explored and so far has disclosed a collection of artifacts that scientists believe to date back as far as the beginning of the first century.

The remains of several humans within one chamber has prompted serious interest by renowned anthropologists and archeologists alike, as it is a perfectly-preserved example of a family burial plot. Paraphernalia, such as tools and clothing and cooking implements, were found in an anti-chamber, while personal possessions, such as footwear and grooming implements were discovered near the bodies.

In a peculiar twist to events surrounding this monumental discovery, authorities have declared that the artifacts found within the burial chamber may have been unduly contaminated and the target of practical jokers. When pressed for further information, Dr. Ernst Bauer of the University of Vienna acknowledged that a contemporary photograph was found in the clutches of one of the skeletons, believed to be a mature male. The document, although appearing to be ravaged by the effects of time, clearly shows the image of two men and one woman lounging against a large boulder in an otherwise barren landscape. A bystander that had reviewed the photograph admitted that one of the men bears a striking resemblance to the late British rock star, Beecher Stowe.

Investigations are ongoing.

MARK WARFORD

Made in the USA
Middletown, DE
30 August 2020

16893345R00210